RED CITY
CASE CLOSED

A TRACTUS FYNN MYSTERY
BOOK 5

by MK Alexander

Red City: Case Closed
By MK Alexander

Copyright 2018. All rights reserved.
ISBN: 978-1720694007

This is a work of fiction. Any similarity between actual persons is purely coincidental.
This work may not be reproduced or electronically transmitted without expressed consent of the author.

Published by KMACK Design, BOX 144, Sea Cliff, NY 11579
Cover art copyright 2018, KMACK Design
Please direct any inquiries to mkalex@optonline.net

Also by MK Alexander:
Tractus Fynn Mysteries
Book 1: Sand City
Book 2: Jump City
Book 3: Low City
Book 4: Cold City

The Farsi Trilogy
Jekyll's Daughter
GenreJam, Volume One: Death & Injury
My New World: A Teenager's WWII Odyssey
Random Sacrifice

note

This, the fifth and final Tractus Fynn Mystery, contains spoilers. For maximum enjoyment, readers might want to read *Sand City*, *Jump City*, *Low City* and/or *Cold City* before embarking on the journey.

PART I

chapter one
rattling stairs

The soft rumble of wrought iron came, or so I thought. Might be thunder from far off. It was one of those steamy nights no cooler than the day's muggy inferno: heat wave, early August. I sat in my apartment by a giant fan. From the screen door I could hear the clatter of dishes and indistinct conversation from downstairs at the Depot Cafe, and maybe music from somewhere. There were some dogs too, barking in the distance, and a few cars rolling by.

Across from me at the table is my cat, Zachary, sitting upright, staring hard. He gave me a slow blink. *Not good, now what?* I thought, and listened harder to hear the familiar sound of my spiral staircase. Someone was bounding up the steps, rattling the metal into a dull musical tone. A head full of silver hair appeared first, then the rest of Fynn. I can't say I was surprised.

That's Detective Chief Inspector Tractus Fynn, retired from the Amsterdam police, my best friend and fellow time traveler. His appearance was less than miraculous since we had walked together along the beach just two days before. Though, where he might have gone between then and now could probably fill volumes. I opened the sliding screen door to let him in.

Fynn seemed a bit over dressed in his well-cut suit and a bow tie tucked under the collar of his shirt. I wondered if we were going somewhere.

"Ah, Patrick, glad to find you home," he said with a smile. "We have a case."

"Do we?"

"Are you game?"

"Absolutely. Where to this time?" I felt the usual mixture of dread and anticipation.

"Give me a moment." Fynn reached into his pocket and pulled out a bundle of folded papers.

"Kind of warm to be wearing a jacket tonight," I commented.

"In your kitchen, yes. It's positively stifling." He walked through to the living room. "I'll say it's even worse in there." Fynn meandered back and stood by the refrigerator.

"The price of living in an attic," I replied.

"Pardon me for asking, Patrick— but what is this date marked on your calendar?"

"Oh… that's when Mortimer returned."

"Returned?" Fynn asked.

"Umm, from when the Arbiter plucked him. Don't you remember?"

Fynn thought for a moment. "Yes, I recall it quite well… a tundra somewhere outside of Reykjavik." He faced me. "But returned?"

"Yesterday… He was in Paris, waiting for a train… and all his memories, I guess."

Fynn laughed. "So he will now remember everything that's happened… and Kali Shunya as well?"

"That was the plan."

"But has he not been arrested?"

"Yes, this time through. Durbin and DC Wilkes made a pretty strong case against him."

"I don't suppose he'll be troubling us then." Fynn gave a tight smile. "There is a cool breeze coming from the ocean. It's a shame we can't sit outside."

"Why not?"

"It's dark."

I flipped a switch and the tiny deck lit up; it was just big enough for two chairs and a small table, almost like an open air dormer cut into the steep roof. "Can I get you something to drink?"

"Such as?"

"I have ice water in the fridge."

"Perfect."

I followed Inspector Fynn outside and lit a citronella candle. The bug-zapper had also come to life, glowing a blue-violet, but so far silent. He was right, it was cooler here, almost comfortable. I had a flash of memory about this place, a memory of the future when it was once wholly submerged.

Fynn sat and sorted through his bundle of papers.

"Another fax?" I asked.

"Several."

"More timelines?"

"From the Arbiter."

"Did he pluck you again?"

"Yes, I've only just been returned." Fynn gave a wince.

"I hate when he does that."

"It's most distressing. He's also overly fond of using the facsimile machine."

"I'd blame Clark for that."

"Clark the clark, Sebastian at the *Hotel de Cirque*?"

"He seems very proud of that machine." I smiled. "It's weird though, that he sends all this stuff to us…"

"He sends his regards as well," Fynn said.

"Miriam is getting mad at me."

"Miriam?"

"From the *Chronicle*. Faxes for personal use and all that."

"I see… Well, I had to install a special line at the house," Fynn replied. "The Arbiter is threatening to send over translations of the Voynich manuscripts. I wanted to be prepared just in case."

"When will that happen?"

"He has so far been rather vague about it."

"Trouble with Geppetto?"

"Not that I've been told."

"And you're absolutely sure you gave him the right books?"

"As far as I know. I took them from my safe deposit box. Why?"

"I just don't have high hopes that it will amount to much."

"Is there something you're not telling me, Patrick?"

"Not really…" I hedged. "But what's all that about talking to plants?"

"In the manuscripts, you mean?" He chuckled. "Some say it's

nonsense… Others would say it's easier to listen."

"What?"

"The wiser course of action is always to listen." Fynn took a long drink. "But I am here to discuss our next case."

He handed me a sheet of paper filled with crazy lines zig-zagging from left to right, each marked with an alpha-numeric identification. The bottom of the graph tallied years up to *2089*.

"The Arbiter drew these by hand?" I asked.

"I'm not sure that's the word I would use."

"It's more like an etch-a-sketch. I expected something high tech—him being from the future and all."

"A good question to pose to him."

"What are these exactly?"

"The top ten timelines," Fynn said.

"What, like the most popular?"

"No, the most probable…"

I glanced again at the wild lines that crossed the page.

"The dips and peaks represent diversity, an amalgamation of the various choices made, or not made," Fynn explained.

"Choices?"

"Sometimes a great many people make the same choice and it is reflected in these charts. These ups and downs, crests and troughs, like a wave, but all moving in the same direction."

"This one has flatlined."

"Yes, marked in red, the one that troubles me the most. It simply ends abruptly."

"When?"

"It looks to be nineteen sixty-two."

"Is that where we're going?"

"Indeed, another historical intervention."

"And the all-powerful Mr Arbiter asked you to do this?"

"He did."

I paused to look at Fynn. "I'm just thinking, he might have an agenda."

"Aside from Kali and her interference?"

"Yes."

"And what might that be?"

"I don't know, but everyone seems to…"
"Seems to what?"
"Have an agenda."
"Hmm… I have not detected anything like this from the Arbiter. What do you suppose he's after then?"
"I couldn't say."
"Well, I can only observe that his methods are subtle, exquisitely so."
"Like our trip to Pasadena?"
"We cannot fault ourselves for those events, and it all worked out in the end nonetheless."
"Until we found out who Charles Whitman was," I muttered.
"A great tragedy, to be sure."
"And last time?"
"You mean to say Hawaii?"
I nodded.
"Granted, that didn't work out perfectly either."
"It's the third time in a month," I commented and took a sip from my glass.
"I thought the other cases easy," Fynn replied with a smile.
"I'm not sure that's the word I'd use."
"Well, except for the arduous and circuitous route home…"
"I'm just glad we both made it back and things seem pretty normal."
"As do I… Well, our labors are far fewer than Hercules faced, and a good bit less strenuous, I might say." Fynn laughed.
"I guess… Last time all we did was go back to the nineteen forties and steal some kid's chemistry set."
"Ah, but by doing so, we made the world a safer place."
"I'm still not sure how."
"That chemistry set belonged to a very young John D. Franz."
"Who?"
"Previously, a chief researcher at the Monsanto Company."
"Previously?"
"His interests turned elsewhere after our visit."
"To what?"
"Interpretive dance."
"You're kidding."

"Probably." Fynn laughed again.
"What did he research… previously?" I asked.
"A chemical compound known as glyphosate."
"What?"
"Known as Round-up."
"The weed killer?"
"Yes."
"And how did that help?"
"A certain cascade of events was halted… This chemical company of questionable ethics no longer had reason to enter the genetically modified foodstuffs business."
"Meaning?"
"Ironically, there was no necessity to modify plants to be immune to the very pesticide they first created."
"That's what we changed?"
"Yes. Tinkering with genetics is best left to others. Perhaps they will take an ethical approach, perhaps they will possess a more benign intent." Fynn paused. "Why, have you noticed any differences?"
"Well, there are more dandelions than I remember." I went to my phone to check Monsanto's list of accomplishments: vanillin, saccharin, DDT, Agent Orange, Dioxin, PCB's, Astroturf, weaponized white-phosphorus… "No Round-Up, no GMO's," I announced.
"Then we have set things right."
I searched a bit further. "Hmm, says they're about to be bought up by a Japanese pharmaceutical firm."
"Interesting, I suppose."
"Well, look who's on the board of directors." I showed Fynn the photo. It was clearly our adversary, Kali Shunya, but her hair was now a different color.
"Can this be printed?" he asked.
"I guess, it's very low resolution though."
Fynn started through his bundle of papers and pulled out several sketches. "It's quite curious that we have no photographs of Kali." He placed the pages on the table as if they were cards: the first was an e-fit composite we had done for Detective Durbin. The second was as Lorraine drew her in an Amsterdam cafe many years ago. And the third was as Monsieur Michel rendered her aboard the *Carpathia*.

"My friend Joey tried to snap her picture at your party, but it didn't turn out— all blurry…"

"The party? Where was I at the time?"

"Oh… Elsewhere…" I went back to my phone.

"It's most curious. Perhaps she feels ready to reveal herself to the world. What name does she go by now?"

"Reimu... And look who else is on the board of directors of that company…" I showed Fynn my phone. "It's Mr Sato, but he looks much older than I remember."

"Hideki Sato, from the *Carpathia*? How is that possible?" Fynn asked.

"It's not. He was eaten by a bear."

"As you say, Patrick, and yet he seems to be alive again."

"Look what he's holding."

Fynn glanced at the screen. "A cane of some sort. I'd say it's the head of an elephant…"

"Do you think—?"

"No."

"Did you know he was a traveler?"

"Not until Kali mentioned it."

"Maybe he didn't die."

"We saw the body, what was left of it, though I didn't examine it very closely."

"You're saying it might have been someone else?"

"Such would be a remote possibility."

"Do you think they're working together? Mr Sato and Kali?"

"I suppose it merits further investigation…" Fynn paused. "But we have a more pressing matter at the moment."

"Okay. So, where are we off to this time?"

"It depends." He raised a smile.

"On what?"

"Your language skills."

Mon Français, c'est bon.

"Spoken like a true Quebecer." The inspector grinned. "How is your Russian?"

"Nonexistent."

"As I thought— then we're off to visit Mr Ming."

"Sonny Ming's School of Language Arts?"
"The very place."
"Where is it?"
"Babylon… and it's the perfect time to travel."
I tried to recall my history. "Babylon… second millennium, BC. Wow, that sounds pretty far."

Fynn laughed. "Not at all… it's in the middle of your Long Island."
"My Long Island?"
"A few states from here, I am meaning to say."
"And why is it a good time to travel?"
"I am thinking there will be little traffic on the roads."
"Oh, you want me to drive us there."
"If you would."
"What about Zachary?"
"Your cat? He can come with us. Does he like to travel?"
"Not really."
"I'm sure Anika wouldn't mind taking care of him."
"What about your dog, Asta?"
"He won't mind either. You mentioned they got along in the past."
"You remember that?"
"I do."
"Okay. How long do you suppose we'll be gone?"
"Difficult to say…" Fynn hedged a bit. "We might return tomorrow or the next day, or even yesterday if you prefer."

I knew what that meant, or didn't. It meant nothing. "Why do I have to learn Russian?"

"We are to save the man who saved the world, Vasili Arkhipov."
"Who?"
"A Soviet naval commander. It's our task to make sure he is aboard a submarine in a certain place at a certain time."
"Sounds complicated."
"Hopefully such matters will take care of themselves. The real problem is with his wife, Olga."
"Why? What's she done?"
"She's been arrested for murder and we've been tasked to find her innocent."
"What if she's not?"

"I've been assured she is."
"By whom?"
"The Arbiter."
"So, you're taking this case for him?"
"Yes. I feel a certain indebtedness," Fynn said. "He's also made a strong argument that a wrongful verdict will alter history in ways which are unfathomable."
"Is it Kali's doing again?"
"It seems likely."
"And somehow all this flatlined an entire history?"
"Yes, as you saw for yourself on the graph."
"You're not going to tell me anything, are you?"
Fynn laughed. "I will say more along the way. We should leave as soon as we can."
"Why would Kali want to erase a whole timeline?"
"To make her own life easier, I suspect. If there are fewer histories to worry about, she can focus on changing the ones she likes."
"*Funneling*, you mean?"
"Yes, as Mr Quandary aptly describes." Fynn gave a small grimace.
"Mr Q is involved in all of this?"
"Well, he was the person who noticed this seemingly small aberration in the timeline."
I was about to say something when my cat came flying out from the kitchen. He gave Fynn and I a meow, then jumped to the roof and clambered across the shingles. In a moment he had disappeared onto an overhanging tree branch.
"How will Zachary get back inside?" Fynn asked.
"Oh, he's learned how to open the screen door."
"How extraordinary."
"Well, I have to leave it open a crack, just enough for his paw." I thought for a second. "Hmm… Better fill up his bowl with food…"

***

Our first stop was the Cove Diner, twice around the Oldham rotary— I missed it the first time. My hope was a giant coffee to go. We parked and moments later a Ford Explorer pulled in along side. It was Chief Durbin and he stepped down from his vehicle with a grin and an armload of papers.

"What a coincidence…" he called out to us. "Fynn and Jardel, good to see you guys."

"Detective Durbin, how are you, my friend?" Fynn greeted him. "I see you are burdened with paperwork, the curse of being a policeman, eh?" He laughed.

"Funny you say that… but no… these days there is no paperwork, it's all gone digital, unless I have to print out a moving violation." He held up his bundle. "A personal thing… history, you might call it."

"Eh?"

"I was going through some old stuff my Grandma Daisy had."

"Old stuff?" I asked.

"From the nursing home… and the attic, all those boxes…" Durbin looked to the ground for a moment. "Oh, hey, and thanks for coming to the funeral last month." He locked his gaze. Fynn and I nodded, then followed him towards the Cove Diner. "So what are you guys up to? Grabbing a late night snack?"

"Just coffee to go."

"To go?"

"Road trip."

"You're kidding." Durbin stared at me. "You're leaving now? This late?"

"Miss the traffic."

"Is it an emergency or something?"

"Not really."

"A case?" Durbin stopped in his tracks.

"Might be."

"Where? If you don't mind me asking."

"Babylon."

"Long Island, New York?"

I nodded.

Durbin glanced back and forth between us. "It's not about the Gilgo Beach Killer, is it?"

"Who?" I asked.

"You never heard of him, Patrick? Ten corpses buried along the side of Ocean Parkway."

"When did this happen?"

"Well, the last body was discovered about five years ago, but the murders probably go back twenty."

"A serial killer— on the loose for twenty years?"

"Ah, I am familiar with that case," Fynn said. "It has gained some notoriety... but such is beyond our capabilities."

"What makes you so modest all of a sudden, Inspector?" Durbin flashed a grin and resumed his pace.

"Well, there is scant evidence, and I have no information about it except what I've read in the newspapers."

"That's never stopped you before," Durbin said with a good natured laugh. "Hey— I have a close friend in Babylon," he continued. "We went through the academy together. She worked that case."

"Never caught him though?" I asked.

"No, but it ate up ten years of her life— nearly ruined her career... I think the Feds took over..." Durbin paused for a moment. "Maybe you could look her up and say hi."

"It would be a pleasure, I'm sure." Fynn smiled. "What's her name?"

"Mitch," Durbin replied with a chuckle. "Kind of a long story as to why... I'll write down her number."

***

The Cove Diner was empty this time of night and dimly lit. Retro-deco, chrome trim and formica. We sat ourselves in a booth with me on one side; Fynn and the chief opposite. The lights flickered for a moment and we all thought the power might go out again. It did, and we sat in the dark.

"The whole town is probably out... right?"

"And the third time in as many days."

"Problems with the main transformer," Durbin said. "That's what I've been told." The words were hardly from his mouth when everything snapped back to normal. "You ever find that woman, the one in the sketch?" Durbin asked.

"No. Have you any news of her?" Fynn replied.

"Still nothing... She's definitely not been seen locally."

The waiter came over carrying coffee mugs and a metal carafe. He nodded and tried to smile but seemed sleepy. He also looked vaguely familiar: a short pudgy guy, dressed in a vest and matching pinstripe pants. An apron covered the rest. He had a mop of black hair slicked down, and a small mustache. He was probably the owner, but tonight he was also waiter and cook.

"So… you're leaving now to get to New York by dawn?" Durbin started and poured out a coffee for each of us.

"That was the idea… miss the traffic."

"It's quite a hike. You might take the ferry."

"What ferry?"

"Outta New London, takes a little longer than driving but worth it."

"We should have a bite to eat, before our long journey," Fynn said and passed along menus.

The waiter returned after a few minutes holding his stubby pencil and a pad. I watched him give Durbin a wink. They seemed to know each other and somehow this did not sit well with me.

"I'll have a bologna sandwich on toasted rye, maybe with a bit of mustard," Fynn ordered.

"An omelet for me, ham and cheese…"

"What kind of cheese?" the waiter asked.

"Surprise me," I replied and glanced up at him with a smile.

"Want green peppers and onions with that? Then it's a western omelet and two dollars cheaper."

"Sure, sounds good."

He turned to Durbin. "Chief?"

"Just the usual, Omar, thanks."

"… So, Richard, tell us about your grandmother and all this history she's left you…" Fynn began with a smile.

"Some old photo albums and a journal."

"Whose journal? Grandma Daisy's?" I asked.

"No, my grandfather, Richard Durbin the first. He was the sheriff in this town a long time ago."

"When was that?"

"The nineteen thirties and forties…"

"It would make a good story for the Chronicle," I said, and did my best to smile.

"Probably. I haven't read much of it… but some weird stuff went on back then."

"Like?"

"Bootleggers, murders, counterfeiters, and trouble at Saint Albans Asylum."

"Asylum?"

"Well, it was a hospital back then…" Durbin grinned and sifted through his stack of papers. "Oh hey, you should see this picture I found," the detective said and put a faded photo on the table. "Some kind of dinner party at Saint Albans. That's Grandma Daisy's sister, Elsie— she worked there as a nurse during the depression. I haven't ID'ed anyone else yet…" Durbin laughed. "Ha, if I didn't know better, I'd say that one was you, Patrick. And that guy in the chair looks just like Fynn."

I picked up the photo for a better look but could tell Durbin was eyeing me for a reaction. I instantly recognized Elsie, Doctor Valenti, Mortimer as Professor Mallinger, two Drummonds, and even Lothar looming in the background. That was a different life for me. I handed the picture to Fynn who barely gave it a glance.

Durbin slid another photo across the tabletop. It was a blurry picture of a man standing in front of the rooming house on Fourth Street. He was posing by a white picket fence in between a very young Grandma Daisy and her sister Elsie Everest— 1933 was written on the back.

I glanced at it but said nothing, though I remembered Elsie fondly, and our life together.

"That guy looks a whole lot like you, Patrick. Don't you think?"

"It could be anyone… kind of out of focus…"

"Yeah… well, that's Grandma Daisy— she was like eighteen or something, and that's her older sister Elsie."

"What happened to her?"

"Elsie? Not sure… long since dead, I guess— but I don't know much about her."

I took a closer look at the picture. "This is a photocopy. What happened to the original?"

"Oh, Ricky's got them… My son… He's putting it all online or something."

"Online?"

"Yeah, he's a crazy social media guy." Durbin grinned.

I had seen plenty of Ricky over the summer, Durbin the Fourth; up at the Beachcomber dance club, cruising around town in his Pontiac T-37, or idling its throaty engine in some parking lot. He also had the job of directing traffic on Long Neck Road. He hadn't mentioned any of this to me.

The waiter returned with our order. Durbin's usual was a stack of pancakes and a side of sausages.

"Do you need your grandmother's manuscript returned?" Fynn asked.

"No hurry on that," Durbin said while pouring syrup.

"Good. I sent it to an expert on such matters, an antiquarian— I hope you don't mind…"

"You think it's worth something?"

"Well, he may attempt to translate it."

Durbin nodded. "You know, I still have custody of the other book."

"Which one?"

"From the Fred Mears trial, in evidence. Mrs Dumont never wants to see it again. Maybe this expert of yours might be interested."

"I can say he would be… most interested." Fynn smiled.

"You can pick it up at the station anytime."

I kept my best poker face but could feel my eyebrow raise slightly and hoped Durbin hadn't noticed.

"And what of the other book?" Fynn asked.

"Still missing from the Yale library, if that's what you mean. Hasn't been recovered." Durbin paused. "Say, Fynn, that might be a good case for you…" He grinned.

"I'm enjoying my retirement, but thank you for the offer, Chief."

***

We returned to the parking lot. I was ready for the long drive ahead, giant coffee in hand. Fynn took me by the arm though. "Do you have a spare, Patrick?" he asked, glancing to the ground.

"A spare what?"

"A spare tire."

"Do you have two?" Durbin added. "They're both flat."

I walked around to the front of the car. "Great, now what?"

"C'mon, I'll give you both a ride," Durbin offered. "And I'll call a tow truck… Ralph's garage is open twenty-four-seven."

I nodded and climbed into Durbin's jet black Explorer. It was well after midnight when I returned to my apartment, and feared the worst when I bound up the spiral steps to find the screen door open. This wasn't my cat's doing. The apartment had been ransacked, things knocked down and scattered everywhere, and it was chaos in the kitchen. The trash had been overturned and strewn across the floor. I saw a pair of glowing eyes in the darkest corner, low to the floor. It startled me to no end. I flipped on the light. There was the culprit: a large raccoon lurking by the cabinets. Moving far from the sliding door, I gave it reason to exit and the creature slinked out into the night.

I heard myself make an odd rhythmic noise and came to realize it was a laugh. I hadn't made that sound in so long, I barely recognized it. Hard to admit, but the summer had been more stressful than I let myself believe. My recent travels with Inspector Fynn and the burden of memory were taking a toll.

A few minutes later I heard a tiny meow. Zachary poked his head through the door. "Hey, little guy," I called out. He meandered over and jumped up into my lap. I felt his claws. He then curled up and started purring expectantly.

chapter two
amusement parking

Next day, Ralph called from the garage in the early afternoon. My car was ready. Flat fixed, both of them.

"How do you suppose it happened?" I asked.

"What do you mean?"

"The odds that both tires would go flat?"

Ralph laughed. "Very low, I guess... Did you hit a curb or something?"

"No."

"Run over a box of nails, a broken bottle?"

"Not that I know of."

"Well, I found a hole in each tire."

"Sabotage?"

"No..." he laughed again. "Luck."

"How is it lucky?"

"If you drove another couple of hundred miles, the engine would have seized."

"What?"

"When was the last time you changed the oil?"

I tried to remember but couldn't.

"I've never seen so much sludge..." Ralph continued, "more like gunk. So, I'd say you're lucky in the end."

"You fixed that too?"

"I did."

"Thanks. How much do I owe you?"

"One twenty-nine for the tow, ten bucks a tire— for repair. Oil change... had to use the synthetic: fifty-nine ninety-five... tax... Well, two hundred bucks ought to cover it."

"I'll be right over..." I paused. "Do you think I'll make it to New York?"

"The Saab will... mechanically speaking."

* * *

I picked up Inspector Fynn from his house on Dune Road just before sunset. His wife Lorraine and his daughter Anika were out again— not that I missed them all that much; we had spent a lot of the summer together, walking along the beach, dining out, or just sitting on the deck to all hours.

"Where's Lorraine tonight?"

"With her sister Elaine, at the cinema, I think."

"And Anika?"

"Oh... Out with Sven again."

"Sven the lifeguard?"

Fynn nodded.

"What do you know about this guy?"

"Very little, except that he speaks excellent Dutch."

I felt a bit flustered and had no reply, but I did have Zachary my cat stuffed into a pet carrier. He was surprisingly patient about the whole ordeal. I dropped him to the kitchen floor and Fynn's dog Asta came rushing over. After just a few moments, they seemed to recognize each other. Zachary sauntered over to Asta's kibble bowl and started to crunch away. The little dog looked on helplessly.

"You mentioned they got along in the past," Fynn said, stooping, petting each creature, and marveling.

"You remember that?"

"I do."

"I'm not even sure they lived through that timeline together."

"Nonetheless…" Fynn smiled and raised himself to his full height. "Ready?"

"I guess."

"And you're sure you don't mind traveling at such an hour?"

"I like driving at night, and missing the traffic."

"Good. I've left a note for Anika and Lorraine." He ushered me to the front door. I had steeled myself for the drive to New York, but still felt a bit anxious when Fynn plopped down in the passenger seat and waved his hand. "Off we go," he said.

"No luggage?"

"We won't be gone that long."

"You're just bringing that?" I glanced down at the bear claw cane that Fynn had brought.

"Only as a last resort."

"And you're positive Pavel has fixed it this time?"

"Mr Mekanos assures me, yes. No doubling, no doppelgängers— I have his solemn promise."

"Did he test it thoroughly?"

"I doubt it."

"Did you test it yourself?"

"No."

"Not exactly a ringing endorsement. What does Edmund say?"

"Mr Fickster gives the same assurances, more or less."

"Uh-oh."

"I consider Edmund to be fairly reliable." Fynn turned to me. "I will admit he has mentioned a few caveats."

"Like?"

"If there is an existing concurrency, and one travels to the past, it is just like a soft jump."

"What happens to the cane?"

"It does not travel with you."

"Where does it go?"

"It remains in the future that has yet to exist."

"What— just rattles to the ground?"

"Edmund tells me that sometimes it's there and sometimes it's lost, like any future event."

"I'm still skeptical. Remember Hawaii?"

"Yes." Fynn gave a pained smile.

"And Pasadena."

"An even worse situation."

"I wonder what happened to those doubles?"

"What do you mean?" Fynn asked.

"The doubles we left behind."

"I'm sure they no longer exist."

"No?"

"We are here in the present and they are not. Their future was irrevocably altered. I believe doubles are removed by traveling."

"What makes you say that?"

"Ah, but only one of us can jump to the future, a future that has yet to exist."

"But that would make them leave-behinds."

"Indeed it would… but if we leave versions of ourselves in the past, and that past is changed, then I suppose they don't exist any longer."

I had to think about this, then said, "When I first made a double, nothing much happened. My future self was still there."

"Yes, but you merely persisted into his present. If you were to jump about from there, things may have been different."

"Hmm, I'll have to trust you on that."

"As I've said, Patrick, we will use the cane only if all else fails."

"Okay…" I paused and put the Saab in gear. "Do you want to stop and get a coffee for the road?"

"If you'd like, though I will confess to a hankering for some saltwater taffy." He smiled.

"Now?"

"If it's not too much trouble."

I suspected Fynn was up to something but played along. "We'll have to stop at the Pier— it's the only place I know that sells it."

"The amusement park?"

I nodded.

"We have time, yes? It seems early."

***

Twenty minutes later I found a parking spot near the Commodore Hotel. We walked up to the amusement pier. It was like a semi-permanent carnival, seasonal though, and crowded this evening. I spotted a copy of the *Chronicle* along the way and grabbed one from its metal box. The headline read: *Fireflies Invade Blackwater Quarry*.

"What's wrong, Patrick?"

"This story in the paper."

"Yes, I've already read it… an ecological anomaly that has baffled the experts. Didn't your friend Joey Jegal write this?"

"Yeah, he took over for me after I left… It just seems weird to me."

"Why is that?"

"I remember seeing dragonflies there, but not fireflies."

"Ah, yes, *vuurvliegjes*… and more than anyone has ever counted, according to the story."

***

The west side of the boardwalk was crowded with onlookers. We didn't find a bench to sit but enough space on the railing to lean and watch the red disk slip below Serenity Bay. As always, a majestic sight. I tried to remind myself it wasn't the sun that was moving, it was us, the earth that was turning.

Fynn nodded up the pier and we started in that direction; weathered planks passed beneath our feet. The fun house, the hall of mirrors, arcades; lights were winking on and most of the rides were in full swing. A modest ferris wheel at the end of the pier loomed, spinning cups were wildly rotating, bumper cars driving recklessly, and a colossal pirate ship creaked back and forth at a frightening angle.

Fynn stopped for a moment to watch the carousel. I could hear calliope music above all the other racket. "A merry-go-round, Patrick," he said solemnly. "Old horses from a century ago; they're carved from wood."

We sifted through the crowd, it was young: kids mostly, some parents in tow, strollers. Everywhere, lots of cries of startled glee and shrieks of delight. Safe scary, I thought, though I'd be the last person to ride the wooden roller-coaster that hung precariously over the edge of the water.

A group of teenagers seemed to single us out, talking and giggling among themselves, but following discreetly while holding up their phones. I felt sure they were taking our picture.

"Friends of yours, Patrick?" Fynn asked quietly.

I shook my head no. We ignored them and continued along the boardwalk, past a kind of midway, and concession stands selling everything from hot dogs to funnel cakes. The smell of cotton candy called me back to the present when a line of booths came to my notice. Games of chance, giant wheels, hooping rings, squirting guns, air-rifles, and plastic bags full of goldfish.

"You two, there," a barker called out. "Care to try your luck?" I would have paid him no mind at all, but there was something familiar in his voice. "I can see your future," he continued, "and I can almost guarantee that you'll win a prize."

I glanced over for a better look. It was Javelin Mortimer— our nemesis, for the lack of a better word. I turned to Fynn though he hardly seemed surprised. This iteration of Mortimer was about my age, if not a bit older. His dark hair was slicked back, and he sported a small mustache with half a beard. He was wearing an eyepatch as well. We strode over to him.

"Shouldn't you be in prison or something?" I asked.

Mortimer smiled. "Yes, well, I served my time thanks to you, but I've returned nonetheless."

"How?"

He glared at me. "Do you really need to know all the specifics?"

"I guess not… but what are you doing here?"

"Nothing sinister, I can assure you, Mr Jardel." He gave me his thin smile and pushed a bucket of ping pong balls in our direction. "Care to try your luck? Ten throws for a dollar— though I'll waive the fee— just bounce the ball into the hole to win a prize," he explained, and did exactly that without even looking.

Fynn tried his luck with less success and was soon standing in front of an empty pail. I stared over at the targets: open mouthed clowns in a row some ten yards distant. Each wore a pointy cap of a different color, and all of them faced slightly askew. Also, I'm almost certain, I saw a pair of large boots poking out from behind the curtain.

I took my shot and it went in directly. Mortimer was surprised. He reached above his head, then handed me some sort of stuffed moose. It was purple. With a nod to a mom, I passed it off to her six year old who had wandered by. I turned back to Mortimer. "I'm still waiting for an answer…"

"Yes, why am I here? Simply, I'm convinced Kali Shunya is now a danger and should be eliminated."

"Then you remember our meeting with the Arbiter?" Fynn asked.

"I do…" Mortimer faced him. "And I was quite astonished when all those memories came rushing back, so to speak."

"Your trials along the tundra?" Fynn continued.

"Aside from the biting cold and my aching legs, I fared well enough. In the end, the Arbiter kept his promise and returned me to the past."

"When?" I asked.

"Seems like just yesterday."

"The Paris Metro?"

"Yes, while waiting for the train."

"To where?"

"If you must know, I was on my way to visit *Père Lachaise*."

"Who?"

"Not who, Mr Jardel. It's a necropolis of sorts."

"A what?"

"A cemetery. Some of my former selves are interred there."

"Oh… But you're here now, today."

"Indeed I am."

"But how?"

"Details, details, Mr Jardel. It's enough that I am in this present, eh?"

"I'm still not sure what you're doing in Sand City."

"Yes, well, I am incognito at the moment."

"Are you married to Melissa?"

"Who?" Mortimer asked, but thought for a bit. "Oh yes, the lovely Melissa from your newspaper. Not this time through."

"You're not the father of Madison?"

"Who?"

"Her daughter."

"No. She was adopted. I have no offspring as it were. If I were to raise children of my own—"

Fynn interrupted. "And the criminal proceedings?"

"Not more than a minor inconvenience. I was detained for a time, placed on remand and then escaped to travel back a few months."

"To here?" I tried to clarify.

"Yes…" Mortimer glared at me again. "But gentlemen, to the point: several of my doppelgängers have ceased to exist, or rather the timelines they were occupying. I will say, I've grown alarmed by this."

"Disappearing timelines?" Fynn asked.

"It's not so much that the timelines are disappearing, it's more that they are empty."

"Empty?"

"Devoid of humans."

"So you are willing to help us?"

"I am."

"How can we possibly trust you?" I blurted.

"I don't expect you can. Our general purposes however have aligned. I will only ask that you judge me by my deeds from this point on." Mortimer began closing up his booth by hauling down a heavy grate. "I am supposing we have a few matters to discuss. Come around to the back and I'll let you in."

Fynn was sanguine about it all though there was a history between the two, more than I could ever know. My dealings with Mortimer were trivial compared to their epic struggles. I did know that he had locked Fynn in a dungeon for nearly twenty years, and stranded him in the Flatlands for who knows how long. The inspector had also been thrown from the rooftops of Paris, hunted down by Denise Drummond. And it was Mortimer who burned down the library.

"Can we believe him?" I whispered.

"Can the fox trust the scorpion who rides upon his back? Of course not, but we might hear what he has to say."

Mortimer appeared at the side door and bid us to enter. It was a dark corridor with black curtains against one side, too narrow to pass except single file. Nor was the ceiling very high, barely enough room for us to stand upright. At the far end I saw a hunched figure, his face obscured by shadow; though I could see he was enormous, perched on a rickety chair and wearing the boots I had seen previously. I also noticed Mortimer's jackal-headed cane leaning against the nearby wall. That explained a lot.

"Pavel can fix that, you know," I said, nodding to the corner of the booth.

"Fix it? My cane? How?"

"So that it doesn't make duplicates."

"I'm not sure fix is the right word then."

"What do you mean?"

"I like having other versions of myself. Sad as it may be, there is no one else in the world that I'd rather converse with." Mortimer swept the curtains aside and pushed against the row of clown heads; they opened like a door on either side, and he found us stools so that we might sit.

"Well, here we all are, eh?" he began rather awkwardly. "In the hopes of better cooperation, I am prepared to overlook all the injustices served upon me by the both of you."

"Injustices?" Fynn asked.

"Yes, I recall neither of you raised a hand to help when I was thrown into the icy Atlantic."

"I'm pretty sure that was your grandfather."

"You may be right, Mr Jardel." Mortimer paced among the clown heads. "And yet, you are traipsing around telling everyone that I burned down the Library at the Palisades."

"Didn't you?"

"I most certainly did not. I have it on good authority it was one of Madame Madeline's guests— careless with a candlestick, I was informed."

"What about the library here in town?"

"Oh, but that was so long ago, I barely recall. Besides it was Mr Mears or one of the Drummond boys."

"Under your direction…"

"I hear you have a brand new library in Sand City these days. Quite lovely, I'm told."

I tried to remember all the other terrible deeds Mortimer had committed, and recalled how he had threatened Elsie all those years ago in 1933. My feeling of annoyance moved towards anger. Fynn sensed it and held me back by one arm.

"You had me imprisoned in a dungeon for twenty years," the inspector changed the subject.

"Not directly." Mortimer smiled. "In fact it was Patrick who sentenced you, am I not correct?"

"What?" I protested.

"Were you not sitting on the tribunal in Modena, hmm?"

"But—"

"No matter," he cut me off.

"And the eternity I spent at the Flatlands?" Fynn asked, daring him to answer.

"Oh Tractus, you must have enjoyed at least a portion of your time there. Lolling on the beach, strolling in the sun… conversing with poets, philosophers and alike. Sounds rather idyllic to me."

"It wore rather thin after a few decades, and I was shackled to a bench for a good part of the time."

"Nonetheless, the island is like a health spa and a holiday resort all rolled into one." Mortimer paused, then took a menacing step towards Fynn. "Certainly you remember tossing me from the cliffs at the quarry?"

"Not until after you stabbed me with that sword of yours," he replied.

Mortimer stood silent for a moment, then said, "On another occasion, you forced me to jump into a disastrous future from the Saint Albans planetarium— and I was nothing but nice to you that day."

"I would say polite rather than nice," Fynn countered.

"And all that time and effort I spent calibrating the cane— eh? That should count for something."

"Do you mean depriving all those hapless patients of their ubiety?"

"Ha, I vividly recollect that you were neither nice nor polite when you accosted me at the fancy dress party, and absconded with my personal property…"

"The cane, you mean to say? That you stole from Pavel Mekanos?"

"I doubt it was his in the first place."

"It was most certainly not yours."

"Yes, well, I don't know what good all this bickering will accomplish."

"Bickering?" Fynn exploded with a scathing tone. "You murdered my wife in cold blood, her sister and my beloved daughter Anika."

"For this I apologize, Tractus, most sincerely. And tell me, are they not all well at present?"

"That is beside the point. These events still live on in my memory."

"They live on in anger, I would say. Recall, in penance, I had to spend fifty years as a milkman."

"What?" I asked, and then remembered the incident: a burglary at Fynn's house, and an idling white truck in the driveway. "That was just to get your cane back."

"My rightful property, I must point out… Fifty years as a milkman— can you imagine what sort of life that was, Patrick?" Mortimer swung around, but then seated himself on a stool. He took a few measured breaths. "I will admit I did not experience all of these events firsthand— but they were well-described to me."

"By one of your doubles?"

"Of course… and he had no reason to lie."

"No?"

"Believe it or not," Mortimer said, "not all versions of myself are as thoroughly evil as you'd like to think. Some of us are quite… benevolent."

Fynn turned to him. "You might convince me of this with your deeds and not merely your words."

"Fair enough," he replied. "I have something tangible. Call it a peace offering, if you will." Mortimer lifted a heavy box to one of the stools and opened it, then drew out a bundle wrapped in cloth. He slowly revealed three musty books. "The Traveler's Guide, the *Dux Viaticum*," he announced. "It may be of some use in stopping Kali."

"From my safety deposit box?" Fynn asked.

"Two of the volumes, yes. The third though is from the Yale library."

"The one that Chloe and Lilly stole?"

"Correct."

"Where are they?"

"The books? Just as you see them."

"No, Chloe and Lilly..."

"Ah, I've not seen them since Amsterdam, last spring."

"And Denise Drummond?"

"Her as well."

"You murdered her."

"I did. She was a danger."

"To whom?"

"Myself of course, and others, certainly Tractus and even you, Patrick."

"You're a killer."

"I am. I have killed people, many people." Mortimer paused and gave us his thin smile. "And this is exactly why you need my help. I doubt either of you have the stomach to stop Kali once and for all."

Fynn took my arm; he could easily sense my rising anger. "Such would be a last resort," he said to Mortimer.

"Yes, it's remarkable what one might do when self-preservation is at stake. And by that, I mean you, me, Patrick, and the rest of humanity."

"You would kill Kali?"

"I'd be happy to, or have Lothar do it."

"Lothar?" I asked, a bit surprised.

"He's quite capable of following my instructions."

I stared harder at the figure stooped in the shadows, and then it dawned on me that I knew this giant. I walked a bit closer.

"Careful there, Patrick," Mortimer warned. "He's not the Lothar you might expect."

"What do you mean?"

"The one who possesses reason. Not to mention, he's a bit leery of strangers."

"Lothar?" I called out.

He didn't seem to recognize me, but when he turned into the light I could see the symmetrical crescent scars on either side of his forehead.

"Where did you find him?" I asked.

"Well, he showed up on my doorstep one day and I took pity on him."

"Doctor... friend," Lothar called out from his shadowy corner.

Mortimer laughed uneasily. "Yes, he still thinks I'm Doctor Mallinger— imagine that?"

"Is this a different version of Lothar?"

"Decidedly so..."

"No, I mean a duplicate."

"Who can say?" Mortimer replied. "He can still cook rather well." He turned to the sad-faced giant. "Food... good, right Lothar?"

"Food... good. Lothar hungry."

"Gracious, I should have never uttered the word. Now he'll be pestering me to no end." Mortimer reached into his pocket and pulled out a wad of bills. He peeled off a few twenties. "Patrick, could you be a pal and walk up to the concession stand? Buy half a dozen corn dogs... And get one for yourself, if you'd like." He turned to Fynn. "Tractus?"

"I'm still waiting for my saltwater taffy."

"Indeed, that's just another few stalls down on the left." Mortimer grinned at me. "Would you be a chum?"

"Patrick... friend. Patrick get food..." I heard Lothar call out again.

"Where's Mr Q?" I asked.

"Last I saw, he was at the *Hotel de Cirque*, waiting for an audience with the Arbiter."

"An audience?" Fynn asked.

"He's a bit like a deity to Mr Quandary, worships the very ground he walks upon."

"And you? What do you think of him?"

"Hmm, haven't given it much thought. The Arbiter can be meddlesome, but for the most part, he rarely hinders my efforts. He usually keeps his promises and I will admit that I admire his reasonable approach to things. Indeed, he can be persuasive at times."

"And the books?" Fynn asked.

"Yes, well, I couldn't find anyone who could make sense of them at all." Mortimer paused. "Still, you may know such a person, and they may shine a light on some of Kali's weaknesses. Don't you think?"

"We will accept your peace offering in the spirit which it is given… Thank you," Fynn said.

"Have you encountered her at all?" Mortimer asked.

"Not as of yet." I heard Fynn answer with a blatant lie, and remembered our journey to Hawaii just a week ago.

"Lothar hungry," the goliath called out from the shadows, stirring in his chair.

"Patience, my loathsome giant. Corn dogs tonight."

"And have you run up against Kali since we've last spoken?" Fynn continued.

"Several times."

"And?"

"It's become clear that she wants to end history as we know it," Mortimer replied. "Though she seems to concern herself with the broad swathes of events, and not the individual threads of people's personal lives."

"That's all you have to say?"

"Very well, I will also admit that a few of my lesser selves have been collaborating with her from time to time. I've tried to warn them about the danger but some of them refuse to listen."

"Some of them?"

"Most of them… and exactly why you are better suited to stopping her, Fynn."

"Why is that?"

"There's only one of you, as far as I can tell." Mortimer paused for a moment. "But tell me, Tractus, how is it that I saw you die? Shot in the heart. Perhaps I'm mistaken to think of you in the singular."

"You are not."

"Yet here you stand before me? You must explain this trickery."

"I'd prefer not to," Fynn replied, tight lipped.

"Well, Kali probably thinks you're dead. Last thing she saw was you being shot."

"Have you noticed any weaknesses in her? Something we might exploit to our advantage?"

"Well… music seems to distract her, if that's any help."

"What do you mean?"

"Just something I noticed. It calls to her like a siren song, and for a moment at least, she seems quite lost."

"And is that why you're here?"

"Yes, it's a noisy environment, full of distractions."

"Anything else?"

"She's rather arrogant, I'd say."

"How so?"

"She might tinker with history here and there, but cares not a whit for the consequences."

"I'm not following exactly."

"She might set things on a different course, but never follows up on it… She's not likely to go back to see the results, the chain of her causality."

"Hmm…" Fynn considered. "Thank you, Javelin. Such is an astute observation and it may prove helpful to us."

"You're welcome… though, I'm not sure how."

"Well, if arrogance is her weakness—"

Mortimer interrupted. "I'm also wondering if there is more than one Kali now."

"What makes you say that?"

"Well, for someone so omnipotent, she seems rather forgetful, and easily confused. Perhaps her memory has limits. I don't think she always remembers who I am, or my counterparts."

"That also may be useful to us. Can you be more specific?"

"No… our encounters have been brief. I for one chose not to linger in any present she might occupy." Mortimer considered further, "I did notice she doesn't seem able to travel geographically, in space, I would say, not unless she uses conventional means."

"It hardly matters if she can soft jump to any location she's been previously," Fynn cautioned. "And that said, we do not know the full extent of her abilities."

"Oh, you mean to say her vanishing act. Well, I suppose she can jump a moment into the future or the past, and to us it appears as if she's flitting from here to there."

"A moment?"

"The tick of a clock, a single tock of the second hand." Mortimer turned to me. "Patrick, the corn dogs, if you would?"

"Right…"

"Oh, and be sure to bring extra mayonnaise."

***

The sky was fully dark now. All along the pier, lights commanded, glowing, blinking, and flashing. Few of them were pure white, rather they glared in color: blues, reds and yellow. A patchy reflection smeared across the still waters of Serenity Bay. All else was in shadow, including the gentle waves that unceasingly lapped against the pylons.

I found the concession stand easily enough. It was more like a pavilion than a booth, with a huge wrap-around counter in the middle of the boardwalk. I ordered half a dozen corn dogs and asked for it to go. The guy behind the counter gave me a look. He was wearing a paper chef's hat and I thought he might be standing on stilts.

"What, like in a big bag?" he asked, peering down at me.

"Perfect. I'll be right back for them…" I walked up to the taffy store. Along the way I had the feeling of being followed and turned to see who was at my back. It was a couple of teenagers and one of them snapped my picture on her phone.

"Hey, you're Patrick, right? Ricky's friend," she called out.

"Ricky Durbin? Sure, I know Ricky…" I smiled.

"I'm following you now."

"I noticed."

"No, I mean on *Insta-Chat*."

"What?"

"Social media…" She held up her phone.

"Oh."

"You're that reporter… and you're friends with that old guy, Fynn. I saw your pictures."

"What's this about?"

"It's just *so amazing* to meet you in real life."

I wasn't at all sure what she was talking about. "Where's Ricky tonight?"

"How would I know?"

"I thought he was your friend."

"Not really... I just follow his stuff... So what's it like?"

"What's *what* like?"

"Umm... immortality."

"I'm not sure I understand what you're saying."

"So, are you like a vampire, or what?" the other girl asked.

"Not that I know of."

"Okay, well, never mind. Nice to meet you anyway," she said, obviously disappointed, and turned to her friend to whisper something. They both smiled at me and then disappeared up the boardwalk.

I returned to the clown head booth with a bag full of corn dogs, knocking on the side door. Lothar showed some enthusiasm at least and ushered me in. Fynn was still conversing with Mortimer and out of earshot. I watched them. I saw Fynn take out his pen knife and make a small cut on Mortimer's index finger. He then dabbed it with something that looked like a magic marker. Mortimer winced in pain. I wondered what that was all about.

I left and strolled down the pier to buy a hot pretzel for myself. The inspector caught up with me a few minutes later.

"Well?" I asked, and handed him a small white box.

"Yes, well... I've asked Mortimer to meet us later, or earlier, as the case may be."

"Where?"

"Elsewhere." Fynn raised a smile.

"Did you mention Hawaii to him?"

"Eh?" Fynn looked at me. "No, it's not something Mortimer needs to know about. In fact, it's best if all that stays between us."

I knew not to ask any more questions for now.

chapter three
lands end

What Mortimer did not know, nor had Inspector Fynn mentioned, was that we had already encountered Kali in recent days. Our previous excursion took us back to the 1940s. According to the Arbiter, she was meddling with history, and it was our job to find out why. Before our departure we debated whether or not to use the bear claw cane. There was the matter of an existing concurrency:

"Tell me, Patrick, do you recall where you were in nineteen forty-one or so?"

I had to think for a moment. "I was living with Elsie Everest."

"Oh yes, the pretty nurse from Saint Albans... and you were in a different hemisphere entirely, if I remember."

"That's right... Rio."

"Well, it can't be helped. I'm sorry to say you'll have to interrupt that life."

"Why?"

"We have a different destination to visit in just the same time period."

"What about Elsie?"

"You can return to her anytime you wish." He gave me a hopeful smile.

"What about you?"

"Ah, I was a much younger man."

"Wait a second... you're talking about making doubles. You want to risk using the cane?"

"Yes, well, I see no other alternative, though we will avoid interacting with our other selves."

"Alright..." I paused uncomfortably.

"And who is to say the past will be as we expect."

"What?"

"How often have we traveled there to find that things are not as they should be?"

Fynn was right but I was loath to think about it.

"Should we become separated, meet me at this address on this day and at this hour." He handed me a note.

"I know this place... sort of... it's familiar to me."

"Yes, it is where Murray lives, his apartment in New York City. He's been in the same flat for most of his adult life. And it's quite near the train station."

"Why would we get separated?"

"Two traveling on one cane... I expect there may be a certain amount of geographic wobble."

With both of us holding on, Fynn and I jumped at dawn from a life guard chair near North Hollow Beach. And while his timing was accurate, we landed somewhere in the deep woods. A hard jump for us both. On arriving, it seemed to be late November, the trees barely hanging on to their foliage, and it was cold. Fynn had warned me to dress well. I found him a few hundred yards away, walking across a clearing and carrying a well-worn valise.

"Why did we land so far away?"

"Oh, that's my doing..." Fynn replied. "I thought if we traveled west we might save some bother."

"Do you know where we are?"

Fynn pointed. There were smoke stacks in the distance, down in a valley by a river, near a large town or a small city. It took nearly a day to hike there and by then I was starving. The backpack I carried had little room for provisions, instead filled with books and files, books that no one from this time period should ever see.

Albany as it turned out was big enough to meet our needs. Fynn exchanged a bag of gold doubloons at a coin shop for local currency, and next we found a quiet restaurant. With full bellies and a few odd stares we came across a clothing store for appropriate attire. In the end, Fynn looked as dapper as usual, stylish; and I was happy enough to wear a warm trench coat, and a wide brimmed fedora.

It was a far cry from the America that I had encountered in 1933. The nation was on a war footing it seemed. Everyone was busy, working, perhaps a bit wary, but a solidarity or common sense of purpose lay beneath their daily lives. Faces were not as grim as I had seen during the depression; they were earnest and determined. I glanced at a headline on the newsstand: *FDR Proclaims*

Thanksgiving Holiday.

This was something of a new experience. What I mean is, 1941 was so very different from 1933, when I was here last, yet only eight years had passed. In my own time, my usual present, I might ask how much difference eight years would make. Not much, at least not in a big sense. That history flowed at a different rate than time itself was becoming increasingly obvious.

***

We were sent here by the Arbiter. Events had been changed in my familiar timeline, not here in Albany, but thousands of miles to the west and halfway across the Pacific. And according to Mr A, it was Kali's doing. "This is no mere fluke, a mishap or random occurrence… it is a deliberate attempt to alter a timeline," he had told Fynn.

I still harbored doubts. The inspector led me to the train station, complaining the whole way:

"Ah… But why choose this place and time? It seems almost cliché… It's nothing more than headline history."

"Maybe Kali doesn't know much about it."

"What are you saying, Patrick?"

"Maybe she only knows about big historical events that are well-recorded."

He turned to me. "Yes, an excellent observation. She may only see the large outlines of things, perhaps as seen from a distant future, or what one reads in a book. Perhaps she fails to look deeply at underlying events."

"What could her intent possibly be?"

"We only know that she is in Hawaii. Of this I've been assured."

"What else did the Arbiter tell you?"

"Not enough, surely…" Fynn grimaced.

"So we still don't know what she did… what she tampered with?"

"No. The Arbiter and Mr Quandary are unsure."

"Mr Q?"

"Yes. The information comes from Mr Quandary, who takes great delight in gathering such tiny details. According to him, on this infamous date, America still enters World War Two, and yet, the outcome of the war has been altered because of some unknown event." Fynn paused. "He theorizes it has something to do with either a radar station or a radio station."

"Didn't we already know about the attack?" I asked.

"Many people say FDR did, and decided to do nothing... It's quite possible, I suppose, in a politically expedient sense. I will imagine they knew about the attack, but not exactly when and where... It might have been at Midway or the Johnson Atoll."

"And you're positive this is all Kali's doing?"

"I'm convinced of it, though if we are very lucky, our paths won't even cross."

Somehow that didn't seem likely.

***

I fell asleep on the train from Albany. Fynn shook me awake at Penn Station. The terminal was jam packed with people, many in uniform, soldiers and sailors, and merchant marines. It was bustling, there were no signs of the great depression, rather, a sense of urgency prevailed.

We ate dinner at a *Horn and Hardart* automat, a kind of giant vending machine. I had a Salisbury steak and mashed potatoes. Fynn chose meatloaf and they seemed suspiciously similar. Afterwards, he sent me to the newsstand to buy a few magazines.

"Why?"

"To be sure things are as they should be, eh?"

I grabbed some newspapers without thinking much about it; and then a copy of *Time*, the *Saturday Evening Post*, and *Newsweek*. The cover of *Life* had a picture of someone vaguely familiar. I read the caption: *King George Vows a Return to His Island Nation.*

They all got stuffed into my backpack. Ten minutes later, we boarded a train to California, first class, a sleeper car, but I was wide awake by now. Fynn and I settled in and sometime later sauntered up to the bar. Everything rocked gently and dark scenery raced by, barely lit, maybe some rural part of Ohio. I recalled the last time we were together on a train; it was 1933 and we were bound for Miami.

"It's hard to believe that you never lived in this present."

"Eh?" Fynn turned to me and took a sip from his glass. The carriage swayed from side to side.

"Nineteen forty-one... that you have no concurrency."

"Oh, I see what you're saying." Fynn smiled. "But I was here before, or I am as the case may be."

"Where is your other self living now?"

"The United Kingdom."

"What are you doing?"

"Working for the allies."

"As a detective?"

"No... a spy of sorts, for the British. "I was using a different identity. I was called Tomás and I befriended a man named Juan Pujol García from Spain."

"Who was he?"

"Garbo, he was called. Also a spy... though for the Germans."

"The Germans?"

"Yes, but a double agent."

"What will happen to that history?"

"It has already occurred."

"But by being here again in this present, you might be changing all that."

"Not if we stay on this side of the Atlantic," Fynn said and smiled. "Though, I suppose I may have to return and relive it."

"Is that possible?"

"Of course, Patrick."

"Won't that change things?"

"We'll have to wait and see." He smiled again. "Tell me, did you find any magazines?"

I pulled out the stack of papers from my backpack and the cover of *Life* immediately got Fynn's attention. A look of concern crossed his face.

"What is it?"

"Things have already gone awry," he said quietly and began to read the article aloud: *Speaking from the Château Frontenac in Quebec City, currently the British Government's provisional headquarters, King George VI declared his intent to rally all loyal members of the commonwealth to arms...*" Fynn paused and looked up from reading.

"I don't recall Great Britain falling to the Nazis."

"Neither do I..." I said, and read from the *Post*: *A year ago, when FDR proclaimed the Corridor of Democracy, my countrymen and I faced our most desperate hour. The seaborne exodus began in Liverpool, Southampton and even Dublin, when a thousand ships sailed east under the protection of the Royal Navy and American forces. We called it the Corridor of Mercy. In the end though, the critics had it right. It was the Corridor of Doom, whereas our convoy was easy prey to German wolf packs that prowled the North Atlantic waters. Tens of thousands of people lost their lives...*

I looked up from reading. "It would have been nice if the Arbiter had mentioned this beforehand."

"I agree. He has been remiss, or he is unaware of these events."

"Kali's doing?" I asked.

"It's hard to imagine she'd be able to cause the fall of Britain."

"Okay, but even if we fix what Kali is about to do, what *about* the rest of it?"

"The war in Europe, you mean to say?"

"Yes."

"But this is already in our relative past. There's little we can do at the moment." Fynn fell silent for a time. The train rocked and swayed along its course. "I say we press on for now."

"Maybe the Arbiter sent someone else to fix things in Europe."

"We can always hope so, Patrick."

***

Inspector Fynn roused me from a deep sleep one night. The train was whistling through the darkness. I only knew we were pretty far west by now.

"Patrick— What say you to a quick detour?"

"Where to?"

"Montana."

"Why?"

"The Mount Rushmore Monument has just been completed— less than a month ago. We might see it in its pristine glory."

"Maybe not."

"There are rumors that they are still tinkering with Roosevelt's mustache."

"Let's just stick to our mission," I said and went back to sleep.

A day or so later we rolled into a rain-soaked Los Angeles, with Fynn insisting that he had a few errands to run. He dropped me off at the Biltmore Hotel, a towering structure just off Pershing Square. The lobby was palatial and overly-ornate.

"We're pretty close to Pasadena," I commented.

"Eh?"

"CalTech, our first errand…"

"Oh… yes, but only geographically."

"Where are you going now?"

"To the hardware store… and a few other places."

"Like?"

"Well, a costume shop for one, and to visit a counterfeiter whom I know about."

"A counterfeiter?"

"Let's call him a document maker."

"Oh…"

"Have you finished all your reading?" Fynn asked.

"Mostly… on the train— Why?"

"We must become experts on the matter. We must know every detail so as to notice what has been changed."

"If anything."

"Do you still doubt this?"

"Well…" I hesitated. "The war in Europe seems more important now."

"I will not disagree, yet our task is to the west. We must focus upon that."

I spent the afternoon in my room reviewing history, specifically, the Pearl Harbor attack and America's entrance into World War Two. Mr Quandary had mentioned something about radio or radar… Fynn wasn't positive what he'd heard. I learned that the Japanese dive bombers had arrived with deadly accuracy by following a civilian broadcast into Honolulu.

The curious radar incident seemed a bit more complicated, and had to do with two novice radar operators in Opana, on the north coast of Oahu:

> Early that fateful morning, Privates Joseph Lockard and George Elliot observed incoming signals and telephoned headquarters for further orders. There was some trouble getting through, but eventually they spoke with Private Joseph McDonald who took the call. His immediate superior, Lieutenant Kermit Tyler, advised there was no cause for alarm. The blips were a dozen B-17 Flying Fortresses due in from San Francisco that morning.

Fynn returned in a good mood, his missions accomplished, and we decided to treat ourselves to dinner and a movie. We ate at Cole's, a few blocks away. Over sandwiches, there was some debate as to which film we should see: either the *Maltese Falcon* or *Shadow of the Thin Man*. And though far from Hollywood, we may have seen countless celebrities that evening, either in the restaurant or the theater. Neither Fynn nor I were likely to recognize them. That said, we did have to sift through some small crowds of reporters here and there, their flashbulbs going off with blinding rapidity.

In the end we watched Hitchcock's *Suspicion* with Cary Grant. While engaging, Fynn found the final scenes dissatisfying and muttered something about the Hays code. It was the newsreel that took our full attention though, and it shocked me to the core. It confirmed what we had already learned, and might as well have been entitled: *The Fall of Britain*.

Filmed in standard propaganda style, the newsreel footage told the story well enough, as did the serious narrator: They had fought on the beaches, in the fields, in the streets, and shop to shop, but in the end they lost. Churchill himself died valiantly; to the last, manning a fifty caliber machine gun perched above Trafalgar Square. He chose martyrdom.

The fall of Britain had actually begun at the end of May 1940, with the *Disaster at Dunkirk*, when more than a quarter of a million men-at-arms were killed or captured, virtually the entire British army. This was a turning point, a crushing blow to morale.

Over the next summer, German Air Marshal Göering saw to it that the coastal radar stations were destroyed. The London blitz was only a secondary tactic. Spitfires were eliminated one by one, many on the ground.

Then came the *October Surprise*... the early days of the month provided calm seas and fog. A full scale Nazi invasion proceeded and beach heads were established near Dover and Brighton.

Two days later, America was firmly entrenched in Iceland and Greenland, strictly as a precautionary measure, it was said; though we stopped short of declaring war on Germany.

There was fierce resistance throughout Britain, yet it amounted to a pull back, ever westward, and to Ireland; civilians mostly, then a mass exodus to the US and Canada... bound for Halifax and Boston.

A vast convoy sailed across the Atlantic, hunted by U-boats; thousands were lost... It's estimated that nearly ten percent of the population evacuated the British Isles, close to five million people: the old, the infirm, women, children, the wealthy, the political class, and those with technical knowledge that could help the war effort; namely, academics, scientists, industrialists, and engineers... But the Corridor of Mercy had become the Corridor of Doom.

***

The following day a hired car took us to San Diego. There, Fynn charted a private yacht to take us to Hawaii. Oddly named the *Cook 'n Dole*, and with no sails and a diesel engine, it seemed more like a small ship, just shy of a hundred feet long. The skipper was a friendly guy, and except for a crew of six, we were alone. There was also a large consignment of pineapples taken on as freight. That seemed counterintuitive to me. "Perhaps they are being returned?" Fynn pointed out.

I had sailed the Atlantic, but this ocean was different, bluer maybe, and deeper. The next afternoon we sat on the deck looking out over a vast unbroken horizon. Fynn tossed me a squeezable bottle.

"What's this?"

"A sanctioned anachronism."

I checked the label: sunscreen.

"Thanks..."

"This is not your first trip on a boat, eh?" Fynn asked with a smile.

"No..." I laughed. "First time on the Pacific though."

"Perhaps we'll encounter a green sunset."

"A what?"

"A rare thing indeed. You've not heard of it?"

"No."

"Something to do with refraction." Fynn sat back. "I feel quite at home on the sea. We are but tiny specks adrift among these endless waves and yet we are able to persist."

Sailing west under calm conditions for the next week was pleasant enough. On stormy days, I studied the books we had brought. And weather permitting, Fynn and I would sit on the deck to discuss the events which were about to unfold. To the tiniest detail, we had become experts on the Pearl Harbor attack. There was no one nearby to overhear our quiet conversations:

"In your favorite version of events, we know that no advance warning was given."

"But they saw blips on the radar."

"True, but the attack was a complete surprise nonetheless."

"It could be important."

"Some would say it's a small footnote in history," Fynn remarked.

"Why is that?"

"Even if the Americans have half an hour of advanced warning, it's not sure the outcome would change much. Perhaps they'll get a few planes in the air, but the warships will still be trapped in the harbor."

"A lot of lives might be saved."

"As you say, Patrick. And we've had this discussion before, eh?"

"Yeah, well, I'm still not totally satisfied this is the right thing to do."

"The treasonous thing?"

I glared at Fynn. "That's exactly what I mean. I feel uncomfortable about this."

"Nonsense, we are here to make certain that events unfold as they should."

"Still, we could probably save a lot of lives."

"We could, but we will save many more lives by ensuring that your favorite timeline persists."

"It's already changed," I protested.

"Well, we can only affect what is to come, eh?"

"How so?"

"Let's say, Kali's timeline unfolds quite differently— if I may call it such."

"Kali's timeline?"

"This is what Mr Quandary and the Arbiter have told me."

"What exactly is it like? This timeline of the future."

"I know only the vague outlines… Society is more uniform, more regimented, and more draconian than you are used to."

"Maybe we should talk to Mr Q."

"You mean to say travel to the Cocos-Keeling Islands, his ivory tower?" Fynn asked incredulously.

"We have a ship, well, a yacht..."

"… and we're halfway there, I suppose." Fynn laughed. "Still, war in the Pacific is just about to begin."

"Right, maybe it's a bad idea."

"It is at that. We'll proceed as planned."

"How are we going to find Kali?"

"Such is our daunting task— how indeed?" Fynn paused. "What ideas do you have?"

"Me? None…"

"Then maybe it's best if our paths never cross."

"She'll probably find us…" I muttered. "So, we're going to the radio station?"

"No, the radar station. It's a simple matter," Fynn replied. "We know all the players involved by name and by photograph. We know also the exact sequence of events, and the exact timing down to the minute. We merely have to cut the telephone wire."

"We still don't know Kali's intent here."

"There seems to be only two possible outcomes: things happen as they did in your timeline with the surprise attack on Pearl Harbor. Or, the second scenario is that the American's have a full foreknowledge of the attack and are able to take defensive measures."

"You mean stop the attack entirely?"

"I cannot think of a third alternative."

"A distraction?"

"From what?" Fynn asked.

"I don't know."

"Now you are supposing Kali is more clever than before."

"Am I?"

"You seem to be…" Fynn replied vaguely. "Though, you're correct. We should not underestimate her intelligence. Kali may only see the broad sweeps of history, but she may tangle with them in subtle ways."

"And she may have done it a thousand times already."

"Eh?" Fynn was alarmed by my remark.

"Until she got it exactly right— for her, I mean."

"That's a most distressing thing to say."

"It's possible."

"Yes, given her abilities."

"So?"

Fynn paused. "Perhaps it's not so strange that she chose this place."

"Why?"

"The Hawaiian Islands are a difficult destination."

"For a traveler, you mean?"

"Yes, the smallest miscalculation lands you in the middle of the Pacific."

"So she chose this place deliberately."

"We might guess it to be true… Though on the other side of the coin, Kali will not expect interference from other travelers. Such will be to our advantage."

"Okay, well, say we do fix everything… What stops Kali from just going back and changing it again? Undoing what we just did."

"I would guess her arrogance."

"That's not exactly something we can rely on."

"No, I suppose not. Still she can't be everywhere at once, eh?" Fynn raised a hopeful smile.

"I think there's more to it than just arrogance."

"Such as?"

"I have no idea."

"Well then, a good question to ponder."

"What do you remember about Kali's abilities?"

"Everything. I've come to dread another encounter. Flitting to and fro in the present like she does."

"By looking at her hand," I said.

"Yes, but what are you getting at?" Fynn turned to me.

"I'm thinking it's some kind of technology built into her palm, like a read-out, a map, or a guide that appears."

"A bizarre supposition."

"Not really. You have the cane and your astrolabe… I have Edmund's pocket compass— like that."

"I see. Some technology from the distant future, you believe."

"Yes."

"But far more advanced."

"Exactly," I agreed. "But I'm guessing her technology only functions in normal time."

"Meaning?"

"She'd be helpless at the library, the bank, Mr Q's tower, or the hotel."

"Not a bad supposition, Patrick, though it doesn't help much at present."

"I guess not… I also remember she's powerless on a moving vehicle."

"To our small advantage, yes. And, I recall she can only travel a hundred years at a time," Fynn observed.

"The Arbiter said that… but how does it help us?"

"I'm not sure it does." Fynn made a face. "She seems to have the ability to travel with such precision, that to our eyes, she's not even moved at all."

"Meaning?"

"If you or I jump to the past or the future, we might return weeks or days later, or at best, hours might pass. For Kali, only an instant goes by before she returns to that exact present."

"That is kind of scary."

"Indeed. One cannot even be sure if she has traveled and returned or not." Fynn paused. "The evidence says she can travel to the past with extraordinary accuracy, but I wonder if she can travel to the future with the same precision…"

"Why?"

"Well, Patrick, the future is always an uncertain place, even for Kali."

**

In my cabin early that evening, I noticed the engines had stopped.

It was dead calm, we were drifting. It brought me topside; Fynn as well. I found him with the skipper on the forward observation deck. They were leaning over the starboard rail. As far as the eye could see, wooden boards filled the water, floating on the surface. "What's left of a ship?" I asked.

"Lost cargo," the skipper replied. "Loose lumber, I'd guess."

"How would that happen?"

"Who can say? A bad bit of weather, a swell, a rogue wave…" He handed me a pair of binoculars. "We'll drift through and I'll start the engines again. He pointed west. "The Big Island, gentlemen."

Fynn and I looked and could see a huge mountain come into view just at the horizon. The captain walked over to the port side and out of earshot.

"Have you ever been here before?"

"To the Sandwich Islands?" Fynn smiled. "Once or twice in the late seventeen hundreds… It didn't turn out so well."

"For whom?"

"For anyone."

"What are those?" I asked with my hand up like a visor, scanning the horizon.

"Ships, perhaps?"

"Sinking ships then…" I said and handed Fynn the binoculars.

"I think they are whales, giants from the deep," Fynn replied after a few moments.

"Whales with conning towers and periscopes."

"Japanese submarines?"

I nodded, then called out to the skipper who was walking back our way. "What day is it?"

"Friday, December fifth," he replied.

"It's too soon…"

"Too soon for what?" the captain asked.

chapter four
hula dance

The next morning, Saturday, we steamed into port at Oahu, though not into Pearl Harbor. We landed a bit further south in Honolulu proper, closer to Waikiki, and I was surprised that despite looming mountains and palm trees everywhere, it resembled any other bland American city.

From our vantage there was little to observe, a few gray ships far in the distance, their stacks at least, and some planes noisily flying overhead. There were serviceman everywhere, sailors mostly, dressed in white or blue, soldiers, and army air corps, all seemingly relaxed if not busy and on the move. It was not touristy in the least.

I looked around. "Well, no ghosts, that's a good sign."

"The phantoms, yes... Perhaps it's too sunny for them."

I laughed. "No, I'm thinking we've never been here before."

"Such may be true, though it might be that this is our first time."

"What do you mean?"

"If it is our first visit to this timeline, surely there would be no ghosts yet."

"That's encouraging... Wait, are you saying we'll have to be here more than once?"

"I fear it is likely."

Our luggage was sent ahead, namely the huge steamer trunk acquired by Fynn in Los Angeles. He checked us into a small hotel right on the beach, really not much more than a guest house.

"No worries," I said.

"Eh?"

I pointed to the sign: *Sans Souci*.

He smiled and told me to meet him back in the lobby as soon as possible. Fifteen minutes later we walked up to Kalakaua Avenue. Fynn had changed into a white linen suit and had a matching panama hat. Binoculars hung from his neck.

"Where are we going?" I asked.

"I hope to find higher ground so that we may have a look about." He pointed to the north. Honolulu was nestled between a series of mountainous ridges that tapered down to the harbor. It seemed pretty far to me.

"If anyone asks, we are coffee merchants."

"Why?"

"Have you not heard of Kona, a special kind of Hawaiian coffee bean?" Fynn asked as we walked to Kalakaua Avenue. He clambered aboard a street car that took us along Kapiʻolani Boulevard. There were old cars everywhere, telephone poles with too many wires attached, and ordinary brick buildings.

"It might not look good, you know, the two of us wandering around in the hills above Pearl Harbor with a pair of binoculars…" I smiled.

"Yes, you make an excellent point, Patrick. Well then what do you say to a bit of shopping instead?"

"For what?"

"An Aloha shirt."

"A what?"

"A Hawaiian shirt."

I laughed at that, unable to imagine Fynn dressed in such a colorful manner.

"The finest silk, the best designs."

"For you?"

"No, I was thinking to bring some back for Anika and Lorraine."

"Oh…"

Fynn jumped from the streetcar and I followed. We were at a busy intersection: South King Street and Kapiʻolani Boulevard. I stopped him on the corner. "Was it a radar station or a radio station?" I asked.

"Eh?"

"What Mr Quandary said."

"I don't take your meaning, Patrick."

I pointed to the flimsy steel structure perched on a building. It looked antiquated, a criss-cross of girders that tapered to a point. "A radio station," I repeated. "Remember? The music guided in the Japanese attack."

"Ah, yes, the dive bombers followed the signal…" Fynn hesitated. "If Kali is anywhere, she is there. Perhaps she means to stop that broadcast?"

"Stop it… or turn it on," I replied. "We still don't know her intent."

There was a marquis outside the building that housed radio station KGU. It pictured the celebrity DJs who worked there, caricature drawings in watercolor, their faces outlined in giant yellow stars, all smiling, some in uniform. At the bottom was a familiar face. The name read: Katy O'Null, the Midnight Owl. I pointed her out to Fynn.

"I shall inquire inside," the inspector said and left me standing on the corner. I looked around at this happy place. It's the only word that fit. And the happiness was infectious. People were smiling, strolling in a relaxed way. I heard laughter and boisterous conversation. The sun was shining and I felt a pleasant breeze coming off the water. A heavily defended paradise.

Fynn returned a few minutes later with a programming schedule in hand. "Yes, I've learned a few things… Kali has a radio program on weekends from midnight till dawn. She plays music by request, I am told."

"Like a call-in show?"

"Yes, and by all accounts she's enormously popular."

"Music?" I asked. "Not coded messages to the Japanese High Command?"

"What?" Fynn was shocked by the idea. "Is such a thing possible?"

I shrugged. "Anything else you found out?"

"I've also learned that Kali is a dancer in a club not so far from here."

"How long has she been in Hawaii?"

"That's a good question, Patrick. It seems she began her career as a broadcaster in early August."

"What now?"

"I will suggest we mingle with the locals."

"The locals?"

"Well, the sailors and soldiers."

"Why?"

"To get a feel for what is happening. Their expectations, their hopes and fears— that sort of thing."

"What good will that do?"

"The general mood might tell us if this history is on track, or if it has been already altered."

When we returned to our hotel, Fynn gave me a parcel wrapped in paper.

"What's this?"

"Some clothes to change into. I'll meet you back in the lobby, say, fifteen minutes?"

I expected a Hawaiian shirt but found a khaki uniform instead. It was a perfect fit. Apparently, I was a corporal in the Army Air Corps. Downstairs, Fynn appeared as an officer, a colonel, cap and all, and he strode over from the reception desk. "Ah, there you are, my driver, at last." He motioned for me to take his duffle bag.

I don't think *Colonel* Fynn had any actual credentials, nor were they needed. A crisp salute along with a good deal of swagger seemed to be enough. He was not timid in the least, and half an hour later he had finagled a Willys MB from the motor pool without a hitch.

We drove out of Honolulu in the late afternoon, north and into the mountains. "Are we heading to the radar station?" I called out while driving.

"No," Fynn replied. "I'd still like to have a look around. Now that we're in uniform there should be no difficulties."

We found a good vantage point just above Pearl Harbor. Gray ships filled the inlet, most of them docked along a central island, and they looked ready for business. I could see swarms of men all about in uniform, tiny like ants. There was an airfield, huge oil tanks, and some sort of administrative buildings.

"Well?" Fynn asked.

"What?"

"Are they preparing for an attack, do you think?"

"It's hard to say for sure… but I'm leaning towards no."

"Why is that?"

"Everyone seems too relaxed."

"That's all you have to say?"

"Well, if we were expecting an attack tomorrow, it's not likely all the ships would be in one place." I paused. "They'd be out at sea or something."

"The two carriers are," Fynn said.

"What?"

"The *Lexington* and the *Enterprise*."

"As they should be," I replied.

"Agreed… well, off we go then." Fynn climbed aboard the jeep.

"Where to now?"

"The radar station at Opana."

It was about an hour's journey along the coast, a stunning drive on a beautiful day. Near Kahuku Point we found the place, though it could hardly be called a station. In reality, it was three trucks parked together on an outcropping that faced the ocean. One truck held a noisy generator, the other a control room, and the third had an ungainly antenna mounted to it. I parked at a discreet distance. Fynn scanned the horizon. "There, I think…" He pointed to some distant telephone poles.

"Too soon to cut the wire?" I asked.

"We will wait till darkness," Fynn replied but drew out a bolt-cutter from his duffle bag.

"Which wire do we cut?"

"All of them."

"And they have no other way to call headquarters?" I asked.

"Ironically enough, no."

***

"Did you notice the little cantina on the way here?" Fynn called out from his seat. "What do you say, we stop on our return?"

It was almost midnight when we pulled into a gravel parking lot. Blue neon glowed: *The Lilo*. I asked Fynn what that meant in Hawaiian.

"It can mean *to become*, or, *to become lost*."

The sign also boasted twenty-five cent beer and private dance lessons for a dollar. It seemed to be a mostly outdoors place with a thatched awning that stretched out into the sand for a good twenty or thirty yards. Under a canopy of palm leaves, the tables were filled with uniforms: navy, army and marines; officers and enlisted men alike. Rank seemed to mean nothing here.

There was a small stage at the back. I heard raucous laughter, hoots and hollers. Hawaiian music drifted in the air, half a dozen tinny ukuleles and a sliding steel guitar. From a distance, I saw a dark, lithe woman swaying to the rhythm, her arms in the air. She danced a hula to the great pleasure of the servicemen watching. Fynn and I had our answer. None of these people were preparing for an attack. None of them had an inkling of what was to come. And some of them, many of them, would be dead by tomorrow.

Fynn found a seat at the bar and dropped a couple of quarters down for beer. We began to scan the crowd, looking for the radar guys, their photos emblazoned on our memory. They were nowhere to be seen and I conjectured that their shift had already begun. We did spot Private Joseph McDonald, the man who took the telephone call; and Lieutenant Kermit Tyler, who advised that the radar signals were a false alarm.

Both men seemed particularly enraptured by the hula dancer on the stage. She was toying with them, obviously, seductively, writhing in her grass skirt and flaunting long slender legs. Quite an audience had gathered. Her face turned to the light and I knew her instantly. "Kali," I whispered to Fynn.

"Yes, but we are lucky that she does not seem to recognize us..."

"She should."

"Perhaps," Fynn answered but seemed distracted. "And, does she mean to seduce this man, the soldier in charge of telephones? Or at the very least get him drunk enough so he doesn't do his duty properly."

"No... look who she's targeting... the man who dismisses the radar warning, Kermit Tyler."

"Why would she do such a thing? Does she want the Americans to have advance notice?"

I shrugged, but we both watched as Kali led the lieutenant into a private booth.

Ten minutes later she reemerged alone and with a satisfied smile. There was something frightening about it. Fynn rose from the bar meaning to approach her.

"Is that a good idea?" I asked as I took his arm.

"It is a necessity."

Fynn spoke to Kali at some length and in a language that sounded awkward to my ear. I presumed it to be Hawaiian.

"What did she say?" I asked on his return.

"Her Japanese is quite good."

"She speaks Japanese?"

"Indeed." Fynn sat again and took a sip of beer. "As far as I can tell, she is declaring to anyone who will listen that there will be an attack tomorrow."

"Really?"

"I told her I was from military intelligence and this seems to have piqued her interest."

"She didn't recognize you?"

"No."

"Are you sure? Maybe she's playing you?"

"I think not..." Fynn replied. "The important thing is that no one is taking her at all seriously."

"How do you know?"

"I sensed her frustration, and it is something she did not anticipate, I am guessing."

I looked over to Kali who was drawing nearer, smiling. She came up to us and put her arms around Fynn and I, and seemed ready to say something. In the blink of an eye though, a look of recognition crossed her face. A scowl then formed and she grew angry. She remembered us now— exactly how much I couldn't say— but she knew us again.

At that moment shouts broke out. A surge of men crowded towards the stage. Soon after, sharp whistles sounded and the Shore Patrol descended upon the cantina with a small army of MP's right behind them. They pushed the onlookers back with rough batons. Fynn and I only caught a glimpse, but we could see Lieutenant Tyler. He was sprawled across the sand; the door to the booth was open and there was blood, a lot of blood. I turned to look for Kali again. She was gone.

"Aren't you going to investigate?"

"What?"

"The murder."

"Hmm?" Fynn replied absentmindedly. "No, I very much regret there's little we can do now."

***

Sunday morning I woke to the sound of sirens. The clock said seven-thirty. I rushed to the balcony of my room on the fourth floor. There wasn't much to see except for a few puffs of black smoke on the horizon. There was lots to hear though: a great commotion, people shouting, and far off thuds that I took to be explosions. I heard engines of all kinds. The sirens continued unabated, joined by loud short blasts from various ships, a plaintive *blurp, blurp, blurp...* klaxons cried out an obvious warning. Urgency was in the air.

Not more than a few moments later, planes flew overhead, roaring just above the palm trees but climbing rapidly, banking to the north, and gaining altitude to avoid the cloud-shrouded mountains that lay before them. Another formation banked south and doubled back towards Pearl. They were our planes, I could see the distinctive US markings. This was no surprise attack, it was to be a battle.

Dressed only in pajamas, I ran down to the lobby to find Fynn amongst the others who all stood about in disbelief. He was again Colonel Fynn this morning, and led me towards the main part of town. Outside, people were pulling on clothes, uniforms, and running up towards the main boulevard to the north. Many crammed onto the street cars.

We had no view of what was happening seven miles to our west. Fynn spotted an idling jeep. We jumped in and set off for our vantage in the hills. Smoke rose from the middle of Pearl Harbor, not from bombs or explosions; they were black columns spewing forth from stacks and funnels. Engines were coming to life and some of the great gray hulks were beginning to steam from their moorings at Ford Island. Overhead, planes roared through the sky and they seemed to be following each other, swooping low and banking high. I could see sporadic tracer bullets falling to earth.

The ships were on alert, guns manned, and they were slowly putting out to sea. The air was soon thick with flack, tiny black puffs appeared in the sky. A different kind of smoke poured from the depots though. There was an oily smell to it. The refineries or the storage tanks were burning uncontrollably, palls of thick black soot rose high into the atmosphere. Hickam Field had also taken a big hit, fires could be seen raging. It was hard to say how much time passed, but an eerie calm soon came.

"What went wrong?"

"We may have cut the wrong telephone wires."

"What now?" I asked.

"We have no choice but to wait till tomorrow."

"Tomorrow?"

"We must read the newspapers to find out what exactly has happened."

"And you think the press will report it accurately?"

"In this particular era, yes. And the early reports will be more truthful. Later, the military will likely step in to censor certain details."

Fynn was wrong about one thing, we wouldn't have to wait till morning. The *Honolulu Advertiser* put out an evening edition and it was snatched up as soon as it hit the streets. I was able to grab a copy at the newsstand.

To the world and to the press, it was a stunning defeat for the Japanese. Our forces were heroic beyond measure. I wondered if it was true or not, or just well-written propaganda. We had fought back valiantly... A fierce battle, some small ships sunk, the *USS Pruitt* and the *USS Tucker*, though there were few casualties in all. There were also reports of minor damage to the submarine pens and dry docks.

I knew some of this to be a lie. All I had to do was look out the window to see the fuel depots still burning. There was little mention of the advanced warning from the radar station, something the military now deemed sensitive information. Lockard and Eliot would not be hailed as heroes after all.

There was also one curious report buried in the back pages: radio station *KGU* had been off the air that Sunday morning due to technical failures. This time there were no signals to guide the Japanese torpedo bombers towards their primary targets.

Another point of history was altered, at least compared to normal. It came to Fynn's attention four days later in the morning edition: Hitler decided against declaring war on America. Further, he condemned the attack as a cowardly failure and threatened to expel Japan from the axis. It was all theater of course, but a shrewd move politically.

"Don't you see? It muddies the waters," Fynn explained. "In your usual history, Hitler made the monumental blunder of declaring war on the United States three days after the attack."

"And?"

"Well, he played right into FDR's hands. It was imperative that the US entered the war in Europe sooner rather than later."

"And you think this was Kali's intent?"

"It seems to be a moot point in this particular timeline, but yes, this is a great mystery."

***

Colonel Fynn was gone the next morning when I came down for breakfast on the veranda. He had set off early to attend a military briefing. Things were approaching normal again. Repairs were underway, the smoke had cleared and warships began to arrive from the west coast.

Fynn returned around noon and in full dress uniform. There was a swath of medals across his chest.

"How did it go?" I asked.

"Yes, the security briefing..." he replied and sat opposite. "The news is dire, I'm afraid to say." Fynn helped himself to a cup of coffee.

"Nothing good?"

"There was a great sense of relief that there was no third wave of attacks, nor did any Japanese forces land on the island."

"That's it?"

"What's quite clear are the unintended consequences of the day."

"What do you mean?"

"Simply put, it was a tactical victory, yet a strategic defeat."

"For the Americans?"

"Yes. According to the military experts, things went badly. The Japanese, having met resistance, instead turned to their secondary targets."

"Meaning?"

"The Japanese did greater damage to the stores of munitions, the fuel depots, refineries, and especially the dry docks and boat yards. There was also a direct hit on the submarine pens. In the end, all this was far more devastating than the sinking of a few battleships."

"Why?"

"It will greatly delay your country's entry into the Pacific War. Untold havoc…"

"Wow…"

"There's worse news, I'm afraid to say. Something that has yet to be revealed to the general public."

"What's that?"

"The carrier *Enterprise* has been lost with all hands, and the *Lexington* is severely damaged— only now limping back to Pearl."

"How did that happen?"

"A disastrous encounter with the returning Japanese battle group."

"What...?" I thought for a moment then asked, "Kali's doing? The radio station?"

"Well within her abilities, yes?" Fynn flashed a grim smile. "It was posited that secret signals were broadcast to the Japanese High Command from a transmitter in Honolulu. They gave the exact positions for the US carriers off the island of Midway."

"There goes the doctrine of carrier superiority,"

"Eh?"

"Oh, something I read in the history books…"

"Rumors are also abound that the Japanese fleet is currently stranded in the north Pacific, crippled and low on fuel, far from the coast of Japan. Though vulnerable, the Americans cannot muster a counter-attack."

"So, history has been changed."

"Yes. Apparently Kali's goal was something neither of us could anticipate. For whatever reason, it seems she wanted a stalemate."

***

Fynn and I had dinner downstairs in the hotel restaurant. The name *Sans Souci* held new irony this evening. There were few other diners, and generally conversations were hushed. A certain sense of disbelief still hung in the air. Fynn pushed his plate away and dabbed a napkin to his mouth. Just then an extraordinary expression crossed his face. It must have crossed mine as well, and at the exact same moment.

It's difficult to describe being on the receiving end of a soft jump. The feeling is odd to say the least. Of course, there's the deja vu that hits you like a ton of bricks, then a flood of memories, but not exactly memories because they were things that never happened in the past. They were from the future.

I turned to Fynn, and if the look on his face was anything to go by, he was experiencing exactly what I was. He stared back.

"A soft jump?" I asked.

"Ourselves returning from a different future."

"That's one way to put it."

"Obviously, both of us have returned because we failed in our mission."

"The Arbiter's doing?"

"I must assume such since we arrived at the exact same moment— eh?" Fynn seemed concerned. "What do you remember of this future, Patrick?"

"Bad things…"

"As do I."

"Why now?"

"A poignant reminder that things have gone awry. If the events of the day stand, then we have jumped back from that future history."

"Just what we needed," I replied.

"Do you remember anything specifically?"

I rummaged through the backpack, the books we had brought had not changed at all, but my memory of history had. "I remember a few things."

"Such as?"

"We were at the *Hotel de Cirque*."

"This also sticks in my memory. But I am meaning something about history."

"It's a little vague… I seem to recall the world was divided into three parts. Europe was one entity, dominated by Germany; the Soviet Union was a shadow of its former self. Asia was under a single economic hegemony… The United States was intact and the center of a large bloc that included Canada and parts of Latin America."

"And what makes it different than your familiar timeline?"

"Not much, except some of the details…"

"And why do you suppose Kali would want the world turned in this direction? What purpose does it serve?"

"No idea."

I rarely saw Fynn in such a state of despair. He sat in the high-backed cane chair and sipped his scotch, brooding for several minutes.

"Endlessly reliving the past few days until we eliminate Kali's interference is not to me a good plan," he said emphatically. "It increases the risk of her knowing."

"Knowing what?"

"That we are present at all."

"But she does know. She saw us at the cantina."

"As you say, Patrick, but we do not know how much she remembers."

"So what's your idea?"

"We will need to change things without attracting her attention. Or we must devise a way for her to leave this place suddenly."

"That sort of sounds like a threat."

"Yes." He thought for a long while, then a smile came to his face and he snapped his fingers. "I have an idea," Fynn said with absolute glee. "Do you have that sketch of her?"

"In the backpack."

"This is something we will need."

"What's the plan?"

"I will jump back to July, to before Kali's arrival."

"What will I do?"

"You will wait for me, if you would."

"Why?"

"We cannot risk such a difficult jump together," Fynn replied. "It is a small island and the altitudes vary wildly."

"We could use the cane."

"I suppose…" Fynn seemed doubtful.

"But, we'll be making doubles again."

"If you are to come with me, it cannot be avoided."

***

It took three days for Fynn to make preparations for our jump back to July. What he was up to, he wouldn't say, but he double-checked the radio station and went to a local printer. I spent my time at the beach wondering if surfing had been invented yet; Fynn's words still ringing in my ears: *"We are surfing the waves of probability."*

Back at the hotel, he wrote out a long letter in Japanese. It detailed Kali's plan and he signed it Mr Hideki Sato, probably as a joke. "This will lend credence to my story," Fynn explained. "Though it might take them some hours to translate." He took me to a rock wall at the beach that seemed to be a suitable height and set the dial. "Are you ready, Patrick?" He glanced at me.

"Now?"

"No time like the present, eh?"

I put my hand on top of the bear claw cane. Fynn's hand came down on mine and he pushed the button. We leapt on a silent count of three.

It was easier than we could've hoped. Traveling back to July, and in his colonel's uniform, Fynn presented himself to Naval Intelligence. He met with a Captain Harding.

"We have uncovered the first snake on the Hawaiian Islands," Fynn said to start off, then presented a stack of papers that were essentially wanted posters. They had a sketch of Kali's face on them, aka, Katy O'Null. He offered the revelation that she was a spy and a saboteur for the Japanese High Command, as detailed in Mr Sato's letter.

"Loose lips might sink ships," Fynn said.

"Indeed," the captain replied, seemingly impressed.

***

"It will put an end to her plans but not to her," Fynn told me later.

"What do you mean?"

"Kali will easily escape given her abilities, but she will not be able to instigate her plans since she is now so recognizable."

It seemed that Fynn's plan worked at least. No future selves thought to jump back and warn us of anything amiss. Of course, there was another possibility: there was no future to jump back from. Fynn dismissed the idea as pessimistic.

The next morning we set sail for the California coast. Fynn's charted yacht however had a different name. Previously the *Cook 'N Dole*, it was now called the *Kamehameha*. I pointed this out but he didn't think it was significant.

"We have a quick stop to make, I hope you don't mind."

"Where to?"

"Nineteen forty-two, Springfield, Illinois." Fynn smiled. "We are in the neighborhood after all."

"Hawaii is not very close to Illinois."

"As you say, Patrick, but nineteen forty-one is very near."

"And?"

"We have to steal a chemistry set."

"What?"

"It's a small favor I've promised for someone."

"Who?"

"The Arbiter, and our mutual friend, Lothar."

I vaguely recalled something about this, something about a scientist who worked for Monsanto. "Where were you in nineteen forty-two— in terms of concurrency?" I asked.

"Hmm, let me think for a moment… I recall that I will be hard at work building the Alaska Highway."

"You're kidding."

"Ah, now that is a concurrency worth reliving… certainly one I would prefer not to erase."

"What happened?"

"I suppose such is difficult to imagine, Patrick, but I will say it was a remarkable experience. Cutting a thin line across the earth for some two thousand miles… leveling the terrain, removing all obstacles from trees to boulders, creating a bed for the asphalt that was to come."

"Wasn't it cold?"

"Bitterly so, but worth the price. I was part of the forward surveying team. We would leave camp early in the morning, and walk for miles into the deep wilderness in order to map out the route ahead. I would not trade the experience for anything else I've ever done."

"Really?"

"There was nothing before us but the grandeur of nature. And all the animals in this place had never encountered a human being before. They came to inspect us with unabashed curiosity. There was no fear in them at all. Nor did they hold any malice. Birds and beasts of every sort... deer, bears, squirrels, wolves even; any woodland creature you might imagine."

"You're saying they were friendly?"

"Yes, and curious. Have you ever pet a squirrel on your shoulder? Or been licked on the side of the face by a doe? Rub the belly of a bear? Quite extraordinary."

"What happened after that?"

"Behind us of course came the ruckus of men and machinery, the diggers and the bulldozers cutting through that swath of frozen forest. Fear and mistrust soon gained the upper hand."

"For the animals?"

"Indeed."

***

We boarded another train in San Francisco, our destination was the midwest. I slept most of the way. Fynn woke me in the middle of the night and we disembarked into featureless blackness, a station in Springfield, Illinois. From there, it was an easy hard jump to the future. I bought more magazines and a newspaper dated October 17, 1942. The news wasn't necessarily good, but it seemed to me that history was back on the right path. A headline boasted: *Reds Make Stand on Volga River*. Several of the magazines spoke about victories at Guadalcanal; and for the British, El Alamein was within sight.

It was an easy errand for us. We found the address on a street of white wooden houses. Young John D. Franz's brand new chemistry set was lifted from an open window and disposed of— the course of his life was irrevocably altered.

On the way out of town, I started to wonder about my own concurrency and asked Fynn about my previous life here.

"You can simply return to Elsie at any point."

"What do you mean?"

"To relive that life, it is an easy soft jump."

"Right, but shouldn't we return?'

"To your usual present?"

I nodded.

"Well, we should be careful. We may have been followed."

"Followed by whom?"

He raised an eyebrow. "Anyone."

"Somehow I doubt it..."

Fynn seemed overly cautious to me. He found a low wall. We jumped again in the middle of the night, and did not use the cane.

When we arrived it seemed to be late afternoon. "So, where are we?" I looked around to see a forest and a tundra, a vast lake, and an industrial outpost in the distance.

"Uranium City, the outskirts."

"Where?"

"Far to the north from where we were... Saskatchewan, Canada."

"Why?"

"It's isolated. No one can bother us here."

"It's cold."

"Yes, and it's August by my reckoning."

"When are we?"

"The present."

"Which present?"

"Your favorite one, as I promised," Fynn said with a smile. "You may not remember yet, but you've spent a lot of time here in the north."

"Did I?"

"You don't believe me?"

"No... I don't like the cold."

"Well, now we face a choice. How do you prefer to return to Sand City? Conventional transport or another jump? We might travel back to yesterday."

"Yesterday?"

"Thereabouts..."

"What's your preference?" I asked.

"Me?" Fynn laughed. "I'd like to bring the Aloha shirts with us."

PART II

chapter five
driving rain

My memories of Hawaii faded as Fynn and I left Mortimer at the amusement pier to begin our long journey to Babylon. We left Lothar too. As we walked along the boardwalk back towards my car, the lights sputtered and switched off in sequence. All the carnival rides ground to a halt. For a brief moment everything fell silent. Darkness engulfed the place and Sand City beyond. I could hear surf lapping against the pylons. Some people who were stuck on their rides began to chatter nervously, though there was no sense of panic yet.

By the time we made our way to the parking lot, the lights had flickered on again. The music started up, and the rides spun back to life. The hour was late, well past eleven, if the clock in my car was to be believed. I put the bundle of manuscripts in the backseat and asked, "What about these books?"

"I suppose we should deliver them to Wilfrid and Geppetto… eventually… As well as the one Chief Durbin has offered to give us."

"It's possible that the copy from the Yale library is a forgery."

"I might say it's likely." Fynn chuckled.

"And the others?"

"Mr Voynich has made such flawless reproductions, it's difficult to say which is real and which is not— not without a thorough translation."

"Well, they seem to exist in at least two of our timelines."

"Yes, because of the entangled safe deposit boxes at the Amsterdam bank."

"And the ones Mortimer just gave us?"

"Surely, they are the false editions you had Mr Voynich create."

"Right. So are any of them genuine?"

"Wilfrid seems to think so… Geppetto, and the Arbiter as well."

Which were the real books and which were fakes came to mind. I could remember 1903 and standing in the middle of Wilfrid Voynich's London bookshop, pages scattered everywhere. I also wondered if there was now more than one copy of each, duplicates from the safe deposit box. It was too difficult to figure out— at least for me.

The inspector unwrapped a taffy and popped it into his mouth. "Peppermint, I think," he announced as we pulled out onto Long Neck Road. It was far from empty, in fact we merged into a giant traffic jam. I could see a long string of brake lights from here to the rotary in Oldham. It was a single lane and no one was moving faster than a walking pace.

"What day is it?" I asked Fynn.

"By my reckoning, Sunday."

"Oh… I thought it was Monday."

"Does it make a difference, Patrick?"

"Well, it explains the traffic. This might take longer than we hoped." I took a piece of taffy from the box and unwrapped it: butterscotch. Then I asked Fynn if Omar the waiter from the Cove Diner seemed at all familiar.

"I've seen him behind the lunch counter a few times at least."

"That's all?"

"I've encountered him elsewhere for certain, though I can't exactly say where or when."

"That's what I was afraid of."

"Afraid? Why?"

"I don't think he's supposed to be there— at the diner— in this timeline at least…"

"I will agree he seems a bit out of context."

I snatched another taffy from Fynn's box. Vanilla with a hint of raspberry. "Okay, so tell me more about this case we're on."

"As I've mentioned, we are to save the man who saved the world, Vasili Arkhipov."

"How did he save the world?"

"Do you recall the Cuban Missile Crisis?"

"I do, a little, from history… October, nineteen sixty-two."

"Yes. Cold War tensions were at a boiling point. The Americans had discovered that some forty atomic missiles were on the island, aimed at their major cities. President Kennedy placed a quarantine zone around Cuba to prevent further weapons from coming ashore. All ships were subject to search, Soviet or not. However, unknown at the time, four Russian submarines already lurked below the Sargasso Sea."

"Beneath the Bermuda Triangle?"

"The what?" Fynn asked.

"Never mind."

"Well, Vasili Arkhipov was aboard one of those submarines, a B-Fifty-Nine. He was not the captain, he did not give orders on that particular vessel; but he was in fact the commander of the entire undersea convoy. Trapped below the waves, they were in a desperate condition and unable to surface."

"Why not?"

"Above them was a vast American fleet, and eventually they were detected. These Soviet submarines were built for cold water, and they had not surfaced in several days. Their batteries were going dead and the air was growing foul."

"Diesel submarines?"

"Yes… It's difficult to imagine, but these were men on the brink of despair. Having survived a hurricane only days earlier, they were unable to communicate with Moscow. The last broadcast they heard was from a Miami radio station, and to them it seemed that World War Three was eminent."

"What then?"

"The most dangerous game of cat and mouse ever played," Fynn said. "American destroyers began dropping practice depth charges, not an overt act of war, but an attempt to make the submarines surface. This was unknown to the captain of the B-Fifty-Nine. Desperate and impulsive, he made the decision to launch his special weapon."

"Which was?"

"An atomic torpedo, approximately a megaton's worth, large enough to destroy the fleet in those waters. And from there, nuclear annihilation would ensue— the end of all life as we know it."

"How was that prevented?"

"Two keys were needed to fire the weapon, one from the captain and one from the political officer. It is said the keys were inserted, but Vasili Arkhipov, as overall commander, refused to give the order to launch."

"Why?"

"A man of infinite wisdom, one might suppose."

"He stopped World War Three?"

"Indeed, he saved the world."

"But we're not going to Cuba?"

"No… The actions of his wife concern us. She was arrested for murder in Zvorkovo, a small village in the Soviet Union."

"That's why I have to learn Russian?"

"Yes, at Sonny Ming's school."

"And?"

"I have no further details about the incident, but the great danger is that Comrade Arkhipov will hear about his wife's difficulties. If he gets wind of the news before his mission begins, he will not be aboard the submarine, and the world could very well end on that day."

"Hence the flatlined history."

"Exactly this."

***

I spotted the cause of the traffic jam: many flashing blue lights ahead. "Probably an accident," I said to Fynn.

A short time later, Ricky Durbin, dressed in full uniform, held up his hand indicating we should stop. He was a carbon copy of his dad, though younger. Nor had I seen the elder Durbin in uniform for years. He walked over and peered through the window. "Patrick, Mr Fynn… How are you guys this evening?"

"Hey Ricky— what's up?"

"Sobriety check point. Have you been drinking tonight?"

"Only coffee."

"You're good to go, I guess. Where are you headed?"

"New York."

"Road trip," he replied and tipped his cap back. "Damn... I'm envious..."

Fynn offered him a saltwater taffy from his box. Ricky grinned and took one. "Okay, well, drive safe, guys."

"Umm, quick question, Ricky... Have you been posting any weird stuff online?"

"Define weird stuff."

"Not sure I can, but some teenagers were following us, taking our pictures, asking questions..."

"Oh that. Yeah, I posted some of Grandma Daisy's old photos last week."

"And?"

"Well, a couple of the people in them looked a lot like you... and Mr Fynn." Ricky grinned but then looked down to the pavement. "Ha, some kids have been speculating, that's all."

"Speculating about what?"

"Hey, listen, I can't talk about it now. Gotta keep the traffic moving. How about you give me a call later?" He waved us on.

"Say hello to your father," Fynn called out as we passed through the barriers. Ricky gave us a small salute.

Traffic eased up at the rotary. I was about to merge onto Route 16 when Fynn called out, "Patrick, go around again."

"What?"

"Go around the rotary again, please."

"Why?"

"I saw a man standing by the side of the road. I think he might need a ride."

"You want me to pick up a hitchhiker?"

"If you would."

I slowed to a stop along the brightly lit shoulder. There was a plump man dressed in a pinstripe suit, standing with his thumb out. Fynn reached behind and opened the passenger door.

"Thank you, thank you, gentlemen," he gave an effusive greeting and hopped into the backseat. "I was beginning to fear there was no kindness left on the face of the earth."

I glanced back. I knew this man. He had a smile and an outstretched hand.

"I am Öde Temsik. It is a great pleasure to meet you."

He spoke with a thick accent, though I could not guess its origin. "Not Omar?" I asked. "From the diner?"

"Well yes, now that you mention it. My shift has just ended."

"Where can we take you?"

"As far as you can. My usual means of transportation has ceased to function."

"We're heading to Fairhaven, then south towards New York."

"And so am I— a happy coincidence."

Fynn eyed him suspiciously. I merged onto Route 16. There was endless traffic in front of us, but it was moving at least.

"You don't recognize me then?" he asked.

"Not exactly," I answered, but noticed his mustache from the night before was gone.

"Ah, if I were wearing a red fez, perhaps I'd be more familiar to you."

We both did a double take.

"You... the man from Cairo..." Fynn could barely believe it and a huge grin formed on his face. He laughed aloud.

"Indeed I am, though I'm not from Cairo at all."

"Where are you from?" I asked.

"Oh, here and there..."

"You've been following me all this long while, all these centuries," Fynn exclaimed.

"No, just dropping in from time to time."

"Why?"

"To see how you are faring."

"But I don't know you, surely— we've never spoken before."

"You ordered a bologna sandwich from me just yesterday."

"True..." Fynn chuckled. "And yet I can recall no other significant conversations despite the passing of millennia."

"I suppose I owe you an apology then."

"For what?"

"For my silence. I've been tempted to say something, but always thought better of it. Best not to interfere. And there have been countless times when you did not notice me. In fact, you only saw me if I wished it to be so."

"What do you mean?"

"I relish my nondescriptness."

"How so?"

"My anonymity, to be invisible."

"Yes, but why?"

"What better way to observe? I am a face in the crowd, a stranger sitting in the theatre, or beside you on a bus... a few tables away at a restaurant." Öde poked his face up in between the seats. His eyes were gleaming. "A car on the highway that passes. A crewman on a ship whom you don't notice. Standing among the ranks of a Roman legion—"

"You seem to be well-traveled," Fynn interrupted.

"Oh yes, and I remember some of the names you've used through the years: Aldus Kenon, Yanni Choros, Janek Jones, Tomás Harris... I like that you've stuck with Fynn, if you don't mind me calling you that."

"And why are you here now, Mr Temsik?"

"Ah, but you must call me Öde, please. And, I am just here to see how you're faring. You as well, Patrick."

Fynn eyed him again. "There is something more to your visit, I will venture to guess."

"Truth be told... I've been scouring the timelines for you both, though it has nothing to do with Sheriff Durbin's fondness for pancakes."

"Sheriff Durbin?" I glanced to the rearview mirror.

"His grandson, I should say."

"What then?"

"Ah, I'm glad you asked," Mr Temsik said. "Indeed, these are dangerous times in which we live. Any semblance of historical causality has flown out the window."

"What are you saying?"

"I can hardly tell cause from effect, or, before from after."

"Meaning?"

"All meaning is lost... Even probability has been thrown into chaos."

"Sounds dire," Fynn commented.

"I have heard you are running errands for the Arbiter," Öde said after a pause.

"You know him?" I asked.

"I do, but I don't like him very much."

"Why not?"

"He has nothing to say that I don't already know."

Fynn had a question: "Why would you call them errands?"

"What would you call them, eh? Tell me, do you trust the fellow?"

"Can you give me a reason why I shouldn't?"

"Ha, reason doesn't enter into it at all."

"What then?"

"Faith, or perhaps belief."

"Faith in what?"

"Call it fate and destiny, or blind luck and randomness… these are what determine history." Mr Temsik laughed. "Ah, but this is a discussion for another time…" He glanced at us both, gauging our reactions. "I suppose it's none of my business, but I don't trust the Arbiter one bit."

"Why?"

"Plucking people from here and there… It's not very polite. And he's argumentative to a fault; not to mention, terrible at answering direct questions."

I laughed at that, Fynn too.

"So, we can agree on something," Öde said. "But all these errands, Mr Fynn. I'm sure his list is quite extensive by now."

"What list?"

"Fixing the timelines. Such an idea is a conceit."

"What do you mean?"

"The very notion that history should follow only one path… that there is only one valid timeline. A sacred timeline, if you will."

"You disagree?"

"The same kind of thinking was prevalent when the earth was at the center of the known universe." Öde seemed a bit worked up. "The sanctity of a timeline, its integrity… as if one were holier than another, or more correct." Mr Temsik sat back in his seat. "A particular timeline may be more pleasant, more hospitable than another, but

that's about all one can say."
"What about this timeline?" I asked.
"Not exactly what I would call utopia, eh?"
"No..."
"I will only say, it would be a great shame if this civilization were to end merely because a tiny minority of people don't like dandelions."
"What?"
"You currently live in a place where it is believed an ever-expanding economy is the only way forward. In the end it's unsustainable," Mr Temsik explained. "We might call it a corporate timeline dominated by short-term thinking. We all sit back and watch the slow degradation of the environment, a sharp rise in social inequality... the concentration of wealth in the hands of a few... and a quality of life that continues to slide for the rest of the people until it reaches a tipping point."
"What sort of tipping point?"
"A revolution, or the general collapse of civilization. Surely we've seen this before throughout history. Such abundance and such scarcity side by side..."
"And the alternative?" I asked.
"There is no profit from a dead planet."
"Still, it might all work out for the best," I countered.
"Well, there maybe infinite variations within a given timeline, but the number of outcomes can be counted."
"What does that mean?"
"Some things seem to be inevitable."
"For example?"
"Broadly speaking, things that are the byproduct of human nature, their curiosity, or their brutality."
"Like technology or war?"
"I suppose... but errands or not, some things cannot be fixed. They are too complicated, a chain of causality which cannot be stopped by any single action."
"For instance?"
"I might say the lightbulb, and everything that's come from it... from television to semi-conductors, from vacuum tubes to cell phones... and this worldwide spiderweb of yours— these were all

inevitable…"

"The murder of Mr Edison would change nothing?" Fynn asked.

"Is that on your list of errands?" Öde seemed surprised.

"No…" Fynn chuckled. "Nor Mr Tesla."

"Is that your cane?" Öde asked and leaned forward a bit.

"Yes."

"Not Mortimer's then?"

Fynn turned in his seat to face him. "No."

"Has the Arbiter had it fixed yet?"

"This remains a question."

"I don't suppose you could lend it to me for a time?"

"I'd rather not."

"I see…"

"You know Mortimer?" I asked.

"Of course I know of him, but I try to give the man a wide berth."

"Why's that?"

"Not the friendliest fellow," he replied with a blank expression. "Mind you, he's no one's fool. A brilliant mind— and wasted in some regard. I sometimes wonder why he is the way he is. All those bitter years of traveling? Or is it his nature?"

"Sounds like you know him quite well," Fynn observed.

"What nature do you mean?" I asked.

"Well, he seems to have an utter disregard for others," Öde replied and leaned back comfortably into his seat. He disappeared from view, but I heard him unwrapping the bundle of manuscripts. "Say… Mind if I flip through these? They look interesting."

I glanced at Fynn and he raised an eyebrow. There wasn't much we could do to stop him.

"Hmm… If I can only find my reading glasses…" he was muttering and the dome light snapped on. It was somewhat of a distraction. Drizzle on my windshield smeared the color of insistent turn signals. Up ahead for some unknown reason, everyone was merging to the right.

"Ah, a language that has not been spoken in many millennia, if at all… And from a timeline so distant as to be unrecognizable to you both," Mr Temsik announced after a while.

"Atlantean?" I asked and chuckled.

"No… there's little truth to any of that, you must know by now."
"So there is no lost city of Atlantis?"
"It is a recollection of the Minoans or Tartessos, perhaps— such myths as that idiot Plato described."
"Why was he an idiot?"
"I'd rather not speak ill of the dead." Mr Temsik paused. "I never cared for the man, all those notions about ideal forms, shadows in a cave, indeed…"
"Not a big fan?"
"Well, I should give him some credit for promoting Socrates."
"What do you mean?"
"Most everything we know about Socrates comes from Plato. The former was absolutely brilliant and had a good sense of humor, the latter did not."
"You can read these books?" Fynn asked, trying to steer the conversation.
"Ha, most of this volume is complete gibberish. It's a poor attempt at a hoax— unreadable."
"And the bathing women?" Fynn asked.
"Oh yes, depicted in the manuscripts," Mr Temsik replied. "I've always been baffled by that. Some sort of preparatory ritual…"
"Preparing for what?"
"Getting ready to travel, I would imagine."
I could hear Mr Temsik flipping the pages. "This other one is better, partially intact," he commented.
"Which one?"
"The pages on botany… Hmm, I might say it's Geppetto's work."
"Geppetto?" I echoed but shouldn't have. Fynn gave me a severe glance.
"Ah, so you've met Geppetto then?" Öde asked.
"I did…" I replied with a slight stammer. "In the Flatlands. He had lost his tongue though"
"Yes, a place to be avoided. I wonder how he's faring, young Geppetto. Last I recall he was in northern Italy. I was instrumental in landing him an apprenticeship with Leonardo."
"Da Vinci?"
"That's right. Do you know him as well? When was it? Early

sixteenth century? I wonder how it all worked out for him."

"Not so well."

"Why do you say that?"

"He was a fish-monger in Florence."

"Who?"

"Firenze," Fynn clarified.

"Oh dear…" Öde fell silent for a time.

The traffic ahead funneled into one lane. We sped along inches away from a concrete jersey barrier. My grip around the wheel was so tight, my hands ached. Fynn sensed my distress and flipped off the dome light, then swiveled to ask: "Is Geppetto a Builder?"

Öde laughed. "Heavens no… He's certainly not, though a scribe perhaps."

"And what do these books tell you?"

"Very little. Have you shown them to Hideki?"

"Who?"

"Mr Sato. He is a great lover of plants."

"You know him too?"

"I know everyone you know, and others whom you don't. I will only say Hideki Sato and I have shared a cup of saké from time to time."

"Where is he?"

"Japan. He rarely strays from the islands, not since… oh, the turn of the previous century. I helped him out of a perilous situation once."

"What kind of situation?"

"The carnivorous kind."

"Do you mean a bear named Ursula?"

"No, a woman named Kali. Do you know her?"

Öde's question was greeted with an uneasy silence from both Fynn and I. He laughed though, and continued, "Fair Lady Kali Shunya, Señorita Cero, the Lady Null, Mistress Nihil, Katy O'Null, Reimu, Comrade Nichego…"

"She seems to go by many names," Fynn said.

"Kali is what she calls herself. And she's made a complete mockery of causality."

"Is that why you're here?" Fynn turned his head to ask.

"It might be."

"Are you working for her?"

"Yes, as a spy," Mr Temsik said flatly.

I shot a dark glance into the rearview and locked eyes with Mr Temsik; then looked over at Fynn. "She's your employer?"

"Far too strong a word. I do things for her, small tasks, if they are not too onerous."

"Why?"

"Someone has to keep an eye on her, eh? It's taken me centuries to build up even a modicum of trust."

"Can you tell us where she is at present?"

"I certainly can, but I'm not sure it's a relevant question."

"Why not?"

"Usually, she hides along the edges of things, the tangents to our usual present."

"But she's here now."

"Yes… Kali has installed herself as a captain of industry, one might say. Wealthy beyond measure, and influential… Last I heard, she owns a large telecom company in India." Mr Temsik paused for a moment. "The Arbiter may know more about this timeline than I do."

"What about the Arbiter?" Fynn asked.

"Oh, I suppose he means well, and I share his concerns, but he's been rather useless thus far."

"Are you spying on us now?"

"Indeed I am, and I have much to report: the subjects Jardel and Fynn were last seen driving along a North American highway in the early twenty-first century…" Öde laughed. "Quite damning, don't you think?"

"And the books?"

"Ah yes, Kali would be most interested in the manuscripts," he replied with an ominous inflection. "I suppose I could lure her to any time or place with the promise of these— should the need arise."

"But you said they were gobbledygook, unreadable."

"Did I say that?" Öde chuckled. "Well, I might forget to mention it to Lady Null."

***

Traffic eased after Fairhaven. A different interstate took us south. We had lost a lot of time between the traffic and the rain. The clock in my Saab read: one forty-two. Mr Temsik had left the back window open a crack. There was an annoying shudder of air so I closed it automatically and glanced in the rearview. He seemed to be asleep for now.

There was no one on this particular stretch of road, though I saw headlights approaching. Soon enough I came upon someone blithely traveling the wrong way in the fast lane, on the interstate. It seemed impossible. I flashed my high beams several times and stayed far to the right. I only caught a glimpse of the driver as he swished by. He was old and oblivious to his surroundings.

Further south and past a historic whaling town, we started up over a large suspension bridge. I was in the fast lane, and traffic was bunching up again. Ahead of me I saw a car, and it seemed to be rapidly approaching, too rapidly. My brain tried to make sense of what my eyes were seeing. The car wasn't speeding towards me. It had simply stopped. We were speeding towards it. There was a man at the back, rummaging through his trunk. He turned and his eyes flashed in panic. I swerved to the right with only a foot or so to spare.

"Hmm, might have used his flashers," I muttered, though my body was coursing with adrenaline.

"Flashers?" Fynn asked.

"Hazard lights, blinkers… for when you break down on a bridge or something."

"We might have been killed," Öde spoke up from the backseat.

***

The pavement had dried out by the time I merged onto I-95. After Providence, traffic was light and we zipped though most of Rhode Island. "We're coming up on Connecticut," I called out, though both Fynn and Mr Temsik may have been dozing. "There's a welcome center… Does anyone need to stop?"

"Connecticut?" Öde asked.

"The next state."

"Will I need a passport?"

"What?"

"At the border…"

"Not really necessary."

"That comes as a relief."

There was hardly another car on the highway. From behind though, I could see headlights approaching at some speed. As they got closer I noticed they were trucks. The first of many rumbled by. I stayed to the right, seventy in the slow lane, and they passed one by one, most with a familiar logo on the side. It was something like a convoy, thirty or forty eighteen wheelers, hurtling south, and at a speed I couldn't guess. I didn't dare clog up their lane.

"What's all this?" Mr Temsik called out from the backseat.

"Trucks, late night deliveries."

"Oh yes, the unintended consequences of Eisenhower. I recall this now."

"What?"

"The interstate highway system that was built so many years ago. In theory a good idea, in practice, less so."

"Why?"

"You just saw for yourself. The trucks… more trucks than cars, it seems to me. I suppose in this timeline there is no longer a functioning railroad."

"Can you tell us more about the books?" I asked once the convoy had left us in its wake.

"Yes, the volume on botany, most enigmatic," Fynn added. "Plants that no one on this particular earth have seen before."

"What?" I asked and swiveled a glance to Fynn.

"You both seem most insistent to discuss this," Öde replied.

"It's kind of strange to me, that's all… talking to plants and all," I said.

"Ah yes, but talking to plants is only a small part of it, a very small part, and most of it involves listening." Öde leaned up between the seats again. "You would have to confer with Mr Sato. He's the expert on all this. I can only say that certain plants depicted in the books, when ingested, alter your perception of how time flows."

"Like a drug?"

"More like a relaxing cup of tea."

"Really? Like slow-time and fast-time?"

"Exactly. The flowers from one plant may slow your perception of time markedly, though to others observing you, everything seems quite normal. Boil the roots of a different plant and time speeds up incalculably. To you, the world would be rushing about in a frenzy while you would remain in a state of utter calm."

"That— someone might notice."

Mr Temsik laughed. "Indeed."

"What does any of this have to do with communicating with flora?" Fynn asked, and had some impatience in his tone.

"Hideki will explain it all, I'm sure."

"But it's just the perception of time, right?" I asked. "Not like—"

"Pavel Mekanos' devices?" Öde finished my thought.

"You know him?"

"Of course. And so does Mr Sato… He's Pavel's leading supplier of yttrium crystals." Mr Temsik sat back in his seat. "Who do you think gave him the inspiration for his inventions? That unusual picnic basket, for example. He got the idea from Hideki's plants."

"It's different though, right?"

"Oh yes, the plants alter your perception of time. Pavel's devices alter time itself."

"Does any of this have to do with Kali Shunya?" Fynn interrupted.

"No, I suppose not, though I can hardly use my cube anymore without running into a blind alley or a dead end."

"What cube?" Fynn asked.

"Oh… Don't you have one of these?" Mr Temsik placed his open palm between the seats. "It was a gift from Pavel."

I glanced over to see what looked like ordinary dice. With one hand I picked it up and turned it in my fingers. It slipped from my grasp and fell on the center console. I found it easily and handed it back to Mr Temsik. A slight tingling sensation traveled up my arm, and I shifted in my seat uncomfortably. "What does it do?" I asked.

"Hmm, well, it's not really for traveling at all."

"What then?"

"It's for exploration, one might say. It takes you to a parallel place, but you remain exactly in the present."

"Like a side jump?"

"Is that what you call it?" Mr Temsik laughed. "I'd give you mine but I only have one, and I find it's invaluable for hiding."

"Hiding from whom?" Fynn asked.

"Anyone who happens to be chasing me…" Mr Temsik paused. "Not for the weak-minded."

"What's that supposed to mean?"

"An exceptional memory is needed to enjoy its benefits."

***

Through an eerie mist, we could see a kind of yellow glow from either side of the interstate. Two giant arches emerged in the gloom, their shape was unmistakable.

"Are we stopping?" Mr Temsik asked.

I nodded and pulled into the exit lane.

"Good. I'm eager to visit this religious shrine of yours."

"No, it's not a church, it's a fast food place."

"I see… and what's that?"

"Like a restaurant, or a cafeteria."

"Ah, so they serve coffee then? One of the few things I like about your timeline."

"So, you're not from around here?"

"Where I'm from, this is called Central Kitchen Twenty-Nine."

"What?"

"A parallel timeline… hmm… which is apparently devoid of marketeers."

"What's a marketeer?" I asked.

"Like a pirate, but they work in advertising."

It felt satisfying to shut the engine off and get out of the car. All of us road weary, stretching, we emerged onto a brightly-lit but sticky parking lot. Mr Temsik took a long time lingering. He seemed to be studying the cars with some close attention. Reflected lights glinted across the chrome and plastic. "The vehicles in this time seem so much more aggressive than I remember."

"How so?"

"Their faces."

"Faces?"

"What do you call it? The front grills and lights. They look as if they would drive you off the road or run you over."

"What are they like where you're from?"

"More docile, surely, friendly looking. And all these vehicles seem larger than necessary."

"It's not like that where you're from?"

"It's hard to say I'm from anywhere else, Patrick— it's more like where I visit most often. I will guess that your particular civilization values wealth and status above all else… And it is probably doomed as such."

"You can tell that by the cars?"

"Of course not. It just reminds me that I have visited this place before." Öde smiled at me. "It's not my first foray into your timeline… All your food is wrapped in plastic, if I remember."

"Is that a bad thing?"

Öde cast a glance. "How could it be a good thing, eh Patrick?"

Inside, Mr Temsik was baffled by the illuminated menu. He stared up at it for a long time. "Tell me, what's inside one of these hamburgers?

"Beef."

"Are you certain?"

"No one is certain."

"What do these cows of yours eat?"

"Corn, I think, and maybe other cows."

"What? Cannibalistic cows?"

"Ground up bone meal— for extra vitamins."

"So they no longer eat grass?"

"Those cost extra."

"And what are the nuggets made from?"

"Chickens, beaks and all."

"Chickens?"

"It's a kind of bird."

"I know what a chicken is, Patrick." Öde gave me a look. "I think I'll have a salad."

Our late-night snack seemed to go on for hours. We sat at a picnic table in the shadow of the rest area, away from the glaring overhead lights. Traffic on the highway passed by unceasingly like static. I would have been happier to eat and drive.

"Tell me, are there any bees in this timeline?" Mr Temsik asked and took out a silver case from his pocket.

"Bees?"

"The insects with stingers that fly about. They make honey and pollinate crops," he said and lit the end of a cigarette with a wooden match.

"Oh… well, they might be under threat."

"As I suspected." Mr Temsik paused and let go a cloud of smoke. "And the blue dogs? Have they arrived?" he asked.

"What blue dogs?"

"In India."

"Not that I know of."

"Ah, then you have more time than I thought."

"What are you trying to say?"

"Well, if I were you, I'd join the resistance."

"What resistance?"

"Isn't there one?"

"Not really, not in any coherent sense."

"I see… Hmm, if I remember my timelines, this one is about to go south very soon. Let's just say things will take a turn for the worse. What's the word? Draconian… yes, yes, very severe measures." Mr Temsik let go a loud sigh. "Kali or not, the timeline you usually occupy is going to end sooner than you might hope."

"How soon?"

"Sorry to say, things won't last much longer. Civilization collapses."

"When?"

"It will all end in a few generations, if you're thinking of raising bairns."

"What?"

"Offspring, children…"

"Why does it end?"

"This is a place where the truth cannot be known…"

"What?"

"Well, perhaps it can be known, but it is no longer believed." He stared at me as if it were my fault. "Tell me, how did it ever come to that?"

"I'm not sure."

"In this place, civilization has fragmented into thousands if not millions of tiny pieces. There is little cohesion between people, nor a common purpose, the will to change things."

"Nothing can be done?" I asked.

"The people will not revolt. They will not look up from their screens long enough to notice what's happening."

"What?"

"Oh, something George told me."

"George?"

"Mr Orwell. Do you know him?"

"From nineteen eighty-four?"

"No, it was nineteen forty-eight... the very opposite of utopia." Mr Temsik snubbed out his cigarette, then reached into his pocket and pulled out a red piece of cloth. He quickly fashioned it into a hat and placed it atop his head.

"Aren't you a little conspicuous with that?"

"I don't always wear my fez. Only when I'm traveling." He smiled. "Well, gentlemen, I would be remiss by not asking you to come with me."

"To where?"

"Ah, paradise of course. It's not so far from here."

"In the past or the future?" Fynn asked.

"I can't say for certain, but it's quite pleasant..." Mr Temsik paused. "Admittedly there's not much for a policeman to do."

We politely declined his offer. Mr Temsik finally rose and stretched. "Well, I'm off. Our little journey has reminded me of an important task left undone."

"What task?"

"I have to put a cat on a fence on a dark night."

"Why would you have to do that?"

"So Percy notices..."

"Percy?"

"Percy Shaw, an inventor of sorts. He's saved many lives over the years."

"What is he talking about?" I turned to Fynn.

"He is meaning the cat's eyes, the reflectors imbedded in the road."

"They are everywhere nowadays," Öde concurred.

"Sure we can't drop you anywhere?"

"No, no, please continue on your way, gentlemen… I'm fine where I am."

"We can't just leave you in a rest area."

"Of course you can." Mr Temsik smiled and shook both our hands.

* * *

We drove on for nearly an hour with barely a word between us when Fynn finally asked, "Well? What do you make of him, Patrick?"

"I think Mr Temsik is trustable."

"Do you? I'm rather suspicious."

"You've known him longer than me."

Fynn laughed. "What wins him your favor then?"

"Well, just about everything he said, but especially the road reflectors."

"Why the cat's eyes?"

"I'm guessing they've saved millions of lives by now."

"Yes, an act of compassion. Still…"

"What can you tell me about him?"

"I've told you all I remember. Only now do I realize I know nothing about the man. All my previous assumptions have been proven incorrect."

"I guess we should wait for evidence then."

"What evidence?"

"Evidence of his intent."

Fynn sat back with a smile on his face. I could see it in the passing lights. "You've come a long way, my friend," he nearly whispered.

I was almost sure there was a bit of pride in Fynn's tone.

"There is something I do not like about the situation, Patrick… Why of all times and all places does he appear now?"

"What's he up to, do you think?"

"I cannot say, but I sense he is greatly troubled. There's something afoot that he is reluctant to share with us." Fynn paused. "And there is another small problem."

"What?"

"It seems Mr Temsik has stolen our manuscripts."

**

A torrential downpour unleashed from the night sky. The windshield wipers slapped furiously but with little result. My view of the road ahead was clear for only an instant. I was driving on instinct, muscle memory, and a few intermittent visual clues. Most every other car had already pulled over to the shoulder.

Fynn spotted a green sign: a graphic boat and car, and possibly the word ferry underneath. I veered to the right lane and took the exit with too much speed. Aside from the small swerve, we found the dock without incident. A dark ferry was waiting as well, but the parking lot was empty except for the pounding rain. I ran to the office. It was closed. I was drenched on my return.

"Well?" Fynn asked.

"First boat, six o'clock."

chapter six
gilgo beach

I heard a sharp tapping on the glass. I looked to my right to find that Fynn was gone, though there was a ferry ticket on the passenger seat. To my left, someone was shouting. I rolled down the window.

"Let's go. You're holding everybody up," a man said and waved me on. Behind was a line of cars waiting. I seemed to have little choice and started the engine. I drove onto the ferry guided in by people wearing orange vests, and all the way to the bow of the ship. Moments later I was surrounded by other vehicles and had a bit of trouble opening my door.

I found Fynn upstairs in the lounge at a window seat. He had ordered breakfast sandwiches and I downed two of them in no time.

I went back to the snack bar for another coffee.

The rain had left clear skies. The morning was cool and the sun was just starting to rise above the Atlantic horizon as we strolled out onto the deck. It was a pleasant crossing. Outside, I asked one of the crewman how fast the boat was traveling.

"Fourteen knots or so," he replied.

I turned to Fynn. "Same as the *Carpathia*."

"Why is that strange to you, Patrick?"

"Well, it's over a hundred years later and we're traveling at the same speed."

"Perhaps progress is slowing down?"

"I'd have to think about that."

"Weren't you wearing a different shirt?" Fynn asked.

"What do you mean?"

"I'm sure it was a dark blue, but this morning it's gray. Did you change your clothing?"

"Not that I remember."

Back in the lounge, I found a row of seats and caught a half hour of sleep. Fynn woke me as we came around Anthrax Island.

"Why would they name this place in such a way?"

"I think they were just making fun. The real name is Plum Island. It's a government research lab or something— a quarantined place."

I set the GPS on my phone to Sonny Ming's address. From Orient Point we drove along the North Fork, west. The day was heating up; we had the windows open, the morning air was still fresh as we passed vineyards and farms along a small country road. Eventually we came to the infamous Long Island Expressway, or the LIE. After just a few miles the traffic began to build and soon snarled to a halt. It was probably an accident ahead or construction delays, but we were stuck for nearly an hour.

Fynn took to calling it the *Big Lie*. "It's hardly an expressway, it resembles a parking lot more than anything."

"I could take the parkway."

"What?" he asked incredulously.

"The Southern State Parkway— it's on the GPS."

"That sounds far worse." Fynn pointed to an exit. It was the service road that ran parallel, and at least the traffic was moving there.

Durbin called my cell and I put it on speaker for Fynn to hear: "Are you there yet?"

"No, hit some traffic... still about an hour out—Why?"

"Just got off the phone with Detective Mitch in Babylon. She's expecting you. Says she could use your assistance."

"We'll be happy to meet with her," Fynn called out from his seat.

"Great. I owe you guys big time, and thanks for helping out."

***

I will admit to being disappointed when we pulled in at Sonny Ming's School of Language Arts. It was a two-story cinderblock building with a tacky facade in a shopping plaza along Sunrise Highway. Adjacent was a nail salon, and across the parking lot, the Leaning Tower of Pizza, Fine Italian Dining. There was also a bowling alley: Ziggurat Lanes.

We arrived, though not at dawn, nor did we miss any traffic. It seemed impossible that our simple drive from Sand City could have taken twelve hours and I started to wonder if there was a chunk of missing time in there. I felt bedraggled, as if I had used up too much adrenaline. Fynn seemed no worse for wear. "Ah, I can smell the ocean," he said as we got out and stretched.

All I could discern was a sweltering parking lot. The asphalt was hot and sticky and so was I. "Not sure I'm in any condition to learn a new language."

"Weary from the road?" he asked.

"Yeah. Should we find a hotel?"

"Hmm, we won't be longer than a few hours."

"A few hours? How can I learn Russian in just a few hours?"

"Sonny Ming has some extremely innovative techniques. It comes with a money-back guarantee, if I recall." Fynn pointed to the entrance. There was a large number five and a small sign that read: *Travelers Welcome Since 1939.*

I tried the door but it was locked.

"They don't open till two o'clock," a voice called out. A tall woman strode across the blacktop and confronted us on the sidewalk. "I guess Mr Ming likes to sleep late." She flashed a badge from inside a dark blue blazer. "You Jardel?" she asked and looked us both over.

"Could be…"

"I know you are. I just ran your tags. That's your Saab Nine-Three…" She nodded over to my parking space. "And, you're Inspector Fynn." This time she added a smile, a small one. "Oh sorry, I'm Mitch, Detective Lieutenant Penelope Mitchell, Suffolk County Police."

"Durbin's friend?" I ventured. She had a sad look to her and smelled of cigarettes and perfume.

"Yeah. Buy you two guys lunch?" she replied and pointed over to the tower of pizza.

"We'd be delighted," Fynn said for us both and we followed the policewoman across sweltering asphalt. There was nothing manly about Detective Mitch. Her hair was long and curly, dark brown, not dyed as there were a few streaks of gray here and there. And she had a pleasant face with an engaging smile, though her lips had an odd shape. There was a weariness in her eyes which might have been mistaken for coldness. She had kept her figure and seem fit for a woman of her years. I also got the sense she was a chain smoker.

"Durbin said you'd show up sooner or later, but I figured later not sooner… Welcome to Babylon."

"Thank you."

"You came about the murders, right?" she asked with a strong south shore accent. I half-expected her to be chomping on a piece of gum but she wasn't.

"The Gilgo Beach Killer?" Fynn asked.

"No."

"No?"

"Well, he is pretty famous around here…"

"Who?" I asked.

"You mean to tell me, you've never heard of the Gilgo Beach Killer, Mr Jardel?"

"Not really. Just what Sheriff Durbin mentioned."

"Sheriff Durbin?"

"Oh sorry, my nickname for him…" I smiled. Fynn chuckled too.

"That's sort of fitting somehow." She laughed. "And what do you know about the Gilgo Beach Killer, Inspector Fynn?"

"I am not privy to police files, only what can be read in the newspapers and such..."

"Okay, well, at least ten victims, mostly women and mostly sex workers, buried up along Ocean Parkway. Five were killed between two thousand seven and two thousand ten. There's another six or seven victims that might be related."

"Has he killed again?" Fynn asked.

"No— not that we know of..." she answered in a voice that was no more than a husky whisper.

"Are you working on this case?"

"Not officially... it's more of a hobby, I guess." She looked down at the pavement. "Some jurisdictional issues at play. The FBI has it now. I doubt it will ever be solved."

"Sadly, not all crimes can be," Fynn replied. "But I can guess you have some ideas about this monster."

"Got that right," she said and looked up with half a smile. "People say he's stopped killing— I don't buy it for a second."

"Nor do I."

"What?" She turned to Fynn.

"It's not in their nature. Once a serial killer begins, they cannot stop. It amounts to a dreadful compulsion that is never satiated. I can think of only three possibilities. One: the killer has grown old and infirm, or two, he has died..."

"And three?" Detective Mitch asked.

"I would guess he is simply burying the bodies elsewhere."

"We're on the same page, for sure."

"And what of this carpenter from Manorville that I've heard about? Wasn't he arrested?"

"Oh, the guy from out east. Well, the county prosecutor wants everyone to believe he's the killer, but I haven't seen any evidence."

"Forensic evidence?"

"No... just means and opportunity." Detective Mitch paused. "I'm not convinced. The case might be related, but I think our perp is a local boy."

"Why is that?"

"Knows the area all too well..."

"I'm not sure how we can help with this," Fynn said.

"You probably can't, but that's not why I wanted to talk to you."

"What's it about then?"

"I have a new case— Durbin said you wouldn't let me down."

"We will do our best," Fynn replied.

Detective Mitch led us into the Leaning Tower of Pizza. I noticed the name *Grimaldi's* in a small scripty font. Bedecked in greasy formica, the inside was level and plumb for the most part. I immediately sensed a battle between air-conditioning and hot ovens, overlain with the smell of fresh dough. She had been here before, that seemed sure, and was greeted by a big guy in a white apron.

"What can I get you today, hon?"

"A grandma's and four knots," Mitch decided without hesitation.

The man turned to us. "How about you, gentlemen?"

I looked to the glass case that held a dizzying array of offerings: pizza with mac and cheese, buffalo chicken, sesame, anchovies and white sauce, veggie delight…

"Two pepperonis," I ordered.

Fynn looked a bit perplexed. "A plain slice— is it possible?"

"Two regs," the big man called back to an assistant. He turned to us again. "Drinks?"

Fynn took a sparkling water, Detective Mitch and I chose iced tea from the cooler. We found a seat in the corner away from the ovens.

"May I ask how you became to be named Mitch?" Fynn said pleasantly as we sat across from her.

"Long story… Guess I didn't want to be called Penny all my life— from my first name, Penelope…"

"Ah, but Penelope is a lovely name. She was the faithful wife of Odysseus."

"I'm not married as far as I know," the detective replied and added a smile.

We all dug into our lunch and the pizza was exceptional. Mitch began to explain her new investigation:

"First case was a couple of months ago, beginning of the summer… Looked like a drive by shooting. Nobody thought much about it, but some of the details bothered me."

"Something that normally doesn't happen in your town?" Fynn asked.

"A drive by? No." Mitch looked up at us. "Seemed like just a regular guy, in a regular neighborhood. Buckshot to the face, both barrels you might say." She paused for a sip of iced tea. "Anyhow, I ran the victim and there was no reason why he should've been shot— no gambling's debts, bad associations, no record, nothing. Just some moving violations. By all appearances, he was just a normal guy: wife, kids, mortgage..."

"Witnesses?"

"Not to the actual shooting... and no trace or forensics at the scene. We did a lot of follow-up though, neighbors, friends, family. We interviewed a few people, but eventually eliminated their involvement."

"The first case, you say. Have there been others?" Fynn asked.

Mitch's face screwed up into a smile. "That's the thing... I ran this 'drive-by MO' through the database and that's when things got interesting."

"What database?" I asked.

"Oh...We have some software in the office that matches crime scene parameters: victims, ballistics, locations, dates..."

"What did you find?" Fynn urged her on.

Mitch rummaged through a stylish carry-all, "I got twenty-seven hits— all the same: single male shot in a driveway, untraceable buckshot... and none of them had a record of criminal activities." She spread a map out on the table. It looked to be the New York area and was marked by a scattering of red dots.

"I got seven hits in Nassau— the adjacent county, four in Suffolk, two in Queens, one in Brooklyn, nine in New Jersey, and three in Connecticut." She paused for a breath. "I was tracking down another one in Pennsylvania just last night."

"All the same?" Fynn asked.

"Pretty much."

"A different kind of serial killer?"

"Could be... I can now see it's a much larger problem. Cases going back at least five years."

"And before that?"

"Could be more, many more, but we don't have them in the database."

"Any connection between the victims?"

"Not at first. Not the workplace, family, locations, community ties... I checked everything." She paused, and a smile crossed the her face. "Then I ran their DMV..."

"Meaning?" Fynn asked.

"Driving records. Every single one of them was horrendous: suspended licenses, a couple of DUI convictions, speeding violations, points on their license, failures to signal, reckless endangerment... all bad stuff."

"You're talking about road rage," I said.

She smiled. "I am."

"You're saying the killer followed them home and shot these guys?"

"Looks to be something like that."

"Perhaps rage is only the catalyst," Fynn commented.

"How did you ever come up with this idea?" I asked.

Mitch sat back in her seat. "Two things... I re-read all the reports, and in some of them, the investigating officer noticed that the engine was still warm— the victim's car, I mean. And that got me thinking, maybe they were followed home."

"What's the other thing?"

Mitch leaned in close. "When I first started on the force, I was assigned to traffic," she said. "Ha, there's this one place in particular: the southbound merge from the Cross Island leading onto the LIE... Do you know it?"

"No."

"Well, the perfect place for road rage. People would be patiently lined up at the exit, and then some idiot would come barreling up the center lane and cut everybody off at the last second." Mitch made a face. "Like they were entitled or something..."

"What did you do?"

"Me?" She laughed. "I'll just say it's a great feeling to pull over some a-hole and give 'em a ticket for reckless driving. Probably snagged four or five people a week." Mitch smiled. "But, I also understand how frustrating it must be for the average law-abiding citizen to get cut off like that."

"You sympathize with road rage?" I asked.

"I guess I do— though most people just bang the steering wheel and curse the other guy out... Most people don't drive around with a sawed-off shot gun in the front seat."

"A sawed-off shot gun?"

"That's what ballistics tells me."

"I must say, it's a fine bit of police work," Fynn complimented.

"Thanks... It's a working theory."

"A very good one." He smiled. "Though, from what little you've told me so far, it's not rage at all. Your killer seems quite deliberate and methodical in his actions."

"I completely agree, Mr Fynn, but my boss doesn't, and neither does the media."

"Why is that?"

"They've dubbed him *Mad Max... the Road Rage Killer*."

"And how can we help?" Fynn asked.

"There was another shooting two days ago, same exact circumstances."

"Where?"

"A couple of towns over... Nassau County. I thought you could take a look at the scene."

"Of course."

Mitch made a face. "I'm on shaky ground, jurisdictionally."

"Why is that?"

"We only have the one crime scene here in Babylon, Suffolk... The rest of the incidents occurred elsewhere, so I had to call in a few favors... State Police took over the case."

"What other details can you give us?" Fynn asked.

Mitch started dealing file folders onto the table. "These are all the same, exactly the same," she announced, and with some pride in her tone. "Victims: solo males. Location: a driveway. Two shot gun blasts to the face and or chest. No shells or casings left at the scene." She paused. "Now, that told me a couple of things: the killer was either really short or remained in his vehicle, probably never left the driver's seat. And, I'm pretty sure the car has electric windows."

Fynn pored through the folders one by one. "Anything that can be traced?"

"It's near impossible to trace buckshot. Could be bought anonymously or off the internet..." Mitch paused again. "Even if we could, it's tough to match it to a particular weapon."

"I see from the reports, there were never more than two shots fired," Fynn commented.

"What does that say to you?" Detective Mitch asked.

"Probably an older model gun that has to be loaded manually."

"That's exactly what I thought."

"What's this?" I asked, holding a close-up photo of an odd emblem splattered in blood. It looked like a "Y" surrounded by a circle.

Detective Mitch turned the picture around clockwise. "A Mercedes logo. Victim number seventeen, Massapequa— not my jurisdiction. Even a face full of buckshot didn't stop him; he was able to yank that off the back of a vehicle."

"The killer's car?"

"We think so…"

"That seems hard to do."

Mitch turn to me. "Funny, I thought the exact same thing. The guy had hands like meat hooks though. They had to pry it from his fingers."

"What happened to him?"

"Died two days later. Never regained consciousness."

"And other witness reports?" Fynn asked.

"Oh, we've got tons of reports. The killer is bold and brazen. I can safely say it's somebody wearing a hoody and a mask."

"A mask?"

"Black ski-mask."

"No one has seen his face?"

"No. Best description we got is a short, skinny guy… Maybe five-four, five-five, wearing a baggy sweatshirt with a hood." Mitch gave off a sigh.

"Ah, the bane of our existence," Fynn said with a smile. "The unreliability of witnesses."

Mitch laughed. "You got that right."

"What about the vehicle used for the crimes?" Fynn asked.

"We have conflicting statements. Could be anything from a Honda to a Mercedes, a Subaru, a Toyota, a Chevy, or a Volkswagen," she ticked off the brands as she tapped each file. "Silver gray, green gray, light gray, dark gray…"

"That's a lot of different cars."

"Yes, but all of them gray." Mitch smiled. "Best I can guess is a late-model sedan, like a million other cars— practically invisible."

"Nothing on CCTV?" Fynn had a question.

"I think the killer is very cautious about that. Like I said, all the shootings occurred in quiet suburban neighborhoods. No cameras usually, but some of the bigger roads going in and out do. I ran all the video I could find, but no joy."

"There seems to be very little to go on," Fynn commented and sat back in his chair.

"It's frustrating, that's for sure," Mitch agreed. "We did get some plate numbers, partials mostly— but they turned out to be ghost plates."

"Ghosts?"

"Not in our database. Lost, stolen, or never turned in to the DMV— some of them ten years old. Of course I checked every single one I could, but it all led nowhere."

"You've been very thorough, Detective Mitchell." Fynn gave a smile. "And what do your instincts say?"

"Well, I'm guessing he's a quiet guy, mild mannered, nondescript… and obviously, easily provoked." She chuckled slightly. "There is one other thing," Mitch said and slid her tablet across the table. It was a blurry photo of a person in a hoody. One hand was on the steering wheel and his elbow was hanging out the window. No face was visible, nor was the car identifiable.

"You think this is the killer?"

"Yup. Right time and place— just a hunch though."

"Where was this taken?"

"A red light camera… He's not the offender— just happened to be in the frame. A lucky break maybe."

"There's something on his jacket," I pointed. "Looks like a circle— a logo or something…"

"Can you enlarge that bit?" Fynn asked. He stared at the screen for a time. "It is the uroboros."

"The what?"

"A snake eating it's own tail. Quite an ancient symbol."

"What does it mean?"

"Many have pondered this question. Perhaps it is the cycle of continuity. The end and the beginning that is always occurring."

"How does it help catch him?"

"I'm not sure it does, other than as a means of identification."

Mitch was interrupted by her phone. She excused herself to take the call, and then came back to the table. She seemed excited. "I just got a hit on possible tags, a two thousand seven gray Honda Civic. You guys want to go for a ride?"

"Where to?"

"It's parked at Tobay Beach,

"Tobay? That's an odd name…"

"Oh yeah, stands for the Town of Oyster Bay on the North Shore… Something about riparian rights to the Atlantic side."

We went back to the sweltering parking lot and Mitch's car, an unmarked blue sedan. "They took away my old Crown a couple of years ago."

"Excuse me?"

Mitch laughed. "My Crown Vic— I loved that damn car."

"What's this?"

"A police interceptor, sedan version… Really, it's a Ford Taurus."

"Pretty roomy back here," I commented.

"You're lucky it isn't piled with junk today."

I was happy enough to have the backseat to myself, sprawled there with my legs up. I could catch Mitch's reflection in the rearview from time to time. I'll also admit to feeling a bit sleepy. The detective was feeling chatty it seemed:

"So, you guys like to travel, huh? That's what Durbin told me."

"You might say that."

"What places have you gone?"

"Oh, here and there."

"I've never left the Island…well, hardly ever. I mean I've been to the City, and even Jersey once or twice."

***

Mitch drove us to the Robert Mosses, and just before the bridge to Fire Island, turned onto Ocean Parkway, a thin strip of road that ran along the edge of the Atlantic. It was a perfect beach day, sunny, hot and humid. There was a fair amount of traffic. We passed a sign that read *Gilgo Beach*.

"The other case we talked about," Mitch said then shot a glance in the rearview. "Is my pad back there, Mr Jardel?" she asked.

"Yeah…"

"Switch it on and hit the file named Gilgo…"

I did, and found a screen full of pictures, the ten known victims. One took my notice immediately: it was Kali Shunya, though somehow that seemed impossible. Her name was listed as Lacy Tipota. I passed the tablet up to Fynn. He said nothing but raised an eyebrow.

"…All the victims were found twenty or thirty feet off the road in the thick brambles there. All within a couple of miles, wrapped in burlap sacks," Mitch was explaining.

"On which side of the road?" Fynn asked.

"The north side, westbound lanes," she replied and pointed to a large bay on our right… "Not much left but skeletons," she added. "Strangulation seems to be the COD."

"Were the victims dismembered?"

"Yeah… Some say they were killed in the summer and buried in the winter. Crowded with beach-goers today, but this stretch of road is mighty desolate in the off season."

"But who would take such a risk? To bury bodies at the side of this highway?"

"Someone who thinks he's a cop, but is not," Mitch replied.

"What do you mean?"

"Oh, like an EMT, or a fireman, or a private security guy. I'm guessing he felt safe on this road, even if he got pulled over…"

"I recall that a woman named Shannon Gilbert brought this case to notoriety," Fynn commented.

"That's right," Mitch replied. "She was here at Oak Beach— we just passed it. Called nine-one-one for help and then just vanished into thin air."

"But her body was discovered some months later?"

"Yeah. December, two thousand ten. A cadaver dog found her…" Mitch swiveled a look into the rearview. "The official report says Shannon was not a victim of the same killer, but it's one helluva coincidence."

"Ah, as a detective, you must agree, there are no coincidences."

"Got that right."

"And yet there is another rather extraordinary coincidence in this case that no one mentions."

"What's that?"

"I remember reading about this police dog and its training," Fynn said.

"Huh?"

"Why decide to train the cadaver dog on that day of all days, and in that location of all locations?" the inspector asked.

Mitch shot him a glance.

"Why a cold December day? And in a patch of impenetrable brambles? Why not along the stretch of open beach on the other side?"

"Wait… you don't think it was just a routine dog training?"

"Hardly seems likely."

"I might have met the guy," Mitch considered. "He can't be guilty though."

"Well, I'm not one to say, but I might guess he was looking for Shannon Gilbert…"

"But the remains he found belonged to someone else."

"Exactly this. If Shannon was found first, there would be no Gilgo Beach Killer. No other bodies would have been discovered. The search would have ended then and there."

"You're saying he's our perp?"

"I am not one to say… but I will speculate he might have had information which he did not share with others."

"Holy crap… the dog handler." Detective Mitch slammed on her brakes and pulled off to the shoulder of Ocean Highway. Iced tea went flying across her shirt and the steering wheel. "Gotta make a quick call, sorry," she announced and took out her cell phone: "Hey Eliza, can you connect me with C.A. in records…? That's right, Mr Dupin… Lunch break, huh? Well, it's a personnel question… No, going back a ways, two thousand ten… You betcha… I'm looking for the name of the K-Nine officer from back then… That's right… Okay, thanks… And can you print it out for me? I'll take a look when I get back to the station."

***

We crossed into Nassau County, a jurisdictional courtesy, according to Detective Mitch. Traffic had all but stopped. Flashing lights and sirens took us the rest of the way up the shoulder. We drove another couple of miles or so and pulled into a giant parking lot. There was a long line of cars waiting to enter. Mitch chirped her siren and rolled through the entrance booth with a flash of her badge. She drove to the far end of the lot, slowly cruising up and down the rows of parked cars.

"What are we looking for?" I asked.

"A silver gray Civic… NY tags: BAB-five, one, one, one."

"Tags?" Fynn asked.

"A license plate."

We found the car in question and Mitch parked along side, blocking any possible exit. She put on the dashboard flashing lights. "Let's have a look…" the detective said and we all got out of the cruiser. There wasn't much to see, just an anonymous vehicle with a carseat and some trash scattered on the passenger side. I noticed the back plates were a little weird. I could see they were magnetic; stuck over the regular plate. Mitch nodded and took out a pair of blue gloves. She carefully removed it to an evidence bag. Now the front and back tags matched. She called it in on her radio but there was some delay— the computer was down or something.

"Let's go up to the ocean," Mitch said unexpectedly. We followed her past a pavilion that housed changing rooms, a snack bar and outdoor showers. A long pedestrian tunnel led under Ocean Parkway and up to the bright sunny beach.

"Somewhere up here is a killer," Detective Mitch said, surveying the expanse of crowded sand.

"More than one perhaps…" Fynn muttered.

I felt out of place, dressed in socks and shoes. This wasn't right.

"I have no wish to be critical, Detective Mitch, but what do you hope to accomplish here? It seems pointless."

"You're right. Sometimes I just like to come out and look at the ocean…" Mitch gave us a smile. "And you never know, somebody might just walk by in a sweatshirt with a giant 'O' logo on it."

There was something in her smile though. She knew something we did not. Far to the south, massive storm clouds were towering into the bright blue sky. A rumble of thunder soon followed.

Mitch chuckled. "Nothing clears the beach faster than a storm… Especially if someone spots lightning."

I could hear the lifeguards now, frantic on their whistles, and waving everyone to shore. It was hardly a rain storm though. A few big drops thudded against the sand here and there. It ended moments later and the sun returned to blaze down on us. Nonetheless, a great exodus began as beach-goers packed up their belongings and headed back towards their cars. We were just slightly ahead of them and sat waiting in the cruiser for the owner of the Civic to return. A woman appeared with kids in tow, beach balls and a wagon, an armload of towels, and a giant umbrella against the sun. It was pretty clear she was not Mad Max the Road Rage Killer.

"He's playing us…" Mitch said with disgust in her voice, and pulled out of the parking lot.

***

We drove to the most recent crime scene, a nameless neighborhood in Long Island, it could've well been Levittown. All the houses were probably exactly the same once… now slightly different, through decades of landscaping and remodeling. Yellow tape was still in place, and a blue tarpaulin covered a patch of road directly in front of a particular driveway.

I watched Fynn and Mitch lift the tarp and examine the spills underneath. Fynn squatted down and put his finger to the pavement as Mitch looked on. I had no idea what they were up to. Something shiny caught my eye. It was beyond the crime scene tape by the curb. I went over to look and found a metallic emblem wedged in the sewer grate. Detective Mitch and Fynn came over. She handed me a pair of gloves and I gingerly wrested it free.

"It's from a Hyundai."

"A what?" Fynn asked.

"A brand of car."

"Okay, that is weird," Mitch said and took it from my hand for a closer look. "Most of these logos are chrome plated plastic… Still, it could be from any car in the neighborhood."

"Well, there's this…" I took the emblem and stuck it to the back of her Taurus. Magnet hit metal with a sharp click.

"Clever," Fynn said as he came over for a look. "One gray car with many medallions."

"Well, I'll be damned."

"Thank you, Patrick…With this bit of new information, I can tell you where to find your killer," Fynn said to Mitch.

"What?"

"Well, his car at the very least."

"How?" Mitch asked.

"I must warn you, it's rather grim and dreadful."

"What are you talking about?"

Inspector Fynn walked back to the blue tarpaulin and lifted the corner. "Fluid from a radiator," he said. "You've done well to cover the drippings from the suspect's vehicle. I see that there is a copious amount on the road— this green sticky liquid."

"How does that tell us where the suspect is?"

"Now, you must check the computers… find a list of recently departed pets."

"What?"

"Cats and dogs," Fynn said and glanced at us as if it were obvious. "Find the place were many have died and you will find your killer— or the neighborhood where he resides."

Detective Mitch looked at Fynn and seemed a bit confused, but she was still listening.

"There may be other creatures involved. Birds, squirrels, raccoons and alike, though I'm not sure they would show up in any reports. I've heard they have a taste for it— it's like a sweet syrup to them."

Mitch stood silently for a long time. Soon enough a smile spread across her face. "Cats drinking antifreeze— it's poison to them."

***

From the quiet neighborhood, we drove back to Sunrise Highway. I could feel myself dozing a little and was jarred awake when we pulled up over a curb. "Just gotta fill up before we head to the other scene,"

Mitch explained. "It's from last week, but we might find something we missed the first time."

I looked around at the gas station, a bit confused. "Why is premium a dollar more than regular unleaded?"

"Isn't it like that where you're from?" Mitch asked.

"I don't think so."

"Damn government regulations… I tell you, I wouldn't put that regular crap in my car… destroy the engine."

I also spotted a CCTV camera at the pumps and asked aloud, "Hey, if we're getting gas, maybe the killer did too."

Mitch shot a glance in the rearview. "You just read my mind, Mr Jardel." She got out of the car again. "Be right back."

There was another crime scene to visit, Mitch told us, also in Nassau county. "It's not far— only take twenty minutes to get there. Let's have a look— what'd ya say?"

Fynn nodded and we set off again. I did my best to stay awake on the ride, but felt myself dosing…

chapter seven
shots fired

The Arbiter had first tasked Fynn with saving our modern civilization at the end of July. It didn't seem like such a big deal, but he asked for my help. We had to travel back in time and save some guy by the name of Clair Patterson. I'll admit I had never heard of him before.

"An easy errand perhaps, yet a tedious journey."

"Couldn't we get Stanley to fly us there?"

"You mean to say in an airplane?" Fynn shot a glance.

"He runs a charter service from Fairhaven."

"Patrick, you know my trepidations about flying."

"It's a long train ride to California."

"Yes, and since we must journey to the west coast, I think it's better that we travel in time first and then in space."

"Why?"

"The trains were nicer in the past. Besides, the Pacific Ocean is vast as you know. I'd hate to end up in the middle of it."

"Think this through for a second, Fynn. Pasadena is a good sixty or seventy miles inland. We should be fine…"

It took me most of the afternoon to convince him this was a viable idea. He finally picked up the phone and called Livingston Aviation. I listened in on the speaker:

"…And expense is no problem?" I heard Stanley ask.

"None whatsoever."

"Okay, there's a nice little Cessna *Citation* I could charter. Get us there in about six hours flying time."

"Are you certain?"

"Not to worry, Tractus, it will all be fine and dandy. Airplanes have come a long way since you were on one last."

"I certainly hope so… Tell me, Stanley, how are they in nineteen sixty-five?"

"What?" Stanley laughed. "More primitive and quite a bit slower."

"Very well…"

"We could land at Van Nuys or maybe Burbank."

"Where?"

"The Bob Hope Airport, Hollywood. It's closer and more convenient than LAX."

"Thank you, Stanley. I'll leave it to your expertise."

"Okay then, I'll file a flight plan… We can leave tomorrow."

The next day Stanley greeted us at Fairhaven airport, a ways away from the main terminal— not that it was much of an airport to begin with. Still, we had to go through security. He led us to Livingston Aviation, a small office with a second door that led out onto the tarmac.

Stanley didn't seem to remember me from the *Carpathia* at all, though he did from Fynn's party. I tried to push the idea that he was recently a drunken homeless guy from my mind. Not a glowing reference for our new pilot. Fynn surely recalled their different adventures together, though neither said a word. I also noticed Stanley had lost most of his brogue.

We had the *Citation M2* to ourselves. I found a fully stocked bar and kitchen. In the fridge were lobster salad sandwiches and I doled them out. Fynn took a glass of single malt to combat his apprehension. I made coffee and took some to the cockpit. Stanley was appreciative. From the panorama below I guessed we were already over the midwest somewhere. I went back to the cabin and sat across from Fynn.

"When was the first time you encountered Kali?"

"It was Africa in eighteen seventeen."

"You were with Stanley, if I remember…"

"Indeed, we were explorers." Fynn paused. "Another man was with us, by the name of Belzoni— an Italian strongman from Padua."

"A strongman?"

"Yes, from a circus. He reminds me of Lothar in some respects."

"Why do you think Kali showed up?"

Fynn chuckled. "Around that time there was a burgeoning interest in ancient Egypt. It was believed that no civilization could be so old… And such antiquity might reveal untold secrets."

"The manuscripts?"

"Indeed. Though she was misguided in her thinking."

"What happened?"

"Hieroglyphs were known but not deciphered until many years later, by Champollion."

"And nothing to do with the manuscripts."

"No. Stanley and I had traveled south on the Nile… far beyond Luxor and the ancient city of Thebes. Further even than Philae… In Nubia, we stumbled upon the temples of Abu Simbel, and except for the local population, they had not been seen for a thousand years. A magnificent sight, hewn from the rock, though half buried in sand along the banks of the river."

"Who built it?"

"The greatest of all pharaohs, Ramesses the second, in the thirteenth century BC."

"Even before your time, eh?" I laughed. "And Mortimer was there?"

"Yes, he went around with a man by the name of Drovetti, who had set out to loot the entire area of its antiquities."

"What about Kali?"

"Stanley came close to losing his life. She threw him from a terrible cliff."

"What happened?"

"He landed in a mountain of forgiving sand and was otherwise unharmed."

"Did she look at her hand back then?"

"I believe so. She certainly had formidable abilities, flitting from here to there and then disappearing."

"Does Stanley remember any of this?"

"You'd have to ask him."

"I'll let him concentrate on flying for now."

"You are learning wisdom, Patrick."

I sat back in my seat. "So… what's in store for us in Pasadena?"

"We are to save the life of Doctor Clair Patterson. It's there in the folders."

"Where did you get all this?"

"From Franny of course. You remember her?"

"Frances Lee— purple hair, steel-trap memory. Not someone I'm likely to forget."

"She's quite thorough."

"She is at that." I started leafing through the files. "Why was he so important to history? Professor Patterson doesn't seem to have lived a very exciting life."

"Perhaps not… but fulfilling, yes? And his actions have benefitted humankind."

"Not so sure how working on the Manhattan Project helped the planet."

"One thing leads to another, I would say. There, he met his wife, Laurie, and they both became experts in mass spectrometry. With that skill he accurately calculated the age of the earth to four and a half billion years."

"Okay, that's sort of important."

"And without those experiments he would not have noticed that there was too much lead in the current environment."

"Franny also said he invented the first clean-room."

"Another notch in his belt," Fynn commented. "But of course we are concerned about his evangelical warnings about tetraethyl-lead."

"That's a mouthful."

"Yes, it is an organo-lead compound."

"What? Something you'd put on a greek salad?"

"No, it is lead bound to carbon, a combination quite deadly to humans." Fynn paused. "After World War Two, right up until the late nineteen seventies, the amount of lead in the food chain and in the atmosphere had reached alarming levels. And at least an entire generation was at risk."

"Right. What happens to this timeline if it's not fixed?"

"Civilization continues on for a century or so, and then trails off to nothing."

"Isn't this how the Roman Empire fell? Lead in their pipes or something?"

"It may have been a small factor, though certainly not the only cause. More likely it was the sacking and pillaging of Rome in the year four-ten by the Visigoths."

"That would do it."

"It is the consequences of doing nothing that frightens me."

"Why?"

"Well, education becomes less of a priority. Science and technology fall into decline. Art and culture lose much of their value. And, how shall I say it? 'Stupidness' is culturally celebrated. It became a trait to be admired."

"The *idiocracy…*"

"What's that, Patrick?"

"Oh, nothing…What's your plan to fix this then?"

"I consider it a simple errand. We travel back and prevent the crime."

"That's it?"

"Yes. I will also provide Professor Patterson some additional information to fuel his noble passion."

"You mean his crusade against lead?"

"One of the very few noble crusades, I might add. He was rather brave and fought fiercely for his cause. Reviled by colleagues, derided as a crank by the press, and demonized by the oil companies."

"What other information do you have?"

"There are three others on the same crusade, more or less.

"Who's that?"

"One from the past and two from the future."

"The future?"

"The relative future— from nineteen sixty-five." Fynn smiled. "It's all in the files that Franny compiled."

I read further about Charles Norris. He was New York City's first qualified coroner, and probably the first to notice the effects of lead poisoning. He was called upon to investigate cases of insanity and several deaths which had occurred at the *Loony Gas Building*, a facility where lead was added to gasoline in order to boost its octane. It proved very profitable for the Standard Oil Company, and as such, Doctor Norris' warnings about lead poisoning met stiff resistance.

"I know this place," I commented while reading, "the meadowlands in New Jersey. An industrial wasteland smack in the middle of the Garden State."

"At present or in nineteen twenty-four?" Fynn asked.

"Probably both... I wonder if he was nicknamed *Chuck*?"

"What's that, Patrick?"

"Oh, nothing... a different kind of hero..."

I also read about two others concerned with lead poisoning: a British chemist named Derek Bryce-Smith, and a pediatrician, Herbert Needleman who worked in the seventies.

***

On our flight west, Fynn pored through the police reports, also provided by Franny.

"It was a terrible massacre," he told me. "Some have called it the first mass shooting in America."

"What?"

"On the second of August, nineteen sixty-five, a man by the name of Whitman climbed to the top of a building and began shooting random passersby."

"Why does that sound so familiar?"

"I do not know, Patrick. But this man killed fifteen people including an unborn child, and injured thirty-one others."

"And our Professor Patterson was among the victims?"

"Yes, the seventh person to be shot. He was strolling across campus."
"Anyone else we know on that list?" I asked.
"Not that I noticed. You should have a look as well."
"I'm no expert," I cautioned, and perused the names.
"Nor I," Fynn replied. "Thankfully, Franny raised no red flags."
"How do we solve this?"
"I hope to prevent it instead; we will arrive a day beforehand." Fynn raised a smile. "The authorities report that the perpetrator was heavily armed, and was seen prowling around the campus for some weeks. There is talk of an accomplice as well, a dark haired woman of foreign descent. They were unable to locate her, nor identify her."
"We can guess who that is."
"Indeed. And firearms are easily acquired, eh?"
"You mean by Kali?"
"By anyone. There is no crime to solve here. I have no doubt that Mr Whitman is the shooter. The police have been competent in this regard."
"What then?"
"He has no apparent motive, so I must assume Kali has influenced him in some way."
"Whispering into his mind?"
"We've seen it before, eh? The way she can so easily manipulate hapless accomplices."
"Victims, you mean."
"As you say, Patrick."

***

It struck me that I had never seen Inspector Fynn asleep before. He had stretched out along two seats and looked peaceful. I put a blanket around him. A few hours later, it was a smooth landing in Burbank.
"Do you want me to wait for you?" Stanley asked at the top of the foldable gangway.
"Oh, for a ride back," Fynn said as he was about to take a step outside. "I hadn't thought about that... Yes, if you would."
"I'll be here." Stanley grinned.
"And so will Patrick," Fynn added.

"What? I'm not going with you?"

"We have only the one cane to use."

"I came all this way, and you're going to leave me at the airport?"

"Alright," Fynn changed his mind. "Come along then." He reached into an overhead compartment and pulled out two hats. "Not that I care for the trilby, but it will help us fit in."

"Fit in?"

"Appear inconspicuous."

The next decision facing us was whether to first travel back to 1965 or take a taxi to Pasadena. We opted for the former, found a low wall and jumped—two on a cane. We landed about a hundred yards west on the other side of the runway. Stanley was gone, as well as our ride. I could only hope he was waiting for us in the future. All the planes had changed from jets to beefy four engine props— passenger liners awaiting take off. It was quite a sound.

Most of the private jets had changed to single engine Piper Cubs. I did see a couple of 707s near the terminal, and the control tower looked primitive by comparison. I saw a sign: *Lockheed Air Terminal.*

The cab to Pasadena was an old fashioned Checker, roomy in the back to say the least, but primitive and bulbous even for this era. We cruised up the flat streets amongst other angular vehicles the size of small boats. It was a hazy summer day in the valley, and I spotted the San Gabriel Mountains looming beyond in the east. The first thing we needed to do at CalTech was find Clair Patterson's office. Fynn had a bundle of files with a note attached which simply read: "Fellow crusaders."

The campus was huge with well-tended lawns and gardens throughout. Everything seemed so orderly, clean and spiffy. It was thoroughly modern for the nineteen sixties; most of the buildings, and surely all the people who strolled by.

"The shooting began there, according to the police reports," Fynn said and pointed.

"What is that place?"

"Throop Hall."

I looked up to the ornate building probably built at the turn of the century. It had columns, a peaked roof, and a small cupola. Oddly, there was a Mickey Mouse clock at the center of the top wall— maybe a student prank. Across the commons was another building, far more modern, a kind of round theatre built from white stone: the Beckman Auditorium.

We strolled across the lawn, but a moment later I heard a gunshot. It was difficult to say from where, as it had echoed a few times. There was another shot, and this time I saw someone on the path crumple to his knees. I could see blood staining his clean shirt. Another shot, and someone nearby fell to the ground. I rushed over and tried to drag them to cover. It was a young woman and I had to wonder if she was still alive. Her blouse filled with a horrible red stain.

More shots followed and people were dropping all around. The rest began shrieking and shouting, and most ran for cover: the few trees that edged the commons. More people rushed out of Throop Hall, but it was a terrible mistake. As soon as they cleared the entrance and came in view of the cupola, they were dropped by expert fire. One of those was probably Clair Patterson. I saw a briefcase hit the ground and spill its contents.

A bullet flew over our heads. It was close, singing as it went past. Fynn and I ducked down. There was little cover though. We scrambled to the trees, breathless.

"What happened?" I asked.

"I'm not sure... though clearly we've arrived on the wrong day. I fear I've made a terrible mistake."

"Maybe you forgot to compensate for leap year or something?"

"Perhaps... What's important is that we are safe and sound so we can proceed with our errand."

Another bullet came, and another— this one hit my shoulder. I felt its sting and looked over to see the fabric of my shirt was torn and charred. Some blood came to the surface. I was lucky to be only grazed. We scrambled into a thick hedge and found another wall. Fynn and I jumped again with the cane between us; a hard jump, this time to the day before the massacre. All was quiet when we arrived, but I was still bleeding. Things were peaceful, birds were chirping, people strolled by oblivious to their fate. It was as if nothing had happened— nothing had, yet.

***

"What about the doubles we just left behind?"

"Not left behind, Patrick. They are one day in the future. But as you mention, they are likely to be dead if that present persists as we saw."

We quickly found Doctor Patterson's office and dropped off the information. He was a quiet, unassuming man, gray and balding with thick glasses. And he was skeptical at first but began poring through the documents as his curiosity took hold. Fynn seemed satisfied, but our task was not quite complete.

We wandered around campus for half an hour. Inspector Fynn was searching for someone. We came across a small garden and a park bench. It was not empty however. A disheveled man sat alone, or rather, lay across it as if it were his bed. He was a young guy in his twenties, probably clean cut on a good day, and had a military bearing. I would've guessed he spent time in the army. As I began to realize who he was, I felt myself filling with rage and loathing. Fynn noticed my reaction and tried to calm me. I did my best to stifle the feelings and decided not to say a word.

"Excuse me, sir?" Fynn called out as we approached. May we share this bench with you?"

He rose bleary eyed. "You're not her," the man stammered.

"No…"

"But she sent you, didn't she?"

"Who might you be speaking about?"

"The dark woman… always smiling at me, always whispering in my ear."

"I may know who you speak of, but I assure you, she is not counted among our friends."

"Who is she?"

"A person to be avoided."

He turned to me. "Hey buddy, you're bleeding, you know."

"That's because you shot me…" I muttered.

"What?"

He hadn't heard. "I noticed, thanks," I said louder.

"How'd that happen?" he asked.

"Tripped and fell."

"And why are you two here?" He searched our faces with a back and forth glance.

"We are just enjoying a pleasant morning on the campus. A lovely sunny day, don't you think?" Fynn responded.

"It's sunny every day— well almost." He looked us over again. "Are you a professor here or something?"

"No, just a visitor. And you, a student?"

"Not anymore…" his voice trailed off.

"I am Fynn and this is Patrick."

"…I'm… Joe… Joe Whitman."

Given the delay in his reply, I suspected this wasn't his real name. "*I was a student,*" Joe continued, "but my scholarship got revoked."

"A scholarship, you say?"

"I was in the Marines; they were paying for it all." The man cast a furtive look around the park. "You sure you don't know this lady who's been following me?"

"What's her name?"

"I don't know… But ever since I met her, I haven't been feeling well. I get these headaches now…"

"Migraines?"

"Yes."

"You should see a doctor, a specialist even."

"I might just do that."

"I'm guessing you're not from around here," Fynn said.

"No… born and raised in Florida. Spent some time in Texas though."

"I see. You must be feeling homesick, yes?"

"Well, now that you mention it, I would like to go back."

"To Florida?"

"No. Texas…" He gave us an apologetic grin. "Kind of low on funds at the moment."

"And what would you do?"

"I was an engineering major at the University… I have family there."

"They must miss you, eh?"

"I guess…" he hesitated. "I've let them down though, something awful…"

"Why is that?"

"Well… I go up to Vegas from time to time…"

"What do you do there?"

"Hit the casinos, see a show maybe…"

"Gambling," I blurted.

"You're right, friend…" He turned to me. "I can't seem to stop myself. It's like a compulsion."

"If I might speak plainly," Fynn said, ignoring me. "I see no future for you here, Mr Whitman— not a good one at least."

"You might be right about that. But I'm stuck till I can find a job… save up for bus fare."

"I see…" Fynn reached into his pocket and pulled out a wad of old currency. "I have eight hundred dollars. Would that be enough for a bus ticket?"

"Back to Texas you mean?"

Fynn nodded.

"It would be more than enough."

Fynn thrust the bills into the man's hand.

"I can't take this," he said.

"Why not?"

"First of all, I'm no charity case, and second of all, I don't know you."

"Ah, this is true on both counts," Fynn replied, then paused. "I suppose I'll have to give this money to someone else."

"What?"

"It's my job," Fynn said.

"Your job?"

"Yes. I've been hired to dispense money to people who seem worthy."

"Who's this boss of yours?"

"I'm sure you don't know him by name." Fynn smiled. "But your benefactor is a Mr John B. Tipton."

"Doesn't ring a bell."

"Well, come along then, we'll give you a lift to the bus station."

"Now?"

"Yes…"

chapter eight
egg rolls

I heard my name called and felt a gentle shake on my shoulder; it was a bit sore. "Patrick, wake up, you've fallen asleep…"

I rose with a start, and in the back of Detective Mitch's Taurus.

"Were you dreaming?" Fynn asked.

"No… remembering."

"Hmm?"

"Pasadena, CalTech." I rubbed my eyes and sat up. "Where are we?"

"Still in Babylon."

"I missed the crime scene?"

"You did… two crime scenes, and a Hittite chariot race."

"What?"

Fynn raised a smile. I was still a bit groggy.

"Did you find anything new?"

"Nothing of note."

"Where's Detective Mitch?"

"She went to get us iced coffee."

"That sounds perfect."

Mitch returned a few moments later and passed out giant coffees, ice cubes rattling. "Well guys, thanks for your help on this today," the detective said. "I'm guessing Mr Ming's school is open right about now." She smiled and shook our hands. "You've given me a lot to think about, and a lot of work to do… so… I'll catch up with you later."

I needed to find my bearings. Fynn and I walked across the parking lot back to the Saab. Inside it was an inferno, baking in the hot sun all day.

"It's lucky we decided against bringing our pets."

"I'll say…"

"Though I fear for my saltwater taffy."

I opened the windows and doors to let the car cool off, then slurped down my iced coffee. "Where or when did you first meet Sonny Ming?"

"Ah… It was many years ago and very far away."

"That's kind of a vague answer." I returned a smile. "He mentioned something at your party… about being a little kid in China…"

"Indeed he was. We first met in a remote province and he cursed at me in Portuguese."

"That was unusual?"

"Of course. How could he ever learn such a word? This piqued my interest and I followed him. When I tracked him down, I tried to speak to him in several languages. He knew at least five. How could this be possible for a young boy in Shanghai?"

"It's hard to imagine Sonny as a boy…"

"He knew far too much about the world for a twelve-year-old."

"So he was a traveler?"

"He didn't see it that way."

"No?"

"He thought of it as a kind of re-incarnation."

"That sort of makes sense in a way."

"Yes, I suppose it does."

"When was this?"

"The twenty-sixth of August, eighteen eighty-three."

"How is it you remember the exact date?"

"The sky grew dark. The sun no longer could be seen— it went on like that for months…"

"What happened back then?"

"Krakatoa erupted…" Fynn paused. "Sonny expressed an interest in exploring the West and I was happy to accommodate."

"You were his guide?"

"You might put it that way. I took him under my wing so to speak. We traveled to the west and he learned about the modern world."

I slurped down the rest of my coffee and we started across the sticky parking lot to Sonny Ming's School of Language Arts. "Oh yeah, I meant to ask: Did Mortimer say anything else to you yesterday?"

"When you went to fetch Lothar's dinner?"

"Yes."

"Nothing important."

"What did you do to him?"

"Eh?"

"I saw you cut his finger or something."
"You've become observant, Patrick… and yes, I gave him a prick with my knife and a black mark."
"How, why?"
"India ink… indelible, one might say." Fynn smiled. "As to why… well, it is so we can identify him when we meet again."
"He agreed to that?"
"He did."
"And when will we meet him again?"
"Difficult to say for certain, though he has promised to help, yes?"

***

I still felt disappointed by Sonny Ming's School. Inside it was more like a dentist's office than anything, generic and sterile. The whole place looked to be newly-remodeled, beige carpets, wallpaper and a faint antiseptic odor. At least it was cool inside. A few framed motivational posters hung on the wall in languages I didn't know, some of them in alphabets I didn't recognize either. There were half a dozen other people in the waiting room, apparently here to learn how to speak English.
I spotted a staircase that led up, though it was closed off by a gate and a sign: *Future Facilities. No Admittance.* There was another door that led to a basement with a yin-yang logo painted on it: *Strictly Forbidden. No Visitors Beyond This Present.* I wasn't sure that was phrased quite right.
Inspector Fynn walked directly up to a glass enclosed reception area. "Excuse me, Miss…" He smiled politely. "Is Mr Ming available to speak with?"
"Is he a friend of yours?"
"I know Sonny very well."
"Sorry, he's with another client at the moment. Can I take a message?"
"You might mention our names: Patrick Jardel and Tractus Fynn."
"I'll see to it he knows you're here."
"And Mrs Ming? Is she present today?"
"Hardly ever— too busy at the restaurant." The receptionist paused

with a smile. "Have you been yet? Everything on the menu is absolutely delicious."

***

Soft music played, emanating from the low ceiling, though none of the melodies were at all familiar. It was also a bit disconcerting to see the corridor filled with phantoms, the ghosts flittering just beyond the corner of my eye. I tried not to look, but it got me thinking this place wasn't quite what it seemed. I was pretty sure Fynn saw them too, but he said nothing to me.

I tried to recall my previous conversation with Sonny Ming, what he had told me about his school during Fynn's party:

"I like to take an immersive approach to language," he had said. "I can guarantee fluency in ten sessions."

"Any language?"

"Any language from the past."

"How long are the sessions?"

"This is a very good question, Patrick..."

I guessed it was a slow-time place. Inside the school, a session might last a month, but outside, only an hour would pass. A slow-time, fast-time kind of thing, like at the Library along the Palisades. The pace of time might creep along in the classroom but outside, barely a few seconds would go by. I supposed you could cram in a lot of learning in a very short amount of time. And I started to wonder how long these sessions were.

Fynn and I sat for nearly an hour. He busied himself in a magazine and I leafed through the brochure:

Enter the exciting world of linguistic immersion. The perfect place to learn a new language. Results guaranteed or your money back. Our proprietary method combines Immersive Hypnosis and Cross-Cultural Cognition...

There was a good photo of Sonny Ming on the back cover, though I didn't recognize him at first. I had never seen him smiling before. Behind him stood a friendly staff, all in lab coats. I read through the many testimonials. They seemed boastful and exaggerated:

Just like a dream... like a dream come true. I was fluent in Italian in less than a week. Grazie, Sonny

I was impressed by the courteous staff... And now, even proper Parisians compliment me on my accent. Merci, Mr Ming

I was so completely immersed in the lessons. I didn't even notice when class was over...

A miracle! I took a class in the morning and by that afternoon I was almost fluent in Portuguese

I was just about to delve into an article entitled, Language Blues: How to cope with creeping despair in three easy steps, when a woman came over to hand me a clipboard and a pen. "Hello, Mr Jardel, I'm Siobhan. I'll be your facilitator today."

She was attractive despite very short hair and a clinical uniform. I looked at the clipboard. It was a questionnaire, a lengthy one.

"If you'll just fill this out for me... and bring it to the desk when you're done." She smiled and sauntered back to the glass enclosed reception room. I started in immediately:

What language do you wish to learn?
Russian.

Speak, read, and / or write? Check as many as apply.
Speak was enough, I thought.

Fluency expectations: conversational, literary, legal.
I checked one.

Have you ever visited any of the following countries?
The list was long. I checked as many boxes as I could remember.

If you answered yes to question three, please fill in the exact dates.
That seemed problematic and it might take a while. I decided to

skip this question for now.

Have you ever been exposed to the following diseases or infections: leprosy, bubonic plague, anthrax, diphtheria, cholera, malaria,, influenza, gangrene, hepatitis A, B or C...

I didn't remember contracting any of these, though it seemed an odd question. I turned to Fynn. "Why all the medical questions?"

"Mr Ming is very thorough."

Please check all and any allergies that apply...

I happened to glance up from the questionnaire and saw a man on a gurney. One of the staff pushed him through a corridor and into an unseen room. I saw his face clearly enough.

"What is it, Patrick? It looks as though you've seen a ghost."

"No, not a ghost... that guy they just rolled by."

"What of him?"

"I'm pretty sure it was Geppetto."

"The author of the manuscripts?"

"Yes."

"Impossible," Fynn scoffed. "Or unlikely to say the least."

"Did you see him?"

"No, I only caught a glimpse of the man."

"I think it was him— but how, and why?"

"I'm sure you're mistaken. Geppetto is at the *Hotel de Cirque* working with Mr Voynich... and far from the reach of Kali, I should add."

"Kali?"

"No doubt she'd like to talk with him, or at worst, dispose of him."

"Probably both." I paused for a second. "Why was he on a gurney? This is a school, not a hospital."

Fynn shrugged. "Perhaps he's not feeling well."

"None of this involves a medical procedure— right?"

"Learning a new language? Not that I know of."

"Have you ever been here before?"

"No, this is my first visit."

I went back to the questionnaire:
Where do you plan to travel in the near future?
I turned to Fynn again. "What's the name of the town we'll be visiting?"

"Zvorkovo in the Soviet Union," he replied absentmindedly.

"Can you spell it?"

"In English or Cyrillic?"

"I'll leave that one blank for now."

When I went back to the questionnaire, to my astonishment, it was just that: blank. All my replies were gone. I flipped through the pages to double check, then walked up to reception.

"Finished already?" Siobhan asked with a smile.

"Umm— there's something wrong with the pen. I think the ink disappeared."

She laughed. "Oh, that's an extra measure of security we have here. No one can look over your shoulder and read what you've written." Siobhan cast a suspicious glance towards Fynn. "I'll get you a new form so you can start again."

It was by far the longest and most complicated questionnaire I'd ever attempted, more difficult than they dole out at any doctor's office. Not all my replies were one hundred percent accurate, and I had left a few blanks here and there. Because of the disappearing ink, I had no idea which. I returned the clipboard to reception and Siobhan scanned it with a black light. I was asked to be seated again.

She sauntered over about ten minutes later. "Ready, Mr Jardel?"

I turned to Fynn. "You'll wait for me?"

"Of course, it shouldn't take long." He smiled. "I see a great many more magazines to peruse."

"Okay then, I'll be right back…" I turned to the attendant.

She smiled too. "This way please, Patrick."

There was some question about payment, my health insurance definitely did not cover this, nor did I have Fynn's magic debit card. It seemed rather steep at nine thousand dollars. I had a plan B though.

"So, Mr Seven's will be paying for the lessons?"

I nodded.

"If you'll just sign this waiver…"

The print was too small to read. "What does all this say?"

"The usual thing... We're not to be held responsible for side-effects, death or injury, emotional trauma, or cognitive collapse..." Her smile faded however as she looked at the screen. "Hmm, this credit card has been declined..." She tapped a few keys and her smile returned. "Oh, there you go, your session has been prepaid after all."

"By who?"

"Doesn't say... Well, aren't you the brave soul," Siobhan said, glancing up from the screen.

"What?"

"You're only scheduled for one session."

"What does that mean?"

"Most of our clients sign up for ten."

"How long are the sessions?"

"They never take more than an hour."

"So... how exactly does all this work?" I asked as Siobhan led me down a sterile corridor.

"A trade secret," she said and ushered me into a private room. "I'll need you to put all your possessions into that plastic container, please."

"My possessions?"

"Cell phone, wallet, whatever's in your pockets." She gave me a practiced smile. "Everything will be returned at the end of the session."

I deposited all she mentioned, some loose coins, a set of keys, Edmund's pocket compass and Pavel's bubble of time, which hopefully looked like a marble.

"And if you'll just change into that," Siobhan nodded over to a teal robe hanging on the wall. "I'll be back in a few minutes." My facilitator smiled and closed the door.

I was forced to wear a medical gown and felt instantly diminished. My humanity, my identity stripped away in a moment, not to mention the feeling of overwhelming vulnerability. A few minutes later a different attendant appeared, rolling an odd looking gurney into the tiny room. It was not unlike a catapult. She asked me to lay down. This was getting strange and I was beginning to grow uncomfortable. A small feeling of panic set in when she started fastening straps around my torso. She also attached a yellow plastic wristband. I looked down; it displayed my name, and "RUSSIAN," stamped in capital letters.

"Siobhan will be back in a few," the attendant said cheerfully and left me in the darkened room.

A few what? I started to wonder, when it seemed that hours had already passed. I also had to reconsider how this might work— learning a new language. I now had the odd notion that it would be like some kind of brain infusion, a download maybe, or learning while you sleep. Or even speeding time up, so I might learn more quickly. I also had a vague fear that all this might involve electrodes to the brain or hypodermic syringes. I consoled myself with the thought that Fynn was still in the waiting room engrossed in a magazine.

The door opened and Siobhan entered with a smile. "Sorry to keep you waiting, I got held up." She rolled me down another corridor and into a medical bay. I was carefully parked, the wheels locked in place and the back of the gurney rose up like a dental chair. On either side was a sort of apparatus, though no drills, happily. She shone a light in my eyes, examined my teeth and ears, then took my blood pressure.

"How long is this going to take?" I asked.

"Not long," she replied, though noncommittally. "Maybe we could go out for coffee when you get back?" Siobhan gave me a flirty smile.

"When will that be?"

"Soon. You seem like a fast learner."

"Why the straps?"

She laughed. "You'll see..."

I voiced my vague fear that all this might involve electrodes to the brain.

"Don't be silly." Siobhan hung a curiously shaped bell around my neck. "Here, read this, please. Your instructions for the instructor."

"What?"

"I know, it sounds awkward." She handed me a small pamphlet. "It's a step-by-step guide to your first meeting."

I read to myself: *One: greet your instructor with a smile but say nothing. Two: present payment promptly. Three: give the instructor your bell.*

"This bell?" I asked.

"Yes. You'll return when your instructor rings it. That tells us you've completed the course."

"Return from where?"

Siobhan smiled but said nothing further and then put a canvas bag on my lap. Inside was a slim Russian to English phrase book, a heavy roll of coins, socks, underwear, and sundries. She adjusted the straps, making them tighter it seemed. Two railings rose from under the chair, a kind of metal harness with padded bumpers.

I held up the coins. "Payment?"

She nodded.

"Who is this instructor?"

"You'll meet him soon enough." She flipped through the pages on her clipboard… "Comrade Grigori Bulgakov."

"What happens when the lesson is over?"

"Well, a quick vocabulary test at the end of the session and you'll be discharged."

"Discharged? You make it seem like a hospital…"

She laughed. "Not at all. We give you a diploma."

"And it never takes longer than an hour— right?"

"Yes, that's right. But the most important thing is: You must not lose the bell."

"Why?"

"It's your way of getting back."

"Getting back to where?"

"Here."

"Am I going somewhere?"

Siobhan smiled again. "Simply ring it and you will be promptly returned."

"How promptly?"

"Two or three weeks. Only Mr Ming can hear its specific frequency."

"Seriously?"

"No." She laughed again. "You'll be returned in a matter of moments. He has an automatic monitoring device."

"Where will I return to?"

"Here, well, downstairs, I should say…" She glanced at my chart. "In your case… room seven." Siobhan held up what looked to be an odd syringe.

"What's that? I don't like needles."

"Not a needle, more like a hypo-spray."
"What's in it?"
"Inoculations and a pain blocker."
"What?"
"You can thank me later." She then put a pair of boots on my feet. They were a snug fit.

"What are these?"

"Boots, Russian boots…" Siobhan replied and locked a mechanism at the bottom of the chair. "If you're not back in fifty years, we'll come looking for you."

"What?"

"Just kidding…"

It finally dawned on me that I was about to travel. By then it was too late, my chair was already moving along some sort of track. I automatically glided down a narrow corridor towards a set of double doors. All my previous ideas about how this might work vanished. It was not a school. It was an amusement park and I was trapped on some death-defying ride.

The doors swung open with a thud and the chair moved along its rails towards a dark room. The mechanism stopped for a moment just in front of an animatronic version of Sonny Ming. Not a very good version, he looked more like a robotic fortune teller at a two-bit carnival. He spoke though: "So glad you have come here to learn…" there was a pause and the voice changed slightly "…Russian… Good luck and see you soon."

My chair swung sharply to the left and quickly glided into a large circular arena. It continued along the track to the center of the room. I was the only one on this ride. I could make out a circle of doors, each numbered— thirty-six of them, I counted. Soon enough though, I was not sure if the doors were rotating, that is to say the whole room, or just my chair.

As I came closer, I realized they were not doors at all, but just painted facades and never to be opened. It was then when the track took a sudden dip. It seemed more like a roller coaster than anything. The chair began to rise up along some hook. I could hear gears clicking and rose to a dizzying height. It stopped abruptly, then tipped by ninety degrees. I was now perpendicular to the floor. The straps released and I was held up only by the metal bumpers. A door opened below me and I stared into a black void. I heard something un-click automatically, and plunged face first into the darkness.

PART III

chapter nine
sputnik too

It was a hard jump but less painful than most. When I arrived, it was clear that I had landed in the middle of a small muddy pond. Wading ashore, boots and all, some children were pointing at me, laughing. I was half covered in silt and still wearing a teal hospital gown. I dragged myself from the water and immediately started to shiver. The children were shouting, "Grigori, Grigori…" a name but clearly not mine. I looked around to notice a few dirt roads, some wooden buildings and a lot of sloping tin roofs. It seemed to be a small village of some kind. There wasn't much more to see, the ground was flat and trees blocked my view of everything else. I could tell one thing, it was autumn; the leaves were changing color.

From up the road, a burly man appeared, now followed by the clamorous children. He walked towards me with outstretched arms and a huge smile, only one tooth seemed to be missing. He grabbed me by both shoulders and gave a double kiss, one on each cheek. "Dobro pozhalovat," he said.

It was unintelligible to me. I was about to reply when he put his finger to his lips. I was about to persist when he put his hand over my mouth. The man held up a knife and then grabbed my arm. He deftly cut the plastic band from my wrist and held it up with a smile. Then he gave a furtive look up the road and hurriedly led me to a ramshackle house. Apparently it was his. I was ushered inside to the dark paneled rooms, built from wide planks sealed with mortar, almost like a log cabin. There were wispy lace curtains on all the windows, though hardly a door in the whole place.

I wondered if this was the past, the present or the future. I looked around the tiny cottage for signs of technology. There wasn't much to see: some kind of coal-fired cooker in the kitchen, a hand pump and a basin, and a single electric light that hung from the ceiling— a shadeless bare bulb. I didn't see a telephone, a clock, or a television, so my question of *when* was not exactly answered. I was leaning towards the past, or some dystopian future. Even the most far flung place in my present would have a cell phone or a TV screen.

A moment later, the man held a newspaper to my face. My first word in Russian: *sputnik*. That's what he kept repeating, tapping on the giant headline. The alphabet was completely unfamiliar to me. My second word in Russian was ПРАВДА. I could almost make out the date: Октября 7, 1957. I turned to my new host and asked, "Grigori?"

His smile returned and he threw me a blanket. "*Da, Grigori.*" He pointed at me. "*I chto?*"

I could tell it was a question. "Patrick," I replied and tapped my own chest.

"Padrik," he repeated with a nod and a rolling "R." He then pointed to himself. "Инструктор, Инструктор," the man kept saying. I had no idea what that meant, though I could almost recognize it. I repeated till it made sense… "*Instruktor.*" Oh, I knew that word in English and felt somewhat relieved.

Grigori had a new word for me: "*zvonok.*" He reached for the bell that hung around my neck. I was about to ring it, but he stopped me with his hand over mine. "*Nyet, nyet, ne zvonite poka. Vy dolzhny otdat' yego mne,*" he said and motioned for me to take it off.

The words were gibberish but I understood what he wanted and complied.

He smiled then handed me a frayed towel and a bundle of rags. "*Vysushites' i sadites' kushat' so mnoy.*"

I had no idea what that meant but dried myself off and changed into the old but dry clothes: a heavy sweater and work pants. I sat next to the man named Grigori at a large kitchen table made of rough hewn wood. He ripped a loaf of bread in half and put it on a plate, all the while nodding and smiling.

"Sonny Ming?" I asked.

Grigori looked back uncomprehendingly.

I pointed to the floor. "Sonny Ming— here?" I asked in an unnecessarily loud voice.

The man smiled and stomped his boots on the planks. "*пол, da,*" he said.

I sounded the word out: *pol.* Apparently that meant floor. It became increasingly clear that Grigori spoke not a word of English. He handed me my bag. I had dropped it in the pond and the contents were soaked and somewhat muddied. I found the few essentials that Siobhan had eluded to: a toothbrush, underwear and two pairs of socks; they were protected by plastic. I gave Grigori my roll of coins which he took graciously.

There was also a Russian phrasebook, though a thin one. I turned the wet pages carefully. It was a rudimentary dictionary, half in English, half in Cyrillic, with the words spelled out phonetically. It seemed to be just for emergencies: food, water, housing; and, I eventually found: where is the bathroom?

"*Gde tualet?*" I asked.

Grigori listened but wasn't sure what I'd said. I repeated it several times.

"Ah," he answered, his eyebrows raised, and then corrected my pronunciation. His finger pointed to the back door off the kitchen. "*Sortir,*" he said.

Not much later I learned that meant "outhouse."

***

It took a while to figure out how this was supposed to work, but it finally came to me: I was deposited here to learn Russian. Grigori would ring the bell when he thought I had. Then I'd be returned to Sonny Ming's School of Language Arts. I'd probably return only a few minutes after I'd left with my memory intact and with new language skills. No wonder Fynn didn't mind waiting. I laughed, a bit giddy about how clever this was… then it dawned on me: How long exactly would it take to learn Russian?

After the first week with Grigori and family, I had no further need of my phrasebook, useless as it was. I could cope with most emergencies. It was a surprising way to learn Russian but effective. My very survival depended on being a good student. In the beginning, I got the general sense of words: *Uzhin* for example. It might've meant *eat* or *sit down at the table,* or *stew,* or *soup*— I wasn't sure yet.

The house was small for five people. Dark panelling, a large kitchen with a hearth. A sitting room with a wood stove, a foyer-like mud room and a single bedroom. Upstairs were two sleeping lofts with separate ladders leading up to opposite eaves. And there was a basement, the cold room, where everything needed for survival was stored. Hot water came from kettles on the hearth, cold water from two sinks with a hand pump, one for washing, one for cooking.

This was my new foster home: Grigori Afanasyevich Bulgakov, the patriarch, his wife Margarita, and my new surrogate sisters, Marta and Valentina. The last three all wore giant napkins on their heads, and Grigori had a baggy cap that he liked to dust off by hitting it against his knee every once and a while. "*Klyanus' prizrakom Stalina,*" he would also shout. A phrase I learned quickly considering how often I heard it, though it would be another year before I knew it to mean, "I swear by Stalin's ghost."

Grigori himself was a big man of about forty or so, and a bricklayer by profession. He looked far older than his years, having spent a good part of his life outdoors. He often boasted he could raise a wall ten meters long in less than a day, though he never said how high that wall might be. For a month, Grigori would repeatedly ask, "*Ponimayu?*"

My reply was invariably, "*Nyet.*" I did not understand…

I was to become a bricklayer's apprentice, and that involved a lot of standing around, rolling wheel barrows full of concrete, mixing mortar and digging trenches. I was expected to earn my keep, although I eventually discovered that Sonny Ming had paid him a hundred rubles a month to keep me as a boarder.

And later I learned, Grigori would disappear for weeks at a time, only to joke he had been *collectivized,* sent off on some huge construction project, mostly a state secret, if anyone bothered to ask.

***

This was the village of Zvorkovo, about a hundred kilometers due east of Moscow, a farming town. Some pigs, cows and sheep, and chickens everywhere. It seemed a lot like Ohio, but maybe Ohio at the turn of the last century. It was flat like the midwest, there were endless fallow fields and a few patches of forest left intact. I couldn't tell what crops might be growing yet, not until the spring.

Zvorkovo was off the beaten track, far from the main highway that went well south of the village. There was however a small paved road on the edge of town. It led west to Moscow and had a bus stop. The other roads in town were dirt, hard packed, except when it rained and they turned to mud. The village had four cars, two of them taxis, one was probably KGB, and the other, a Party official's. Another thing I noticed: Women seemed to outnumber men about two to one.

"Nearly a whole generation is *pogibshiy*," Grigori explained very patiently.

"*Pogibshiy?*"

"The war, Padrik. The Americans lost many thousands, but we lost millions of souls."

Zvorkovo was a place where nothing ever happened, not really. There was no TV, no news from the outside world except for a few radio broadcasts and the daily newspaper from Moscow. Events were passing us by, it was almost palpable. It was a place where you knew life was going on elsewhere: the world was turning, progressing, changing, but not here; things only happened someplace else. This was my new life among the peasant farmers. They wanted the same as anyone else in the world. A quiet life, a safe place for their kids, and a little bit of fun now and then.

***

Eventually I got pretty good at pantomime. More often than not I would act out a task and learn the Russian word for it. Simple things like: sleep, walk, wash... Grigori and family would do the same. He repeated his words very slowly and deliberately, annunciating each syllable. It was painful to hear and probably painful to speak.

One of my first vocabulary words was *Porucheniye*, "work" or maybe "errand." Early one evening, Grigori took me up to the main part of the village. Along the way he stopped to talk with everyone we met. He seemed eager to introduce me. To my ears it was all still incoherent, though I occasionally heard my name, "Padrik."

Grigori soon decided I needed additional ones. He dubbed me *Padrik Stephanovich Kuznetsov*, the last name I later learned meant Smith. More commonly, I was just *comrade*— another word I recognized. He often joked that I looked exactly like his uncle's sister's third son. He also seemed to have an inexhaustible supply of cousins, all who had unpronounceable names.

Some of my new neighbors seemed horrified by my very presence, others were more friendly, and a few gave me a double kiss on the cheek and a wide smile. We even ran across Deputy Boris Ivanovich Popov— no one ever called him Boris, except behind his back. I could barely see his eyes in that slab of a face, and when he did look at me, the feeling was one of impending malice. In actuality, he could be quite expressive and friendly, especially after a *troika*. I was loath to get too close, he smelled like cat's breath mixed with vodka.

"*Uchastkovyi militsioner*," Grigori told me. I later learned that meant local police. "Pals around with Comrade Malinov." I also found out Deputy Boris rides a bicycle around town, and lives above the police station, a house with a jail cell in the basement, mostly used as a drunk tank.

Grigori and I came to the central square, a cobble-paved park with a few shrubs and benches. Across the way was some kind of shop. It had large windows in front and a few tables and chairs on the sidewalk.

"*Ya by i sam poshel, no ya uzhe dostig moyu dnevnuyu kvotu*," Grigori said, though I had no idea what he was talking about. He pointed to the store. "*Magazin*," he repeated over and over until I echoed the word. Then he thrust three coins in my hand.

"*Rubles?*" I asked.

"*Da. Troika.*" He held up three fingers, "*Troika*," he repeated slowly. It probably meant three.

"*Vodka,*" he said and pantomimed drinking from a bottle.
I understood that.
"*Butylka.*" He held up one finger and then motioned to the store again. My mission was clear enough.

The village market, or what passed for a mall, was really like a series of shops all connected along one side of the town square. Over time, I learned it was operated by a single family. They had the only refrigerator in the village. There was a general store with a few items: dry goods, soap, clothes, medicines. There was another section that was a grocery store with canned goods mainly. The shelves were usually bare, and the few pitiful items that were there might sit for weeks at a time: dusty boxes and tins filled with unidentifiable products. The butcher shop was almost always empty, certainly devoid of meat, except on Tuesdays when there was a line for sausages.

The shop doubled as a community center; maybe what could be construed as a cafe or restaurant. It had a few rickety tables and chairs where people would often sit for the day drinking tea, or eat something from the bakery next door. Today it was just a half liter bottle of vodka for Grigori. Mission accomplished.

I didn't learn till later that pretty much everything in the village cost a *troika*, three rubles, goods and services. Fix a fence? A *troika*… Mend a sweater, a bicycle, a broken window or a leaky faucet— a *troika*… A taxi ride to the next town over? Bus fare to Moscow? It was no coincidence that a *troika* would buy you a half-liter bottle of government vodka.

When we started back to Grigori's house, I noticed a derelict church at the far side of the square. It looked abandoned, though I saw a flicker of light coming from the tall narrow windows. It also had a couple of onion domes. At the other side of the square was a large house. It seemed oddly out of place, having stone walls and two stories with a slate roof. There was an iron gate surrounding it and a well-maintained garden. I asked Grigori about it as we passed.

"*Kto tam?*" I asked but struggled to find the right words.
"*Vasili.*"
"*Kto?*"
"*Comrade Vasili Alexandrovich Arkhipov, bol'shoi chelovek v voenno-morskom flote.*"

I was baffled by the reply but heard the word *navy*, and I recognized the name: *Vasili Arkhipov*, the man who saved the world, or would... Not a coincidence, I reckoned. It was suddenly clearer why I was in this particular location. I remembered most things, not as much as I hoped, but over the coming weeks, everything came back to me, including the fear that the world would end in a few short years.

***

I lived my first month in Zvorkovo in a state of utter frustration. The simplest tasks required a huge amount of linguistic effort. Odd to say, but the inside of my brain felt fizzy, there was almost a discernible popping noise coming from inside. To me, Russian seemed to be a language with too many syllables. I spent much of the time at the kitchen table with Grigori's family. They all took turns, teaching me to read from grade school primer books: *See Ivan run,* or *Videt Ivan beg*. There was no Russian Doctor Seuss, probably no American one either, not yet at least. Complex things were difficult to understand and express. I yearned for the day when I could take on more challenging topics.

By the time Laika the dog circled the earth on November 3, 1957, my Russian was on par with a three year old's, not that I could read or write, but I understood a lot of what was said, so long as you said it slowly and clearly. An nostalgic thought crossed my mind while looking at the newspaper. I recalled Brigadier Thomas at Fynn's party and his cynical comments about Laika, the sepulcher dog... It was a small comfort. I could picture Thomas in full uniform, living in the stone cottage along the Palisades Cliffs, half a world away. Still no Sonny Ming, no Fynn, nor anyone else I knew. I almost expected Öde Temsik to appear, and kept a careful vigilance.

***

"My lovely wife Margarita works at the school where she teaches Soviet history," Grigori told me at dinner one evening, and for the first time I understood what he was saying. We all broke out into smiles. "My daughter, Marta, is sadly a widow at such a tender age. Her husband was killed in an industrial accident," he continued. "Though happily, she is expecting her first child in the spring."

I bowed, saying, "Congratulations."

Grigori added, "And Valentina, my baby girl, has just graduated from agricultural college. She works at the horticultural center."

I wasn't sure about all the words but nodded anyway. Valentina gave me a special smile. She had a pretty face under her wire rim glasses. I looked shyly into my goulash.

***

The cold was coming, my first winter here. "We need to get you dressed for the weather, Padrik," Marta told me one morning and handed me a bundle of rags, among them I found many scarves. I almost fit into her late husband's clothes. He was a bit shorter than me. The trousers hung around my ankles and I didn't like the idea of wearing a dead man's attire.

In December, Grigori announced that I was ready to contribute to the collective, the greater community of Zvorkovo. I protested that I was still a stranger and that people might be suspicious. Grigori laughed it off as nonsense. "I've told everybody you're my long lost cousin visiting from Estonia. And who has not believed me, eh?"

There was to be no argument, I was to be set to work.

"I spoke to Deputy Popov and frankly he's delighted," Grigori went on.

"Why is that?"

"It used to be his job."

"What is this job?"

"I have even acquired permission from our party leader, Comrade Nichego, the Bureau Secretary."

"Who's that?" I asked.

"Best you stay clear of the Party Boss... If you're lucky she won't even know you're in town."

"Where is she?"

"Hardly ever here, so don't you worry. She leaves everything to her second-in-charge— now, there's a piece of work. Best you stay clear of him too." Grigori laughed. "Lucky for us, he's drunk more than half the time."

"What's his name?"

"People's Commissar Malinov."

"Commissar?"

"It's an honorific title. Mr Big, he would call himself. The man's a bloody Cossack." Grigori smiled. "Old Russian proverb: He'd be better off if his mother had a barren womb."

My new job: I was up before the roosters. Every morning at dawn I would hike down to the main road about a kilometer from town. A truck would leave a bundle of newspapers by the bus stop. I was tasked with bringing it up to the market. There weren't enough copies for everyone, though it hardly mattered. Many couldn't read and most were willing to share.

One of the first things I experienced were the dogs of Zvorkovo. I wasn't entirely sure if they were strays or pets, but every morning I'd encounter a pack of them on the road. Some were friendlier than others, and this was not something Grigori had warned me about. Apparently they held an elevated status in town ever since the exploits of their canine comrade, Laika.

I learned to carry an old bone with me or whatever other inedible scraps of meat I could scavenge. I would toss it to those who followed. By the spring I had a pack of new friends and they were linguistically undemanding of my attention, speaking only in single syllables. There were probably just as many stray cats around town as well, but they were more furtive and largely unseen.

One dark morning I was coming back from the market with a half-liter bottle of vodka and a plucked chicken. People's Commissar Malinov pulled up alongside in his Volga sedan, the only one in town. Beside him in the passenger seat was Deputy Boris. I was startled to say the least. The driver was Mortimer— some iteration of him— he had a glass eye that stared off in a slightly different direction. *Coincidence number two.*

It was soon apparent this version of Mortimer had absolutely no recollection of me. I looked carefully but could see no black mark on any of his fingertips.

"Ah, so you've taken to the bottle?" Comrade Mortimer asked, and he seemed slightly sodden himself.

"No, it's for a friend..."

"So you won't be opening it here?"

"Here on the path?"

"So we might all have a swallow." He laughed and then whispered something to the deputy. "You're one of Grigori's many cousins, eh? So, how do you like our little village?"

"It's quiet, peaceful."

"And why are you here exactly?"

"I'm an apprentice to Grigori."

"Learning a trade, eh? Oh yes, bricklaying, if memory serves. A valuable skill to be sure." Malinov gave me a thin smile and it sent shivers up my spine. "I'll take the bottle, and you may leave the chicken for my friend here."

"What?"

"Buying vodka before eleven in the morning is strictly forbidden."

"And poultry might be deemed illicit goods— you wouldn't want to be arrested, would you?" the deputy put in and laughed.

"Please give our kind regards to Grigori and his family," Mortimer added before he drove off in a cloud of exhaust fumes.

***

I had learned never to ask what was for dinner. It was almost always soup or stew, cold or hot. It wouldn't be chicken tonight. We ate a lot of potatoes and cabbage, venison on occasion, and sausages were a real treat once a week or so. Fruit and milk were in short supply, butter as well— none of these things were sold at the one shop in town, sold by the government. Cheese was pretty much non-existent except for a kind of tasteless curd called *zernyony tvorog*, or "grainy quark." There was also a pink substance that Marta would sometimes buy, though cheese was too strong a word. It was called *Korall*, a processed, shrimp flavored substance. I grew quite fond of it.

Bartering was the necessary skill to obtain such things from the shop, and both Marta and Margarita were exceptional at it. There might be nothing on the shelves, but there might be something to be had from the back room, if one asked correctly and was willing to pay.

That night I came home to find Grigori and his wife arguing, and to my surprise I could almost understand their conversation. There was one word I didn't know: *veterinar*, but I could guess what it might mean.

"Ah, the man's a horse doctor. Not fit to examine a human being," Grigori said with disgust.

"But it's important for the baby, important to Marta."

"At the clinic?" Grigori asked. "He's only there once every month or so."

"Once a month is better than nothing."

"No, we will go to the *doula*, the midwife to us all."

"She's too old, and too old fashioned," Margarita protested.

***

The first winter was brutal. I didn't adjust well. Snow would fall and there was never any thought as to plowing it or shoveling the walkways. It sat where it lay until spring. I spent a lot of time indoors reading, huddled in blankets by the wood stove, usually with a candle since the electricity was spotty at best. Valentina had found an old dictionary for me. It was missing a few pages here and there, but my vocabulary was increasing one word at a time.

There was no holiday season as far as I could tell, though New Year's was recognized with a small celebration. A few people gathered at the church, candles were lit, and the bells were rung. Grigori gave me a handful of coins. "What's this for?" I asked.

"Fifty kopeks. Spend it wisely."

"How much is it worth?"

"Not very much at all," Grigori replied with a grin. "It's for the children," he said, and glanced over to a gaggle of kids who had gathered at the curb. "Take them to the shop and buy them some sweets, eh?"

As winter continued, my new job took a turn for the worse. Finding the bundle of papers at the side of the road was now a challenge. It was hard to tell if they'd been delivered or not, or if they lay buried under a foot of snow. I usually dragged the frozen bundle to the store, where Dimitri the shopkeeper would let me in and give me a hot cup of tea. There also seemed to be fewer dogs in the neighborhood.

Shivering or *drozha ot kholoda* was my new vocabulary word. I don't think I felt warm once the whole season. Well, at least once, when Valentina came to my bunk dressed in little more than a huge bear fur. She was up against me in a moment, skin to skin, warm, smooth and delicate.

***

It wasn't until spring that I realized how beautiful Valentina was, especially when she chose not to wear the giant napkin on her head. She had short blond hair just to the top of her shoulders, pale blue eyes and a shy smile. The season brought another surprise. No crops were planted; instead an explosion of flowers filled the fields.

"Oh yes, we grow flowers exclusively. Sold in Moscow," she explained.

By the summer, Mikhail was born. He had the sweetest expression on his tiny face, a look of curiosity and wry wisdom about the world. Life changed in the Bulgakov house. Marta moved into the sitting room to sleep nearer the cradle. We all took turns helping.

I hardly remember the rest of that year, 1958. Events in the world passed by the village of Zvorkovo. Only a few things filtered in from the outside: There was one of many Berlin crises, Alaska was made into a state, and Khrushchev was elevated to Premier. He was now the First Comrade of the Central Committee or the Presidium, or something.

"Ah, little Nikita, he only wants what's best for us all," Grigori announced with enthusiasm.

"Our very own little dancing bear— we're quite proud of him…" Margarita added.

I did learn that one hundred and fifty centimeters was not very tall. "What does he mean when he says, *We will bury you?*" I asked.

Grigori laughed at that. "Oh yes, it makes those Americans very upset." He dusted off his cap. "Old Russian proverb. It means we will outlast you long enough to attend your funeral."

***

One morning, Valentina was chatting away and used a word wholly unfamiliar to me. I asked if she might pantomime its meaning. She turned bright red and giggled. "Here, you mean to say, in the middle of this field?"

That evening I asked Grigori what *lyublyu* meant. "Not a word you've run across yet, eh?" he replied but would not say more. He found a bit of charcoal from the fireplace and drew a large heart on the kitchen table. I didn't take it literally but came to think of the word as "love." And later I learned, it was one of many used.

I had grown fond of Valentina, almost to say, I fell in *lyublyu*. But she had different ideas. She didn't want to marry or have children... She was a thoroughly modern Soviet woman, and her career meant everything. Sex was just sex. Next year she planned further college, advanced studies into the genetics of plants. Gregor Mendel was like a god to her, though a Czech. And even Watson and Crick was required reading, despite her insistence that it was the Russians who discovered how DNA operated.

"Can you imagine, Padrik, all the colors of the tulip imparted to a humble daisy... the world will never be the same."

I had enough trouble with flower names in English, in Russian I was completely lost. All the while, I felt she cared for me, always ready with a smile or a laugh if I was feeling low. And I supported her fully, her ambitions and studies. Her father seemed to have little inkling about our liaisons. When Grigori was away, she'd sneak up the ladder to my sleeping loft and stay till dawn, until I was up and out of the house, on my way to pick up the newspapers.

***

By now I was able to ask more questions about Vasili Arkhipov. I eventually came to learn he grew up here. "Not that we'll be building a statue of him or anything," Grigori remarked with typical cynicism. "But yes, the whole village knows Vasili, a local boy who has done well for himself. He's famous, a real hero to us all."

"Is he here?"

"No."

"Where then?"
"Murmansk, far to the north. Better him than me."
"Why?"
"It's cold there."
"I meant Comrade Arkhipov."
"Oh... He's probably out at sea somewhere in a submarine."
"And his..." I struggled to find the right word... "*devushka?*"
"You mean his young daughter?"
"No, Olga... his wife."
"Ah, she has a fine house at the center of town. You've seen it for yourself."
"I remember."
"A family home, I think. Goes back a ways... something the state forgot to seize and collectivize, Stalin and his goons." Grigori paused. "But she's hardly ever there either."
"Why not?"
"Olga runs a stable at the edge of town. She keeps the horses... gives pony rides to the children every summer, sleigh rides when it's cold... A nice lady."
"How many horses?"
"Six, or maybe five now— we had to cook one a few winters ago."
"Does Comrade Vasili ever visit town?"
"Of course he does." Grigori laughed. "He has his own car, a two-cylinder Moskvitch... though they stay in the city most of the time."
"But you've met him?"
"Sure... we got drunk together lots of times."
"Really?"
"Him and Vadim."
"Vadim?"
"Vasili's brother. They grew up here— ha, I could barely tell them apart as youngsters, fighting all the time..."
"Where is he now?"
"I don't know. Also a big man in the navy... Has a wife and young daughter. They have a flat in Moscow."
"He visits too?"
"Of course... they still like to argue, the brothers."

"About what?"

"Ships. I've heard Vadim say many times: 'I'd prefer if we had a proper navy, but that Khrushchev, all he wants to do is build submarines…'"

"I'd like to meet him someday."

"Who? Little Nikita?" Grigori laughed but took my meaning. "Sure, I'll introduce you next time he comes to town."

***

It was impossible to believe that the years were passing. I could count them. And except for two coincidences, there seemed little reason to be here. My thoughts turned to leaving. I felt abandoned, stranded, and I felt angry about it sometimes, but it was a useless feeling. At worst, I'd learn enough Russian so that I could bone up on my astronomy and jump back to my present… I'd ask Grigori to buy me a compass. Some nights I thought I'd just jump at random, just to escape… it didn't matter to where… I'd find a way back home… eventually. In the end I thought better of the idea.

No Fynn, no Arbiter, no word from Sonny Ming, or even a face in the crowd that could be Öde Temsik. I'd even welcome Mr Quandary's company by now. Kali was no where to be seen, and this particular Comrade Mortimer hardly seemed a threat, unless state subsidized vodka was suddenly banned. I could count only one small accomplishment: my Russian was improving. I was nearly fluent despite Grigori's criticism of my accent. "Sounds like you grew up in Estonia," he'd complain.

So far, I had visited Moscow only once. The bus came every other day and took about four hours. Valentina and I rode together and stayed overnight in a hostel. She was attending a horticultural seminar the next morning. The city was impressive in some ways, not in others. The Kremlin topped the list, but everywhere in the outskirts, huge apartment blocks were going up… towering concrete boxes with little windows.

I had also picked up a handy new skill: bricklaying, and I guessed that the Moscow suburbs was where Grigori disappeared to during his long absences. There were a lot of bricks to be dealt with. When we returned a day later, Grigori introduced me to Vasili Arkhipov, totally by chance. I was only able to stammer a few words when we met him in the market buying a newspaper. He shook my hand. I was in awe. The man who saved the world, or would. He was a short guy in this thirties, stern-faced, but with kindness in his eyes, a friendly smile, and a splendid uniform.

***

Resigned to my fate, I had settled into a simple life, a life without luxury or even appliances. I heard over and over about the Americans, almost with a sense of envy. Some dared to whisper, "god has gone over to their side because we've outlawed him here." People saw Americans as privileged— a bitter irony, according to Grigori, "Our motherland bled so much for the victory while they suffered but a pin prick. Many millions to mere thousands of men. I lost two of my brothers to the war, in Stalingrad." I felt relieved that Grigori had never asked where I was from.

It all came to a head during the *Kitchen Debates*. That summer in 1959, the American Vice President appeared in Moscow.

"Ah, blast this Nixon, he's like a traveling salesman showing off his grand appliances. Toasters, refrigerators, vacuum machines. We have no need of such things."

"Marta and Margarita might," I replied.

"The Americans are arrogant braggarts, know-it-alls down to the last, and they no nothing of sacrifice."

"What about the English?"

"Oh, that's a different story. For a nation of shopkeepers they seem to be quite brave, and fierce fighters." He turned to me. "Lucky for you, I happen to know you're a Canadian."

***

That autumn, Nikita himself was traveling to the United States for a goodwill tour. Over dinner, Grigori complained, "I for one would never board such an airplane."

"What plane?"

"Comrade Khrushchev's *TU-One-Fourteen*."

"Why not?"

"My cousin was there when they built it— he told me everything."

"And?"

"It's not safe. It's liable to shake apart into little bits. Twelve hours flying in the air?" Grigori scoffed. "It's a death sentence, surely."

"What are you saying?"

"He'll never make it across the Atlantic."

The Premier's visit was widely covered in *Pravda*, though the news was one or two days old. Grigori grew concerned one morning. "Padrik, you know something about America, eh? Will Comrade Khrushchev be imprisoned at Camp David?"

"What? No… it's a presidential retreat."

"Oh, so it's a great honor to be invited?"

"Yes…"

"And Disneyland? Why will they not let him go to this place? Are there missile bases there?"

"Not that I know of."

"Why is it forbidden then? He only wants to visit with his children."

I tried to explain that it was as crowded as Red Square on May Day, but in the end, the best I could do was make Grigori understand it was where Mickey Mouse lived, and he didn't like strangers. Khrushchev himself didn't help matters when he told the press: *We can make missiles like sausages…*

"A boast that may come back to haunt him," Grigori told me. "It makes the Americans nervous to hear such a thing." He loved this particular quote from his fearless leader, and often joked, "In reality, we are not very good at making sausages either…"

chapter ten
new decade

I remember the year 1960 for three reasons: I read the name John Fitzgerald Kennedy for the first time in Cyrillic: Джон Фитцджеральд Кеннеди. The town got its first television set, and our May Day celebration was interrupted by the man who fell to earth. Some first speculated it was a Soviet cosmonaut who fell from the sky, though with a large parachute. It was not. It was Francis Gary Powers, an American spy, pilot of a U-2 that was shot down by Soviet Air Defense. We didn't hear about it until weeks later, but we saw it on May First. That day, we all came out of our wooden houses to watch the contrails of jets streak by at altitude and leave a frightening din. He had landed in the village of Sverdlovsk.

"Well east of here, on the other side of the Urals," Grigori explained.

***

"Big meeting, you must come along, Padrik."
"Why?"
"Television is coming."
"Really?"
"All Soviet Union has television, of course, but not all Soviet Union has a television set, and we must decide where to put it."
"Where do you think it should go?"
"Well, our sitting room is too small. And I don't relish the idea of having so many visitors… It will have to be put to a vote."

The entire town gathered that Saturday evening, filling Party Headquarters to capacity, crowded into chairs and lined up against the back wall. At the front of the room I saw Commissar Malinov, aka Mortimer, seated on a raised platform. Deputy Boris paced back and forth to keep the rabble at bay. A hush came to the place when a small woman made her way to the podium. I recognized her at once: Kali Shunya, though here in Zvorkovo, she was known as the Party Boss, Comrade Bureau Secretary Nichego.

Coincidence number three.

She was dressed smartly, her hair severely tied back, most of it collected under a somber gray cap, and all held together by an ornate hatpin.

I kept my head down, happy to be leaning against the back wall. She saw me though, and I'm not sure if there was a flicker of recognition on her face. A curious sensation crossed through me. In one instant I saw her standing at the podium, but in another, it felt like she was standing right next to me, gazing into my eyes and stroking my face with a delicate hand. I looked straight ahead, ignoring her the best I could, pretending she wasn't there at all. Luckily she lost interest, and certainly, no one else in the room noticed any of this. When I looked up again she was back at the podium. Not that I could say she had actually moved. If she had, I alone had realized this. The harrowing incident left me unsettled.

Arguments began about where to put the village's new television, and they were long and fierce. Some said party headquarters, others preferred the village shop. I realized my new language skills were not as good as I hoped. Mumbled Russian was still difficult to understand. Even when shouted, I only caught half the words, words spoken quickly and with passion— quite different from Grigori's patient pronunciations.

In the end it was decided the television would be installed at the "cafe," and a few weeks later in October we were treated to a show. TASS broadcast footage of Premier Khrushchev at the United Nations. He took off his shoe and started banging it on the table.

"Is this something Russians usually do?" I asked.

"What?"

"Bang their shoes on the table."

"It's something Khrushchev does."

"But this guy too…" I pointed to the screen.

"Oh yes, Comrade Gromyko. He does the same only because Nikita does it as well."

***

Nineteen sixty-one came and went. JFK took power in January

yet we heard little about it. By spring, Yuri Gagarin became the first human to journey into outer space, and he was no taller than Khrushchev. Crammed into a Vostok capsule, he completed an orbit of Earth on April 12, though the news of his success came to us a few days delayed. It then filled the pages of *Pravda* for weeks. Also around this time, we heard about the Bay of Pigs invasion. A secondary story, though apparently it was a great victory for socialism. Events were simmering.

As for Vasili Arkhipov, he was gone the entire spring and most of the summer. "Oh well, you've just missed him, he's traveled north again," Grigori explained. When Comrade Arkhipov returned in August, he was visibly shaken, and some said gravely ill, spending all his time in the bedroom at the house on the square. His wife Olga was pale with worry.

"Something has happened this time," Grigori observed.

"What do you mean?"

"He's a broken man. Perhaps there was a terrible accident at sea, a mutiny even, or maybe he lost some of the sailors under his command. Who is to say? Those submarines," Grigori said grimly, "they are widow-makers, eh?"

That same summer, there was a strange occurrence: "Why have they all sprouted beards?" I asked Grigori as we walked to the bus stop. He had been tasked to build a new one, orders from the Party Secretary. It was late August and along the way we passed fields filled with sunflowers and droves of men lounging about.

He laughed. "Yes, why indeed? And why do they sit half-naked in the sun all day?"

"Well?" I persisted.

"They want to be *barbudos*."

"What's that?"

"The bearded ones."

"Why?"

"Ah, they're all off to Cuba next month, as technical advisors."

"Doing what?"

"It depends who you ask. Some say they are rocket experts. Others say they are agricultural agents."

"What do you say?"

Grigori dusted off his cap and laughed. "Don't worry, comrade, you won't be joining them. It seems they have no need for bricklayers."

***

A certain despair filled me when 1962 rolled around, and by autumn I felt completely abandoned; not having an inkling of what to do next. I couldn't just leave, not with the end of the world coming. I owed something to Grigori, his family, and especially Valentina. And yet, all these years later, I could still imagine Fynn sitting in the waiting room perusing a stack of magazines.

I had watched little Mikhail grow from infant to toddler in what seemed like no time at all. He was nearly five now and would sit on my lap to read from the very same books I had used to learn Russian. Grigori and Margarita would tease me that I was a bad influence, teaching him my terrible accent.

It was impossible to believe so much time had passed. The fifth anniversary of my arrival was less than a month away. And as absurd as it seemed, I would soon be returned to my former present. Fynn would be waiting for me. This was just a phantom life, like the one I had with Elsie Everest in 1933— that had lasted almost a decade. I had lived it surely, and the best I could, as I had done here. One of Fynn's rules of travel came clearly to mind: *stay as long as you can.* In the end, I understood it was for the sake of sanity. It's a wonder Fynn hadn't gone mad after all this time.

I was also acutely aware that things were coming to a head. Events were aligning. *Pravda* reminded me daily: The "Caribbean Crisis" had begun, but I alone knew it would lead to World War Three. It was late September when Grigori first uttered a word in English. Early one morning, he came up to me outside the barn where I was chopping wood and said, "You Canadians… haven't you ever used an axe before?"

I was surprised to say the least. "You speak English."

"Of course I do…"

"But—"

"I was instructed not to speak in your mother's tongue."

"Instructed by whom?"

"Mr Ming, of course..." Grigori smiled.

"He told you I was Canadian?"

"Yes, but don't worry, your secret is safe with me. I'd be the last person to say a foreigner is living under my roof."

"But how did you learn English?"

"Long story," Grigori said with a grin. "During the war. I worked as translator." He took me by the shoulder and led me back to the house with happy news. He had acquired a tin of coffee for a *troika*. "Cuban coffee," he explained with a certain pride. I took it upon myself to prepare it for us both. Grigori even mustered fresh cream and a bit of sugar, pinched from Margarita's precious baking supplies. I took my first sip in years and it was absolute heaven.

Grigori was less impressed. "Why anyone would want to drink hot coffee on such a warm morning is beyond my understanding." Nonetheless, he seemed to enjoy every sip. He looked up from his cup with a smile and spoke in English: "Ah, Padrik, I have found you a new job..."

"Where?"

"At the de-Stalinization plant."

"What?" I wasn't sure I heard right.

Grigori laughed a bit too loudly. "The place that takes salt from the water."

I thought about what he'd said for a moment, then I laughed too. It was a joke that would only make sense in my language.

He did have a new job however. This one entailed digging a new basement. "Old Russian proverb: You can only dig a cellar when the ground has thawed."

"Is that really an old proverb?"

"No, but it does describe what I do very well. I've built many a cellar in this town. And this time I need your help."

"Before the ground freezes again?"

It was grueling work, digging out a basement by hand. We had shovels of course, and a wheel barrow, and picks for unearthing the large rocks that we found every few feet. Most of the time we labored with scarves over our mouths. It was hot, dusty work. It started as a hole, then a crawl space, and after a few days, we could nearly stand. After a week, the space was about ten yards square. "Now for the wall," Grigori announced and began mixing mortar. "You can start bringing the bricks closer, if you would."

Maybe I was distracted, but somehow I managed to drop a load of bricks on my foot. At least one of them slammed onto my second toe. I wasn't wearing work boots, but flimsy sandals, and felt sure it was broken. I sat on the ground for a while. Grigori came rushing over to look. There was blood everywhere.

"That's a nasty gash, Padrik. We should get you to the doctor."

"The doctor?"

"At the clinic, Doctor Zadarsky. He's only there once a month, so you're lucky to be injured today."

I guess that passed for Russian optimism.

"Every Soviet citizen has the right to free medical care."

"I'm not a citizen exactly."

"Ah yes, then you'll have to pay through the nose. It will cost you a *troika*, no doubt."

"Zadarsky?" I wondered aloud; it seemed familiar to me. "What's his first name?"

Grigori shrugged. "Hmm… Doctor, I think." He laughed and the next thing I knew I was sitting in the wheelbarrow, rolling through the streets of Zvorkovo, and into an empty medical clinic.

An orderly and a nurse seemed to appear out of nowhere and I was ushered into the office, placed on a metal bed, and told to wait. My back was to the door that soon opened. A man walked in, presumably the doctor, and he asked, "What seems to be the problem?"

I couldn't see his face at first but the voice was known to me. I gasped slightly at the sight of him. He was short and wiry with a head too large for his body; his features, prominent and exaggerated. He looked down at me with a smile. I was astonished to see such a familiar face staring back. *Coincidence number four.*

It took me a moment to find words: "Doctor Zed, of all the people to meet," I said maybe too loudly, and in English.

He shushed me and looked about the empty room.

"How did you get here?" I continued in Russian.

"I emigrated."

"But you should be about sixty years older than you look."

"I'll take that as a compliment." He smiled and his large eyebrows rose to a pinnacle. "I was summoned, and told to come here."

"By the Arbiter?" I guessed.

"Yes."

"And Fynn— have you seen him?" I felt some excitement at the idea.

"Not a trace," he replied, but also read my expression. "Don't despair, Patrick. He'll be here soon enough."

"When?"

"Who can say? Perhaps he got lost along the way?"

I had no reply.

"I, myself, got lost… I spent many months wandering the streets of Žarkovo looking for you."

"Where?"

"It's a similar sounding village outside of Belgrade, along the Seva River— but you weren't there."

"No, I'm here."

"As I can now see, Patrick."

"You're saying that's where Fynn is?"

"I doubt it." Doctor Zed's eyebrows fell nearly across his eyes. "I'm sure he'll turn up soon."

"When did you first meet Fynn?"

"Ah, you were there, you should know."

"Aboard the *Carpathia*?"

"The very place."

"But you never mentioned anything… about traveling, I mean."

"An unlikely topic for conversation— don't you think?" Doctor Zed smiled. "You didn't mention anything either."

"Right… Wait— you did say something about the Venetians who stole all your trees…"

"Ah, so you were paying attention." He laughed. "Now let's see about these toes of yours, eh?"

"Should I get them X-rayed?"

"I would advise against it, here, and at this time."

"Why?"

"How much trust do you put in Soviet machinery?"

"Primitive?"

He nodded, then gave my foot a thorough if not painful

examination. "Go shoeless for a few days and walk gingerly. You'll be fine in a week."

"Should I use a cane?"

Doctor Zed's eyebrows arched severely. "Definitely not. Use the foot as close to normal as you can. And wiggle your toes often, no matter how much it hurts."

"What about the pain?"

"I may have some Soviet aspirin laying about."

"Soviet aspirin? Is it different than regular aspirin?"

"Harder to swallow."

I felt myself smiling and started laughing as well. "I am glad to see you."

"Consider me your very own sputnik."

"What?"

"Your fellow traveler, your companion, one might say in English. I doubt you'll be doing much *libra lapsus* with that foot."

***

It was a sunny afternoon in the last days of September when I had a sit-down with Grigori at the kitchen table. Supper had been cleared away. Valentina, Margarita, Marta and little Mikhail had all gone out for a stroll.

"Your Russian is quite good now, even though your accent is atrocious," Grigori began, and rather formally. "And you've made strides with reading and writing. You are finished here, Padrik. You may leave now, if you wish. Go back to Mr Ming."

"How does that work?"

"What?"

"Do I have to jump or anything?"

Grigori gave me a stare. "Not that I know of. The instructions say to ring the bell for a prolonged period, ten to fifteen seconds. Place the bell around the graduate's neck and he will be returned."

"Returned how?"

"I don't know. You're my first student."

"And how did I arrive?"

"You were dumped right in the middle of the pond." Grigori

laughed.

"And nothing strikes you as odd about that?"

"What do you mean?"

"That I just appeared out of nowhere."

"I assumed you took the bus from Moscow."

"And Mr Sonny Ming. There's nothing unusual about him?"

"Aside from being a Maoist, you mean? Well, no, we have a business arrangement, that's all."

"But you've met him?"

"Indeed. I am told to ring the bell, and put it around your neck. Someone will come to fetch you, bring you home." Grigori paused to reach into his pocket. "I almost forgot… Here, you're supposed to take one of these tablets…" He handed me a pill.

"Before I go?"

"That's what I was told."

"When will I be returned?"

"He did not say exactly."

"Don't ring it."

"Why?"

"I'm not sure I want to leave yet."

Grigori sat back with a grin on his face. "Ah, because you have fallen in love with my beautiful Valentina?"

"That's part of it…" I admitted. "I also have to stay because, well, something terrible is going to happen and I have to fix it."

"Something terrible will always happen, it's called living."

"That's not what I mean. I'm afraid the world will end. You'll all die, Margarita, Marta, Mikhail, Valentina."

"What?" Grigori scoffed with a laugh but then stared hard at me. "What are you saying, Padrik?"

"The end of the world, a war."

"Hmm, how would you know? A war… Should I be calling the KGB?"

"You wouldn't do that."

"And why not?"

"You love your family too much. It would only cause them grief."

"Yes…" he considered.

"I'm from a far away place and I know about what will happen in the future."

"Far away, yes. But how do Canadians know such things?"

"We just do."

"When will this happen?"

"Before October ends."

"So then, are you a spy? What great secrets might you uncover? The success of our flowers perhaps... Now that's a secret worth telling the West, eh?" Grigori laughed and dusted off his cap. "What's to be done then? You, Padrik, here to fix the world? That's quite boastful, even for you. I'll tell you what, first thing tomorrow—"

We were interrupted by a persistent sound. It started as a slow winding noise, building in speed and volume until it was a full blown siren, like an air raid.

Grigori's jaw dropped. An expression of shock and disbelief rose on his face. "The alarm!" he shouted. "I haven't heard that since the war." He was on his feet in a flash. "Quickly, Padrik, come along..."

"To where?"

"The center of town."

"You go, I'll catch up," I replied, not able to muster a good pace.

I arrived about fifteen minutes later; it took that long to hobble there. Already a crowd had gathered outside Vasili Arkhipov's house on the square. Apparently there had been a small fire in the downstairs kitchen. It was quickly extinguished by the volunteer fire-brigade.

"Mostly smoke, something left too long on the stove," Grigori explained when he came over to me. "But the fire is the good news."

"What's the bad news?"

Grigori nodded over at the house. I could see a body wrapped in a blanket being loaded onto a cart.

"Who is it?"

"It was Vasili Arkhipov. He's been killed."

"Are you sure?"

"He is still in his uniform."

"Who killed him?"

"I'm not one to say... but Deputy Boris has arrested his wife, Olga. Soviet justice is swift and sure."

Shock and panic filled me. The man who saved the world was dead.

This was it. Kali had won. Everything would end in a matter of weeks.

"What's the matter, comrade, you look as if you've just eaten a cat."

"Where are they taking the body?"

"To the butcher shop."

"Why?"

"Hmm… I suppose the doctor will have to take a look inside of him."

***

Grigori was not happy when someone started banging at the door later that night, much later. "It's well after midnight I would guess, Comrade Doctor. Why are you here?"

"So sorry to wake you, Grigori Bulgakov. I've come to see Padrik… my patient."

"Are you suddenly worried about his foot?"

"It may become infected. I won't be but a moment."

I had already heard the ruckus and hobbled down from my loft. Grigori went back to sleep. Doctor Zed took me outside. It was chilly and drizzling so we sat on the small porch.

"I am growing concerned, Patrick. Terrible events and no sign of Inspector Fynn or the others."

"You're sure he's coming?"

"Yes, we all knew something dreadful was about to happen— Mr Q lectured us at great length."

"When was this?"

"More a matter of *where*… The Arbiter summoned us all to the *Hotel de Cirque*."

"Who else was there?"

"Edmund, Pavel, Lothar… and the lovely Miss Chloe."

"What about Vasili?"

"He was not there."

"No, I mean, did you examine the body?" I looked down at his bloody apron.

"Oh yes… I performed a cursory autopsy— not a pretty sight— not something anyone should see…"

"And?"

"I have not determined the exact cause of death, though I believe he has been murdered."

"How?"

"I don't know yet. I had the remains moved to the clinic for a more thorough examination." The doctor paused. "Who do you think killed him?"

"It had to be Kali, Comrade Nichego."

"But she's in Moscow with Commissar Malinov. I might consider that an alibi."

"Maybe to the rest of the world… but given her abilities, she could pop back anytime and do the deed."

"I've only heard about her prowess… but I don't really believe any of it."

"Well, you should. She can be scary."

"How so?"

"Remember all the victims on the *Carpathia*?"

There was a long silence. Doctor Zed finally spoke again, "It seems to be up to us then— to set things right."

"I'm not sure what to do."

"Somehow, I would guess, we have to jump back and stop this woman Kali before the murder takes place."

"It might be too late."

"Why?"

"She might know we're here."

"And that makes a difference?"

"Yes."

"Well, it's probably not her first murder," Doctor Zed considered further. "I've run across three dead bodies since I've been here."

"How long is that?"

"Three years— ah, that's a body a year."

"Who were they?"

"Damned if I know."

"Why?"

"No one seemed terribly interested. None of them were from the village it seems."

"Are you sure? Did you talk to Deputy Boris?"

"Of course, and he warned me to mind my own business. I've been told no one is missing, but all of the victims were impossible to identify. Half-eaten by animals; cats or dogs, I would guess."

"People's pets?"

"Perhaps pets no longer."

"Are you still a veterinarian?"

"Of course."

"Maybe you can help me with something."

"I already have."

"What?"

"Your foot. I've given you a bandage, aspirin, and good advice."

"Thanks." I smiled. "My question is about dogs."

"In the village?"

"Yes."

"Ah, so you've noticed as well."

"Noticed what?"

"That they are disappearing one by one, the old dogs at least, there are always new puppies to be had."

"Why do you think that's happening?"

"It was the beginning of the summer… I noticed several dogs had died; strays, I suppose, rather than pets… Though being a veterinarian, it piqued my interest. I observed each of the dogs had blood coming from their ear… and thought it strange."

"Some kind of experiment?"

"I gave them only the most cursory examination, but I would say they all had something jabbed into their ears."

"That's horrible."

"I agree."

"What kind of thing?"

"Long and sharp, like a skewer or a needle."

"A hypodermic needle?"

"Ah, you may be onto something… but it would be a very long needle, one that might be used for knitting." Doctor Zed held out his fingers and measured off a distance of nearly a foot.

"How could someone do that?"

"You mean to say morally?"

"Yes, of course, but physically… You can't just sneak up on a dog and shove something into its ear."

"I agree, most baffling."

I paused to consider for a moment. "What about the bodies you found? Were they killed in the same way?"

"Hmm... sorry to say, I did not examine the bodies."

"What about Vasili?"

"Yes. Now that you mention this, it is something worth checking."

chapter eleven
olga

There was rain again the next morning. I lugged a wet bundle of newspapers up to the market and was probably an hour later than usual. It seemed like half the town was already awake, inside the cafe and sipping tea. Everyone was chattering about the events of yesterday. Grigori called me over to a rickety table. He was about to comment when we saw a Zil limousine prowling up the muddy streets to stop out front.

Two high-ranking party officials emerged. I recognized them immediately and with great relief: Comrade Fynn and Mortimer, the latter looked just as I had seen him at the amusement park: a mustache and an eyepatch. He also had his jackal cane. Both men wore trench coats, and large fedoras pulled down against the downpour. Mortimer took his jacket off and handed his cane to Fynn, then deftly clambered up the wet telephone pole to snip the wire, the only wire that led to the village of Zvorkovo.

"Uh-oh," Grigori muttered.

"What? You've seen this before?"

"Sure. KGB does it all the time. We might be in for it now."

"Not to worry, I know these two men."

"Friends of yours?"

"Comrades at least." I hobbled outside to Fynn and Mortimer the best I could and gave them a cursory greeting. We found shelter under an awning.

"Why did you cut the telephone wire?" I asked.

"We have heard Mrs Olga Arkhipov was arrested. News of this must not reach Vasili," Fynn whispered.

"Vasili? You're too late, he's dead, murdered."

"What? Are you certain?"

I nodded.

"Then all is lost," Fynn replied with a grim sigh.

"What now?"

"I suppose we must travel back a few days to before the murder," Fynn said, but paused. "So… Kali is here already."

"Yes, she's the Party Boss, Comrade Nichego."

"Has she seen you?"

"She has, but I don't think she recognizes me."

"Are you certain?"

"No… Well… hard to say…" I hesitated. "There's a Comrade Mortimer here as well, called Malinov. He's the People's Commissar."

"Ah, my other self," Mortimer said. "I can hardly wait to meet him."

"I'd keep a low profile for now."

"Why?"

"People around here might get suspicious. Except for the eyepatch and the beard, you two look pretty similar."

"Where are they at present?" Fynn asked.

"Oh, Moscow maybe? There's a party conference."

"And when are they due back?"

"This afternoon, I think."

"We have only heard that there has been a murder and Olga has been arrested," Fynn explained. "What other news can you give us?"

"She's the prime suspect, but I don't know much else…" I pointed to the house on the square, one of the windows still blackened by smoke.

"We will visit the crime scene directly," Fynn said, "and then we must speak to Olga."

"You should probably talk to Doctor Zed, too."

"Yes, I heard he would be here. Where is he?"

"With the body, I think, at the medical clinic."

"No, I am not. I am standing directly here," the doctor spoke up from under his umbrella. None of us had noticed him until that moment. "Before you go traipsing back to the recent past in order to change things, I suggest you examine the body," he announced.

"What good will that do us, eh?" Mortimer glared at him.

"There is a discrepancy."

"What?"

"The medical records state that Vasili is one hundred and seventy-five centimeters. The body is not. It is one hundred and eighty centimeters. Surely, he hasn't grown in that time."

"Are you so trusting of Soviet records?" Mortimer asked.

"No, but it is a discrepancy nonetheless."

"Who has identified the victim?"

"Everyone says it's Vasili. Who else could it be?" I answered.

"Doctor?" Fynn turned to him.

"I can only say the laundry marks on his uniform say *B. A. Архипов*. Curiously though, I did not find his hat."

"His hat?"

"The cap that goes with his uniform."

"No identity papers were recovered? A photograph? Fingerprints?" Fynn asked the doctor.

"We might contact the navy for such things."

"Hmm, I'm loath to get the military involved..." Fynn's voiced trailed off, then he asked, "What does his wife say?"

"She has said nothing at all as far as I know."

"Well then, where is she?"

"Deputy Boris has her in the basement of the police station."

***

We walked up to the house on the square. There was no crime scene tape, nor was the front door locked. "Not exactly what I would call a *dacha*," Mortimer commented.

"What do you mean?"

"It looks to be rather a splendid home."

Fynn stopped by the front gate and immediately drew our attention to a bicycle parked against the iron railing.

"What's up with that?" I asked.

"You may observe there are the tire marks of four bicycles all parked together— yes?"

I nodded, but was unsure of the significance.

"All the bicycles are gone except one. It seems curious to me."

"Why?"

"It is recently splattered with mud."

"Where do the tracks lead?" Doctor Zed asked.

"The stables, maybe…" I said.

"What stables?" Fynn turned to me.

"Vasili's wife Olga runs the stables up that way."

Mortimer waited on the stoop. "I'll keep watch," he said sullenly and took the doctor's umbrella.

"Remain inconspicuous if you can. Your doppelgänger may be out and about."

"It is exactly him I am watching for."

The rest of us trudged up the steps. It was an old house probably built at the turn of the century. Downstairs was a sitting room, a formal dining room and two kitchens, one more like a pantry.

"I was called in shortly after the body was discovered," Doctor Zed spoke as we entered.

"And who discovered it?"

"The victim's wife… said she was sleeping upstairs and smelled smoke… Came down to find a body in the parlor."

"What did she do then?"

"Called for the police… Deputy Boris."

"There is a telephone?"

"Yes." Doctor Zed nodded over to the foyer.

"Did anyone take photographs?"

"Not that I know."

"Signs of a struggle?" Fynn asked while scanning the sitting room.

"None."

"Was there anyone else in the house?"

"No, only Olga was present."

"And the door— locked?"

"The fire brigade had no trouble getting in."

"How did you find things then?"

"Vasili was there, half on the sofa, half on the floor." The doctor pointed. "Someone had pulled his trousers up— give him a bit of dignity, I suppose."

"And the manner of death?"

"Yes, well, that's the curious part… The dogs are telling us something," Doctor Zed went on.

"What dogs?" Fynn asked.

"It was Patrick's idea."

"What idea is that?" Fynn glanced at me.

"Kind of a long story…"

"And…?" Fynn turned back to the doctor.

"I examined the remains again to find his eardrum has been pierced."

"This caused his death?"

"Indirectly… Something long and sharp entered into his brain. It should not have necessarily caused death though. I must run a few more tests…." The doctor made a face. "The clinic is woefully ill-equipped for such a task."

"How about the horticultural center?" I offered.

"What's that, Patrick?"

"Oh, where Valentina works… There's a lab filled with test tubes, equipment, and all kinds of chemicals."

"Ah, it seems worth a try. I could—"

Fynn interrupted, "What sort of murder weapon might we be searching for?"

"As I said, something long and very sharp. A skewer perhaps, like for a shish-kebab."

"What about a knitting needle?" Fynn asked and stooped near a basket of yarn. The doctor came along beside him for a closer look.

"Yes, there's a bit of blood on this one…" Doctor Zed carefully put it into a handkerchief. "I will run some tests."

"When was the time of death?" Fynn asked.

"The night before, I would say, or the very early hours of the morning."

"What?" Fynn turned to him.

"Yes… We must presume Mrs Olga Arkhipov waited a long time before she called the police."

"Anything else?"

"Vasili was bitten on the left hand, just below the thumb— the meaty part here…" Doctor Zed demonstrated on his own.

"A defensive wound?"

"More like an offensive one. I would guess Vasili had his arms around someone's neck and was bitten for it. Some one fending him off."

"An unwanted advance?"

"Or an unwanted attack…"

Fynn moved over to the fireplace and sifted through the ashes with an iron poker.

"What's in there?" I asked.

"Burned letters. Correspondence between a husband and wife."

"Vasili and Olga?"

"Yes… though they are mostly unreadable now… and if I had to guess, they were burned not last night, but weeks ago."

Upstairs, Fynn examined the bedrooms. There were three; one large and the others small. One for guests and the other a bit like a nursery. The master bedroom seemed undisturbed, the bed neatly made. The guest room had an extra cot, and the nursery as well.

"I might say someone was expecting visitors," Fynn commented.

"Why?"

"All the beds are out and neatly made."

Downstairs, Fynn took a quick look at the kitchen. It really wasn't much of a fire at all, more like a cooking accident. He was unimpressed. "It looks rather more deliberate to me," Fynn muttered.

***

Outside the house, we came across a Moskvitch-402 still parked at the curb.

"Who's car is this?" Fynn asked.

"Comrade Arkhipov's."

At Fynn's urging, Mortimer and Doctor Zed walked off to the clinic. "Go along with the good Doctor, please. It's best if you make yourself scarce for now."

We decided to investigate the vehicle and found some documents inside. "It's a navy car… and look who it's signed out to: *B. A.*

Архипов."

"The signature is an unreadable scrawl," Fynn countered.

"Well that's a B for *Basili* and that's an A for *Arkhipov*."

"Let me take a closer look…" He pored through the papers. "If I'm reading this correctly, these documents are out of Odessa."

"Where's that?"

"Far to the south."

"Vasili is stationed in the north, Murmansk, the Kona peninsula—I remember Grigori told me."

"Grigori?" Fynn asked.

"Grigori Afanasyevich Bulgakov, my language instructor…" I stopped to think for a moment. "Vasili had a brother, Vadim… also in the navy."

"This is interesting to us, eh?" Fynn gave me a smile. "Tell me, is Vadim married?"

"Yes, a wife and a daughter, I was told. They have an apartment in Moscow."

"Might they visit the countryside, do you think?" Fynn stuffed all the documents he could find into his pockets then rummaged around the backseat. There were some blankets and a stack of books. I spotted several paper wrappers.

"Somebody has a sweet tooth," I said.

"Why is that, Patrick?"

"The wrappers, I recognize them: sweets from the market."

We continued on towards the police station, a few streets down from the square. "Aren't you supposed to be waiting for me, reading a magazine?" I asked.

"Am I?" Fynn laughed. "I'm sure I will be when the time comes." He slapped me on the back as we walked. "I do apologize for the delay… our arrival. The logistics were more complicated than anticipated."

"You knew this whole time."

"What?"

"That Vasili grew up here, all about the murder… Comrade Mortimer and Kali being here…"

"Of course I knew. The Arbiter told me all about it."

"You could've said something, warned me…"

"What good would that do in the end, eh? Do you regret the

experience?"

"No… but still…"

"I apologize, Patrick. I could think of no other way to get you here and learn Russian at the same time."

"But you were in the waiting room, reading magazines."

"Yes. And if all goes well, that's where we will find ourselves again."

I followed in silence for a time. "It's hard to stay mad for five years— even though I tried."

Fynn laughed and clasped my shoulder. "I'm rather proud of you, Patrick… It seems you've risen above the devastating cycle of fear and inertia that dominates many people's lives."

"Thanks, I guess…" We walked on a few steps. "How did you get here?" I asked. "Where is your cane?"

"I left it at the hotel."

"The *Hotel de Cirque*?"

"Yes, I've just come from there. By the way, Miss Boole sends her regards…"

"Chloe?"

"Yes, I suspect she's quite fond of you, Patrick." He stopped to rummage through his satchel. "Ah, I brought you a few things…" Fynn gave me a newspaper, the *London Times*, though dated several months ago. Funny, the alphabet looked strange to me. I hadn't read anything in English for years. A sad headline pronounced the death of Marilyn Monroe— it was very far from this reality. There was a jar of instant coffee, and a book. I flipped through the pages. It was mostly in the language of mathematical formulas: *Wave Mechanics Without Probability*, by Hugh Everett.

"It's recently published," Fynn said over my shoulder.

"What's it about?"

"The multiverse as described by mathematics."

"Maybe it's something Lothar would like?"

"I'm sure you're correct. Perhaps you can lend it to him."

"Is he with you?"

"No."

***

Deputy Boris Popov was not dozing in his chair when we entered the police station, though it was not always easy to tell if his eyes were open or closed.

"Ah, the big man from the Moscow Oblast. Here to take over my case, eh?" He greeted Fynn with outright hostility. "Wife kills husband in small village and they send a detective..." he continued with a tone of disgust. "And who is this with you? Padrik, Grigori's cousin... Why is he here?"

"He's a potential witness. I've asked him to come along."

Boris eyed me suspiciously. "Who was the other man with you this morning? And where's he gone now?" the deputy continued with his questions.

"What man?" Fynn replied.

"In the big car, when you pulled into town."

"There was no one with me."

"But I saw him, the driver—"

"He has no name. I can only say that while this is a civil matter, the KGB is interested nonetheless."

Deputy Boris was silenced and reluctantly led us to the musty basement that housed a single large cell.

"I will speak to the accused alone," Fynn said.

"Pretty as they come, but she's said nothing to me— like a stone wall, that one... What makes you think she'll confess to you?"

Fynn glared at the deputy until he finally trudged upstairs. Olga sat alone on one of the cots straight as a board, and was a bit wary as we entered.

"Mrs Olga Arkhipov, I am Detective Plavnik from the Moscow Oblast. Have you been well treated?"

"What a question, and why should you care?" she responded coldly.

"I care because an innocent woman should not be jailed for a crime she did not commit."

"And what makes you say this? Deputy Popov is fully convinced of my guilt."

"Well, I am not." Fynn tried to raise a smile.

"And why is he here?" Olga gave a sharp glance in my direction.

"He knows your husband. And he has been my eyes and ears in this town."

"You knew something bad was going to happen then? Are you KGB, GRU, or some party official?"

"But I am none of these things. I am a policeman only. I want to know the truth of the matter."

"An honest policeman, eh?"

"Surely, I'm not the only honest policeman you've run across in your life?" Fynn sat beside her.

"Maybe not…" She gave a small sigh.

"Tell me then, your version of events from yesterday."

"I've said everything to Deputy Popov."

"Indulge me, please."

"I was asleep… I smelled smoke, and I came downstairs to find Vasili in the parlor…"

"Vasili, you say?"

"Shouldn't I know my own husband?"

"Indeed you should, but the dead man is not your husband."

"Why do you say such a thing?"

"He is too tall," Fynn replied. "And we found these identity papers in the car parked outside your house."

Olga glanced at the documents then cast her eyes to the ground and shifted uncomfortably. She seemed inclined to say nothing more. Fynn broke the uneasy silence, "I'm less concerned for you than your daughter."

"She has nothing to do with this," Olga shot back.

"Where is your daughter at present?"

"Safe from you."

"I don't believe you've killed anyone."

"Why not?"

"You have no motive. Though, there is certainly something you're not sharing with us."

"How can you tell?"

"I've had many years of experience, that's all. I would prefer that things went well for you."

Olga gave Fynn a searching glance but said nothing more. He broke the silence again, "Answer my questions honestly and to the best of your ability, and I'll let you go home with your daughter."

"Home? No, I will not go back to that house."

"Where then?"

"The stables, on the outskirts of town."

"Very well... I'll make arrangements."

"When?"

"It may take an hour or so..."

"And what of Deputy Popov?"

"He is under my authority. He must do what I say."

Olga sat with her hesitation. She finally looked up at us and in a choked voice, said, "You are correct. It is not Vasili. It is Vadim who was killed."

"Are you certain?"

She simply nodded.

"Vadim. Your husband's brother?" I asked.

"Yes. How many times must I tell you?"

"So where is your husband then?"

"It's a state secret."

"Why have you not mentioned this to Deputy Popov?"

"And why should I say a word to him? He's drunk all the time and he'll forget what I say by the next morning."

Fynn sat quietly for a moment. "Mrs Arkhipov, though I have many more questions, I shall not burden you further. I beg a bit of patience though. I'll see to it that you're released before the end of the day." With that, Olga finally managed a small if not grateful smile.

Upstairs in the office, Fynn confronted the deputy again: "Prepare the prisoner for transport."

"What?"

"She is to be taken elsewhere. I'll send my driver along."

"Where are you taking her?"

"It's best you don't know," Fynn said with absolute authority.

"I suppose you'll want to visit the crime scene," the deputy said and attempted to smile.

"I have done so already."

"Then you'll need fingerprints as well. I've called Moscow, they'll send a specialist. Should be a day or two."

"I doubt that will be necessary," Fynn replied.

"What?" Deputy Boris was incredulous. "You're the first policeman in all of history who doesn't want fingerprints."

"What good would it do? Whose fingerprints do you expect to find? Only Comrade Vasili's, Olga and their daughter's."

"You have a point, but it's the necessary protocol."

"I leave such matters in your capable hands then," Fynn replied and whisked me out the door. He had a broad smile on his face, unseen by the deputy, and stopped me in my tracks. "Well, Patrick, there is little more to be done. Happily, Kali has made a great blunder by killing the wrong brother, and the world will continue on as it should."

"More or less," I observed. "There's just one problem. Olga, that is, Mrs Arkhipov, is still the prime suspect… If Vasili finds out…"

"Ah, but we've cut the telephone wires," Fynn replied. "Records indicate his submarine will leave its base on the first of October. We need only sequester Vasili from the news until he sails from port."

"That's it? No investigation?"

"I see no need for one. It's obvious that Kali is our murderer."

"Still…" I muttered. "We should figure out what happened."

"As you say, Patrick. It is perhaps that I am blinded by relief."

"Why did Olga lie about her husband?"

"I'm not certain, though there is more to her story."

"What?"

"I would guess she is protecting someone."

"Her daughter?"

"Yes, and someone else… Well, I must keep an open mind and see where the evidence takes us."

"Why no fingerprints?" I asked.

"I think it's best if we find no trace of Vadim in the house, eh?"

"What about Kali's prints? They might be there too."

"This might work against us. We shall see."

***

We found Doctor Zed and Mortimer at the clinic, both enjoying tea, and bread with jam. They were relieved by the happy news, but Mortimer was most curious about his doppelgänger. "When do you say he'll return?"

"This afternoon, or this evening at the latest."

"I'm anxious to speak with him."

"What good will that do?" I asked.

"He can tell me things he will not say to any other."

"Do you trust him?"

"No. Why do you ask?" He turned to Fynn.

"We must keep this news from Kali, that the wrong man has been killed… at least until the matter is thoroughly investigated."

Mortimer complained, "There's no reason to solve this case, Tractus, to save Olga from her fate. Clearly, she is guilty according to the evidence."

"But we must come to the truth of the matter," Doctor Zed stammered.

"Why must we?" Mortimer looked over.

"Clearly, it's a fragrant violation of the law."

"Do you mean to say flagrant?"

"Odorous."

"Odious?"

"Both."

***

The black Zil was waiting for us outside as we left the clinic. The window rolled down and Mortimer stuck his head out. "Well?" he asked at large.

"First, we take Doctor Zed to the horticultural center," Fynn said and we stepped into the back seat. "Then, you will take us to the stables. Patrick knows the road… After you drop us there, go to the police station and fetch Mrs Arkhipov."

"From her cell?"

"Yes, and be sure not to be recognized."

"What do you suggest?"

"The eyepatch is in your favor. Keep your hat low and flash your credentials… And Javelin, I beg of you, treat her with respect."

"I will be nothing but a gentleman."

Dr Zed was to perform his forensics in the state-run agricultural lab. I smoothed things over with Valentina. She was delighted to have him present— the very same doctor who had delivered little Mikhail some years ago.

"Not the best facilities, no... but I will be able to test for certain things: chemical compounds, PH levels, toxins and such." He smiled. "There are test tubes, beakers, and microscopes. I will make do."

Mortimer then dropped Fynn and I at the stables and drove back to the village to pick up Olga. The place seemed more or less abandoned, certainly run-down and in disrepair. I had the feeling that no one was here, though after a few minutes we could smell and hear the horses in their stalls. We started down the path and I stooped as something caught my eye.

"What have you found there, Patrick?"

"More candy wrappers."

A trail of them led to the stable doors. We could also see three bicycles parked outside. A little face peeked out— two eyes— and then two hands clutched the edge of the door.

"Hello?" I called out in a friendly voice.

A girl of eight or nine stepped out into view and gave us a look of distain. She was defiant, hands on her hips.

"Don't be afraid little one, we are here to help. Your mother sent us," Fynn said.

"My mother? But she's inside..."

"I mean to say your aunt Olga." Fynn squat to one knee... "Here you are, a candy... and one for your cousin." He doled out some saltwater taffy.

"Might she have two?" the little girl asked.

"Of course, but why?"

"She's been crying today, feeling very sad."

Fynn reached into his pocket and gave her more wrapped taffy, more than she could hold in two hands. We followed her inside to find Natasha Arkhipov hiding in the stables. She sat on a bale of hay. A large blanket had been set down and she had been reading to the girls.

"Mrs Arkhipov, hello... There is no cause for alarm. We are here on behalf of Olga..."

"My sister-in-law?"

"She is on her way as we speak..."

Olga arrived with Mortimer, and not much later. There was a tearful reunion and much was said in whispering tones. The two girls were overjoyed. Meanwhile, Fynn looked around the stables for anything of interest, but only found some grooming equipment, brushes and alike. In an old rusty cupboard he came across some medical supplies and what looked to be a very long syringe.

"I notice there is a small cottage in the woods. Is it yours?" Fynn asked Mrs Arkhipov.

"No, it does belong to the stables though," Olga replied.

"I suggest you take Natasha and the girls there. You should be safe enough until this matter is resolved."

Olga nodded and began to gather their things. One of the young girls took Fynn by the hand. His expression softened and he smiled down at her. "Perhaps we can walk up to the cottage together? We may find some more sweets along the way."

***

Inspector Fynn had few questions for Natasha. She seemed unable to cope at present, distraught, often breaking into tears and then looking away so the children might not notice. He sat down with Olga instead and spoke in nearly a whisper, "Please, my dear Mrs Arkhipov, you must tell me all that happened on this dreadful night."

"I heard some noise and came downstairs."

"What noise?"

"Someone crying out in pain."

"Vadim?"

"Yes."

"What did you see?"

"Hardly a thing, it was dark."

"You saw something, surely."

"Yes… I saw Vadim lying on the floor, and there was a woman squatting over him, doing unspeakable things."

"What things?"

"I couldn't tell for certain… It was dark. I didn't see her face and she was dressed in a black coat."

"What then?"

"The woman had disappeared when I looked again, like she vanished into thin air." Olga stifled a sob. "I thought at first, it might be Natasha."

"Why would you think that?"

"She hasn't been getting along with her husband lately…"

"Surely, she wouldn't kill him?"

"She doesn't suffer easily."

"What next?" Inspector Fynn asked.

"I woke Natasha and the girls."

"They were asleep?"

"Soundly, difficult to rouse. Then I sent them packing."

"To where?"

"To here… on the bicycles we have outside."

"You stayed in the house?"

"No, I returned later to clean things up a bit. Then waited till morning when I set the kitchen aflame and called the fire brigade."

"And this?" Fynn asked holding out a large syringe in his hand.

"What of it? It's for the horses…We give them vitamins from time to time."

Fynn said nothing for a long while, presumably deep in contemplation. "Light no fire until the sun goes down and draw all the curtains," he finally said to Olga. "It's best if no one knows you are here."

"Why?"

"There may be others who wish you harm." Fynn forced a smile. "Have you provisions enough?"

"For how long?"

"Only for a day or so, rest assured. I can acquire anything you might need and have it sent here."

I heard another car pull up outside and peeked through the grimy window. It was a Volga sedan. "Your double is here."

"Eh?" Mortimer turned to me.

"People's Commissar Malinov. The one who's working for Kali."

"I see, well, we should have a chat then. Leave this to me."

Fynn and I stayed well back when one Mortimer confronted the other by the stable doors. At first the meeting seemed amicable, though only snippets of their conversation could be heard. It was difficult to tell which Mortimer was saying what:

"…God forsaken place? No, I'm here with Kali. You remember her? She has great plans… Seems some naval commandant has it in mind to start the next world war. I'm here to help stop him."

"Not so well versed in history, eh?"

Quite suddenly, one of the Mortimers drew a sword from his cane. "Sorry, old chum," I heard him say, and he thrust it deep into his doppelgänger's chest. "One of us has to go…"

A body slumped to the ground. Fynn and I went rushing over. I was sickened.

"Help me get rid of him," Mortimer said.

"What?" I stammered, staring down at the fresh corpse.

"Any ideas?"

"I- I…." My brain was shutting down.

Mortimer looked around. "There, the compost pile. We'll bury him at the bottom. That should buy us sufficient time. Find a shovel and pitchfork."

I was horrified. Fynn seemed somewhat less disturbed but said nothing and made no move.

"I'll need his clothes as well, everything but the shirt at least. And I rather like this shiny leather coat." Mortimer rubbed his own face. "I'll need a razor as well." He leaned over the body and plucked from it the glass eye.

I felt my stomach rumble and retched by the wall. I had never seen anything so brutal… The rain was pouring down now, it seemed like I just noticed. After some minutes of long hesitation Fynn and I helped haul the body onto an old wooden cart. We were accomplices to murder.

"I had no choice," Mortimer explained. "He would have betrayed our presence to Kali. What would you have me do?"

"What now?" I asked.

"I shall take his place. Everything Kali knows you will know. That is my plan and my vow."

* * *

I took one of the cars back to town and parked it near the police station. No one noticed and I trod along the path back to my house. It was more than disconcerting to arrive and find Bureau Secretary Comrade Kali and Deputy Boris Popov sitting at the kitchen table.

"Where's Grigori?" I asked immediately.

"Grigori Bulgakov and his family have taken a promenade… A lovely afternoon, don't you think, Padrik Stephanovich Kuznetsov?" The deputy added a sneer.

"It's still raining…" I muttered and looked around, now seeing two other men lurking in the parlor. "Who are these comrades?" I asked.

"Such does not concern you." The deputy gave a smile. "Comrade Nichego has a few questions, as do I… Please join us, have a seat."

"Where is the Commissar?"

"He has driven to the stables."

"Why?"

"You are here to answer questions, not ask them."

"What questions?" I glanced at Kali, wondering if she recognized me or how much she knew. She was certainly looking at me with great interest.

"This comrade detective— how well do you know him, eh?" the deputy asked.

"I've never met him before," I lied with ease.

"Hmm, you seemed quite chummy to me. Well, we're having his credentials checked. Where is he now, do you know?"

"I think he's at the clinic with the doctor."

"What do you suppose they're up to?" Kali spoke for the first time.

"Trouble, I'd say," Boris replied.

"I don't like this doctor at all. He's far too curious." Kali turned to me. "And you… you seem out of place here, and yet very familiar to me. Surely, we've met before?"

"I've been here for five years."

"Why?"

"Visiting my cousin, Grigori."

"That's quite a long visit."

"I like it here. It's peaceful. Nothing ever happens in Zvorkovo."

"Except murder," the Deputy cut in.

"Where do you come from?" Kali asked.

"Estonia."

"Estonia, eh?"

"Reval."

"You mean to say Tallinn?"

"Yes…"

"And where were you the other night?"

"Asleep in bed," I replied but didn't care to mention that Valentina was beside me.

"The other night?" Deputy Boris asked Kali. "I thought Comrade Arkhipov died yesterday morning."

"Can we know when he was killed exactly?" She turned on Boris.

"I suppose not… though the doctor may—"

"He is a dangerous incompetent," Kali barked. "Haven't you more important matters to attend?"

"No, I've already contacted the naval authorities," Boris said.

"Why?"

"To inform his brother Vadim of the tragic news."

"His brother?" I asked.

"Yes. Vasili had a brother, didn't you know?"

I lied again: "*Nyet.*" Neither did Comrade Kali know, if the expression on her face was anything to go by.

"He grew up here, I've heard, but it was well before my time." Boris turned back to me. "We have been told you are a witness— what have you seen, eh?"

"Early that morning I saw a man on a bicycle."

"What man?"

"I didn't recognize him. He was wearing a ushenka," I replied, and cast a glance to Boris' hat on the kitchen table.

"Where was he going?"

"He turned onto the Moscow road..."

Before any more questions could be asked, Comrade Mortimer swept into the room— the new version to be trusted, at least somewhat. I could see the black mark on the tip of his finger. He roughly took my shoulders and made me stand.

"Where are you taking him?" Boris asked.

"To an isolated location. I have some questions of my own— I'm sure you don't mind."

***

"No need to thank me, Patrick," Mortimer said as he drove me back to the horticultural center.

"For what?"

"Saving you from *losya i belka*."

"Moose and squirrel?"

"Boris and Kali…"

He dropped me off and inside I found Fynn and Doctor Zed. The latter had set Valentina to work. Wearing a white smock and swishing some liquid at the bottom of a test tube, she put it down and came rushing over with a greeting.

"The doctor is quite an extraordinary man," Valentina whispered to me. "I believe he's found a way—"

Doctor Zed walked over to us. "Miss Bulgakov has been a great help. She is a capable researcher." He smiled then took me aside. "Ah, Patrick, I need a favor from you."

"Sure."

"I need a good piece of cheese. There's nothing to be found at the market… probably doesn't exist in all of Russia."

"What kind of cheese?"

"A hard cheese: a gouda or a munster. Even Swiss would do in a pinch."

I turned to Valentina knowing she was an expert at procurement.

"Yes, I might be able to find such a thing, but it would cost you more than a *troika*," she said.

Fynn came forward with a wad of rubles. "Will this be enough, my dear?"

"More than enough," Valentina replied with a smile and took off her smock. "I'll be back in no time at all…" She hesitated though. "May I ask what the cheese is for? That is, should I bring some bread as well?"

Doctor Zed laughed. "It's for science, Miss Bulgakov, the science of forensics… Though a loaf of bread would also be most welcome."

Once Valentina departed I asked about the cheese.

"Ah, it is to check the bite marks we found on the body, the distinctive patterns left by the teeth. I will test Olga and her sister Natasha. If they don't match, they can be eliminated as suspects."

"What about Comrade Kali?"

"This may be more difficult. Do you suppose she is fond of cheese?"

"Doctor Zed has found the cause of death," Fynn came forward and urged him on.

"Yes. Upon further examination, I found a terrible necrosis to a large portion of the brain. As if the tissue had been eaten away."

"Eaten away… like bugs?"

"No, like acid, I'm speculating. A horrible way to die. I couldn't think of worse."

"Painful?"

"No, not in the least, well not in itself— perhaps a slight headache."

"Why is it so terrible then?"

"Well, if the victim were conscious, he would feel his facilities slipping away until nothing was left. For your brain to be eaten away like that slowly, your senses disappearing one by one, all your thoughts and memories dissipating like smoke…"

"You're saying someone injected a substance into his brain?"

"Yes."

"Why would anyone— why would Kali do this?"

"I could not say… unusually cruel though."

"Painful then."

"Well, having a long needle plunged into the brain through your ear— I imagine it would hurt a bit."

"What substance do you think it was, Doctor?" Fynn asked.

"My best guess is chlorine."

"Who might have access to that?"

"We use it at the clinic as a disinfectant."

"So it was a syringe after all."

"Yes, not the knitting needle. It left so little blood, I can surmise it was very thin indeed."

"How is such a thing possible?"

"It would take some doing, getting all the way through to the brain from the ear is not easy. One has to go through the bone where the nerves attach. The victim would have to be sedated first, or strapped down in a chair."

"Are there any signs of either?"

"No…"

"It seems like something only Kali could do," Fynn said.

"What do you mean?"

"She seems quite adept at manipulating time. Perhaps she slips into the future to commit her act of cruelty."

"Before the victim is even aware?"

"Yes."

***

Mortimer returned with news. "An inquest has been set for tomorrow."

"Tomorrow?" Fynn was appalled. "We must delay this at all costs. News of it might still reach Commander Arkhipov."

"When is he scheduled to depart?" the doctor asked.

"I was told, the first of October."

"That's next Monday," I said.

Mortimer went on, "And these two new KGB officers may prove troublesome."

"Who do you mean?"

"They're more like Kali's bodyguards than anything else. They never leave her side."

"What's to be done about them?" the doctor asked.

"There's little we can do," Fynn replied.

"Not at all," Mortimer said with a thin smile, "I've already read their dossiers. It's easily remedied." With that he adjusted the dial on his cane and climbed to the top of a desk. He took a leap and disappeared entirely.

Mortimer returned about an hour later to announce, "Yuri and Ivan won't be bothering us any longer."

"What do you mean?" I asked.

"They've been erased."

"Erased?"

"From history."

"How?"

"Must you know all the details?" Mortimer glared at me. "No one was harmed in any way, if that's where your concern lies."

chapter twelve
courting disaster

That night the four of us sat down together in Doctor Zed's clinic. The doors were locked. Mortimer pulled out a bottle of vodka and glasses. "When in Russia, one must partake…"

"I don't like vodka much, especially after five years."

"I must insist. Even Tractus here, who enjoys nothing but a single malt will join us in a glass, eh?"

"I will."

"I don't care for the stuff either," the doctor said, "but I have come prepared." He took something from his pocket.

"What's that, a lime?" I asked.

"Sadly, only a lemon that is not quite ripe. Valentina procured it for me." He cut it into sixteen pieces with surgical precision. We all downed a shot.

It was clear to us that Kali had committed this murder. The discussion turned to how we might catch her in a physical sense, especially given her ability to manipulate time, to hop about in the present like a phantom. Mortimer was first to speak: "We shackle her post haste, or even better, cut her achilles tendon like we used to do… Perhaps the doctor can perform this surgery for us."

"I'll do nothing of the sort."

"You must understand she is a madwoman bent on destroying the Northern Hemisphere in a matter of days. Surely you can bend your ethics here."

"I am sworn by a sacred oath to do no harm."

"Think of all the lives you'll save—"

"It's a moot point," Fynn interrupted.

"How so?"

"I'm sure shackling or cutting her achilles tendon, as you suggest, will not work on Kali."

"It's a tried and true method," Mortimer replied.

"It's been well-observed that Kali does not need to jump in order to travel."

"Oh, the disappearing act…" Mortimer said. "Yes, I've seen this and it's most disconcerting."

"I agree."

"Your thoughts, Patrick?"

"I think she's not quite in normal time."

"What?" They both turned to me.

"Like Pavel's marble. Time is flowing at a different rate for her, faster maybe. We probably seem like slow pokes to her."

"Seems unlikely," the doctor responded.

"Okay… well, maybe she can run time in reverse… maybe just for a few seconds," I said.

"Wouldn't this be something we'd notice?"

"And Pavel Mekanos would certainly take issue with that concept," Fynn added.

"I'm just throwing out ideas…"

"She seems to have the ability to anticipate future events. I would surmise she travels ahead in the blink of an eye and then returns to the present."

"That does make more sense…" I agreed. "And why she is hard to catch on camera."

"Meaning?"

"She's impossible to photograph."

"I can't see how holiday snaps will help us in this regard," Mortimer growled and then poured out another four glasses.

"Perhaps we can sing to her then."

"What?" Mortimer turned to Fynn.

"You mentioned that music seems to distract her."

"Yes, though a lullaby does not constitute a strategy."

"I believe she doesn't exist in the immediate present as we usually think of it," Fynn continued. "Instead, she oscillates between our present and a few seconds in the future."

"Travels back and forth?"

"Yes, and so quickly, it is barely noticeable. In such a way, she can anticipate our actions and avoid injury."

"She'd see an attack coming, you say?"

"Exactly this."

"But only if she can see her hand," I spoke up.

"What's that, Patrick?"

"I don't think she can do anything unless she's looking at her palm."

"Yes, I've noticed this as well. How do you suppose we might prevent that?"

"Handcuffs. Hands behind her back."

"While I agree this might be effective, how do we go about getting her in this position?"

"Indeed. How do you suggest we combat someone with absolute prescience?" Mortimer slurred.

"How far in the future can she see?" I asked.

"A very short time, I would guess," Fynn answered. "What good would it do her to look ahead a day, or even an hour? Much could happen in a volatile situation. The future may unfold differently than she expects."

"So you're saying it's a very short time."

"Yes. If she finds herself physically threatened, she would only need a few seconds to avoid the danger, to return to her past and avoid harm."

"So, it's a hard jump to the future and a soft jump back to her immediate past?" I asked.

"Yes. She cannot soft jump to the future. None of us can."

"Are you sure?"

"Of course. One cannot re-enter a place that does not yet exist. It's common sense, eh?" Fynn smiled. "And, she seems unable to hard jump to the past, with her concurrency so filled-to-the-brim as it were."

"Perhaps she is impossible to catch," Doctor Zed put in.

"I say get in close with a sharp knife and put her out of her misery. I'm more than capable of doing so. And we'll be done with her once and for all." Mortimer gave his thin smile. "The question then becomes how do we kill someone who can see their own demise."

"Kill her?"

"Have you a better idea, Patrick?"

"No."

"I'll use my cane," Mortimer said.

"I'm not sure you're a match to her abilities. At best you can jump an hour ahead or an hour behind," Fynn cautioned. "She can slip in and out of the present for seconds or less."

"I can jump back and double myself. In half a day she'll have a dozen Mortimers to contend with."

"I appreciate the sentiment, but that would be in the past. We must deal with her in the present and going forward."

"Can we alter time… make it so she can't see the future?" I suggested.

"How?"

"Pavel's marble might do the trick."

"It doesn't work very well, given what you've told me," Fynn replied.

"You're right… but it might work just long enough."

"Do you have it with you?"

"No."

"Exactly how far in the future does she oscillate?" the doctor asked.

"This is so far unknown to us. And it would be a good bit of information to have."

"I'd say it's at the very heart of any plan we might conjure," Mortimer said.

"He's right," I agreed, then asked, "How about a diversion?"

"I'm skeptical such a thing would work," Fynn replied and belted back another shot.

"Tag team," I said.

"Meaning?"

"Well, she might know what one of us will do in the future— but all of us? And at different times?"

"Explain yourself."

"Something like one of us confronts her in a big way, but the rest of us do something more subtle."

"You may be onto something," Fynn said with half a smile. "At the very least we might determine how far she can skip ahead…"

"What sort of concerted effort do you mean?" Mortimer asked.

"Well… She can't anticipate four different distractions."

"What do you have in mind, Patrick?"

***

The following morning, we walked up to the police station. "Who's to say Boris will even listen to us?" Mortimer asked along the way.

"We are in authority. Our evidence is overwhelming, and he is in the end, a policeman. How can he disagree with us?"

"The evidence is circumstantial at best. You should know that better than anyone, Tractus."

"We shall see."

"Besides, he's already questioning your credentials. Are you sure they'll hold up to scrutiny?"

"I only ask that we make no mention of Natasha for now, nor Vadim. It would only confuse matters for the deputy."

It didn't go as well as Inspector Fynn had hoped. Deputy Boris was probably asleep as we entered his tiny office. He roused himself quickly enough and his eyes widened a bit when we presented our new evidence. He listened patiently about the bite marks and the evidence of the cheese— how it completely exonerated Olga.

"You want the Comrade Party Leader to bite into a piece of cheese?" the deputy asked more than once.

Fynn also talked about the missing cap, Comrade Arkhipov's— a cap which had never been found— and a new witness who had come forth.

"Who is this witness?" Boris asked.

"Someone to be protected for now."

"You say they saw Comrade Nichego enter the house?"

"Yes."

"But she is beyond suspicion," Deputy Popov balked.

"Why?"

"She's the Bureau Secretary."

"Nonetheless, it is our duty to ask her a few questions, eh?" Fynn responded.

"I don't think so."

Mortimer intervened, "I have a question for you, Comrade Deputy Boris Ivanovich Popov."

"Yes?"

"What is Comrade Nichego's given name?"

"What? I'm not sure I've ever heard it."

"And her middle name?"

"What are you getting at?"

"You know me as Drotik Brakovich Malinov." Mortimer paused to give his thin smile. "But Comrade Nichego? What names does she have? I'm not at all convinced she is who she says…"

"I don't know his full name either," Boris complained and pointed at Fynn.

"I can vouch for him. Detective Plavnik is well known around the Oblast. "

"And his other names?"

"What a question, comrade. Of course they are withheld for security reasons."

With great reluctance, Boris took us over to party headquarters. He had a question along the way and directed it to the doctor: "Tell me, comrade, when exactly was Commander Vasili killed?"

"The night before he was discovered."

"Are you certain?"

"Of course I'm certain. I'm a doctor."

***

It was true that the KGB agents were no longer present. Mortimer had erased them. Though two uniformed officers from the GRU now took their place. At the sight of them, I wasn't quite sure if they were wearing huge military caps or had tiny heads. Mortimer had made things worse, though he'd never admit to it.

"And why are you involved?" Deputy Boris demanded of the two uniformed men.

"It is a matter of military security," one of them answered, but both barred our entry into Kali's office. "We are waiting for the fingerprint expert to arrive from Moscow. He should be here at any moment."

"To what end?" Fynn asked.

"Of course, to confirm the identity of the deceased."

Comrade Nichego heard the arguing outside her office and burst through the double doors. "What is going on out here?" she challenged, her voice shrill. "You… the policeman…" Kali glared at Fynn and then the rest of us.

"We are obliged to ask you a few questions, Comrade Party Leader," Fynn responded.

A smile crossed her face. She seemed bemused and led us inside her cramped office. It didn't appear that Kali was doing much work. The light on the desk was off, and the covers on the settee had been thrown to the floor without care. In all likelihood she had been napping.

Deputy Popov helped himself to the sofa as Comrade Kali sat behind her desk. The four of us took our positions with Mortimer at the door, Inspector Fynn in the only chair, and the doctor and I flanking either side.

Fynn wasted no time in leveling his accusation: "We've come to believe you murdered Commander Vasili Arkhipov."

"But this is completely absurd," Kali replied and glanced around the room. "I was in Moscow on the evening in question… at the Party Conference… with Commissar Malinov. He will certainly vouch for me."

To Deputy Popov it was a very convincing alibi. The rest of us knew that meant nothing. Mortimer made a loud smacking noise. "I hate to be the one who disagrees, Comrade Party Leader. But you were not in Moscow on this night. You informed me personally that you were returning here."

"What?" Kali shouted and was surprised by the turn of events. She glared at the would-be commissar and immediately grew suspicious. I wondered if she'd start to flitter around the room, out of sync from normal time. If she did we were ready.

"Are you calling me a liar, dear Comrade?" Mortimer goaded her.

"I've never known Commissar Malinov to speak an untruth," Boris said from the sofa. He glared at Kali. "And why is this in your office?" he asked while picking up a naval cap from the table. "It belongs to Commander Arkhipov— it's written so inside."

"Comrade Arkhipov must have forgotten it here."

"He visited you— when?"

"I'm not sure I remember. We had important matters to discuss, not that it's any of your business."

"You mentioned to me that you'd never before met him," the deputy persisted.

Doctor Zed found a radio on the table and switched it on. Russian folk songs filled the office and Kali was distracted for a moment. Her eyes went blank and her face flaccid. A second or so later, she glanced around the room and then started from her chair. Fynn lunged first, heaving himself across the desk. I counted to five and swept my arms out as if to catch her. The doctor counted to ten, and stood with a hypodermic at the ready. Mortimer barred the door. Kali could not avoid all these possible futures and ended up in Fynn's grasp. He drew her hands behind her back and handcuffed them. As an extra precaution I covered them with some furry mittens I'd found.

Deputy Popov was slow to rise and slow to comprehend what had just occurred, though his face held a small satisfied smile. Doctor Zed then came forward and gently removed Comrade Kali's ornate hatpin. Her cap came off and with it, a long tumble of dark hair followed. "A perfect match to the murder weapon," he announced. "And there's still a bit of blood on the tip. This can be tested."

***

A small, quiet man stood in the doorway to Kali's office. He had both hands on a large valise. "Excuse me, comrades… I was sent here to take fingerprints."

I glanced over to Fynn; he was crestfallen, but spoke to the man, "Yes, we will start with the Party Secretary."

With some difficulty, Comrade Kali's fingerprints were taken. We took great care to ensure her hands remained behind her back. To everyone's surprise, she had no prints at all, just smudges, at least on her left hand.

"Have you ever seen such a thing before?" Fynn asked the expert.

"No, though I have heard stories about people using acid on their fingertips to erase the ridges."

"And you believe this is the cause?"

The man simply shrugged. "I am here primarily to identify the murder victim. Can you tell me where he is?"

"We have him on ice, at the butcher shop," Doctor Zed spoke up but looked over at Fynn.

"You should first check the scene of the crime, eh?" Fynn replied in a useless attempt to stall for time. "The Deputy can show you the way."

***

That afternoon, the four of us met at the police station to ensure that Comrade Kali was safely installed in her cell. In Deputy Popov's empty office a brief conversation ensued:

"Does anyone have a gun?" Mortimer asked.

"That's not like you, Javelin," Fynn responded. "I've never seen you use a firearm. And no one here has a gun, not even Deputy Boris."

"What are you thinking?" the doctor asked.

"Expedience. That we end this here and now. Strike while she is vulnerable. Mission accomplished."

"No life will be taken," Fynn said. "Even Kali's."

"Too bad Lothar isn't here with us," Mortimer growled and started down the stairs. "I'll do the job myself." He unsheathed the sword from his cane. Fynn's hand came down on the handle.

"No. We will not kill her like this."

"Then how…? What would you have us do, Tractus? Ask the Arbiter to fetch her to the hotel?"

"I don't think that's within his ability," the doctor spoke up. "Our course of action is quite simple. She must go on trial. She has murdered, and you will bring a case against her. When she is found guilty, the Soviet justice system will take care of her."

"Fair enough," Mortimer said and gave a thin smile.

Fynn had lingering doubts. "Should something happen, should she get free, things would go badly for us. As of now, she still thinks it is Vasili who is dead. If she learns it is Vadim, we will have a problem on our hands."

***

We kept a careful vigil until October first, until we were sure Commander Arkhipov was aboard his submarine. There were times when I'd glance into the cell and think that Kali was not in the present— but she always was, slouched in the corner, hands behind her and covered with mittens. Sometimes she'd look back at me with a twisted smile. It was a disconcerting feeling. For now it seemed,

"Detective Plavnik and Commissar Malinov will be immediately arrested for harboring the fugitive and obstructing justice."

The two GRU men rushed forward under her orders. Boris lumbered over to make the arrest. Kali herself came close and whispered into Fynn's ear, though I could not hear what she said.

Mortimer however, took the news badly. He lunged at Kali, brandishing the blade from inside his cane. She stepped aside deftly, and in the next moment he had been stabbed by his own sword. It clattered to the ground in the confusion as the GRU officers led Fynn and Mortimer from the courtroom. It was pretty clear that things had gone south.

***

A few hours later I accompanied Doctor Zed to the jail cell. Mortimer was in a bad way.

"He'll bleed to death if he doesn't get medical attention."

"So?" the guard answered.

"You'll have no one to put on trial if he dies," Doctor Zed responded defiantly.

"Who's this fellow with you?" The guard looked me up and down.

"My assistant."

We found Fynn and Mortimer in the cell, chained to their cots, the latter laying there, doubled over in agony.

"Where's your cane?" I asked.

Mortimer could offer no coherent response and Fynn gave me a troubled glance. "When did you see it last?"

"On the floor, after Kali stabbed Mortimer."

"Did you see her pick it up?" he asked.

"No… there was a lot going on."

Moments later, someone else came down the steps to the basement. It was Comrade Kali. She had with her the morning edition of *Pravda* and displayed the headline through the bars: *American Piracy on the High Seas*.

She glanced at the guard, then the doctor and I, but generally ignored us, turning back to the prisoners. "Well, gentlemen, before I go, I wish to offer my thanks," she said in English.

"For what?" Fynn asked.

"Without your intervention, my plans might have failed."

"Killing the wrong brother, you mean to say," Fynn said.

"Yes… and then having someone to blame for the crime."

"Natasha?"

"She was perfect for the situation. Motive, means, and opportunity— eh, Mr Policeman?" Kali laughed. "I've whispered in her ear for weeks now. I've told her all about that husband of hers, having a wild affair with her sister-in-law."

"But that's not true at all."

"Of course it's not," Kali said.

"What have you done with her?" Fynn asked.

"I've done nothing. She's had a complete mental breakdown it seems."

"And?"

"What does it matter? For now, Boris sent her to the stables to be with her sister." Kali laughed and walked through the open cell door. "You've made the mistake of revealing yourselves. I won't forget you. I understand your plans and there's nothing for you to do— you cannot stop me."

"What now?"

"Vasili is not aboard his submarine as you had hoped. He has been notified about the tragic events that have befallen his family. I've seen to it. He's likely on his way here already…." Kali laughed again. "But none of it matters, as you'll all be dead by the end of the week."

"And you?"

"I'll be far from here, of course."

"But why destroy an entire world?" Fynn asked.

"Let's say I've grown weary of this battle between ideologies, Capitalism versus Communism. Neither is very effective."

"But to erase civilization— why?"

"The people get what they deserve, on both sides." She laughed. "And it saves me the bother of keeping track of this depressing timeline. I need not return again."

"Surely, there's more to it than that?"

"In the end, it compels people to live in the place I have chosen for them." Kali flashed a hideous smile.

"And him?" Fynn asked, glancing at Mortimer on the cot.

"My next task will be to resurrect the more helpful version of Comrade Malinov from the past... or whatever name you go by." She looked down at the wounded man. "I will say thank you for the cane however. Quite an interesting device." Kali then walked directly up to Fynn, simply staring at his face. "I remember you, policeman. Our paths have crossed before... but they won't again."

"What about the dogs?" Doctor Zed spoke up.

"The dogs?" Kali turned towards him. "Oh yes, well, canine or not, they were for practicing my technique."

"What technique?"

"Piercing the ear into the brain. Trying different substances to see which works the best..."

By now Deputy Popov had made his way down the stairs. Kali's demeanor changed somewhat and she switched back to Russian. She turned to face me. "I don't know why you've been helping these men, but you don't seem the dangerous sort... And even Boris will vouch for you..."

The policeman was nodding, perhaps even smiling.

"What should we do with him? I wonder. What say you, Deputy Popov?"

"He's done nothing wrong, technically speaking."

"Very well, let him wander about freely, but keep a close eye on him. The doctor as well." Comrade Kali gave a smile. It wasn't a friendly one. She was toying with us again.

***

Over the next several days, I paid regular visits to Fynn and Mortimer. Not a hard thing to do. Deputy Boris was usually upstairs snoozing in his chair. I brought them bread and whatever else I could find to eat. I passed things along through the wide bars of their cell. We spoke in hushed tones.

"Can't we jump back and stop this crime?"

"There's nothing to be done. If any of us try to set things right, Kali will be waiting. She will only redouble her efforts."

"That's it? We just give up and let the world end?"

"The game is over. We must consider it a tactical defeat but a strategic victory."

"In what way ever is this a victory?"

"We know of her exact plans, they are deeply rooted in one time, one place, and one person. We might travel to before these events take place and stop her then. It's quite simple."

"Simple?"

"We will have to take a different approach entirely."

"Like?"

"It will take some careful thinking…"

"What do you suggest?" Mortimer grumbled. "Impugn her character so she does not become Party Leader?"

"She has recognized her mistake and will return, no doubt, a thousand times if she has to."

"So this is not the first time we've been here?" I asked.

"It's the first time I remember…" Fynn tried to raise a smile with no success. "There is no way to win against her as it now stands."

"What then?"

"We need to come up with a new strategy."

"No, there's nothing to be done here," Mortimer said in a harsh whisper. "We must eliminate Kali at her source."

***

"What's troubling you, Patrick?" Doctor Zed asked and put his hand on my shoulder.

"Everything," I replied. "Mostly though, I'm worried about Grigori and his family."

"You've grown close over the years?"

"Yes."

"What's to be done? They will die no matter what you do, in some timeline. You cannot fix them all, eh? You have only the present to enjoy their company. You must console yourself with that."

Somehow it was not very satisfying. I drove the black Zil over to Grigori's house and parked out front. He was sitting on his porch and his face held a wide grin. I handed him the keys to the car.

"What's this?" he asked.

"You have to go— as soon as you can. Pack up anything you need, get the family, and leave immediately."

"Why?"

"Something terrible is going to happen, probably the end of the world."

"You've told me this before, but we are still here, eh? When will this happen?"

"Sunday."

"And where shall I go?"

"Go south, as far as you can. Cross the equator if you're able."

"What? You're joking… besides all the roads lead east and west."

"Go east… then south. Stay far away from any military bases if you can, and don't look back."

"Don't look back? You make it sound like Lot and his wife. Will I turn to a pillar of salt?"

I had no reply but Grigori read my expression well enough. I helped the Bulgakov family gather a few possessions and loaded the car. Grigori and I scrounged up as much gasoline as we could find, provisions as well.

"What about the rest of the people in my village?" Grigori asked.

"Tell anyone you want. I doubt they'll believe you."

"And we will be safe?"

"I don't know. I don't know what will happen… maybe nothing at all, and you can just drive back." I knew I wasn't really saving them. There might be no hope, but I couldn't bring myself to tell Grigori that. I might be giving him a fighting chance, or worse, condemning him to a horrible ordeal.

Even though the family was ready and sitting in the car, Valentina refused to leave my side. She held on so tightly, I felt she'd never let go.

"You can't stay," I whispered.

"I will not leave you, Padrik."

"Please, go with your family."

"No," she insisted and cast a defiant glance at her father.

"You keep her safe, Padrik, or there will be hell to pay," Grigori said reluctantly.

"She can't stay," I repeated and reached into my pocket to pull out the pill Grigori had given me. I put it in Valentina's mouth, bidding her to swallow. She was surprised but complied. Then I rang the bell for a full ten seconds and hung it around her neck. "This might hurt like hell," I cautioned, "but you'll be fine. Take a deep breath. I promise we'll meet again, and sooner than you think."

I kissed her, and just like that she was gone, disappeared.

To say Grigori was astonished was to say little. He stood there mouth agape, and blinking. "By Stalin's ghost, I swear."

"She's safe, I promise…"

"But… but—"

"You need to go, Grigori Bulgakov. Now."

We embraced.

"I'm going…" he replied but stopped to scrutinize me. "You are not from Canada, are you?"

"No."

"From where then?"

"From the future," I replied. It didn't matter what I said at this point. He had no one to tell, nor would anyone believe him.

He nodded and walked towards the car. He turned though. "One last thing, Padrik. About your friends…"

"Yes?"

"I know Boris all too well. The jail cell is not locked."

"What?"

"He lost the keys some years ago." Grigori laughed. "The prisoners never expect that."

***

I ran to the police station and hurried downstairs. Deputy Popov was no where in sight. I found the cell door unlocked just as Grigori said.

"You could've left at any time."

"Eh?"

"The door to your cell. It's not locked."

"That may be, but we are still shackled here," Fynn replied. "Fetch the doctor," he said with some urgency. "Mortimer has taken a turn for the worse. He will not survive without medical attention."

I ran again and returned with Doctor Zed and a stretcher. Fynn had already freed himself from his chains, Mortimer as well. "He is in a bad way," the doctor confirmed. We carried our failing comrade to the clinic and the doctor treated his wound with what he had available. "There's an infection starting. Shame we don't have any penicillin." Doctor Zed looked around the room. He spied an old piece of bread on the shelf. "Ah," he said. "Just the thing…"

I watched him break up the moldy loaf into a mortar and add water to it. He started grinding with a pestle to make a thick paste. Minutes later he was dressing the wound with a bluish goop. "If he survives the night, he should recover," Doctor Zed announced and injected something into Mortimer's arm. "I've given him something to sleep and an extra dose of vitamins."

***

The next morning, a disheveled man wandered into town, up from the Moscow Road. He was in uniform but it was covered in mud and grime. His face held a rough beard as if it had not seen a razor in weeks. Fynn and I watched him slowly march towards the house on the square, Olga's house. We met up with him at the gate.

"Mrs Olga Arkhipov is not at home," Fynn called out. The man turned to us and I recognized him at once: Commander Vasili Arkhipov.

"Where is she?" he asked with an expression of terrible concern.

"At the stables. She is safe, and your daughter, I assure you."

Vasili immediately started up the path that led out of town. We kept pace with him.

"And you are?" he asked.

"Detective Plavnik. I don't know what you've heard but there has been a terrible miscarriage of justice."

"My brother, Vadim?"

"Murdered yes, I'm sorry to say, but not by your sister-in-law, nor your wife."

Vasili seemed relieved to hear that at least. "Who has killed him then?"

"Comrade Nichego, the Party Boss," I answered. He turned to me with disbelief. "You walked here from Murmansk?"

"More or less," he replied and gave us a beleaguered grin.

"You're supposed to be the man who saved the world."

"What?" he asked with a questioning glance.

"Aboard the submarine, you—"

Fynn cut me off by squeezing my arm. "Enough, Patrick," he whispered, and in English. "You needn't say more. Let him live out his final days in peace, and not with a great burden of unnecessary guilt."

Vasili had not heard me. Up along the path was Olga. He spotted her. She was soon running towards us. They met and locked in a long embrace.

***

In the clinic, Mortimer sat up on his gurney, clutching his side. Doctor Zed noticed. "Feeling better, eh? Well, don't get too excited, the world ends in a few hours."

"Are we obliged to wait till the very last moment?" he asked.

"No. We should leave immediately, if you can walk and jump," the doctor replied.

"Agreed. But to where?"

"The future," Fynn called out from across the room.

"What? That's utter insanity."

"It is a place where Kali will dare not follow, eh?"

"Any sign of her?"

"No, it seems like she's disappeared."

"Little wonder," Mortimer commented.

"Party headquarters is all locked up," I went on. "The village is a ghost town."

"I won't be jumping to the future," Mortimer said. "What will be there? Clouds of radiation, a few pathetic stragglers, pestilence and torment? No, this world will surely end."

"Where then?"

"To the past again."

"And yet we must take care not to be followed," Fynn cautioned. "Best we leave separately. It's less likely that Kali can follow all of us. It may throw her off the scent."

"Let us agree to meet at the hotel," Doctor Zed suggested.

"The *Hotel de Cirque?*"

"The very place."

"When?'

"It hardly matters, we'll run into each other in the lobby, sooner or later."

From outside, I heard singing, a tune from a distant memory and it was in English: *We'll meet again... Don't know where... Don't know when...* The voice was also familiar. I ran out to the street. A tall figure appeared from around the corner, walking up the cobbles towards the village square. It was clearly a female by the way her hips swung. She was dressed head to toe in tan fur and wore a high fuzzy hat. I could see shiny boots to her calf, and she carried a matching black bag over her shoulder. Then I caught a glimpse of her face. She was beautiful; wide eyes, pale skin and lips flush with red. *Wait... I know this woman.* I called out, "Chloe?"

She turned with a smile and ran towards me. I was showered with kisses. "Oh Patrick, I'm so happy to see you again..." She seemed a bit flustered though. "I'm not quite sure why I'm here... give me a moment to remember..." Chloe glanced at her surroundings. "Where are we exactly?"

"Outside Moscow, nineteen sixty-two."

"Oh yes, and where is Fynn, the Doctor, and Mr Mortimer? I was told to fetch them as well."

"This way..." I led her to the clinic.

"The Arbiter thought you might be in some trouble."

"What, so you're like our ride?"

She laughed. "Yes, I guess I am." Chloe greeted my comrades with a big smile. "Gentlemen, I've come to take you back to the hotel," she announced.

"Why can't the Arbiter just pluck us from here?" Fynn asked.

"Presently he's residing in the past. He can only fetch you from the future. But I've brought these..." She rummaged through her bag and held up several brass keychains, oval in shape, room keys to the *Hotel de Cirque*.

"Are you sure they will work?"

"Of course, Sebastian has promised."

"I seem to remember it's like a rubber band."

"Clark says they'll take us right back to the lobby."

"Thank you, my dear," Mortimer said as he snatched one of the keys from her hand and started out the door, though rather stiffly.

"Where are you going?" Fynn called out.

"To find my blasted cane. I won't leave here without it." He turned to give us a smile. "I'll meet you later."

"Gracious me, I only have three keys remaining," Chloe said.

"What?"

She handed a key to Doctor Zed and another to Fynn. "I must have forgotten one… Patrick and I will have to jump together."

***

It was a crisp October morning with the sky bluer than it should be. The four of us crossed the town square and found a brick wall that seemed to be the perfect height. The doctor climbed up, gave us a friendly wave and jumped off to oblivion. Fynn was next. He gave me a hug and gave Chloe a kiss. "Till we meet again," he said and disappeared. For a moment it seemed like Chloe and I were the last two people on earth.

That was not quite true. A figure appeared in the middle of the road. She walked towards us. It was Kali, still dressed in her party clothes: a small gray hat and a black coat. I noticed she did not have Mortimer's jackal cane. She stopped some distance away, and held an eerie smile. She simply stared, as if waiting for us to leave.

Over our heads, and lit by the morning sun, I could see contrails, a dozen or so thin needles of smoke at the top of the sky. They traveled in from the west, gently curving towards earth, and presumably Moscow. I heard the village siren start, a mournful wail. All the while Kali stood apart, but still grinning.

There was a blinding flash in the west. Instinctively, I held my arm up to cover my eyes. A wind began, slowly at first as a gentle breeze, but within moments, it felt as if the very atmosphere was being sucked from this place. A low rumbling came. Kali still stood before us wearing her hideous smile. I felt someone tug on my hand. It was Chloe. I followed her up to the wall and we jumped. I felt the usual searing pain as her hand slipped from mine.

PART IV

chapter thirteen
no vacancy

  It was a hard jump, I could tell by the searing pain, and my broken toe still ached. I landed and looked around, not quite sure where I was. As far as the horizon lay a huge sea, calm and barely blue; no distant shore could be seen. I had been here before, though I won't say I had the feeling of deja vu. Then I started to wonder where Chloe might have landed. Something had gone wrong, not terribly wrong I hoped, but slightly wrong, and reckoned I was near to the hotel.
  I stood for a while on a beach, sand and pebbles. In the gentle waves lapping against my boots were thousands of tiny fish. They weren't swimming; they were floating and staring up at me with lifeless eyes. Everything else around me was dead or dying, some scrubby dune grass and a few dry bushes; the rest of the area seemed to be a desert.
  The ground was littered with the desiccated carcasses of unknown grazing animals, goats or sheep. There were flies everywhere and the stench of decomposition. I felt sure I had traveled to the future, the atomic future, the aftermath of a timeline we failed to stop. A kind of dull panic set in.
  Behind me I saw some low hills and headed in that direction. After about fifteen minutes of hard walking, a dusty trail appeared. A vehicle was kicking up sand and it now moved towards me. A sort of military jeep, it seemed, and it pulled up along side. Two men

got out, both armed, wearing gas masks and primitive hazmat suits. They trudged over.

"Was he exposed, do you think?" one of the men said, but not to me. "I don't see any blisters on his skin."

"Well, he's still alive…" the other replied, his voice muffled by the mask.

"Hey you, how are you feeling? Are you sick?" one of the men asked.

Lucky for me my Russian was perfect. I could certainly not see their faces, only their eyes flickering behind thick, grimy goggles. "What year is it?" I asked.

"See, he's delirious already," one of the men said.

"It's nineteen sixty-two," the shorter of them answered.

"Is it the end of the world?"

"It is for you."

"You shouldn't be here, you know. It's dangerous… We're conducting experiments," the other man said.

"What kind of experiments?"

"Hmm, a state secret. We're going to have to arrest you."

"Why?"

"Like I said, you shouldn't be here. We'll have to take you back to town."

"What town?" I glanced around at the wasteland.

"Kantubek, Aralsk-Seven… it's over those dunes."

I could see the sun on the horizon, but couldn't tell if it was setting or rising. I pointed. "Is that east?"

"No, west," he replied.

"Say, where did you come from?" the other man asked.

"The hotel."

"What? That abandoned ruin?"

"It's just the off-season… We still have a backgammon tournament every Monday night."

"Backgammon, you say?" He turned to his comrade, presumably with a smile.

"Any women there?" the other man asked.

"Sure…" I lied outright. "Lots of women, pretty women."

"And booze?"

"You can bring your own, or sit at the bar."

"A bar, you say? Well, that does sound like fun… maybe we'll see you there next week, if you're still alive… if you're feeling alright."

"What about the hotel? Do you know what direction it's in?"

"Just travel north, you'll find it eventually."

"It's pretty far," the other man added.

"So you're not going to arrest me?"

"What's the use? You'll be dead in a few hours and we'll save a lot of paperwork."

"What will I die of?" I asked.

"Anthrax."

***

It took hours to reach the *Hotel de Cirque*; walking along the sand was harder than I anticipated, especially on a broken toe. Make that limping. There was enough of a moon to guide my steps and it was a happy sight when lights appeared on the horizon. I quickened my pace as the hotel came into view.

Everything looked about the same. It was nearly three in the morning if the giant clock in the lobby was to be believed. I could also see Sebastian Clark through the giant windows, rolling in his chair back and forth behind the reception desk. I saw a tartan blanket draped over his footless legs.

I knew better than to use the revolving doors at either side of the main entrance. I knocked on the glass instead. Clark spotted me, startled and squinting at first, but eventually a smile came to his face. I heard the lock click open and in I went. The towering marble colonnade held little warmth but Clark made up for it.

"Ah, Mr Jardel, good to have you back. Do you have a reservation?" He looked up at me, even though his eyes peered in slightly different directions.

"No, sorry." I was parched, barely able to find my own voice.

"No matter, I think you're expected," Clark said and put a glass bottle of water on the counter. It was icy cold and perfect.

"I'm happy you decided against using the revolving doors this morning."

"So am I…" I replied, remembering well how those doors had

swept many people to oblivion. "Don't you ever lock them?"
"Never."
"Tell me something, Clark, how far do they take you?"
"Depends on how hard you push and how fast the door spins."
"Where do they take you?"
"Depends which door you choose and if you're entering or leaving."
"Wow, sounds confusing."
"Yes, it is, very," Clark admitted. "Still, it's been an effective against intruders."
"Who?"
"Visitors without a reservation."
"So, Kali has never made it into the lobby?"
"Who?"
"Lady Cero, Mistress Nihil..."
"None of them have, I can assure you of that— such would be a great disaster and something I would have noticed."
"Well, that's good at least."
"Seems like months since you've last visited, eh?"
"Seems like years to me."
"Traveling?"
"Learning Russian."
"Well then, *dobro pozhalovat*."
"*Blagodarya* ... Anyone else around?"
"They're all here... but asleep at the moment."
"Do you know what day it is?"
"Saturday."
"How about a year?"
"Outside, you're meaning?"
I nodded.
"Nineteen sixty-two."
"So the world didn't end after all."
"What's that?" Clark asked, somewhat alarmed.
"What month is it?"
"September."
"Did Chloe make it back okay?"
Sebastian hit the bell on the desk and gave it a sharp ring. Chloe appeared a few moments later dressed in her bellhop uniform, and

with a huge smile. She seemed ready to pounce.

"Luggage?" Clark asked.

"Not this time."

"I suppose you'll be needing a room?"

"If you have any vacancies." I glanced around the empty lobby.

"Hmm, you may have to share a suite— if that's alright. Will you be taking another excursion with us?"

"Hopefully not…"

Chloe led me to the kitchen with effusive apologies. "I have no idea what went wrong, but I'm so sorry, Patrick."

"It wasn't your fault. I'm just glad you made it back."

"Back from where?"

"Zvorkovo… Russia…"

"Where?"

"Don't you remember?"

"Sorry, no… I only recall we were supposed to return together. Two on a key— never a good jump." She draped herself around my shoulder. "Let me make you something to eat. Hungry?"

"Yes."

"What would you like?"

"Anything that isn't soup or stew."

"Hmm, you look a bit older than I remember," Chloe said and slid her finger down the side of my face.

After a tasty snack of cold kebabs and sardines from a can, Chloe led me to her room on the ground floor, back behind the kitchens. It was different than the others I had seen; one wall had a definite curve to it. It was also windowless and had more doors.

"I'm sure you'd like to change, even though you're cute as a proletariat." She smiled. "I think I have some of your old clothes laying about. Clark had them laundered. Now, where did I put them? Be a dear and check the closet."

I opened the door onto a dark swirling void.

"Wrong closet, Patrick," she said with a laugh and pulled me back a step. I turned and she wrapped herself around my waist. Chloe gazed up at me and I felt her palm across my cheek. We kissed. "I remember you," she said in a whisper, then pushed me away gently. "Ah, now I recall. In the armoire, second drawer down."

I found a set of tennis whites, a shirt, trousers, shoes and a v-neck sweater all of the same color. I remembered wearing them in 1903.

"Aren't you going to change?" Chloe asked with a devilish smile. She handed me the straw hat.

"Hmm, first a shower, if there's enough hot water." I smiled back.

Sometime later, I found Chloe sitting on the edge of the bed staring into space. I sensed something wrong and called out her name several times. She was unresponsive. "Are you okay?" I persisted.

She finally reached over and took my hand. "Sorry, Patrick, I was elsewhere…"

"Where?"

"I'm not sure. I am on the threshold of remembering something, but I can't think what it is."

"Are you back?"

She laughed. "I'm not sure I went anywhere, but I could feel Lilly for a brief moment."

"Your sister?"

"Yes… it's troubling." She turned to me. Tears streamed down her face. I held her tight until she fell asleep.

***

The next morning in the lobby, I noticed that Clark had dragged a sign in front of the main entrance. It read:

Sunny, 89 degrees
High tide, 2:05 pm
Air quality today, lethal

"Ah Patrick, there you are… Good morning," Clark got my attention as I strode through the lobby. "Someone has left you a message."

"Who?"

"I'm not sure… I found it on the counter." He handed me a folded scrap of paper. *Be seeing you*, it said, but was written out in morse code. "Didn't you give me this once before?"

"I pass on many messages on any given day."

"Right… I remember getting this in nineteen-oh-three from

Mortimer… Is that possible?"

"Possible?" Clark was baffled by my question.

"In terms of how the lobby works… how time passes here."

"Oh… Well, time certainly doesn't flow as normal."

"How does it flow?"

"I'm not sure it does at all. It's better to think of it as a place where the past, present, and future intersect with each other."

"How do you keep track of it all?"

"Well, there's that over there…" He glanced to the giant lobby clock. "And as long as I know what day of the week it is, everything else takes care of itself."

I found Inspector Fynn alone in the dining room just finishing breakfast. He rose with a broad smile and gave me a hug in greeting. "Ah, there you are, Patrick. I was growing concerned. The rest of us have been back for days. Tell me about your harrowing escape."

"I'd rather not, not this second anyhow." I sat and helped myself to coffee. "Glad you're okay…"

"All is well."

"Is it?"

"No. Admittedly, even I feel a bit unsettled. I've had to break every one of my rules of travel in the last few weeks.

"Except for *the only timeline is the one you remember*."

"Even that seems to be in question, I'm afraid to say."

"Well, not the last one, about *dying*…"

"Thankfully not… though, I cannot say the same for some of our colleagues."

"Who's been killed?"

"That remains to be seen," he replied. "But all of us are succumbing to despair, I fear. We are under siege."

"From Kali?"

"Of course…"

"Well, she might have been incinerated."

"How do you mean?"

"My harrowing escape, with Chloe… We jumped away seconds before the blast."

"And?"

"Kali did not. She just stood there smiling."

"We cannot assume she's dead. It may be a game of chicken, as I've heard you describe."

"Why would she do that?"

"To be sure you departed." Fynn paused. "Did she have Mortimer's cane when you last saw her?"

"No."

"It's not something I would mention to the Arbiter."

"Why not?"

"Let's see what he has to say first." Fynn tried to raise a smile, but sat quietly for a long moment. "Well, I was thinking of taking a stroll down to the seashore… perhaps I'll take a swim."

"Hmm, you might want to ask Clark about that."

"Why?"

"Doing some sort of experiments outside. Not sure it's safe today."

"Who are you talking about?"

"The Soviets…"

"So you won't be joining me?"

"My foot still hurts. And I'm wondering why I'm not dead or sick from anthrax."

"You might thank Sonny Ming for that."

"What?"

"One of the inoculations you were given before traveling to Russia."

"Oh… Clark tells me it's nineteen sixty-two— well, out there." I nodded to the desert. "How does that work?"

"You mean because we failed to stop Kali?"

"Yes."

"I've been wondering that myself," Fynn replied. "Though I am happy to hear our memories coincide."

"An alternate timeline?"

"Perhaps… I will admit the hotel can be disorientating. I'm not even sure what day it is."

"Saturday, according to Sebastian."

"I am wondering more about the month."

"I think he said September."

"Well, then this world is yet to end, I would say…Have you seen anyone this morning?" Fynn asked.

"The Arbiter, you mean? Not yet." I slurped down my coffee.

"It seems we've all been summoned again."
"What do you mean?"
"He's called for a meeting of minds."
"Do you think he's an AI?"
"A what?" Fynn asked.
"An artificial intelligence, a machine, like a computer."
"The Arbiter? Hmm, I suppose it is within the realm of possibility."

As I reached for some toast and jam, I heard a slight whirling noise from behind. I turned and the black-robed, hooded figure glided up to our table. He was wearing his usual porcelain mask— certainly a frightening sight in any other context. "Gentlemen…" the mechanical voice intoned, "I see you've returned of your own accord."

I looked over at Fynn.

"I thought you rescued us."

"Have I now? I can't think why… Oh yes, I must send you back to Hawaii again."

"Again?"

"You failed at your mission."

"But we fixed that."

"Did you? Well, that's good news." He paused. "Are you absolutely certain?"

"Yes," Fynn replied. "But things did not go as planned in Zvorkovo."

"A terrible mishap. An entire timeline virtually erased. Still, you did your best, I imagine…" The Arbiter hovered nearer to the table. "Another item for tomorrow's agenda."

"A question…"

"Yes, Mr Jardel?"

"Why didn't you just pluck us back?

"I cannot fetch someone from the future."

"This is the past, right now?"

"From my perspective, yes."

"So the world is still going to end next month?"

"Unless we can prevent it some other way."

"Could you fetch Kali?"

"Why would I want to?"

"Hypothetically."

"No. She is beyond my reach."

"And what about Chloe?"

"What about her?"

"Is she alright?"

The Arbiter paused to consider my question. "In what way do you mean, Mr Jardel?"

"She seems a little off— maybe a little forgetful."

"I'm afraid her memory is fraying at the edges. I blame myself, sending her on too many errands. She can remember people well enough, but events are vague and she hardly knows where she's gone, or when to return."

"And you're sure it wasn't Lilly Boole who has returned?" Fynn asked.

"Who do you mean?"

"The other If-Then sister," I said.

"I'm not aware that she was ever here."

I had another question: "Where's Geppetto and Mr Voynich?"

"Their task is complete. Mr Voynich has been returned to nineteen-oh-three. He remembers nothing."

"And Geppetto?"

"He was sent along to Sonny Ming's school, there to learn English."

"Oh... How did it go with the books?"

"Satisfactorily. Did you not receive the faxes?"

"The translations?" Fynn asked. "Not as of yet."

"You must speak to Clark then."

***

After breakfast I found someone buried behind a giant newspaper. The headline was in German, I guessed, though the reader could not be recognized. There was a great rustling and folding of paper. Doctor Zed looked up at me with a smile.

"How's the foot, Patrick? Have you been wiggling your toes?"

"Yes, and it's feeling better, thanks." I sat opposite. "Glad you made it back okay."

"So am I."

"What are you reading?"

"Oh, just catching up on the war."

"Which war?"
"The Great one."
"How's that going?"
"Depends who you're rooting for."
"I'm trying not to take sides."
"Well, I've just read an interesting story about Vladimir Lenin. Seems the German authorities have given him a special train through their territory. He's on his way to Finland now."
"Finland?"
"Oh, it's an article from nineteen seventeen. He's en route back to Russia to start the revolution."
"Are you saying we can thank the Germans for communism?"
"It would seem so…" Doctor Zed gave me a grin. "Perhaps that will be on the agenda?"
"What?"
"It seems we've all been summoned. A sort of council is scheduled for tomorrow."
"What day is it today?"
"Saturday."
"And what year?"
"I'm not entirely sure…"
"Neither am I."
"Well, I'm happy to say I've done my part already."
"What do you mean?"
"Oh, an errand for Mr Arbiter."
"And?"
"Nothing much. I had to travel to London and open a few petri dishes."
"When was this?"
"The summer of nineteen twenty-eight."

✶✶✶

Sometime later, I came across Lothar and Mortimer in the game room playing billiards. Not the same Lothar I had left in Sand City, and perhaps not the same Mortimer. The giant's head nearly brushed the low ceiling. He lumbered over with a greeting. "Thank you so much for thwarting Monsanto."

"What?"

"You and Mr Fynn… we can now live in a time where dandelions may flourish."

"Oh right, I remember now. I'm not sure that's happened yet… and it was mostly Fynn's doing."

"Well, I'm sure you'll set history along a better path."

"Ah, Patrick, there you are," Mortimer called out. "How goes the bricklaying?"

"I'm a full-fledged mason now."

"I see… Well, what say you to a game of tennis, eh?" He stared at my clothes with a smirk on his face.

"How's your backhand?"

"What?"

"The stab wound."

"Oh yes, still smarts a bit." Mortimer clutched his side and winced for a moment. "Thanks for asking though."

I tried to get a good look at his finger, to be sure it had a black tip, but didn't get a good view. Then I started to wonder if his eyepatch should be on the left side or the right. "Did you find your cane?" I asked.

"Yes… It's safely stowed away."

"And what happened to your eye?"

"Oh, a terrible mishap on the journey here."

"By the way, thanks for the note," I added.

"You're welcome."

That was hardly the reply I expected, but decided to say nothing more for now.

On my way back up to the lobby I found Clark struggling with the elevator. I helped him open the heavy iron door. He was carrying a tray of cucumber sandwiches in his lap. "Have you seen Pavel or Edmund by any chance?" I asked, and helped myself to a sandwich.

"I've seen them both. They're in the workshop."

"Where's that?"

"Next to the chickens."

"Chickens?"

"It's not safe for them outside. I herded them into a room on the lower level, next to the pool room."

"Billiards?"

"No."

"You mean the game room?"

"The next level down. *The Grotto*. We have an indoor pool, filled to the brim."

***

If anyone knew the gossip, it would be Pavel and Edmund. I took the stairs to the basement, a huge circular place that was probably the foundation for the dome at the center of the hotel. The walls gently curved out of sight. Across the corridor, I could see a shimmering reflection from the pool. It was illuminated with green and blue lights. I peeked in through the porthole windows. It reminded me of the planetarium at Saint Albans. Steam swirled off the water, but no one was swimming today.

I knocked on the door to the workshop and let myself in. It was filled with chickens, clucking and preening. I closed it hurriedly and tried the next door in line. It was a dingy place, ill-lit, except for the workbench. Neither Pavel Mekanos nor Edmund Fickster seemed the least bit surprised by my arrival, and greeted me warmly:

"There he is, the man of the hour," Mr Mekanos said and gave his double laugh.

"What?"

"It's just an expression, Patrick. How are you, my boy?" Edmund raised his goggles and shook my hand with some enthusiasm.

"What are you working on today?"

"Ah, something quite out of the ordinary. A new sort of communications device."

I looked on the bench and saw a thin rectangle about the size of a laptop. It had a closable lid but I could see no keyboard. It was just a smooth grey surface, almost glossy. "How does it work?"

"Ah, one takes a stylus and writes the message here," Pavel demonstrated by writing a few words.

"It's made of wet clay," I said.

"Yes it is," Edmund concurred. "We've used a design that harkens back to the Mycenaean era. A clay tablet in a box which can be written upon."

"Not exactly high-tech."

"Submerging it is an effective way of erasing the message. Good for keeping secrets."

"It's for the Arbiter," Pavel Mekanos went on. "He's traveling to a time where nothing works, nothing but analog devices."

"Why not?"

"Some sort of storm, I think he said."

"When is this?"

"Oh… not sure, a few hundred years from now."

"What do you have for the present?"

"I'm glad you asked. Here, we have a device for traveling through space but not time." He presented me with a round disk. It looked exactly like a poker chip.

"What does it do?"

"It is designed to allow one to travel in space, well east to west at least…"

"And a bit to the south or north," Edmund added, "depending on one's latitude and the earth's obliquity."

"How far does it take you?"

"About a quarter of a mile. It stops one parameter of inertia: the earth's rotation. Of course, you're not really moving at all, it's the earth spinning beneath your feet."

"Sounds dangerous."

"I suppose one has to look before he leaps, eh?"

"Ingenious… How does it work?"

"Let me demonstrate…" Pavel took the chip, flipped it into the air and caught it again.

"That's it? Nothing happened."

"Not within the confines of the hotel… You might try it outside though," Edmund offered.

"Do you have to jump or anything?"

"No, that would be rather dangerous. Works best if you're standing still."

"There is one drawback of course," Pavel cautioned.

"What's that?"

"It prevents you from traveling in time."
"Meaning?"
"If one has it on his person."
"Like in your pocket?"
"Exactly."
"Hmm... that is kind of a drawback."
"Well, I suppose the chip could be sequestered from proper time."
"How?"
"A bit of aluminum foil should do the trick."
"Like wrap it up?"
"Yes."
"Do you have any?"
"No— you might try the kitchen," Pavel suggested. "Take as many as you'd like. I have a whole pile over there…"
"How did you ever come up with this?"
"Geppetto gave me the idea… He has the extraordinary ability to do this without any trouble at all."
"Where is Geppetto?" I asked but knew what the Arbiter had told me.
"Oh, the Tower of Babel."
"Where?"
"Sonny Ming's school… I don't know why, his English was quite good already. He's an absolute wiz at languages."
"You've been to Sonny Ming's?"
"Seems like we're always there… something or another is always breaking down," Edmund added woefully.
"What about Mr Temsik? I ran into him the other day and he mentioned that he knows you."
"Öde?" they both asked in unison. "Well, we haven't seen him in ages," Pavel said further. "Why do you ask?"
"No reason… but he does say 'hello' to you both."
"He actually spoke to you?"
"Yes."
"What did he say?"
"More than I want to remember."
"Well, watch yourself around Öde, he's a tricky little man," Pavel said.

"Not to be trusted," Edmund concurred.

"Why not?"

"He's a bit of a gossip. Always has his nose in other people's business."

"Is he dangerous?"

"No, I wouldn't say that. He's good company and never brought us any harm." Mr Mekanos grinned from behind his mustache.

"A bit dispassionate, I've always thought. Holds himself above the fray," Edmund commented.

"Meaning?"

"A bit of a fatalist, I'd say."

"He mentioned something about a cube you gave him."

"Oh… that…" Mr Mekanos said as I sat next to him and Edmund. "One of my lesser inventions." Pavel brushed his mustache nervously.

"A miserable failure, you mean to say," Edmund taunted.

"The road to success is paved with failure, don't you know," Mr Mekanos replied and drew a small black cube from his pocket.

I noticed it was blank on all sides. "What does it do?"

"What was it intended to do, or what occurs?"

"Either or both."

"It was meant as a way to travel in the present. And in this regard it functions perfectly. Trouble is, it takes you to an entirely different present."

"How does it work?"

'Technically speaking?"

"No."

"Ah, the *Dice of Destiny*…" Edmund put in, and there was some sarcasm in his tone.

"I prefer calling it the *Cube of Parallels*. It takes you to one of six different timelines."

"One of six? I'm not sure I understand."

"Surely you've experienced such a thing before, eh?" Pavel asked. "Don't you see the phantoms?"

"Sometimes."

"Do you understand what they mean?"

"Well, I've been told they are people flitting through another present, like a parallel present."

"That's an accurate enough description, I suppose."

"And?"

"This device makes you into one of those phantoms."

"Why would I want to do that?"

"Well, traveling to a parallel reality is quite a common occurrence— meaning, every time you ever jump," Edmund pointed out.

"This keeps you in the present, always, but the closest parallel place," Pavel explained. "Given your extraordinary memory, you may be one of the few people who can appreciate it."

"Like slip sideways into a different present?"

"Exactly," Mr Mekanos replied with a double-laugh. "Technically it's a die, though no one likes the sound of that, so they are, or, it is, a dice."

"Like Einstein's?"

Edmund smiled. "Indeed, or like those of Brigadier Thomas."

"How does it operate?"

"You must touch all eight corners to activate it."

"How do you turn it off?"

"Off?"

"Deactivate it."

"Oh, I hadn't thought of that," Pavel said and ran a hand across his hairless head.

"Of course its shape is ironic," Edmund put in.

"Meaning?"

"You can't say exactly where it will take you, so it's just like rolling."

"Rolling?"

"Rolling the dice. First, find a flat surface… then shake the cube in your hand, and finally, let it fall and come to a stop."

"Then what?"

"When you pick it up again, you are in a different present."

"How different?"

"Hard to say," Pavel replied. "The device itself has no intelligence. It simply takes you to the nearest of six parallel tangents— those are dictated by the choices you've made… Some of those choices could be rather minor."

"So— it's like my own personal parallel timeline?"

"Indeed— that's not a bad way to look at it."

"How minor?" I persisted.

"Well, say you chose to have a bagel for breakfast. You might roll the dice and find a croissant on your plate instead."

"That doesn't sound so bad."

"He's leading you astray," Edmund spoke up.

Pavel gave his double laugh. "Admittedly, your own choices matter of course, but so do others."

"Such as?"

"Well, some timelines have such small differences that you might not even notice."

"Like?"

"Hmm… let me think of an example… Say, your favorite team might not have won the World Cup for instance… but everything else is largely the same."

"That's sort of comforting."

"Not if you follow soccer."

"Or if you're a football hooligan," Edmund muttered.

"Go ahead, try it," Pavel offered with a smile.

I took the dice, shook it in my palm and rolled. When I picked it up again there was a slight tingling in my hand. "Nothing happened," I said.

"Hasn't it?" Pavel asked and added a double laugh.

"You mean I'm in a different timeline right now?"

Pavel smiled. "Undoubtedly. You're in my timeline."

"But what's different?"

"Who can say?"

"It's not marked," I complained.

"What do you mean, Patrick?"

"Each side looks exactly the same… there's no way to keep track of where you are or where you've been."

"What are you suggesting?"

"Maybe paint each side with a number?"

"Oh, that's rather clever. I hadn't thought of that."

"When Mr Temsik showed me his, it had numbers on it, just like regular dice."

"Did it?" Mr Mekanos paused for a moment. "Hmm… I never knew where one would be starting from, so I thought numbers would be of no use."

Edmund snatched the cube and started over to the other workbench. "I have a paint brush and a steady hand… and, I like Patrick's idea."

"I haven't worked out all the kinks exactly." Mr Mekanos turned to me.

"What does that mean?"

"Well, the trouble is, the cube rarely takes you back to your original timeline."

"Make that *never* returns you," Edmund called out from the other workbench.

"Why not?"

"Because rolling the dice in the first place is a new choice that you've made."

"So there's no way to make it back to exactly where you left?"

"None. Infinite variations… finding one timeline in particular can be rather difficult."

"Easy to get lost?"

"How could you become lost? It's not really traveling at all, you merely slip between presents," Pavel replied in a huff.

"Lost, yes…" Edmund affirmed. "If you roll a dozen times, you're a dozen timelines away from where you began."

"So there's no going back?"

"That's it exactly. And why it's such a disastrous invention," Edmund concluded.

"What happens if I keep rolling a six, say?"

"It's a good question, but I have no answer for you. Maybe Öde Temsik knows."

"Most of the time you won't even notice what's changed," Mr Mekanos continued.

"Most of the time?"

"Well, a hard jump to a parallel timeline would be easy to recognize."

"So it's usually a soft jump?" I asked and laughed a bit nervously.

"If it's a hard jump, you'll know; but it's rare to end up in a timeline that you've never been to before."

"How rare?"

"You'd have to ask Öde about that. Of course such a jump might have disconcerting results."

"How so?"

"Well, say you're dead in a particular timeline and you go there... your friends and associates would be rather alarmed."

"To them, it might seem as if you've just appeared out of nowhere," Edmund clarified.

"So it's a soft jump."

"Calling it a replacement jump might be better."

"Why?"

"You replace the person in that timeline— so to speak."

"The cube comes with you, if that's what you're asking," Edmund added.

"Is it painful?"

"Not at all, you will only feel a slight tingling in your extremities."

"Does anyone else have one of these?"

"I'm firmly convinced that Carlos Santayana has... though he denies me giving him one."

"The paint's dry. Here, take it, if you'd like," Edmund offered.

"Thanks, but no... I don't feel like becoming a ghost."

"It's your choice." Pavel smiled.

"When did you invent this?"

"When was it? Hmm, do you recall, Edmund?"

"It was two hundred and fifty years, if it was a day."

"Yes, but two hundred and fifty years from now, or back in the past?"

"What day is it today?" Edmund asked in reply.

"Saturday."

***

Later that afternoon, I came upon Mr Quandary sitting alone except for a giant rhododendron bush beside him. He was upstairs in the Conservatory, which was an arboretum filled with plants and lit by a glass ceiling. There was a late-Victorian feel to the place. I saw his cape draped over a nearby chair that was also occupied by his top hat.

Mr Q was reading a book but put it in his pocket as I arrived. I'd never seen him looking quite so despondent, though he was smoking his pipe and sipping from a glass of wine.

"How's Mr Toad faring?" I asked and came over to sit next to him.

"Eh?" he asked, as he hadn't quite heard me.

"Here all by yourself?"

"Yes, Lothar is at home guarding the tower."

"Guarding?"

"Indeed. Haven't you spoken with the Arbiter?"

"Just briefly."

"It seems we're under attack… all the circles at least."

"Who's attacking?"

"Not a question you need ask, surely?"

"Kali…"

Mr Q nodded. "She's on a rampage."

"What's going on then?"

"All the places where time flows other than normal are being systematically destroyed."

"How?"

"The same in every case, nearly: explosives. The Bank in Amsterdam has been blown to bits. Mr Vanderhoot is beside himself."

"When was this?"

"Difficult to say. The bomb may have been placed in a safety deposit box at anytime during the last two hundred years. It was the corridor to the past that was destroyed."

"When did the explosion happen?"

"Twenty eighty-nine."

"What about rising sea levels, floods?"

"The least of his worries, I should say."

"And it's Kali doing this— you're certain?"

"That's the question, Mr Jardel. And perhaps only Tractus Fynn can answer it."

"What?"

"I am meaning in his investigative capacity."

"Oh… And the other places?"

"We've already lost the Library on the Palisades, as you know— a terrible fire. And the circle by the Hudson has ground to a halt."

"When?"

"Nineteen fifty-five."

"Brigadier Thomas was there, I'm pretty sure…"

"If he was, he failed to catch the saboteur." Mr Q paused to puff on his pipe. "Now I've just heard that Sonny Ming's School was utterly destroyed, and many people were injured."

"When was this?"

"A terrible gas main explosion, I'm not sure when."

"But I was just there learning Russian… a few days ago… sort of…" my voiced trailed off as I stopped to work it out.

"That you completed your language lesson is beside the point."

"There's a circle there?"

"Yes. In the basement."

"This is all relative though, right?"

"In what way?"

"These attacks have or haven't happened from the perspective of this present."

"This present?" Mr Quandary turned to me.

"Now… this moment."

"Hmm… Undoubtedly."

"You don't sound very sure."

"I won't say we are outside of time at the moment, but I will say time is in flux within the confines of the hotel."

"Clark says it's nineteen sixty-two outside."

"Does he? I doubt he's correct. Besides, it's the fact that these events occur at all is the terrible news."

"What about your place in the Cocos Islands?"

"It's safe for now. Lothar is there. I can think of no better deterrent."

"But I just saw him."

"Who?"

"Lothar."

"Where?"

"In the game room, playing pool with Mortimer."

"Are you certain?" Mr Quandary rose suddenly and with some anxiety.

***

I saw no one for the rest of the day and I can't say that was a bad thing. I felt weary, depleted and confused. I decided to take a nap in Chloe's room. She woke me with smiles and kisses in the early evening and brought along a tray with dinner. We chatted about this and that but she soon grew tired and fell asleep. After a few hours I returned to the lobby, now feeling a bit restless. Clark was on duty as always and I asked where the other guests were.

"Most are probably asleep. Mr Fynn is out on the veranda, having a nightcap."

"Is it safe outside?"

"Quite safe once the sun goes down and the winds pick up." He smiled. "Can I get you something?"

"A cold beer would be a real treat."

"I may have a few bottles of *Zhigulevskoye* somewhere."

"What?" I asked but then remembered the word. "Oh, Soviet beer."

"I can't promise it's cold though."

Fynn seemed to be waiting for me on the patio. I had a few questions about Mortimer:

"Well, no, something went awry. As you remember, he didn't return with Dr Zed and myself."

"But I saw him."

"Where?"

"Playing pool with Lothar."

"I wasn't aware he had arrived. Does he have his cane?"

"He says he does."

"And the mark on his finger?"

"I couldn't see very well. Maybe it rubbed off?"

"No, it's indelible."

"There's also this…" I showed Fynn the note.

"He gave you this?"

"No, Clark did. But why would Mortimer give it to me a second time?"

"Perhaps you can ask him."

"I'm thinking it's better that I don't."

"You are suspicious then?"

"Always."

"You're right to be wary, Patrick."

***

"Ah, Mr Jardel," Clark called out to me as I started back to my room.

"Chloe asked me to give you these." He patted a bundle that rested atop the counter.

"What are they?"

"Trunks, I think, and a towel. She's waiting for you at the Grotto." He gave me a wink. "She always likes to take a midnight swim."

I made my way down to the lower level again and could hear singing, echoing from a long way off. It was Chloe's beautiful voice. The song was familiar, just on the edge of recollection: *Blue moon... you saw me standing alone... Without a dream in my heart... Without a love of my own...*

I entered the pool room. Steam rolled off the water. It was spooky still, but on the other side I saw Chloe on the diving board. She gave me a friendly wave and then tucked a few strands of dark hair under her bathing cap. She took a step and sprung headfirst into the water. There was hardly a splash and she swam the entire length of the pool submerged. I watched her shimmering form until she surfaced right next to me. I gave her my hand and helped her over the ledge. She sat down beside me.

"Not afraid to jump, eh?"

Chloe laughed. "No, not inside the hotel at least." She took off her cap and a long tumble of dark hair followed.

chapter fourteen
meeting

We convened early the next morning in the hotel cafe. It opened up onto the marble lobby and west facing floor-to-ceiling windows. Sebastian Clark had pushed several tables together to make a larger one, and covered it with a cloth. Cheese had been laid out, and fresh fruit for anyone who wanted. Clark had also provided an extensive array of breakfast offerings: toast and jam, scrambled eggs, and sweet pastries, though coffee was in short supply. It seemed like a time travelers anonymous meeting.

"Good morning," the Arbiter greeted in his mechanical voice, "I trust you all slept well and without incident?"

"Incident?" Chloe asked.

"Unpleasant dreams or other interruptions."

Clark rolled by and complained in a whisper: "I do hope we'll finish things up by tomorrow."

"Why's that?" I asked.

"Monday night is the backgammon tournament."

The Arbiter sat at one end of the table, or rather hovered restlessly. At the other end, Mr Quandary, aka the Quantifier, had positioned himself. On the left side was Chloe; she sat between Fynn and I. Next to him was Doctor Zed. Facing us, was Mortimer, Edmund, Pavel and Clark. The giant Lothar sat slightly apart so that he might stretch out his legs.

I looked over at Mortimer. It was hard not to notice bandages on two of his fingers. I made a comment.

"Oh, an accident suffered while playing foosball with Lothar." Mortimer smiled and held up his hand. "Doctor Zed fixed me up in no time."

I turned to the doctor.

"Yes, there was a danger of infection. I swabbed the wound and gave it a proper bandage."

Once we had all settled, the Arbiter began with an announcement: "This morning we have but one topic of conversation: Kali."

"Who?" Edmund asked.

"Señorita Cero, Mistress Nihil, Mrs Nil, the Fair Lady Null… She goes by many names," the sad-faced giant clarified.

The Arbiter glided nearer to Lothar. "She may go by many names, but Kali is what she calls herself."

Mortimer began with a complaint: "All this historical hide and seek… It's little more than a game to her. She's probably greatly amused. I don't think Kali by whatever name sees us as a threat at all."

"Nor is she a threat, so long as we stay within the confines of the hotel," Clark replied.

"I'm not entirely convinced," Mr Quandary said while waving a jam laden knife like a baton.

"Why not?"

"It's like Fynn's party, all of us sitting at the table. Ten travelers gathered in one place… I wouldn't be surprised if we started dropping like flies."

"Yes, like the ten little indians," Lothar agreed.

"I think we are eleven," Clark observed. "But he's right, only ten travelers. It seems I never get to leave the lobby."

"If we might begin our meeting…" the Arbiter said in his inflectionless tone. He hovered up and down the length of the table, pausing by the pastry tray. "I have a strategy to stop Kali at her source, but I will say nothing more until my plans are ready."

"And yet this would be of great interest to everyone who has gathered," Mortimer protested.

The Arbiter glided over to loom above him. "It is not a topic of discussion this morning."

"Why not?"

"I have not completed the preparations as of yet."

"I'm forced to agree with Mortimer," Mr Q spoke up. "Following Kali through history and repairing the damage she does hardly seems like a good use of my time," he said. "The thing is, we have to put a stop to her meddling in the first place."

"It's quite simple, if you ask me," Mortimer persisted. "We banish her to the Flatlands."

"What?" I asked.

"She'll never escape and she'll never bother anyone again. She'll be trapped in nineteen sixty-four."

"I escaped," I pointed out and took a sip of coffee.

"That was a fluke." Mortimer glared at me.

"Fynn escaped, Edmund too… Geppetto doesn't live there anymore— and he has a tongue."

"The boy makes a valid point," Edmund said.

"We will accomplish little if we descend into such an argument," the Arbiter intervened. "We have other questions to ask, other tasks to consider."

"Such as?"

"Kali's intent is our most important topic. From this everything follows."

"Utter nonsense," Mr Q scoffed. "We need only be resolved to save the circles from Lady Null's destructive wrath."

"Are we positive this is her doing?"

"It's Kali, surely."

"I don't believe so… Not directly." Fynn stirred his tea and looked up at the rest of us.

"What are you saying, man?"

"I will agree it's her intent, but wouldn't Mr Vanderhoot recognize her if she walked into his bank. Similarly, Mr Ming, at the school? I doubt Madeline or Brigadier Thomas would allow her into the library."

"Maybe she wore a disguise," Chloe suggested while munching on a pastry.

"A possibility, I suppose." Fynn nodded, then turned to the Arbiter. "Do I not have your assurance that they've all been warned?"

"They do view Kali as a danger." He hovered nearer. "But there is something in what you say, Policeman Fynn. It may be someone acting on her behalf."

"So, our saboteur might not be a traveler?" I asked.

"I won't go so far as to say that." Fynn turned to me. "Only another traveler would know about these places or have a way to gain access… Who would be permitted into the bank or the library with impunity? Certainly someone familiar to us all."

"A traitor among us?"

All eyes turned to Mortimer.

"I readily admit some of my lesser selves may have been collaborating, despite my ardent cautioning against it. But that excludes me personally— Tractus will vouch for that."

"You were helpful in Zvorkovo, regardless of the outcome, and I thank you," Fynn replied.

"You see?" Mortimer spread his thin smile across the room. "And not that I keep close tabs on them, but several of my other selves have already disappeared."

"How many?"

"Six currently, by my count."

"I keep track of them as well," the Arbiter said dully. "I'm not always sure which is which, but there were eight Mortimers in total. Six of them have died by my reckoning."

"How tragic indeed…" Mortimer gave a sigh. "Might there be others?"

"Others?"

"Accomplices."

"Everyone present is beyond reproach," the Arbiter declared and glided back to the head of the table.

"Can we be sure?" Doctor Zed reached for a handful of grapes. "Kali has a way of manipulating people that is difficult for us to understand. I think anyone might be susceptible."

"I disagree. Her machinations may work on an unsuspecting person, but it is more difficult to influence a traveler," Fynn observed.

"Why is that?"

"They know better than to linger and are able to jump away from her grasp."

"Even so…"

"It's best if we begin with the process of elimination," Fynn continued. "If we ask who Kali's accomplices cannot be, our list gets considerably smaller."

"We might start with who has already perished," Mortimer said. "Or is about to…"

Fynn turned to him. "I take your point, but it is not something we can exactly rely upon."

"Why not?"

"I myself have returned from the dead with Patrick's help. And if you recall, she attempted to kill all the travelers at my birthday party with a large bomb."

"Perhaps you might compile a list of guests?" the doctor suggested.

"There are others as well… I saw Mr Sato die in nineteen-oh-three, and yet he seems to have been resurrected in recent days," Fynn responded.

"Oh yes, Hideki Sato…" Mr Quandary looked through his notes. "I have his dossier… A horticulturist, some expertise in geology… and it seems he has a penchant for baseball…" Mr Q paused. "He resurfaced off the coast of Smyrna in nineteen twenty-two."

"What was he doing there?"

"Aboard a Japanese ship, saving Greek refugees from the Turks… Since then, he hasn't left his own islands."

"What islands?" I asked.

"Japan," Mr Q replied. "And who else was aboard the *Carpathia?*"

"Our friend Stanley was there…"

"Yes, I remember, a patient of mine, but he made a full recovery. What's become of him?" Doctor Zed turned to Fynn with a smile.

"Died in July nineteen ninety-nine… his airplane went down in the Atlantic," Mr Q reported.

"But he was at Fynn's party almost twenty years later," I said.

"Yes, he was recently killed."

"After the party?"

"No, before. A case of encapsulated causality. His future was altered, but your memories remain intact."

"I don't quite understand this." I went to take a sip of coffee but my cup was already empty.

"Our perspective is different from yours. To the Arbiter and I, all these events have occurred in the distant past."

"How about Myra Hatchet?" I asked.

"Oh, she's very much alive, living in Amsterdam with husband number nine."

"Also killed in nineteen-oh-three was Herr Hinkley Martin, the German Professor aboard the *Carpathia*," the doctor pointed out.

"Irrelevant to the situation. I'm quite sure he has not been resurrected," the Arbiter said.

"I have observed Kali enjoys killing people simply for sport," Mortimer remarked.

"Sport?"

"For the fun of it."

"That's an odd definition of fun, is it not?"

"She might extinguish a life as easily as she blows out a candle." Mortimer took a piece of toast and scraped some butter on it.

"We are all at risk. Kali will kill any traveler on sight," Lothar cautioned. "We've already lost a few dear friends…"

"Like?" I asked.

"Well, Sheik Abbas is no longer with us. Burned alive in a refinery accident, along with half of Yemen."

"It's true what he says," Pavel spoke up, and in an upset tone. "And now Brigadier Thomas is dead."

"What?"

"Killed in the Crimea War… Usually though, he isn't."

Edmund was nodding.

"What about Madame Madeline? Is she alright?"

"Oh, she's in a dreadful state, a withered old woman wandering the streets of Paris."

"What happened?"

"She went traipsing off to the past to try and save her brother— but to no avail. She returned, but as I've said, she's now in a terrible state."

Edmund agreed, "A sad and convoluted story. She's stuck on this side of the Atlantic. Tried to—"

"Anyone else?" the Arbiter interrupted.

"Tragically, Queen Zalika has been erased, or will be," Mr Q reported.

"How do you mean?"

"The timeline she occupies has flatlined more or less."

"The one without coffee?" I asked.

"Yes."

"And sadly, Doctor Zed has been murdered."

"But I have not been. I am sitting right here."

"Lilly Boole has also been killed," Mr Q continued, ignoring him.

"Mistaken for me," Chloe added.

"Yes, your poor sister," Mortimer said.

"I don't miss her at all."

"What happened?" I asked. "How was Lilly killed?"

"Oh, shot by that tedious Drummond woman and dumped into an Amsterdam canal." Mortimer turned to me.

"What about her, Drummond's daughter?"

"I can assure you, Patrick, she is quite dead."

"Anyone else?" Chloe asked.

"Well, Carlos has not been heard of in ages," Lothar replied to her, then went back to his mountain of scrambled eggs.

"Carlos? Mr Santayana?" I asked.

"Yes…"

"Have you checked his Viking Empire? He may be—"

"Mr Santayana's whereabouts are irrelevant at the moment," the Arbiter interrupted in his mechanical voice.

"Is it? He might be a great help to us," Pavel said.

"Yes, what about Carlos' world?" Edmund echoed.

"It seems intact, but it is quite far from here, almost to say inaccessible."

"And what's the difference between what Kali is doing and Carlos?" Mortimer asked. "They are both creating history by design."

"What are you trying to say?" Mr Q shifted in his seat.

"I'm thinking of Kali as a thief, stealing bits from here and there, as if she wanted to build her own world. This is exactly what Mr Santayana does."

"Carlos is expanding timelines. Kali is contracting them, or worse," Fynn observed.

"But surely there is a comparison here…"

"All this tinkering with history," Mr Q said with contempt. "No good will come of it."

Lothar seemed to disagree. "I suppose in the end Carlos does us a great favor, establishing alternate timelines, should we need to flee to them."

"It comes down to a very basic question: What does Kali want?" I looked around at the others.

Edmund came to my defense. "I agree with the lad. There's no sense in tip-toeing around the issue."

"Oh, it's all just a harmless game to her," Mortimer remarked.

"You think so?" I was astonished. An awkward silence filled the room. "Well… I'm still not clear on her ultimate goal."

"Nor I," Fynn admitted. "What is her intent? The larger picture, the thing under the surface which we cannot see— What binds all her actions— eh?"

"In a word, I would say *funneling*," Mr Q stated and reached across the table for a ripe banana.

"In what way?"

"Some timelines she makes defunct, uninhabitable. Others she means to bring under her control. If she is successful at eliminating timelines one by one, all that will be left is the place she's chosen."

"Three of us here, myself, Mr Q and Chloe have a unique insight into that. We've all lived in her world." They both nodded, remembering the future and Siren City. "She's all about control."

"Paradoxically, for all her reverence for the present, she seems unduly anxious about the future," Mr Q commented.

"What do you mean?" Mortimer asked.

"Should it turn out differently or unpredictably— this is what worries her. She seems only to want stability and routine. The present must be continuous."

"I also have lived in her world and I concur," the Arbiter remarked.

"She must be constrained in some way," I said.

"In what way?"

"In her actions, I mean. For instance, she can't do anything so dramatic so as to wipe out her own future. You know, like stop science from existing."

"I understand what you're saying, but it isn't so," the Arbiter considered. "Even if her future is erased by some unknown dark age, it wouldn't matter. She has already left that place. She does not exist there, nor will she again. She is here in this present. It is all..."

I heard something else other than the conversation. I stopped to listen to the background noise. A sort of creaking came to my ears. "Does anyone else hear that?" I asked. The room fell silent for a moment and it became obvious now, the sound of a winch and scraping metal.

"Someone is using the lift!" Clark called out and wheeled himself in that direction. We rose separately and followed him across lobby, the Arbiter glided past us all. The elevator was descending from some upper floor.

"Is anyone else here?" Fynn asked.

"No, everyone is accounted for," Clark replied.

"No unwanted guests?"

"None."

The elevator came to rest on the main floor. The door slid open automatically, and the iron grate behind it, yet no one appeared. The Arbiter hovered closer to inspect the scene.

"An invisible ghost?" I asked.

"A visitor, I shall say. But one whom we cannot perceive in the present."

"Has that ever happened before?"

"No."

"Should we be worried?"

"If we cannot discern the visitor, it's likely they cannot see us either."

"Are all the keys accounted for?" Fynn asked.

"All but one," Clark answered.

"Which one?"

"Sixteen."

"Whose room is it?"

"No one's, it's vacant."

"As a precaution, I suggest we all turn in our keys," the Arbiter said. "It would be a great disaster if Kali infiltrates our group, or gains access to Pavel's workshop."

"Can we even be sure this has not happened?"

"I can be sure," Clark replied and glared at the doctor. "She has not set foot in the lobby."

***

When we reconvened it was almost lunchtime. Clark returned carrying a tray of little sandwiches, all with the crusts cut off.

"It is clear that Kali wants to end history as we know it," the Arbiter began again. "Her perfect world would be a place where nothing changes. The timelines she cannot destroy, she will seek to control."

"Perhaps she's doing us a favor… When has history been anything but brutal, violent, and chaotic?" Mortimer posed the question.

"Are you agreeing with her aims?" Fynn asked.

"No. I am saying the allure of order, calm and peacefulness is very powerful indeed."

"No matter how it is enforced?"

"There are a variety of ways to control the world, some more successful than others… Which she chooses probably has to do with expedience."

"For example?"

"Well, a strongly religious society might be easier for her, one with little science, little education. A population that's docile, compliant to her wishes, one might say." Mortimer smiled.

"And why would she want that?"

"In the end she wants her world to be static— a place where only the present can be experienced," the Arbiter answered instead.

"It might be she's just trying things out to see what sticks… There might not be any real plan at all."

"Patrick makes a good point," Fynn agreed. "I don't necessarily see any consistency in her plans, no grand stratagem is discernible. She may be hop-scotching about, trying this and that, to see what suits her liking."

"It's more than obvious that she's bent on destroying the circles," Mr Q said.

"Okay, but that's not what I mean. My question is why is she changing history." I turned to him. "What's she after?"

"It seems to me, she wants to erase all the other parallel timelines," Lothar said.

"But aren't they infinite?"

"There are infinite variations but a limited number of outcomes," the Arbiter responded.

"How so?"

"Random fluctuations tend to follow a larger direction," he explained further. "There are fewer than ten major branches remaining. A healthy history has dozens, if not hundreds of such branches."

"She's been consistent in one regard… all the changes we are noticing seem to be within the last few hundred years. She hasn't gone back to the distant past as far as I can tell," Mortimer said and reached over for a sandwich.

"Can you be sure though?" Mr Quandary asked. "Can you say she hasn't meddled with the distant past? The records are spotty at best… and our own experiences of these events is highly localized, I would say."

"What do you mean?"

"Many of us here may have lived through those times, but we did not see the broad sweep of history until much later. We were more often than not immersed in our own affairs."

"I have to agree with Mr Quandary," Fynn said. "One might guess

Kali is responsible for burning down the library at Alexandria. That certainly threw progress back several hundred years."

"We've established that was Mortimer's doing— have we not?" the Arbiter said.

"I don't remember being there," Mortimer put up a half-hearted defense.

The Arbiter hovered nearer. "It's impossible to discern all the things Kali may or may not have done. Indeed, the things we take for granted in this particular timeline might be her doing."

"Where is Kali now, at present?" I asked.

"A difficult question to answer. Which present do you mean, Mr Jardel?"

"Oh… the early twenty-first century."

"Rather shadowy. Enormously wealthy," Mr Q reported. "Has her hand in many industries: television, newspapers, and the internet… On the board of several large corporations… pharmaceutical, construction, mining firms."

"Mining?" I asked.

"Yes… in China, Australia, India and Brazil."

"What do they mine?"

"I don't know," Mr Q replied then looked down at his notes again. "Seems she also does quite a lot of charity work.

"Charity, really?"

"Contributes staggering sums to various religious groups across the world. Nor is she very discriminating it would seem. That is to say, she doesn't favor any deity in particular. Vast monies funneled to evangelical groups, muslims, or anyone else who comes with their hand out."

"Anyone with a radical agenda?"

"There might be something in what you say."

"And that brings us to the second item on our agenda," the Arbiter spoke up. "Why is she meddling with history as of late?"

"Can you be sure she is?" Mortimer asked.

"Yes."

"How?"

"Mr Quandary and I have compiled some lists."

"What sort of lists?"

"I've made two: the improbable and the inevitable," Mr Q replied. "I fear there's little we can do about the latter. Some things cannot be fixed. They are too complicated, a chain of causality which cannot be stopped by a single action."

"These are events we cannot influence, but they are also events beyond the reach of Kali," the Arbiter concurred.

"Perhaps we should consider these things nonetheless," Lothar cautioned.

"Railing against the inevitable? It would be no more effective than beating the ocean with a stick to stop it from making waves," Mortimer scoffed. "The futility of it all…"

"What do you mean, inevitable?" I asked.

"Well, for example, the proliferation of plastic was inevitable no matter who discovered it accidentally."

"What else?" I persisted.

Mr Q paused to consider further. "I suppose every vehicle that has been mechanized was also inevitable: carriages, bicycles, boats, airplanes and alike."

"What about in a cultural sense?"

"What do you mean?"

"Oh, like slavery… poverty, injustice…"

"Ah, those are much larger questions, Mr Jardel."

"I meant in terms of Kali's interference."

Mr Q turned to me with a smile. "I see what you're saying… such as all the money pouring into religious groups as of late. It can be traced directly to Kali, but there is little we can do short of eliminating her in the first place."

"Why would she do that?"

"Religious wars throughout the ages have proved divisive and violent. There's no better way to make one group oppose another."

"A divide and conquer kind of thing?"

"Yes, coupled with distraction, and the fact that zealous faith is an extremely good motivator."

"Yes, well, we'll get to that," the Arbiter said and almost seemed impatient, if such was possible in his mechanical monotone. He passed out the list of timelines with an arm-like appendage.

I had seen these before. The pages were filled with crazy lines zig-zagging from left to right. Each was marked with an alpha-numeric identification. "You drew these by hand? I expected some kind of sci-fi computer hologram."

"When they were made the only devices that operated were analog. A storm has wiped out humankind's technology."

"What kind of storm?"

"From the sun," he replied and glided back to the head of the table. "I'll turn this over to Mr Quandary."

"Thank you, yes. I've had access to the Arbiter's records, some of them at least, and I've come up with a list of half a dozen anomalies which require minor repair, if history is to stay on track. These events are correlated to direct evidence of Kali's involvement, or, her likely interest thereof…"

"That implies she has an intent," the doctor protested.

"She most certainly does…" Mr Q looked around the room. "I've had better luck with the improbable… focusing on timelines closest to the present and those with the high probability of occurring. Those in the distant past have been made largely inaccessible."

"Why is that?"

"They are now branches which are difficult to access by any means."

"How about an excursion from one of the rooms?" Clark suggested.

"If I might begin," Mr Q said. "There is of course the Pearl Harbor incident…"

"But I have Fynn's assurance this has been rectified," the Arbiter commented.

"Fixed, yes, but even though Fynn and Patrick saved the timeline in Hawaii, a tangent was created and it's competing rather strongly with this current, familiar one."

"What?"

"In terms of probability. The alternate World War Two timeline is changing from unlikely to inevitable."

"It's an utter waste of time. None of this does any good unless Kali is dead in the first place," Mortimer said abruptly. "She'll simply go back and undo what we've done, or re-do what we've undone."

"He makes a valid point," the doctor said. "The failure of Zvorkovo is a perfect example."

"Is there a remedy?" Chloe asked.

"No. It simply re-affirms what I've thought all along. Kali must be eliminated at the source," the Arbiter replied.

"And you have a plan for that?" Mortimer questioned.

"I do, but I will not discuss it today."

"There's also the missing cane. Kali may have taken it," I pointed out.

"Why did you not mention this?" Mr Q turned to me.

"I just did."

"I don't think Kali has any interest in the cane. She called it a blunt instrument, if I recall," the Arbiter dismissed my concern.

"Such may be true, but she does have an interest in doppelgängers; creating them, I should say," Fynn added.

"Hasn't Pavel fixed the cane?"

"Not that one."

"Such would be a disastrous outcome, though it might explain why we have failed to clearly understand her motives," Mr Q said.

"Why?"

"If there is more than one Kali, each may have a different intention."

"Where is your cane?" Fynn turned to Mortimer as did everyone else in the room.

"Safely hidden, I assure you all," he responded and gave us a thin smile.

"Kali already took it from you once," Fynn persisted.

"Yes, well let us not dwell on our failures." Mortimer replied but fell silent for a time.

Mr Quandary broke the silence, "I think it's easiest if we check off the things already accomplished, or will be." He shuffled through his papers. "First, thanks to Doctor Zed for fixing penicillin."

"Fixing?" I asked.

"Seeing to it that it was discovered."

"You're most welcome, and of course it was a great pleasure."

"Wait, Kali tried to stop antibiotics?"

"We cannot be sure of course, but better safe than sorry." He paused. "If I may continue…" Mr Q smiled politely. "There was also the matter of the two brothers from the bicycle shop."

"What two brothers?"

"I've forgotten their names, but Lothar and I remedied all that."

"How?"

"Well, in the end, Lothar gave their contraption a good push and it took to the air."

The giant was grinning from across the table.

"When was this?"

"Nineteen-oh-three," Mr Q replied and looked to his notes again. "Next on the list is Clair Cameron Patterson."

"Who?"

"He was the first to notice tetraethyl-lead in the atmosphere which had been building up since the nineteen twenties."

"Well, that's a good thing."

"Yes. Trouble is, he was killed before the discovery was publicized in nineteen sixty-five."

"How?"

"Gunned down by a so-called campus shooter."

"Where?"

"California."

"And?"

"Well, by the turn of the twenty-first century, lead concentrations had reached dangerous levels."

"How so?" Fynn asked.

"In the atmosphere, in the water supply, and the food chain itself. It affects urban dwellers most of all, and the Western world. Fertility rates fall dramatically..." Mr Q glanced down at the page. "It became statistically significant by the year nineteen eighty, as evidenced by the decision to—"

"But it begs the question," Mortimer interrupted. "Even if it's not remedied, you're saying that from the nineteen twenties to the nineteen sixties there is a whole generation of people exposed to such."

"You'll have to excuse them, all those people breathing in toxic fumes— it certainly affected their intelligence."

"The baby-boomers," I commented.

"Is that what you call them?" Mortimer asked. "A generation of idiots..."

"Let's call them impaired."

"Well, in any case, the timeline falls to nothing by twenty-fifty," Mr Q continued.

"Falls to nothing?"

"No sign of any coherent civilization."

"Patrick and I will take on this task," Fynn volunteered as he gave me a smile and a nod. It seemed to me we had already accomplished this, or would, though admittedly my recollection was vague.

"Next up is Percy Shaw in nineteen thirty-four," Mr Q said, glancing down at his notes.

"The guy who invented road-reflectors?" I asked.

"The very man."

"Already taken care of…"

"What? By whom?" the Arbiter questioned.

"Mr Temsik."

Fynn nodded in agreement. "Why does this affect history so greatly?"

"Well, aside from the millions of lives saved, apparently some of them were notable personages who seemed to have an impact on things. I have a list somewhere—"

"Who is Mr Temsik?" the Arbiter interrupted.

"Öde…" I replied. "Fynn and I met him in Sand City."

"What was he doing?"

"Working as a waiter. He says he knows you… umm, just about everyone here…" I looked around the table and saw a few nods, as well as furtive glances.

"Perhaps he goes by another name?"

"A short guy, pudgy, thick accent, sometimes wears a red fez and a pinstripe suit."

"He is not at all familiar to me."

"He may have shaved his mustache."

"And he claims to know me?"

"He said something like that."

"Perhaps this is a topic best left for later," the Arbiter intoned mechanically and hovered back to the head of the table.

"He might be able to help."

"It seems he already has."

"What happens if that timeline is not fixed?" the doctor asked.

"It ends abruptly in twenty-one twenty-nine."

"The cause?"

"World War Five."

"Clearly, we will need to enlist more help," Mortimer spoke up and his comment surprised me.

"Like?"

"We need to resurrect the Drummond family."

"What?" I asked, astonished.

"Drummond was most skilled. If you remember, he created a prodigious number of duplicates." Mortimer turned to Fynn. "When was it exactly that you went back to erase Drummond?"

"He wasn't erased," Fynn replied. "We simply stopped him from doubling in the first place."

"Yes, but we might have to undo this. We should enlist this army of Drummonds to battle against Kali."

"How could that possibly be a good idea?" I asked.

"He had an excellent network in the Americas. It could be of use to us." Mortimer gave me a thin smile. "As a last resort, you understand."

"And what of an army of Drummonds doing Kali's bidding. That's not an alliance I would like to witness," Fynn grumbled.

The was a long silence broken by Mr Q again: "Last on our list is the introduction of Sweet Water in twenty twenty-one."

"Sweet water?" I asked.

"Something is lost in the translation. We might say *Savory Water* instead. The Japanese word is *umami*."

"What is it exactly?"

"Seems rather innocuous: ordinary water flavored with a few drops of honey, monosodium glutamate, and various plant extracts."

"What makes it such a danger then?"

"Ah… well, it's attractively priced and becomes alarmingly popular. By twenty twenty-five, more than six hundred billion bottles of *Sweet Water* had been consumed worldwide."

"And?"

"And, as you can see by the chart, that particular timeline fizzles out to nothing a few years later."

"Is it carbonated?" Doctor Zed asked.

"Not that I'm aware."

"A poison of some kind?" Fynn questioned.

"Not in the strict sense of the word… Though surely it merits investigation, eh?"

I turned to Mr Q. "Who invented this drink?"

"Not a question you need ask, eh?"

"If Patrick is with me, I will take this on. We will travel together and speak with Mr Sato," Fynn volunteered.

"Mr Sato?"

"He seems to be intimately involved with Kali."

"In what way?"

"They are both on the board of directors of the same pharmaceuticals company—"

Our conversation was interrupted when Chloe cried out, "Look..." She pointed outside and we could all see a dark figure approaching. At first I thought it might be a Soviet soldier here to play backgammon, but he was fully robed in black. We watched as he trudged up the steps towards the lobby door. Clark wheeled himself to reception, hoping to lock the main entrance before the intruder could enter. I heard a sharp click. But he was too late.

The man had already strode into the lobby. He wore a turban and scarf that covered everything but his eyes. He then doubled-over, coughing and sputtering. The air outside had taken its toll. He finally caught his breath and stood upright, and began to unwrap the vast swath of fabric from his face. It was Mortimer... another Mortimer.

All eyes turned to the one sitting next to us, his expression was unreadable except for a thin smile.

"He is an impostor," the newly arrived man called out and pointed an accusing finger. I immediately saw it was tipped with black ink. Fynn noticed as well.

"No sir, it is you who are the impostor— indeed, if such a word even applies," the seated man countered.

The other Mortimer dropped his robes to the floor and leapt across the table. Dishes clattered everywhere. "Where is my cane?" he demanded, and seized the other by the throat. "Even though Kali has resurrected you, comrade, I've killed you once, and I will again."

"*Do smerti!*" the other Mortimer shouted in Russian, and the two doppelgängers were upon each other trading blows. One threw the other to the floor and was kicking him savagely in the side. He had the clear advantage, as he had not been stabbed. I sought to intervene, but Fynn held me back. Lothar and the Arbiter also had the same idea, but both men were already back on their feet staring each other down.

One Mortimer fled, though his only means of escape was the revolving door. He leapt through and disappeared. The other Mortimer hesitated and turned to give us all a smile. "Wait not for me, though I vow to return." He bowed graciously then followed himself through the doors, and into oblivion.

"Where have they gone?" I asked

Clark shrugged. "It's hard to say for certain, though quite far from here."

chapter fifteen
saving circles

About an hour after Mortimer's sudden arrival and subsequent departure, Clark laid out tea and biscuits. From the floor-to-ceiling windows, I could see the sun beginning to settle just above the horizon.

"We may now turn to our most pressing concern," the Arbiter began and glided nearer the table.

"What's that?"

"The systematic destruction of the circles."

I glanced over at Mr Quandary. He had already mentioned this several times. "What's the plan?"

"Simply, we must find the person responsible for these deeds and put a stop to them."

"Foremost on my mind is the culprit," Fynn concurred.

"Surely it's Mortimer working on behalf of Kali," Mr Q said. "We must fix things at the library, the bank, Sonny Ming's, my own tower… and the hotel."

"The hotel?" Clark asked.

"They will seek to destroy us here, no doubt."

"Haven't we eliminated Mortimer as a threat?"

"He was more of a spy. I don't believe he had it in mind to set fire to the lobby," Fynn responded and glanced over to Clark.

"Nor would Kali," I said. "I don't think any of her special powers work inside a place where time flows out of the ordinary."

"Your thoughts, Mr Jardel?" the Arbiter asked.

"She would have to do it old school."

"Meaning?"

"Some conventional way."

"Or it is not Kali at all," Fynn said.

"So who then?"

"We have no evidence as of yet… though leaving aside who our perpetrator might be, we are left with a similar *modus operandi*."

"To that I will agree," Mr Q said and continued, "All the associated buildings were blown up with an incendiary device of some kind. A fire at the library, an explosion at the bank, at Sonny Ming's school, and reports of smoke pouring from my tower."

"What about here, the Circles of Null?" I asked.

"They are currently in a state of disrepair, buried under a great mound of sand. I doubt they hold any interest to Kali," the Arbiter said. "Besides, they are well guarded by the Soviets."

"The Soviets?"

"Inadvertently. Few can survive the toxic wasteland they have created outside."

"How about the magnetic circle in Mongolia?"

"Which do you mean, Patrick?" Lothar turned to me.

"The one that draws you in if you get too close, geographically speaking."

"I'm not sure that qualifies as a circle, more of a nuisance than anything," Mr Q replied instead. "Besides, I think it's on the border of Kazakhstan."

"Does Sand City have a circle?"

"Where?"

"Where I live."

"Not that I know of. It's just a very convenient place to jump from."

"I remember seeing some carvings there, glyphs…"

"When was this?" The Arbiter hovered closer.

"Hmm… had to be the future, the distant future."

"And?"

"My recollection is very dim, sorry."

"There are also the standing stones in Caledonia," Chloe spoke up. "My sister Lilly and I spent some time there."

"An anomaly at best…" the Arbiter considered.

"What kind of anomaly?" I asked.

"It is a place where the present cannot exist."

"Not a place Kali would be interested in?"

"It's doubtful."

"I'm just thinking out loud, but there are probably other circles that we don't even know about."

Lothar caught my eye and nodded in agreement. "But where are they?"

"I don't know, but it seems likely— right?"

"If none of us know about them, then we might guess neither does Kali," Mr Q remarked.

"Any other weird explosions in the world? Suspicious fires?" I asked at large.

"Such is too long a list to make sense of…" the Arbiter replied. "We will first turn our attention to Madame Madeline's Library along the Palisades. We have two problems: the fire, and the circle grinding to a halt."

"There's little we can do about the circle. The *Temple*, as you call it, fell prey to vandals. I don't believe it was Kali's doing. This event shows up in a large number of timelines," Mr Q explained. "Though surely, they can be warned in advance of the fire."

"Yes. The question is whom do we send to notify them. Any volunteers?" the Arbiter hovered across the floor. "Chloe?"

"I'm not sure Madeline and I are on speaking terms," she replied softly. "And I mostly blame my sister Lilly for that."

"I for one have never been to America and relish the opportunity," Doctor Zed spoke up with enthusiasm.

"We need someone who already has a concurrency there," the Arbiter said and drifted in my direction.

"I'm not sure I want to take that risk," I said. "And neither should

Fynn, or for that matter, Mr Q."

"I can appreciate this is a delicate timeline for the three of you. And I will not attempt to alter it more than necessary. However, the library must be saved."

"Won't that just change everything?" I blurted out with frustration. "Especially American history, saving FDR and all."

"But this has already occurred, Mr Jardel. There's no need to worry. Any changes we might make will be after the fact. That bit of history will remain largely intact." The Arbiter loomed above me.

It was a relief to hear, though I wasn't sure I believed him. "What about Sonny Ming?" I asked. "He was definitely there at the library."

"He has a different task."

"Which is?"

"His School of Language suffers a terrible destruction and Mr Ming has been asked to prevent such."

"What happened exactly?"

"The authorities report an explosion due to a faulty gas main. As a precaution, Sonny Ming is going green," Mr Q explained.

"What?"

"He's switching to a windmill, a turbine."

"Might be tough to get zoning for that," I said.

"Solar panels on the roof then?"

"We will rely on Mr Ming's competence. I'm sure he'll think of something," the Arbiter concluded.

"Yes, well, back to the library... Why not fetch Madeline or the Brigadier? Either of them seem the logical choice," Mr Q said.

"Since they spend so little time outside the library in proper time, they are difficult to extract," the Arbiter replied.

"Edmund was there, I remember," Fynn pointed out.

"Was I?"

"Absolutely."

"Well, Mr Fickster, what do you say? Will you volunteer?" The Arbiter glided over to him.

"I suppose…"

"I can send you there easily enough."

"Can you?" Edmund asked with a bit of trepidation.

"Yes. Tell me exactly where you were before you entered the

building."

"The front door."

"And before that?"

"It's difficult to remember… I was looking for Pavel, I think… Oh, yes… I took a long hike along the cliffs. They were building some sort of bridge nearby."

"And when did you leave the confines of the library?"

"Not sure about that either." Edmund paused to remember. "I think it was when Mr Drummond kidnapped me and brought me to Sand City."

"Drummond?" I asked.

"I believe so."

"It was Thursday, the ninth of February. I remember the date of the fire quite clearly," Mr Q spoke up.

"It's decided then," the Arbiter announced and raised an appendage-like arm. I heard a soft whirring, like an engine warming up. In the following moment, Edmund blinked from the present.

***

When Mr Fickster returned some minutes later, he was wearing his goggles and holding a screwdriver. He gave us all an embarrassed smile. "Sorry for the delay, I was asked to repair the clocks…"

"What have you learned?"

"Well, it was a simple matter. Brigadier Thomas seized everyone's matchsticks and cigarette lighters. He forbade smoking and turned the stove off in the kitchen. We sat in the dark and ate cold food for two weeks straight."

"That's it?"

"Yes, no fire."

"It's a relief, certainly, but we still have no idea who Kali's accomplice may have been," Fynn said. "Did you see her there?"

"Who?"

"Kali Shunya."

"No."

"Anyone else you didn't recognize?"

"Well, there was that Raj Ashoka chap, seemed nice enough until he fell off the balcony and turned to dust."

***

"Let us consider the bank in Amsterdam. Who should we assign to remedy this disaster?" the Arbiter asked.

"What disaster?" Chloe looked up at him. "Another robbery?"

"Not this time… something worse," Clark explained in a near whisper.

"Can you not just pluck Mr Vanderhoot here?" the doctor asked.

"No. He rarely leaves his office. I can't remember the last time he was out and about."

"At Fynn's party," I blurted.

"But that is some years from now… I cannot fetch someone from the future."

"Has Mr Vanderhoot been warned?"

"Not yet." The Arbiter paused. "I'll send Chloe and Patrick. They can lure him outside the confines of the bank— then I can bring him here. A hop there and a hop back, simple as that."

"Well, before we go rushing off, let's think this through first," Fynn sounded a note of caution.

"Your thoughts, Policeman Fynn?" the Arbiter asked.

"It's the very impossibility of this event that intrigues me." He sat back in his chair. "What are the facts as we know them?"

"A large explosion took place in the year twenty eighty-nine. The damage however is centered around the turn of the previous century. The corridor to the past was utterly destroyed."

"A large explosion?"

"If you recall, the safe deposit boxes are also quite large."

"It was some kind of bomb then?"

"Yes."

"Edmund can whip you up a sensor," Pavel Mekanos said, nodding to his friend.

"What kind of sensor?"

"One that would locate explosive devices," Mr Fickster replied.

"A bomb it may be, but how was it detonated?" Fynn asked.

"He's right. Any explosive device would not be on a timer," Pavel considered. "Given the nature of the boxes— suspended from time, as it were— no clock could count down. It would never go off."

"What else might trigger it?"

"Remote detonation is an old favorite."

"No," I disagreed.

"Why not, Patrick?"

"No signals inside the bank— I remember Mr Vanderhoot mentioning that."

"What was the exact date of the explosion?" Fynn asked.

"The fourth of August, twenty eighty-nine," Mr Quandary reported.

"Seems to me, we only need to ask Vanderhoot who was in the bank on that particular day."

"No one," Mr Q continued.

"What?"

"Closed for the Bank Holiday."

"That's it," I said.

"What, Patrick?"

"Mr Vanderhoot told me that once a year, the box from the present moves into the past corridor… and one from the future moves into the present."

"How extraordinary," the doctor commented.

"A giant mechanism in the basement, he said. That must be what set it off."

"Movement, you're saying?" Fynn turned to Edmund. "Is such a thing possible?"

"Not exactly. Motion is too strong a word for how the bank operates. *Spacial displacement* might be a better description of what goes on. I doubt it would set off a bomb."

"Nonetheless, I think Patrick has stumbled upon a vulnerability. The only part of the bank that remains in the present is the entrance corridor and the main office."

"What are you saying?" I turned to Fynn.

"This one box that moves to the present… we might guess it is not sequestered from time like the others."

"But it wasn't the present corridor that was obliterated," Edmund observed.

"Then we are left with only one conclusion: the bomb was not in a safety deposit box."

"When it was detonated, you mean to say?"

"Yes, the box had to be opened in the past corridor and then exploded."

"A person then," I said.

"What do you mean?"

"A person had to be there to take the bomb out of its box and set it off."

"Yes… and a person with a key." Fynn nodded.

"But who, and where were they hiding?" Pavel asked.

"It's not beyond the realm of possibility that someone slipped inside the bank without Vanderhoot's knowledge," Mr Q said.

"It's unlikely though," Clark countered. "He's not some bulging-eyed Belgian, I'll have you know."

"I agree," Fynn replied and sat forward. "But the difficulty for Mr Vanderhoot is to recall a single visitor over the span of some two hundred years—"

"I think someone made two deposits," I interrupted.

"Why?"

"They put the bomb in one box and deposited themselves in another."

"Deposited themselves?"

"Sure… They hid in a box that went to the future and waited. Eventually, they *wake up* in Mr Vanderhoot's present, during the bank holiday, and when no one was there. They get out of the box, walk to the corridor in the past and set the bomb off."

"Are you saying there is a bomb in the past and a person in the future?" Pavel asked.

"Pretty much."

"But this goes against all the rules," Clark protested.

"You mean the laws of physics?"

"No, Mr Vanderhoot's rules: no explosive devices and no livestock of any kind."

"I guess they broke those."

"I agree with Patrick. It's safe to say whoever did this cares little for Mr Vanderhoot's protocols." Fynn paused. "We can then guess which box contains the person: it had to be number twenty eighty-nine.

When it moved into the present corridor, the deed was accomplished."

"It's a simple matter to find out who is the owner of that particular account. Mr Vanderhoot is scrupulous, if he's nothing else," the Arbiter said.

"He does keep excellent records," Mr Q concurred. "We must contact him immediately."

"This is the problem. We usually do business by post," Clark said.

"How long does that take?"

"Months or weeks at best."

"Can you call him and warn him?"

"Hmm… He's never been known to answer his telephone."

"What about a fax?" I asked Clark.

"All we have is a telex machine at present."

"And what would you tell him?" Fynn complained. "We still cannot say who the perpetrator is, or when this plan originated. These deposits could have been made at any time."

"Well, there is box eighteen ninety-nine…" I said.

"What?"

"It was mine, but Mortimer was the last person to have that key. He stole it from me."

"There you have it; Mortimer after all," Mr Q concluded.

"Perhaps, though it was not Mortimer who set off the explosion. He was not hiding in the box. He is at large as we've seen." Fynn sat back in his seat.

"Who then? And how did this mad bomber exit the bank? Surely the front entrance is locked," Doctor Zed remarked.

"If I remember right, there's a door at the end of the hall of mirrors. Leads to the basement," I said.

"No, the basement is a dead end," Fynn commented.

"Hmm… maybe they didn't exit."

"What's that, Patrick?"

"A suicide bomber."

"I agree. Despite all our speculation, this is the most likely explanation."

"But if it was Kali herself— our problems would be over," the doctor said.

"Someone else then?" Chloe asked. "But who would make such a sacrifice?"

"Perhaps some hapless victim of her incessant whispering," Doctor Zed replied.

* * *

"The final circle in jeopardy is at Mr Quandary's tower. I doubt there's need for discussion, only action at this point."

"I agree," Mr Q said and glanced up at the Arbiter. "I'll ask that Fynn and Jardel accompany Lothar and I to remedy the situation." He looked to the three of us and we all nodded.

"What happened exactly?" I asked.

"What will happen, you might say." Mr Q turned to me. "My tower was set ablaze and the obsidian circle was taken by the sea."

"When you say *taken by the sea*… is that Kali's doing or just a tidal thing, like global warming?"

"Well, it is of course the tower's destruction that I wish to prevent."

"When was this?"

"Ah, there's the rub. We only know it did happen, but we can't be sure when."

"Why not?"

"If you recall, the tower exists in slow-time compared to its surroundings."

I had to think about that for a second, and remembered how the world outside the windows could race by at a frightening speed.

"Given that the Cocos Islands are difficult to access geographically, we might suppose Kali traveled there only once in that respect," Fynn observed.

"Meaning?"

"She journeyed by ship or airplane and then through time. Can you narrow it down a bit?" he asked.

"Well, no one even knew we existed until Captain Keeling spotted the islands in sixteen-oh-nine. And we had no visitors at all until John Clunies-Ross sailed ashore in eighteen twenty-five and took over the place, wives and all."

"Wives?"

"A harem of sorts."

"When did you first get there?" I asked.

"Hmm, when was it? ...sometime in the twelfth century, I think."

"What did you live on?"

"Meaning?"

"What did you eat?"

"Oh, coconuts and fish for the most part. Lothar also brought a few chickens with him."

"And my garden," the giant reminded. "There is an abundance of fresh water— it falls from the sky," he added with a smile.

"Did anything else significant happen in the time since?" Fynn asked.

"Nothing of note," Mr Q replied.

"Are you sure?"

"A few boats visited from time to time."

"Such as?"

"Well... Darwin made a brief stop over."

"As in Charles Darwin?"

"Yes, do you know him?"

"Not personally."

"Hmm... What else?" Mr Q considered. "There was a minor naval battle during World War One... And an airport was built during the Second War."

"The queen paid us a visit," Lothar added.

"Which queen?"

"Elizabeth."

"The second?"

"Yes, her too."

"The Australians took over in nineteen fifty-five," Mr Q continued. "But it wasn't till the jet age that people began arriving in droves, holiday-makers."

"And no one noticed your giant white tower the whole time?" I asked.

"It was quite invisible back in the day."

"It's hard not to spot, if I remember right."

"Oh yes, it's visible now in your usual present; the tourists seem to love it."

"Why would you want them to see it?"

"Increases traffic to our little museum."

"But not back then?"

"Not at all, except on rainy days..." Lothar explained unhelpfully.

"Well no time like the present, eh? What's the weather like outside, Clark?" Mr Q asked.

"You're in luck, I'd say... The atmosphere is only slightly noxious this evening."

Fynn, Lothar and Mr Quandary went back to their rooms to gather what they might need for the journey. Clark called me over to reception with a finger and a smile. There was a bundle on the counter wrapped in brown paper. He glanced down at it and then up at me.

"What's this?"

"Some clothes I gathered for you... from the lost and found. Should be something in there that fits, and a warm jacket just in case."

"Thanks."

"Oh and here, bring these with you..." Clark said and slid a couple of room keys in my direction. It should make your return easier." He smiled. "I can only spare two— and please don't mention this to the Arbiter."

"Why not?"

"He's a bit possessive of the keys. With any luck, you'll end up right back in the lobby..."

***

The sun had all but set when Fynn and I followed Lothar and Mr Q up a paved path half covered in sand.

"No cane?" I asked.

"I left it with Pavel— he promises to fix it for us."

"Again?"

"We shall see..." Fynn raised a smile.

The four of us stayed well clear of the Arbiter's circle, the Circle of Null. It seemed to be just a low mound in the distance. Lothar carried a small backpack and I recognized it as one of Pavel's coolers. The giant led us to the cabana cafe, where we had once shared a picnic. This time the umbrellas were intact and gentle waves from the Aral

Sea lapped at our ankles. "Shame the cafe isn't open," he muttered and smiled down at me.

There was a perfect wall to jump from. Tried and true, according to Mr Quandary: "Lothar has done an amazing set of calculations which allow us to travel with great accuracy," he said and climbed up the wall, though his black cape snagged on a branch. "It's quite convenient." He took off his top hat and called out, "First stop, Mongolia—that's unavoidable I'm afraid to say."

Mr Q and Lothar jumped in quick succession and blinked from the present. Fynn and I climbed the wall and followed. We landed near enough to each other, and close to the circle in Mongolia, about a quarter of a mile away. There was no sign of anyone else, let alone our giant and his companion.

"When are we?" I asked Fynn, who sat on the huge slab of rock with his legs dangling over the side.

"Sorry to say I have no idea… only where."

The minutes went by and I grew increasingly impatient. I stood on the highest outcropping to scan the horizon.

"Anything?" Fynn called out.

I shook my head. "It's been over an hour. Maybe they got lost or something."

"It's possible, even likely… And no others in sight, eh?"

"You mean Mongol hordes?"

Fynn laughed. "Well, we have a decision to make: go back to the hotel, or onwards to the Cocos."

I spotted something in the distance, a black bag, I thought it was, and jogged over to fetch it. Returning, I handed it to Fynn. "Pretty sure this belongs to Lothar."

"Ah, fresh fruit and sandwiches," he said after rummaging through.

"What should we do now?"

"I suppose we'll have supper."

"Doesn't this mean they've been here and left?"

"It might, though they did say they'd wait for us."

"Maybe we were late, very late…"

"The sandwiches appear quite fresh."

"One of Pavel's coolers— whatever's inside might have been in there for years."

"I see..." Fynn replied vaguely because his attention had turned elsewhere. He pointed to the ground. A few yards below our perch was a gleaming object, a white fist-size rock. It seemed to be perfectly round. I clambered down to look and Fynn followed. Up close it was recognizable as a billiard ball, the cue ball no doubt.

"Mr Cue," I said with a smile.

Underneath was a handwritten note. It had a set of coordinates, marked in longitude and latitude. It was signed: Lothar. Fynn carefully placed the ball back to its exact location and beckoned me up to the stone slab.

"Alright then, off we go to the Cocos Islands. Aim for that when you jump," he said. "We will hope for the best."

"When will we arrive?"

"It matters not, only where we arrive is important."

**

It was another hard jump. Fynn landed on a green lawn and I ended up on the beach, though we were both very close to the obsidian circle. I recognized the place immediately; the white sand, palm trees and the hot, thick air. This time there was no iron fence around the circle, nor was there a gleaming white structure.

"Where's the tower?" I asked the obvious question.

"Most baffling that it has disappeared," Fynn agreed. "Perhaps we've arrived too late?"

Just then a man appeared out of nowhere and came dashing towards us. He was dressed in a faded tunic and some kind of turban. It was Mr Q, though perhaps ten years older than I remembered, and he had an angry look about him.

"What the devil are you doing here, eh? And who are you?" he demanded.

"Don't you recognize us?"

"Of course not."

A moment later, Lothar also popped out of thin air and came rushing over. He was smiling at us but took Mr Q aside and spoke in soothing tones. "It's alright, they are our friends..." Mr Quandary cast more suspicious glances at us nonetheless. Lothar turned. "Sorry for this... he's completely forgotten about the future... a soft jump I think. It happens sometimes... he'll be fine in a few hours."

"He doesn't remember the hotel?"

"Sorry, no..."

"What's the plan then?"

"We can go to the tower and wait for the present to catch up to us."

"What tower?"

"Oh— it's right where it always is, you just can't see it."

"What do you mean?"

"Pavel gave us some sort of special paint. Makes things invisible." Lothar reached into his pocket and pulled out a tiny remote control. He flipped a switch and the tower reappeared in a shimmer.

"How does that work?"

"You'd have to ask Pavel. Something about reflecting photons at a precise angle, a hundred and eighty degrees, I think."

"Any sign of trouble? Any strangers about?" Fynn asked.

"Not a soul... still, it's early days."

"When is it?"

"Thursday, I think, early twelfth century." Lothar smiled and ushered us inside. "All we have to do is wait. Let's go upstairs, it will make the time go by more quickly."

"Hang on, you're saying that we just sit and wait in the tower for nine centuries to pass?"

"It might only be seven."

"That's a comfort."

"We can climb to the top and see who arrives... I have a pair of binoculars laying about somewhere."

The four of us started up through the ramp-like rooms in single file. From the few windows that overlooked the circular courtyard, I could sense time was speeding up outside. The days were passing in a flicker, as if one were blinking. Outside the tower, years passed in minutes. Also, as we ascended, Mr Q seemed more like himself.

We rested about halfway up and Lothar opened one of the doors to the outside. I saw a white shape on the horizon. Sails— a ship speeding towards us, however at a rate no ship could travel.

"That's Captain Keeling," the giant said. "He always shows up around this time..." Lothar pointed, and after a few more minutes another ship arrived. "And here's Mr Ross, come to take over the place."

"What year are we looking at outside?" I asked.

Lothar did a quick mental calculation. "Coming up on eighteen thirty-six."

"Darwin," Mr Q commented.

"What?"

"It's the *HMS Beagle*. Darwin is arriving."

"We should go back down and meet him," Fynn said.

"Are you mad?"

"Certainly not. I now suspect he may be Kali's target after all. The very reason she is here."

"That was not on the Arbiter's list," I complained.

"And why would she want to do him harm?" Mr Q asked.

"His ideas surely changed the way we view the modern world, eh?"

"Well, I suppose you're correct on this, Fynn. His theory was co-opted by everyone else on the planet, from capitalists to governments…"

"He may be in peril then," Fynn replied.

"I doubt it. At best, his original theory is a moot point."

"What makes you say that?" I asked.

"It's no longer the environment that fuels evolution."

"No?"

"Well, I suppose it is, but we humans are now in control of that environment. We are making the choices about what survives and what doesn't. It can hardly be called *natural selection*."

"What do you mean?"

"It's humans who make all the selection decisions these days."

"Like?"

"Well, for the last few thousand years, domesticated crops and animals, selective breeding with our own aims in mind; and in the next hundred years, genetic manipulations that we cannot even begin to imagine."

"So, not the survival of the fittest?"

"No longer."

We hurried down to the bottom of the tower and walked back out into proper time. It was decided that Mr Quandary would stay behind to guard the tower, even though it was rendered invisible again. Lothar led us to the other side of the island where two small boats were dragged up onto the sand. They were primitive to say the least, but serviceable. Lothar used one for himself and Fynn and I followed. The giant paddled across the strait towards the main island, then maneuvered through a small channel and drifted towards the shallow bay. At anchor in the pale blue was a large two-masted ship, about fifty yards off shore. It seemed like you could almost walk out to it, though it lay in deeper water.

Along the beach I could see a longboat, big enough for a dozen people. A few sailors were milling about, all in white shirts and wearing straw hats. Further inland I saw a number of huts with thatched roofs. Fynn and I waded ashore and walked up to the first person we saw.

"Mr Darwin?" I asked.

"No, I'm Syms… Syms Covington." He gave us a once over. "And you are?"

"I am Mr Fynn and this is Mr Jardel. We're part of the Ross colony."

He shook hands. "I didn't see you at dinner last night."

"No, we were out… fishing… but we would very much like to speak with Mr Darwin this morning."

"Well, I'm his personal assistant. Anything you might say to him, you may say to me." The man named Syms looked us over again. "Mr Darwin is not to be disturbed this morning."

I glanced up the beach. There was a serious looking guy with a receding hairline and generous muttonchops. He was stooped over, collecting something into a jar. I started in his direction but Fynn held me back by the arm. "Wait," he said softly.

"What? We have to save him."

"Yes… but if Kali is here— and I don't see her as of yet— we would lead her straight to the target."

I thought for a moment. "Let's take Syms then."

"What?"

"Take him back to the ship."

Fynn smiled. "An excellent idea, Patrick." He turned to the other man. "Mr Covington, your life is in peril; you must come with us at this very moment."

"What?" He seemed astonished. "And why? if I might ask."

"We will take you back to your vessel where you may find safety."

"What about the others?"

"We will fetch them as well." Fynn took Syms by the arm and started leading him towards our primitive kayak. We hadn't gone more than a few yards when Kali appeared out of nowhere, standing in front of us with a grin on her face. She was oddly dressed though, almost as if in uniform, and they were modern clothes: a short skirt just to the knees and a patterned blouse under a blazer. A small peaked cap with wings emblazoned on the front matched the piping on her jacket. She was also holding a cane, this one with the brass head of an elephant.

"If it isn't Fynn and Jardel… and who's this? Mr Darwin, I must suppose."

Covington seemed to sense Kali's malicious intent and luckily said nothing more about his own identity.

"And why would you wish to harm Mr Darwin?" Fynn asked.

"I promised someone a favor."

"Who? Mr Lamarck?"

"No, someone more religious, if you must know…"

We tried to approach the boat again but Kali blocked our way. There was little we could do against her. She blinked from here to there, always impeding our path to freedom.

"Who is this woman?" Syms asked.

"One of Mr Ross' wives, I might guess," Fynn replied. "She doesn't take kindly to strangers."

Kali grew tired of our attempted escape and cracked the elephant cane against Covington's leg. It made a terrible sound. He cried out and fell to the sand. Further down the beach Mr Darwin seemed oblivious to our skirmish. Others were not however; a group of men came rushing towards us, calling out in alarm. They were probably members of the Beagle's crew.

We had only a moment while Kali was distracted. Fynn grabbed one of Syms' arms and I took the other. We hoisted him above the low surf and began wading out into the shallows. To our surprise and relief, Kali stayed put on the shore. She seemed unable or unwilling to follow us into the water. I turned to watch. She stood there motionless, though smiling perhaps. Up the beach I could see the sailors clambering into the longboat with Mr Darwin in tow. They were pushing out into the bay.

A few minutes later Lothar came along side in his kayak. He helped us climb aboard.

"If we see him to his ship and it sets sail, he should be bothered no more," Fynn said, a bit breathless. "Mr Covington, there is great danger here. Tell your captain to sail away at once."

Not all was well however. Kali had disappeared. Just after we got Syms aboard the *Beagle*, the air was suddenly thick with smoke. A huge pall appeared to cover the surrounding sky. It floated upwards and outwards, then seemed to dissolve into nothing but a few wisps. At that moment there was the sound of stone against stone, and we presumed the invisible tower had collapsed into a heap. Lothar paddled wildly, back towards the tiny island with Fynn and I following.

***

We found Mr Quandary head in hands. He was as his tower, a pile of rubble. Lothar ran over to give comfort. Inspector Fynn ignored him for the most part and began to inspect the damage. He was paying special attention to the charred, burnt bits.

"The fire was started with kerosene," Fynn announced.

"What makes you say that?"

"It leaves a distinctive odor."

"How does that help us?"

"It narrows down the timeframe somewhat. This occurred in the relative future."

"Wait. How did it happen in the future? We just heard it collapse…" I protested. "In the present… or the past…"

"The tower does not exactly reside in proper time." Fynn raised a smile. "Best not to dwell on it, Patrick."

"Why the future then?"

"Kerosene was introduced in the eighteen fifties, when, I assume such lamps were in common use."

"Yes, lamps of one sort or another… but for hundreds of years," Mr Q spoke up having regained his composure.

"So you would have an ample supply of kerosene?"

"No, we use whale oil for the lamps," Lothar said.

"I remember seeing them at the souvenir shop last time I was here— in my recent present. They were like replicas or something."

"Such lamps were for sale to the tourists?" Fynn asked.

"Of course."

"And one could buy fuel as well?"

"I doubt it. You'd never get past security."

"What about the locals?"

"The power is not always reliable," Mr Q considered. "But most people rely on propane, or batteries in modern days."

"Patrick, where else might one find kerosene?"

"Hmm, the airport maybe. I think they use it for jet fuel."

"That makes some sense," Fynn replied with a smile. "Do you recall how Kali was attired?"

"Like a stewardess."

"How could she get through the door? It's locked at all times," Mr Q protested.

"You mean to say that you never open it?"

"Well, not often…"

"You must think of Kali as a person who is present always."

"That's an absurd notion."

"Yes, but likely, the one time the door was left open is when she slipped inside."

"And how do you intend to rectify this, Mr Fynn?"

"First you must jump back to before the tower was a pile of rubble."

"And then?"

"Wait until Kali again arrives to destroy it."

"But how can you say when this will be?"

"The clues tell us everything: it is in the jet age."

"What clues?"

"The kerosene and how Kali was dressed… I would wait until the mid-sixties. It should be a simple matter to see who arrives, most likely at the airport."

"What about Darwin?" I asked. "She might come after him again."

"Forewarned is forearmed. We'll think of something," the giant said with a menacing smile.

"Hmm, we'll all have to jump at the obsidian circle to reset things. Lothar can easily do the calculations."

"We won't be coming with you," Fynn said.

"No?"

"Patrick and I have an errand to run in Japan."

"To find Mr Sato?"

"Yes."

"We'll meet back at the hotel then?"

Fynn nodded and gave them a small wave as the two men set off towards the obsidian circle. He confided his worst nightmare to me: jumping from here. "This place constrains time but not space, if I recall what Lothar told me."

"And?"

"I fear that I'll end up dangling in a cold vacuum with no earth beneath my feet."

I held up a room key from the *Hotel de Cirque*, and Fynn was greatly relieved.

chapter sixteen
a visitor

Fynn and I returned to the hotel without incident. Sebastian Clark was behind reception as usual and greeted us with a nod. "I trust all went well?"

"For the moment, yes," Fynn replied.

"Any sign of Mortimer?" I asked and gave him back his keys.

"Which one?"

"Either or both."

"No."

"Anyone else here?"

"Lothar and Mr Q have already arrived. They're waiting in the Conservatory."

It was difficult to understand how they returned before us, but I saw a familiar top hat as we entered the room. Mr Q was all smiles. "A great success, thank you for your assistance, gentlemen."

"Where's Lothar?"

"In the kitchen rounding up champagne and local caviar. We shall celebrate our victory."

"Not too local, I hope."

"What do you mean?"

"The caviar," I replied and remembered all the dead fish by my feet.

"Yes, well, Kali is gone and the tower is intact. We've locked the door and the place is impregnable. It was much as you said, Fynn. She appeared in the early nineteen seventies, posing as a stewardess… Kiwi Airlines, I think it was."

"The kiwi is a flightless bird," Lothar commented as he entered the room carrying a silver tray.

"It's also a delicious fruit, but that's beside the point… Kali Shunya arrived at the airport and made her way to the tower with a can full of kerosene. It was all we could do to stop her before she took a match to it."

"Violence?" Fynn asked.

"Regrettably, yes. Lothar had to stuff her out one of the windows into the courtyard."

"You mean she fell?"

"Yes, and a long way down… a terrible mess."

"Quite dreadful," Lothar concurred, and popped open the champagne bottle.

"She was easier to apprehend than I expected. No special powers in evidence," Mr Q added.

"Did she have the cane?"

"Which cane?"

"Any cane."

"None that I saw."

"You may have killed a Kali, but not *the Kali*," Fynn observed. "Though, my congratulations on saving the tower. This is good news."

"And what do you mean, *the Kali*?"

"I've come to believe there is more than one."

"What about Darwin?" I asked.

"There is only one Darwin," Fynn replied with a grin.

"Okay…" I laughed. "But that's not what I mean."

"Yes, well… it was a simple matter to keep him aboard his ship. He complained bitterly, but no harm came to him," Mr Q explained.

A few minutes later the Arbiter glided into the room with Edmund and Pavel following. "I have heard the news," he said in his mechanical voice. "However, I will not join in celebration."

"Why not?"

"I fear our recent actions are for naught. Eventually she will undo all that we have done. The only way we can stop Kali is at her source."

"And where is that?" I asked. "Far in the future?"

"No, far in the past."

"How far?"

"To the time when she was first banished, before the Pharaohs."

"When is that exactly?"

"To my best recollection, three thousand, one hundred BC."

"That's pretty far… How do you plan to get there?"

"I am rebuilding the Circles of Null."

"I don't see any signs of construction."

"Nor would you, Mr Jardel. They are being restored in the future, two hundred years hence, but the work is progressing nicely. In fact, we are slightly ahead of schedule."

"That doesn't make sense to me."

"Let us say different components are constructed at different times, some in the past, and some in the future. When completed, they function together with a kind of synchronicity."

"In the present?"

"Yes. The circles, once completed and functioning, encompass all timelines."

"Not before?"

"No."

"And why the delay in going back?"

"There is one more component I have yet to procure."

"What is it?"

"The central disk. The very thing that makes circles operate with precision."

"How did you figure all this out?"

"Mr Mekanos and I have discovered much from reading the manuscripts."

I turned to Pavel.

"We've looked over the translations… Edmund and I… and yes, we've found schematics on how to build all sorts of circles."

"All sorts?"

"Ways to slow time down, or speed up its flow, constrain space, movement, energy… and so forth."

"Anything else?"

"Well, there's the *ever-present*," Edmund chimed in.

"What's that?"

"We're not entirely sure," Pavel replied instead. "Something has been lost in translation… it could be the *always-now* or the *never-now*."

"What does that one do?"

"It seems to be a way of combining timelines."

"Is that even possible?"

"I'd say no off the top of my hat." Pavel gave a double laugh.

"It's not like that at all," Edmund disagreed. "You might liken it to a difference engine."

"What's that?"

"The differences between two timelines are calculated and then combined."

"That doesn't sound good. Are we talking past, present, or future?"

"It's not really for traveling at all."

"And what about here, the Circles of Null?" I asked.

"We are waiting on Lothar to finish a few calculations," the Arbiter responded.

"How long will that take?"

"It shouldn't be long now, a few years or so."

"A few years?" I was surprised by his reply and looked over to the giant who returned a sheepish grin.

"I'll notify you all when we are prepared," the Arbiter said and started back towards the lobby.

"By notify, do you mean to say you'll pluck us?" Fynn asked.

"Yes, if it's not too much of an inconvenience," the Arbiter replied. "Don't worry, I know where and when you'll be. I'll send for you."

"We'll be in the past?"

"Yes, relatively speaking. You are all invited to attend. I will see you then."

The Arbiter spoke with such finality, I expected him to simply blink from existence. Instead, he glided to the elevator and pushed the call button.

Even the veranda was off-limits tonight; some sort of lingering toxic cloud, according to Clark. The rest of us retired early. I found Chloe half naked and waiting in her room.

***

Late that night I suffered from a terrible thirst— maybe from eating too much caviar. I staggered out to the lobby, hoping to steal a bottle of water from reception. The hotel was dark and quiet. Even Clark was asleep. I was startled to see a lone figure seated by the backgammon tables, his silhouette at least, set against the moonlit desert. A dim light came on. It was Öde Temsik.

"You again," I called out as soon as I recognized him, though he wasn't wearing a red fez.

"Again?" he asked and looked me over. "Oh yes, we met at Fynn's party... not formally perhaps, but with a mutual nod and a smile."

"Which one?"

"Hmm?"

"Which party?"

"Don't you recall?" he asked and gave me an eye. "Oh..." then he laughed, "I see what you're saying now... Yes, it was his funeral not the birthday party. I'm glad it all worked out in the end."

"How well do you know Fynn?"

"Know is certainly the wrong word, but I can tell you quite a bit about his life."

"Like?"

"Yes, I liked Fynn from the moment I met him... I could see he had a good mind and a sense of fair play."

"When was that?"

"Oh dear, it was so long ago, I've almost forgotten. I'm quite sure he has." Öde leaned back in his chair, his face returned to the shadows.

"How did you get here?"

"I knew enough not to use the revolving doors." He leaned forward again and smiled. "But I have been here the whole time."

"What?"

"In parallel, let us say."

"The elevator?"

"Yes."

"You were watching us, listening to everything?"

"No… you could not see me, nor could I see you. I was no more than a phantom. The hotel is filled with them. Haven't you noticed?"

"No…" I replied and took a long sip from my water bottle. "Why are you here?"

"Best you don't mention it."

"Why not?"

"I wouldn't want to alarm anyone… nor do I have a great desire to become embroiled in the situation."

"What situation?"

"Thwarting Kali and her plans."

"Don't you remember being a hitchhiker?"

"Not recently. Why do you ask?"

"We gave you a ride once."

"Did you?"

"You also stole the Voynich manuscripts from the back of my car."

"Did I?"

"Yes, don't you remember?"

"It's essential that they do not fall into Kali's hands."

"Well, the copy you took was a forgery, so, no worries."

"It's for the best in the end. Everything happens for a reason, even if that reason is no reason at all."

I was growing increasingly frustrated with the conversation, but reminded myself that Mr Temsik was not the most slippery character I had ever run across. I knew to change tacks. "What can you tell me about Fynn?"

"Tractus? Hmm… In the beginning he was rather inept at traveling, Oh, he'd flop from here to there, but very much at random. He was however, a keen observer, and soon enough began to suspect there was a pattern to his jumps."

"Past and future?"

"Yes, indeed." Öde grinned and settled back in his seat. He took out a cigarette from a silver case and lit the end, then shook the match until it finally went out. "I will say he took the time to learn Greek and Latin, and schooled himself in the philosophy of the day… I always thought he'd end up as a scientist. I never guessed he'd be a policemen— well, a detective… Not to say anything bad about scientists, but they can be rather detached at times, dispassionate. I suppose that's not in Fynn's nature; he has that desperate sense of fairness."

"What happened next?"

"Things really changed for him around sixty BC."

"Why then?"

"He took passage on a ship, a voyage from Rhodes to Epirus, and found the *Antikythera* mechanism, as you call it."

"What's that?"

"A decidedly geocentric device… a sort of early astrolabe that measures the movements of the stars and planets." Mr Temsik paused to puff out a long cloud of smoke. "…Well, soon enough young Fynn began to figure out which way was which. And as impetuous as ever, he made a bold move. He jumped far to the future, very far, to the seventeenth century."

"You're kidding…"

"No. Can you imagine? A few short jumps and he found himself in the sixteen hundreds. I could barely catch up to him. He landed in France, understanding nothing of himself or how he got there."

"I would guess he had trouble communicating."

"At first, it's true, but people took him as a kind of novelty, speaking ancient Greek as he did. It wasn't too long before he learned several new languages. He might have made a good diplomat."

"Where did he go next?"

"Oh, heavens, I lost track of him for a long while. Eventually, he found himself in Scotland, at Culloden… and on the wrong side, some would say. Poor Fynn, he had absolutely no inkling about firearms… charging head first into the line. Terrible wounds, almost cost him his life. But I'm sure you remember that better than I."

"Me?"

"You were there. I always thought it was the first time you two met."

"I don't remember that at all."

"Perhaps it's yet to happen for you."

"Why was he there?"

"A futile attempt to fix history."

"Who's idea was that?"

"Not Fynn's…" Mr Temsik laughed. "I'd never interfere in his life, you understand."

"Until now."

"Yes…" Mr Temsik took a puff from his cigarette. "And even after all these centuries, he does not give up on his beliefs."

"Which beliefs?"

"That the future is shaped by hope, and the choices we make."

"Isn't it?"

"No, it's cut in stone. It unfolds the way it does because of events which have occurred in the past, and in the present. Neither of these are separate things. Time is not at all how you believe it is."

"How is it then?"

"Unlike what Fynn and the others have told you, the future has already happened. How else would I be able to travel from there? It has already been determined— though I hasten to add, there is not only one future."

"How many are there?"

"As many as you might imagine."

"Fynn says there's only one timeline, the one you remember."

"This is certainly true when it comes to traveling."

"And what are you talking about?"

"All the parallel presents… the ones you are so far unaware of." Mr Temsik held up a single dice. It was black with white dots.

"That's Pavel's."

"Indeed it is… and my gift to you." He placed it on the table with a flourish.

"No thanks."

"Would you prefer white with black dots?" He set another dice next to the first. "I must insist that you take one."

"Why?"

"Despite what you've been taught, parallel lines do meet. There are many Patricks out and about, just waiting in the wings."

"I'm not sure I want to meet them."

Mr Temsik snubbed out his cigarette and stared at me. "A single timeline cannot hold two choices… Like the cat in the box, it must be dead or alive; it cannot be both." Öde grinned. "And so it is with you, Patrick. There are choices you must make."

"What choices?"

"Well, you might choose to travel with me. I live in a paradise. You'd be much happier…"

"I'd miss my friends."

"Most of them are there already."

"Really?" That took me by surprise.

"Of course, and you can make new friends."

"What about Fynn?"

"Hmm… not many murders for him to solve."

"What other choices do I have?"

Öde laughed. "I might ask you to hide Geppetto instead."

"Where is he?"

"In Babylon, as you well know."

"Protect him from Kali?"

"Yes… but you will need the dice."

"I'm not sure…"

"If Kali has one weakness, it is that she cannot exist in more than one timeline."

"Can any of us?"

"Of course, we all exist simultaneously in unlimited parallel worlds."

"We do?"

"In infinite variety."

"But not Kali?"

"No. She remains in a timeline tangent to our own, appearing only when she wants."

My arm reached out, my fingers moved to the black dice, holding it on two sides. I hesitated then picked it up. I felt nothing though, no tingling up my arm. I did see a small smile pass Öde's lips. "So I'm guessing Kali shouldn't find out about this."

"Under no circumstances… It would allow her to slip between presents, and the outcome would be dreadful."

"And you?" I asked, but put the dice back down. "Why do you like traveling between presents?"

"Ah, I enjoy having a bit of fun, that's all." Öde gave me a wide grin.

"Fun?"

"Let's just say I like arranging things."

"What kind of things?"

"Events, situations, coincidences…" He was still smiling. "I play the role of *Fate* as it were…"

"Wait, you're saying you like to mess with people so they'll believe in destiny?"

"I do. I find it amusing at the very least, and rather engaging much of the time."

"I'm not sure I like this idea."

"Most people in the world prefer to believe in fate, one way or another." Öde laughed. "I simply intervene in small ways. I've made many a person get on the wrong bus for the right reason… say… to fall in love… I consider it my duty to convince others that destiny is alive and well."

"So you're a matchmaker, like a cupid?"

"On occasion, yes."

"You take pleasure in that?"

"Great pleasure, simple as it is… And this is a consolation to people. It makes them happy and full of hope… usually."

"So like, you dispense karma?"

"There is a dark side to it as well," Mr Temsik said in a different tone of voice. "I am also death."

"Death?"

"The grim reaper. Some lives deserve to be taken."

I was speechless for a few moments. Öde leaned back into the shadows and took another cigarette from his case. He tapped the end several times. A wooden match flared up in the darkness.

"Do you believe in fate, Patrick?" he asked. "Destiny, pre-determinism?"

"Not really."

"What then?"

"Happenstance, I'd call it."

"I see… Luck, you mean, randomness, chance."

"It's more than that, but I can't quite explain it."

"Probability then?"

"Maybe…"

"Ah, you'd prefer to live in a Boolean world?"

"A what?"

"In place of causality, I mean to say. If something happens, *then* something else will follow, with *if* being the operative word."

"I never thought of it that way."

"Yes, well, the *ifs* matter little. It's only the *then* which counts in the end."

"If wishes were horses, beggars would ride…"

"What's that, Patrick?"

"An old saying."

"Wishes… well, perhaps it's the choices you make instead?"

"I doubt it."

"And would you make these choices out of free will?"

"I wouldn't say that exactly." I laughed at the thought. "Some of my choices are better than others, some are deliberate, some ill-advised, some in the heat of the moment, and some are probably genetically programmed."

"You take a rather sophisticated view of this…" Mr Temsik smiled but then looked about the dark room. He rose abruptly.

"What's the matter?" I asked.

"I see a light on in the Conservatory." He pointed down the long corridor. "I wonder if there's someone there?" He started in that direction and I followed. Our footsteps echoed against the glass and marble colonnade. I found that I had to walk more slowly than usual to keep pace with him.

"How about you? Do you believe in fate and destiny?" I asked.

"Me?" Öde chuckled. "But I am a leading purveyor of both…"

"There seems to be a lot more randomness to things than most people admit."

"Well, I consider it my job to make people think otherwise." He paused. "Tell me, Patrick, is one destined to win the lottery, or lucky to do so?"

"I'm not sure."

"In either case, you would first need to buy a lottery ticket, eh?"

That was hard to argue with. "What's the difference between

destiny and fate?"

"They are largely synonymous these days." Mr Temsik gave me a glance. "Though I suppose, strictly speaking, they are slightly different."

"How so?"

"Aside from the connotations imbedded in each word?" He looked up at me.

I nodded.

"Destiny is largely under your control; fate never is."

"Really?"

"One must throw random coincidence into the mix before we can truly tackle the question."

"You mean luck?"

"I do."

"Isn't that the opposite of fate?"

"It depends what you mean by fate."

"Some higher power that predetermines events."

"Surely not all fate requires supernatural intervention."

"Like?"

"An ill-fated war, I shall say. The consequences of which are entirely in the hands of politicians, generals and soldiers." Öde snubbed out his cigarette on the floor. "Death is the simplest example of destiny."

"Why is that?"

"As living creatures, all of us will die. It is our destiny."

"And our fate."

"I won't disagree, though we rarely choose the manner of our own death."

"And destiny?" I asked.

"It is merely the sum total of all the choices you make in your life."

"But that's after the fact." I looked down at him.

"Ah, yes, it would appear so. Who can know with certainty where a choice you make in the present might lead?" He laughed. "I will only say, destiny is a localized phenomenon."

"What, like geographically?"

"In a sense, the geography of your own ego. All that it can see and dimly comprehend. Destiny is an egocentric concept designed to give one's life some modicum of meaning."

"It's an illusion, you're saying."

"When it comes to destiny, we are all Nero: emperors of our ego, fiddling while the world burns."

"That's pretty cynical."

"Do you think your destiny is important to another being that lives half way across the galaxy, in another arm of the Milky Way? It is a conceit to think such a thing." Öde stopped walking and looked up with a smile. "Let me tell you a story, Patrick: There is an alien I know, a kind of intelligent crustacean, and he lives on a planet that is like a sauna— an atmosphere of steam and methane. He is however a firm believer in destiny. When he met a female of his species, it was love at first sight, kismet, fate, destiny. He was besotted. They had a lovely wedding and later spawned a thousand offspring. You should be happy for them."

"I am…"

"Is his sense of destiny different than yours? Does it affect you in any way, on this side of the galaxy?"

"You're making this up."

"Yes, but you understand my point nonetheless." Mr Temsik smiled again. "His destiny only becomes yours when his brood of hatchlings decides to cross the galaxy and invade the earth."

I couldn't help but laugh at Öde's story.

"Destiny is surely something that only exists in the eye of the beholder. Far fewer people can live their life knowing there is none… It takes more courage than most have."

"So we're back to randomness and luck?" I asked.

"It depends how you define luck. I prefer the word chance. To me, luck is neither good nor bad, it is only a matter of perception."

"You're saying there's no such thing as bad luck."

"Yes, nor is there good luck. It is only your reaction to a chance event in the present."

We walked on a few steps. "It has to be one or the other," I considered. "It has to be a deterministic world or a random one, a glorious accident."

"Can it not be both?" Öde asked.

"I don't think so."

"Two camps then: the determinists and the believers in randomness."

"Not indeterminists? Or non-determinists?"

Mr Temsik chuckled. "Let's call the them believers in free will. If there is chance, then there must also be free will, eh?"

"Okay, that sort of makes sense."

"Ah, but we are sloppy most times when we use the word random— very few things truly are."

"An example?"

"Let's say static…"

"Static?"

"From a television set, a radio, or background signals from space. At first, it certainly seems to be random."

"You're saying it's not."

"I'm saying its exact cause might be determined, given enough effort. What seems to be random might have a structural nature in the end."

"So, everything is determined? It's all just an endless series of cause-and-effect since the beginning of time?"

"To suggest that the universe is either this way or that is a grave error in thinking. Both camps are wrong."

"What do you mean?"

"Are we ruled by fate or free will? Neither is exactly true, as both aspects seem to be operating." Mr Temsik stopped at the end of the corridor. "Not all things which we don't understand can be said to be random… nor predetermined; and neither needs to evoke a higher power."

"What then?"

"Probability will suffice." Öde paused. "I shall say, from my experience, things are mostly predetermined. Free will is exercised only on rare occasion."

We came upon the Conservatory. The door was unlocked and except for the giant rhododendrons, empty. The light came from far across the room. A chessboard was set up and it looked to be a game already in progress. Öde walked over and stared at the board for a few moments. "White can win in seven moves," he declared.

"So… it's just a theory, all this…" I persisted.

"No."

"A philosophy?"

"It's more akin to a belief."

"How so?"

"Neither camp is supported by much evidence, so it's a matter of faith as to which you believe. If determinism is true, then everything has already been decided… Ah, but such a notion makes fate into a mindless series of events which has led to this particular present. It seems no different than randomness to me."

"Is it?"

"There is little difference between those who think the world is determined or those who espouse randomness… Both views operate with an a priori assertion: cause and effect. Such, to them, is nothing less than the expression of time. One thing comes before another, on and on, to the end of days. But to view time this way is their first mistake."

"Why?"

"Both camps enshrine causality."

"And they shouldn't?"

Mr Temsik turned to me. "What if we live in a universe that is completely simultaneous?"

"That's hard to imagine."

"Indeed it is… Most would have us believe we are riding the present into the future— but this is not so at all. Where does one end and the other begin? It is impossible to say." Öde had another question: "At what point does the past become the present?"

"What?"

"I can understand how the present might flow into the future, but when does the past become the present?"

"I'm not sure anyone has ever asked that question."

"Surely, no one has answered it." Öde smiled.

"Then both camps are wrong?"

"The first can never hope to determine all causes and effects. Such a task is impossible since even the smallest causes can lead to the largest effects."

"Like chaos theory?"

"This, and complexity theory, are a blind alley in the end. Only developed in service to determinism."

"And indeterminism?"

"As I've said, the second group, those who insist on randomness, too often apply this label to things that could be understood, but they fail at the task, either out of laziness or expedience."

"So which is better?"

"Clearly, determinism is very effective in small, tightly controlled models, something we might call science... though even that is changing."

"Science is changing?"

"New science is beginning to see the fuzziness of creation..." Mr Temsik sat in front of the chessboard. "This noble game is the best example. As soon as the match begins, the outcome has already been decided. There are no random moves, only errors that your opponent may seize upon. Even in your time, primitive computers can win a game against almost any human."

"And..."

"And it is because all the moves are knowable. It is quite an easy task for a computer to calculate every outcome and come up with an appropriate strategy. The parameters are narrowly defined. The real world however does not operate like that."

"Are you implying you could beat one of these chess computers."

"Easily."

"How?"

"I might move my pawn three spaces instead of one." He laughed.

"But that would be cheating."

"You would label it such, but I have simply changed the parameters to something the computer cannot comprehend. This is the essence of free will." Öde laughed again. "The real problem with determinism is that all the variables can never be accounted for."

"Why not?"

"Your model of the universe is flawed to begin with, your assumptions are incorrect."

"How so?"

"The way time seems to be. There is no past, present, or future, they are all the same thing, they are simply viewed from different perspectives." He looked up at me. "Join me in a game, Patrick?"

"No thanks. I don't play chess very well."

"Not even if I let you use invisible pawns?"

"What?"

"Your model of the cosmos is incomplete, we can only see a tiny fraction of it, that which emits photons. No one has yet to calibrate dark matter or dark energy as you quaintly call them in this age. So, in the end it is an impossible task to account for each and every variable, when you are not even seeing a tenth of what comprises the universe. In that regard, randomness is a better model, or at least a more efficient one."

"I'm starting to feel depressed."

"Sorry for that. In either case, or should I say, in both camps, these models are necessary for survival, if not only to assuage their ego, their sense of self— it's a kind of buffer against the vastness of creation when compared to their own insignificance."

Mr Temsik switched off the light and we strolled back to the lobby. "Clark will be happy," he said quietly.

"What?"

"To save electricity."

"You know Clark?"

"Everyone knows Clark, though he might not know me."

Mr Temsik and I walked back up the colonnade in silence. He had said too much, given me too much to process. My head was buzzing. When we sat again at the backgammon tables, Öde opened a small drawer and drew out a stack of chips. He started setting up the board. "Will you join me in a game?" He held up the two dice.

"Not with Pavel's *Cube of Destiny*."

Mr Temsik laughed. "Ah, but we played once before, you and I. Don't you recall?"

"Not really... When was it?"

"Fifth century BC, Babylon."

"Doesn't ring a bell."

"It was called *nard* and the rules were a bit different... Still, both games employ strategy, or thinking ahead, one might say."

"Like chess?"

"This game is also a good model of the way things are... Not entirely accurate, but it contains elements of predetermination, chance, and free will. The rules are well established, and indeed all the possible moves can be counted. And yet, there is an inherent unpredictability to contend with. How will the dice fall? Or, who can say how your opponent might move his pieces? Perhaps in an unexpected way?"

He held out the pair of dice for me to see and then dropped them into a container. He began to shake and they rattled inside. "The simple act of rolling the dice demonstrates everything we have been discussing quite well." Öde rolled. "Ah, double sixes..." He looked up at me with a smile. "A determinist will say it's a forgone conclusion, it is something we can predict once we isolate all the variables— this is key to their philosophy, their view of the world: predictability. And here lies its failing. There are too many variables to account for, it is an impossible task."

"Well, given a smart enough person or a computer, you might be able to," I countered.

"Indeed… the amount of oil from my hand, the way I shake the dice, for how long, the angle at which they fall, the surface on which they bounce before landing— all these variables might be tallied. And yet someone who believes in randomness, would say the result is never predictable."

"Who is right?"

"Neither, I would say, and both. We seek the solace of predictability and order." Öde rolled double sixes again.

"So it comes down to belief?"

"Yes. All philosophy does."

"And free will?"

"Something that is rare and hardly ever exercised."

"Can you put that in the context of the dice?"

"Not exactly… free will would be for me to assess all the variables and make a choice not to throw the dice at all."

"That's just like cheating at chess."

"You are catching on." He smiled, shook the container and let the dice spill out. "Ah, double sixes again."

"That's the third time in a row."

"Is it?" He smiled.

I picked up the black dice and this time felt a tingling up my arm. I looked up to Öde, but he had vanished. There was little left to do but go back to bed.

***

"Where's Pavel and Edmund this morning?"

Clark glanced up at the giant clock then turned to me and said, "It's two in the afternoon."

"Oh, I must've slept in…"

"Well, Mr Fickster and Mr Mekanos had an errand to run, left at the crack of dawn. Didn't even say good bye, nor did they touch their breakfast."

"Lothar, Mr Q?"

"Also departed… back to their usual hemisphere."

"Fynn?"

"He's gone for a swim."

"Outside?"

"Heavens no, he's down in the Grotto."

"Chloe? Doctor Zed?"

"Playing checkers in the Conservatory," Clark replied and paused to chuckle.

"What?"

"An unlikely couple, don't you think?"

***

With his hair still a bit damp, Fynn caught up with us in the Conservatory. He seemed refreshed and in a good mood. "Ah, the last of us indians remaining," he joked and sat down beside Chloe and Doctor Zed. "I have an important task for anyone who cares to volunteer."

"What would that be?" Clark asked.

"Who wants to go back and fetch Carlos. We could certainly use his help at this point. Does anyone speak Old Norse?"

"I do," Chloe replied. "Well, I remember a few words of Swedish at least."

"I've always fancied a trip to America," Doctor Zed responded with enthusiasm.

"You've never been there?" I asked.

"Not that I recall."

"Well, Carlos' America is slightly different than mine."

"Is it?"

"Room twelve," Clark said.

"What?"

"The easiest access to Carlos' world. I'll get you the key."

"What should we tell Mr Santayana when we find him?" Chloe asked.

"Tell him everything we've learned and ask him to join us in our battle against Kali."

"Here in the present?"

"Wherever it suits him best. He can be quite fierce. And I would call him a powerful ally."

"Can he be trusted?"

"Of course," Fynn replied.

"I'll just stay and hold down the fort, shall I?" Clark said, then fell silent. He had noticed something moving out in the shimmering wasteland. The rest of us turned to look. A curious figure was making its way towards the hotel. He was difficult to see at first with the sun against our eyes, but I could discern a person trudging along, getting closer. It had to be Mortimer, I thought, but as I stared it became apparent that two people were walking in single file. I could now see both heads bobbing up and down. Two Mortimers returning? That didn't make sense.

Clark seemed to have a better understanding of the visitors. He hurried back to reception. I heard the main entrance unlock, and he quickly pulled on his boots of illusion. The two figures trudged into the lobby and began to remove their protective gear.

"Gentlemen, *dobro pozhalovat*," Clark welcomed in Russian. "I expect you're here for the backgammon tournament, eh? Well, you're a bit early, but make yourselves comfortable, please."

I recognized them: the two Soviet soldiers I had first met when I arrived. They gave us some close inspection, especially Chloe.

***

"We will need to return to our former present," Fynn explained to Clark once he was no longer occupied by the Russians. "I was wondering if you had any suggestions?"

"Room nineteen might do the trick."
"Where does that take us?"
"Just at the beginning of World War Three… quite close to your usual present."
"Any other suggestions?"

Clark reached under the counter and produced two gas masks with a slight thud. Fynn and I took what was provided and trudged to the cabana cafe that lay along the shore of the Aral Sea. Conversation was pointless, breathing was difficult enough. We climbed a high wall, Fynn adjusted the dates on his cane and we jumped painfully into the future. When we arrived, the sea was gone, dried up to the horizon, but the air was breathable.

"Where are we?"
"Some many years in the future. Now it's a simple matter to jump back to our usual present and our usual location."
"Using the cane?"
"No. I think not… we need a soft jump, eh? Besides, it should still be there when we arrive."
"You're just going to leave it here?"
"Perhaps I will bury it," Fynn replied and set to the task of digging a hole in the sand.
"Mr Temsik paid me a visit last night."
"Did he?"
"Everyone was asleep. I came to the lobby for some water."
"I see. What did he want?"
"Just to talk, I guess… and we played backgammon, sort of."
"What did you talk about?"
"Fate, destiny, mostly."
"I suppose he had much to say."
"Yes… I'm still processing it. He also offered to take me to utopia."
"Well, I've been there once or twice— it's quite pleasant, though there's not much there for me to do."
"How do you mean?"
"There's little need for a policeman."
"Maybe a good place to retire?"
"From traveling, you mean to say?" Fynn smiled.
"Another thing… He's asked for my help."

"What's that?"

"He wants me to hide Geppetto from Kali. Keep him safe."

"That's a large request."

"I agree. It's a big planet though, lots of places to hide."

"Where is Geppetto now?" Fynn asked.

"It's hard to say where *now* is exactly… But I know he was sent to Sonny Ming's for safe keeping, and to learn English… Remember I told you that I saw him there?"

"Yes. You were correct after all."

"So I know where and when he is at least. I'm just not sure how to get back."

"You are willing to do this for Mr Temsik?"

"I'm thinking about it… Of course, I could use your help."

"You shall have it. And yet, we still need to visit Japan."

"To help Mr Sato?"

"If help is the right word, yes." Fynn paused. "It seems for now, our paths coincide… traveling back to your usual present is our best choice."

"Sonny Ming's?"

"Yes… and travel to Japan is easiest in that era as well."

"Good." I smiled.

"While we're at Mr Ming's school, I might brush up on my Aramaic."

"Seriously?"

"I'm told it only takes an hour or so."

"Mr Temsik gave me this…" I held up the dice.

"Pavel's cube, eh? Have you used it?"

"No, I'm afraid to."

"Fear might not enter into it. Call it good judgement or prudence. How does it function?"

"It takes you to the present, but a parallel present."

"I will offer only one small bit of advice. Do not hide Geppetto in Sand City."

"Why not? Hide in plain sight, I was thinking."

"No. If anything were to go wrong, we would not want Kali's wrath to descend there of all places."

"So… how do we do this?"

"A simple soft jump."

"Are you sure?"

"And you do not trust that I can get us back to the correct moment? Oh Patrick, I am deeply hurt by this."

"Sorry… If we soft jump, it means I can't bring anything with me, like the dice…"

"Yes."

"Does that mean I'll also forget my Russian language skills?"

"That's not likely."

"What about everything else we've done? Will we have to do it again?"

"Not to worry, Patrick everything that has happened since, has happened in your past. We are from that present. It is a matter of record."

"You're sure?"

"No. But stopping Kali is the only goal we have."

"I also found this… I think Öde gave it to me— a lottery ticket, but I don't recognize the language."

"It's Greek," Fynn said after a glance. "I will guess you've won ten thousand drachmas in the national lottery."

"How much is that in dollars?"

"About three hundred."

"When's the drawing?"

"The first of November, nineteen sixty-two."

"That's a day after the end of the world…"

PART V

chapter seventeen
geppetto

It was a soft jump just like Fynn promised. I found myself back at Sonny Ming's School of Language Arts, though still strapped to a chair. My facilitator Siobhan was looking down at me while holding a high-tech hypodermic at the ready.
"Wait," I said.
"What?"
"I've…umm… changed my mind."
"About having coffee?" She smiled.
"No. About learning a new language."
Siobhan stared at me. "Well, that's never happened. Are you sure?"
"Very sure. Can I get a refund?"
"Hmm, I'll have to check with my supervisor."
"Can you unstrap me at least?"
There was some delay before things were sorted out, and that obliged me to remain seated for another hour at least. I was happy enough not to fill in the questionnaire again. Siobhan returned eventually and seemed a bit flustered. "Sorry for the delay, Mr Jardel, we had a minor emergency…"
"Is everything okay?"
"Yes, an unexpected arrival, that's all."
Back in my usual clothes, I headed upstairs to find Fynn in the waiting room.
"Ah, Patrick, finished already? That was quick. I've just been reading a fascinating article about pollination. I never knew that bees

were responsible for virtually all the food we eat… "

"Mr Temsik mentioned that."

"Who?" Fynn asked and gave me a wide smile. I knew immediately he was teasing, or hoped so. A moment later, Sonny Ming walked over. He had an anxious look about him.

"Is everything alright?" he asked.

"Couldn't be better."

"But you've cancelled your session."

"Yes and no…" I replied. "*Moy russkiy sovershenen.*"

"Your Russian is nearly perfect," Mr Ming echoed in English and a slight smile crossed his face.

"Where's Valentina?" I asked.

"Who?"

"The woman I sent back from Zvorkovo."

"Oh… This is something we should discuss in private, in my office… Mr Fynn?"

"I'll be along," he replied but did not rise. "I'd like to finish the article I'm reading."

Sonny Ming led me down the corridor to a modest office. We sat opposite, his desk remained unmanned.

"Well?" I asked.

"Oh yes, Valentina Bulgakov…" A dour expression came to his face. "We were unprepared for this contingency," Sonny admitted.

"Is she okay?"

"She seems no worse for *where*."

"What happened exactly?"

"We received the signal as usual… the bell…"

"And?"

"It wasn't you returning. Instead, this woman was transported back to our facility. It was decidedly a hard jump, and to her own relative future."

"Is she alright?"

"Yes. Luckily she took the pain pill before returning."

"And?"

"The staff was not sure what to do. It was all quite unexpected."

"Where is Valentina?"

"Sent away again— but she's yet to return."

"What do you mean?"

"She hasn't rung the bell… and it's been well over an hour. It seems she's decided not to return."

"Why would Valentina do that?"

"Perhaps she likes where she is."

"Explain, please."

"Well, after Ms Bulgakov arrived… it was agreed that she should learn English."

"Where?"

"Odessa… oh, sorry, no…" Sonny flipped through some pages of a notebook. "It's Little Odessa."

"Where's that?"

"Brighton Beach in Brooklyn. I have an address if you want."

"She's still there?" I thought for a moment. "In this present?"

"No, she was sent to nineteen eighty-seven."

"Why then?"

"Many Russians live there."

"But you're sure she's okay?"

"Yes, as far as I know… Ms Bulgakov runs a successful florist shop. I visited her personally."

"How is that possible?"

"I traveled back to check on her."

"It seems like a paradox to me."

"Why?"

"I haven't left for the Soviet Union yet."

"True enough, though the bell was logged onto the system once you signed up for a lesson. It rang in nineteen sixty-two and the automatic retrieval system was activated."

"What about Geppetto?" I asked.

"Who?"

"The Arbiter's referral."

"You know about him?" Sonny cast a glance.

"I do. In fact, I'm supposed to hide him."

"Hide him, you say?" Sonny Ming squinted as if in pain. "Yes, the Arbiter may have said something like that."

"Well?"

"He's right in the middle of a lesson. He may be gone for some years."

"Can't you bring him back any sooner?"

"I cannot, not until his instructor rings the bell."

"Where is he?"

"Vermont."

"Why there?"

"It's quiet, peaceful."

"How long will I have to wait?"

"It never takes more than an hour. He should be up and about shortly."

"How does this whole thing work exactly? Your school, I mean… like for a regular person, a non-traveler?"

"Have you read the brochure?"

"I did."

"We usually offer a course of ten sessions," Sonny began. "It's a two-part process. First a hard jump to the past…"

"A medicated jump?"

"Yes, our clients are sedated just before departure to mitigate against the pain." Mr Ming smiled. "Second, the bell rings at the end of your session, and you are returned to the present."

"Like how the Arbiter can pluck someone?"

"Somewhat," Mr Ming replied and gave a slight wince.

"Where do you arrive?"

"The center of the basement."

"What happens then?"

"The client is tested briefly, and then returned to everyday life."

"And what do people remember about the experience?"

"Very little. It's like a dream to them, I suppose."

"How do they remember what they've learned?"

"It has to do with how the human mind works, it's physiology. Lucky for us, the brain is hard-wired for language, so that knowledge seems to stick for most people… Memories on the other hand are a bit more ephemeral."

"A lot could go wrong…"

"I pride myself in being thorough, hence the lengthy questionnaire." Ming smiled. "And if anything does go wrong, I personally see to it that things are made right."

"By traveling there?"

"Yes. I enjoy the excursions for the most part… though usually the destinations are the major capitals of the world. You're the first person ever sent to Zvorkovo— I would have thought Moscow a better destination."

"How did you know to send me there?"

"I don't really understand the physics behind it all," Sonny admitted. "For example, when you were sent to Russia and nineteen fifty-seven, in reality you were sent many millions of miles through space. Certainly the earth was in a different location, not to mention the sun, and the rest of the solar system."

"You're saying I was lucky?"

"No. We are very thorough. If I were to send you to the same coordinates, but in the present. You'd be floating in the vacuum of space."

"You mean, I'd be dead."

"Yes."

"How did you ever figure all of this out?"

"The tricky bit is compensating for the earth's varying orbital velocity. Lothar did the calculations for us." Ming forced a smile. "We've never lost a customer."

There was a noise in the corridor and I was only somewhat surprised to see Pavel Mekanos emerge from a utility closet. He was wearing khaki overalls, a red cap, and as always, his outrageous mustache. Behind him came Edmund Fickster, dressed similarly, though with goggles, and carrying a large toolbox.

"All fixed?" Mr Ming called out as they walked by.

"Right as rain," Pavel replied, and they came into the office. "Hello, Patrick. What brings you here?" He greeted warmly.

"Weren't you just at the hotel?" I asked.

"Not that I know of."

"Oh… We were just talking about how this place works."

"A marvel, eh?" Edmund chimed in. "When it *is* working."

"I'm still not clear on any of this."

"Once you jump from here, you are returned to here. Space is constricted, one might say," Pavel explained. "Though your first departure might take you anywhere."

"It's random?"

"Not at all, thanks to Lothar's calculations table, Mr Ming is able to send you wherever he chooses."

"And this place?"

"It's a locus."

"A what?"

"A focal point that brings one back to a very specific location."

"We've built the whole school on top of a circle," Mr Ming clarified.

"What circle?"

"It was discovered after a terrible storm."

"Discovered?"

"Unearthed, one might say."

"When was this?"

"Just after the Great Hurricane of nineteen thirty-eight."

"And what about the bell? How does that work?"

"Entangled in the past, and it emits a standing wave," Pavel replied.

"A what?"

"It has no motion, so it is impervious to time…"

"Or, more simply, it's a simultaneous signal from the past and the future," Edmund added unhelpfully.

***

Back in the waiting room I asked Fynn about Geppetto. "I'm trying to remember… Did you ever meet him?"

"Yes, though I doubt he'll know me."

"Why not?"

"I had quite a long beard," Fynn replied.

"When?"

"Where is more apt. We were together in the Flatlands… Even if he does recall, I wouldn't say a word."

"Why not?"

"Best we spare him the indignity."

"You mean the whole tongue thing?"

Fynn nodded.

Sonny Ming kept his promise. Geppetto was led into the waiting room and introduced, all spruced up with a haircut and newish clothes.

"Hello there... remember me?" I asked.

Geppetto looked me up and down then gave a wide grin. "Oh yes, I do. You bought a fine *Branzino* from me in Firenze."

"Not that I recall..."

"Or was it on that island with Edmund?" He turned to Fynn. "I may have seen you there as well."

"Best not to think of it," Fynn said quietly.

"Yes..." Geppetto considered and turned back to me. "Ah, then it was at the hotel, with Mr Voynich."

"That's right... How did you two get along?"

"Mr Voynich has taught me much."

"Like?"

"I picked up a bit of Mandarin. I have a knack for language."

"Well, your English is excellent... I'm Patrick."

"Where is Wilfrid?"

"Umm, not here at the moment." I put on a hopeful smile. "What's your real name by the way?"

"Oh, Geppetto is fine. I've grown used to it and I rather like it as well. Besides, my real name is difficult to pronounce." He shook my hand and I noticed a terrible scar pretty much in the middle of his palm. It almost looked as if a bullet had passed through and healed up badly. I stared at it for too long and Geppetto noticed. He also looked down.

"I'm not sure how I got this wound," he said, and gave me a pained expression. "It seems as if I've always had it— though for the life of me, I cannot remember the injury."

"Hungry?" I asked, changing the subject.

"Ravenous..."

Fynn, Geppetto and I left Sonny Ming's school agreeing that a bite to eat was a good idea. "How about pizza," I said and nodded across the shopping plaza to the leaning tower.

"Pizza?" Geppetto repeated.

"An Italian delicacy."

"I don't recall ever eating such a thing in Firenze."

"No... it wasn't invented until after the tomato was discovered."

"The tomato... oh yes, this red fruit with seeds, I remember it from my days in Vermont. Sounds delicious."

As we walked across the parking lot, I heard a deep heavy thud and a low rumble coming from behind us. The ground shuddered for an instant. I looked over my shoulder at the school. It seemed to breathe with smoke, and a moment later all the windows flew outwards, followed by a scatter of dust and debris.

We stood in disbelief, then the three of us rushed back inside and began hauling people out. Most were startled more than injured, though their hearing was certainly impaired from the explosion. "Is there anyone upstairs?" I had to shout into Sonny Ming's ear. He shook his head no. I dragged him past a gaping hole in the floor; I could see the basement, and perhaps the remnants of a stone circle.

I helped Siobhan to the door and went back for any stragglers. Pavel and Edmund seemed in good shape; Fynn had dragged them out, and Geppetto was tending to the rest of the staff. A few moments later, flames erupted and soon engulfed the entire building. Smoke poured from the roof.

Sirens sounded and a slew of emergency vehicles pulled into the lot, fire trucks, ambulances, and police cars. Among them was Mitch in her dark blue Taurus. After conferring with colleagues and local officials, she came over to us. "What— I leave you two alone for an hour and you try to blow up my town?"

I laughed but said, "It wasn't us."

"No, it wasn't." She turned to Geppetto. "Who's this?"

"A friend of ours."

"I'll have to hold you all, sorry guys. You were inside, you're material witnesses."

"We are heroes, we've saved lives here. But we cannot stay," Fynn replied.

"You have to. It's procedure. You know, make a formal statement."

"Detective Mitch, we have done you a favor and now one is owed to us," Fynn said and added a smile.

Mitch was shaking her head.

"We promise to be back first thing."

"Okay... go..." she said, and we started towards my car. "Wait a second," she called out, "there's something you should know."

"What?"

"It's a she, not a he," the detective said.

"What?"

"Mad Maxine, not Mad Max."

"How do you know?"

"From the CCTV footage at the gas station…" She took out her tablet to show us. "Look at the way she walks… that's not a man."

It was hard to disagree.

"What about the logo?" Fynn asked.

"Oh yeah, the snake eating its own tail. I searched the internet… only thing I found that might be relevant is some construction company… But it's based overseas, Asia, someplace…"

"The same logo?"

"Looks like it."

"What's the name of the company?"

"Otas Construction. They have a satellite office in Garden City. I was thinking of swinging by to see what's up."

"Could you call us if you find anything?"

"Sure thing."

***

"It's best we go our separate ways… just in case we are being followed," Fynn said as Geppetto scrambled into the backseat of the Saab.

"Followed? You think Kali is here?"

"I suspect this is her doing."

"But how?"

"Perhaps Detective Mitch will discover such."

"Where to then?"

"If you'll just drop me at the station."

"A train?"

"Of course. I like trains… and I'll be safe from Kali should it come to that."

"A moving vehicle— one of her few weaknesses…" I laughed. "You could rent a car."

"I'd prefer not, given our travails on the way here." Fynn gave half a smile.

"You could always use the cane," I said to him.

"I'd like to remain in the present… Take Geppetto to the library. I'll meet you in Sand City in a few days."

"A few days?"

"Well, take as much time as you need. That should give Geppetto a chance to settle in."

"And he'll be safe there?"

"I cannot think of a better place. As you've said, Kali's abilities are likely thwarted by an area where the flow of time is not normal."

"Okay…"

"By then I should have booked passage to Japan. It's high time we pay a visit to Mr Sato."

I thought for a moment. "What kind of passage?"

"I'll see what sort of boats go there."

"Are you kidding? It makes perfect sense to take a commercial flight."

"You may fly if you like… and I'll meet you," Fynn said with an optimistic grin.

"How will you get there?"

"By other means…"

"I'm not sure I like that plan. We should go together."

"You know I don't like to fly."

"You were fine when Stanley took us to the West Coast."

"I was not fine, but at least I knew the pilot."

"I remember we rode a zeppelin together not so long ago."

"And I recall it didn't work out at all…" Fynn paused. "Alright, Patrick, it may be necessary to take an airplane, even though it's against my better judgement. Let us call it plan B. I will ask Anika to make the arrangements. Your passport is in order?"

"Mine or Gary Sevens?"

"It hardly matters." Fynn rummaged through his jacket and handed me a wad of cash.

"What's this for?"

"Gas money… and any unexpected contingencies."

It was a quick drive to the intersection of Railroad and Deerpark Avenue. Geppetto said little along the way, his head swiveling from side to side as if to take in all the marvels to be seen. We pulled into the LIRR station; tracks loomed overhead.

"Were we followed?"

"Hard to say, a lot of traffic."

"Good luck then," Fynn said. "See you in a few days…"

***

Once I dropped Fynn off, Geppetto climbed into the front seat, literally. He scrutinized my every move as we set off towards the Southern State Parkway, westbound.

"I would very much like to learn how to operate such a fantastical conveyance."

"Sure… it's not that hard. In fact, it becomes second nature after a while."

"That's hard to believe…" Geppetto stared at me. "Such speeds; we are surely traveling faster than the wind."

He began his driving lesson by opening and closing the electric windows from the center console, then the sunroof. By the time we were on the parkway, he had accidentally turned off the Saab. It took me a second to understand why my car just suddenly died. "That's the key, it keeps the engine going. Please don't touch that."

"Sorry," he replied.

I glanced down and noticed a dice sitting on the console, Pavel's dice. I could only guess that Mr Temsik had left it, and crammed the cube into my front pocket.

Geppetto moved to the controls on the dashboard. "What are these?" he asked.

"Climate control… heat and air-conditioning."

"What's that?"

"Cold air for hot days, like today."

"But we have all the windows open." He smiled and began rolling them up and down again. "And this?"

"That's a cup holder."

Geppetto pointed to the sky. "You have creatures here that fly?"

"No, that's an airplane, a mechanical creature."

"So many marvels…"

By the time we were on the Clearview Expressway, Geppetto had found the radio and turned it on. A hip-hop tune blasted through the speakers but I turned it down and found a classical music station instead. It was Gustav Holst: *The Planets*, and Geppetto was delighted.

"Very nice indeed…" he approved.

The first movement, *Mars*, seemed to add unnecessary drama to changing lanes in the heavy traffic. We had a good view of Manhattan as we crept over the Throgs Neck Bridge. Geppetto was transfixed by the vista. The skyline rose in a distant haze.

"And all these boxes I see on the horizon; what are they?"

"Buildings. That's New York City. It's even more impressive at night."

"Why is that?"

"All lit up, like a million stars."

"And why are we going to bypass this wondrous place? I was told we are going to the library."

"Yes, but this particular library is not in the city."

"You have more than one?"

"Almost every town has one nowadays."

"I am at your mercy, Mr Patrick."

"So… what's it like being here in the future?"

"I haven't decided yet, though I admit to being overwhelmed." Geppetto turned in his seat. "Some things I like about your era… I've noticed sanitation is more advanced than what I'm used to. Clothes are easier to don, especially what you call trousers. And everything I have so far seen appears quite miraculous."

"Not like home, eh?"

"I am so far from there, you cannot even begin to imagine."

"Florence, you mean?"

"Who?"

"Firenze, Italy."

"No, even that seems closer to here…"

"So, where are you from originally?"

"This is something I cannot say."

"Why not?"

"It is something I can barely recall. I only remember there were no cities."

"No?"

"We lived in burrows."

"Burrows?"

"Yes, beneath the earth. On the surface lived horrific beasts that would eat you in a single bite."

"What kind of creatures?"

"Oh, something between a lizard and a bird."

"Where were you before this? To learn English, I mean."

"At a Joss House, someone called it."

"A what?"

"Like a monastery."

"How long did you live there?"

"Two or three years it seems to me."

"What religion did you say?"

"Some deity named Buddha, I think… or was it Mr Zen?"

"Sounds peaceful."

"It was a sheltered existence. Quite beautiful…"

"When was this?"

"The late eighteen hundreds, someone said. I did read many books while I was there. Many books on history, so I'm quite up-to-date on things."

"Hmm, late eighteen hundreds… that was a century ago at least. A lot's happened since then."

"What year is it now?"

"We're sneaking up on twenty-twenty."

"As in a calendar date?"

"Yes…"

"That's more than five hundred years since I last remember."

"Italy, you mean?"

Geppetto nodded but fell silent… "Tell me, Patrick, where is Mr Voynich these days? We became good friends at the hotel. Is there a chance we might pay him a visit? I would very much like to see Wilfrid again."

"I'm afraid he's dead."

"What happened to him?"

"Died of old age, I think, sometime in the nineteen thirties."

"Ah… Well, couldn't we travel back to see him?"

"Are you a traveler?"

"I used to be, and I thought, quite good at it… But no longer…"

"Why not?"

"I cannot say, but very many years ago, I woke up, decided to leap— and instead of finding myself in a different era, I was merely half a *miglio* to the west… Ever since that day, I cannot travel."

"A *miglio*? Is that like a mile or a kilometer?"

"I couldn't say, sorry."

***

Our drive took a turn for the worse shortly after we crossed the bridge. We merged onto Interstate-95, southbound, the signs said, but surely we were traveling west. Once we hit the Cross Bronx Expressway, traffic snarled to a halt. The highway was filled with lumbering trucks; they outnumbered passenger cars ten to one. Geppetto asked about all the rolling cabinets that surrounded us on every side.

"The what? Oh, they're called trucks. It's almost rush hour," I tried to explain.

"What does this mean?"

"Traffic."

"And what is this?"

"Many cars moving very slowly."

"Cars— what is this word?"

"Like carriages without horses… all these vehicles you see around us."

"I thought the big ones were called trucks."

"You're a fast learner."

"And what is in these trucks, as you call them?"

"Freight, cargo, boxes…"

"And inside that?"

"Stuff… food, clothes, furniture… gadgets…"

"Machines?"

"Yes."

"Even trucks that carry cars," Geppetto said.

"Crazy world, right?"

"A few of these I can guess, as I see beautifully painted murals on their sides."

"Advertising," I replied.

He repeated the word, obviously unfamiliar to him. "And what makes them go?"

"Truck drivers," I said but he was hardly satisfied with my reply. "An engine... most of them use diesel."

"There are many new words for me to learn, eh?" He grinned. "And these cars, I notice they are subtly different from each other."

"What do you mean?"

"Of course they are of different colors, but I see variations in their shapes and sizes... Why are they not all the same?"

"A good question... I guess they're a reflection of the driver's personality."

"And what does your vehicle say about you?"

I chuckled. "Me... well, I guess it means I'm on my way to becoming defunct."

"Why is that?"

"They've stopped making this kind of car."

"I remember what the Romans called roads. Ha, they were roughly cobbled foot paths, certainly not expressways as you call them now."

"They'd be envious, huh?"

"Perhaps... though I'm sure an entire legion could travel faster than we are at the moment." Geppetto was so fed up with traffic, he opened the door and started to get out of the car.

"No, no, you can't do that," I shouted, though helpless to stop him.

"I'll meet you up ahead— I just want to have a look around..."

Geppetto didn't anticipate a sudden eruption of honking horns, nor the noxious fumes. The stench of diesel hung heavy in the air. He was choking and sputtering. I caught up to him a few yards ahead, just before a dark overpass. He seemed reluctant to enter the tunnel, and heard me calling out from the driver's seat. He climbed back inside, now a little cowed by the experience. Geppetto settled again as we crept through the Bronx. Not much later, traffic began to pick up speed.

"All these buildings? They are workshops, yes?"

"Apartments, mostly. Dwellings."

"Who lives in them?"

"People... just everyday people."

"And what do they all do?"

"Various things. They keep civilization running."

"That is their duty?"

"No, it's their life."

"Do any of them sell fish?"

"Sure... seafood is very popular."

"Do they care about each other?"

"That's a good question... not so much, probably."

"What holds your world together then?"

"Momentum."

"And this civilization is based on these vehicles of yours?"

I had to think for a moment. "Pretty much, yeah...cars and cell phones."

"Ah yes, these little blocks that I see, that everyone carries with them. You are all connected to each other."

"In theory. But most people just talk to people they know."

"Friends?"

"Friends and family... maybe colleagues at work."

"I see...so it's not really a civilization at all. It's a kind of tribalism, people only stick to people they know."

"Pretty much."

"I suppose then, there are many, many chieftains."

"You'd be right."

"I don't think I wish to live here."

"Why not?"

"Despite the many wondrous marvels I have seen, something is lacking."

"What's lacking?"

"I cannot put my finger on it." Geppetto sat quietly for a long while. "Do they all know each other?"

"What?" I swiveled a glance.

"Do all these people know each other?"

"No, not really. That would be impossible."

"And yet they all share the same fate more or less."

"I suppose that's true."

"And how many did you say?"

"In the whole world, around seven billion now."

"That is not a number I've heard of, nor can I conceive what it means."

"Well, it's a lot…"

"Your city looks so shiny and splendid from afar, but up close it is a disappointment."

"How so?"

"Everything seems to be crumbling and filthy." Geppetto paused for a time. "Where are we going now?"

"The Bridge."

"Yet another bridge? But I see so many already here, they cross this river of cars."

"This bridge goes over water, the Hudson."

"Ah, there is a small taste of home," Geppetto said and pointed to the left. Just at the East River there was a medieval looking tower built of bricks and topped with a green copper roof.

The approach to the George Washington Bridge was utter chaos. We were flanked on every side by merging trucks, inches away it seemed. One in particular appeared like a wounded beast, stuck in its lane with blinkers on, desperately trying to merge left, back into the herd. We entered a narrow, pitch black tunnel filled with the bellows of these traveling cabinets: the sound and fury of hydraulic brakes, grinding transmissions and throttling engines. There was the asphyxiating stench as well, the relentless stop and go, and then surging ahead, all accompanied by echoing thunder.

I glanced over to see an expression of abject terror on Geppetto's face. "How's my driving?"

"I am impressed by your skills to steer clear of these enormous beasts… It's little wonder you can keep your sanity, let alone your focus and ability to safely guide us through such incredible peril."

"Not too worry, we're getting close and the rest of the drive is… well… more scenic."

***

We arrived at the Library on the Palisades later than I hoped. The sun was close to setting, and the cliffs along the Hudson were in deep shadow when I pulled up to a familiar iron gate.

"Sorry sir, this facility is for faculty only. We're not open to the public…"

"Stanley?" I asked, and with a smile.

"Patrick." He recognized me. "I'll be damned."

"I thought you were dead."

"Not that I know of." Stanley laughed.

"Oh, maybe it hasn't happened yet."

"You might say the same thing to anyone who is alive."

I nodded over to the other guard, a goliath of a man sprawled in a tiny chair. It was Lothar, crescent scars and all.

"Mr Mortimer dropped him off a few days ago," Stanley replied to my unasked question. He opened the heavy iron gate and waved us through.

Brigadier Thomas came rushing down the hill and maybe for the first time I'd ever seen, he was out of uniform. He was older than I expected. "Good heavens, it's Patrick, a sight for sore eyes. How are you, my boy?"

"All things considered, not so bad…" I smiled and took his handshake. "This is my friend Geppetto."

"Ah, Mr Geppetto, a great pleasure… my sister Maddy and I have heard a great deal about you. Please, come along. I'll take you up to the house."

"How is it that you know Stanley?" I asked the brigadier.

"We fought together during the war, side by side." Brigadier Thomas slapped him on the back with great affection. "He's saved my life on more than one occasion, and I, his."

Stanley beamed back nodding, but said nothing.

"Considering our dire situation, I asked him here. All hands on deck— eh?"

I saw many other buildings that were not here before, built recently. It looked more like a campus now. Geppetto stopped for a moment to read a small blue sign: *Lamont-Doherty Earth Observatory, Columbia University*

"Things are quiet here in August… until the next semester begins," the brigadier explained as we trudged up the hill.

"If this is an observatory, do you have a telescope?" Geppetto asked along the way.

"Sorry, no... it's an earth observatory. They look downwards not upwards."

"How do you mean?"

"Seismic sonar, core samples, that sort of thing. They store long tubes of dirt in that building." The brigadier pointed to a sugar-cube-shaped structure.

"Things do look different," I commented.

"Oh, had to sell off some of the land for financial reasons. Mr Lamont bought up the place after the war. A damn shame... Gave up the waterfall, and Einstein's dice..." Brigadier Thomas resumed his pace up the hill that was flanked by a familiar row of uniform trees.

"What about the temple?"

"Gave that up too... The circle ground to a halt some years back. Hasn't functioned since the flood of fifty-five."

"When?"

"Nineteen fifty-five. And then there were vandals some years later... I came down one morning and found the whole place smashed to bits. Broken beer bottles everywhere. You can't imagine how difficult things are for Maddy and I."

"How is your sister?" I asked

"Oh, poor Madeline, she's in a terrible state... Spends most of her time in an apron, baking gingerbread men."

"What?"

"Well, now that Cook is gone."

"For Lothar, you mean?"

"Yes. His appetite is insatiable."

We came to the clearing at the top of the hill. The library stood alone much as I remembered, though unscathed by fire.

"The library is still out of bounds— it's considered our private residence."

"No one notices the slowly rotating building?"

"No one has said anything to us."

***

We decided to spend a few days. I was hoping Geppetto would take to the place so I could head back to Sand City and meet up with Fynn again. He was suitably impressed as we entered the giant library that spiraled down to the depths like a nautilus. He seemed overwhelmed by the sight of all the books.

"Ah, I could spend my entire life here," he declared.

Madame Madeline gave off a sharp laugh. "Well you may, Mr Geppetto, and to our great pleasure."

Brigadier Thomas and his sister were perfect hosts as usual. It was a very young Madeline who was present, and no less flirtatious, seizing every opportunity to sit closer than necessary.

"We finally got electricity..." the brigadier announced proudly.

"No elevator though," Madeline said. "Pavel advised against it."

"A *death trap*, I think he called it, my dear."

I warned Geppetto not to go down into the stacks, not too far at least, and especially not to linger in the corridors. "Time is a bit strange down there. Runs faster than it should."

"Yes, I can remember writing something about the pace of time, how it might be made to ebb and flow at different speeds."

"Did you write these books yourself?" I asked.

"No, no, I was just a scribe. I only wrote what I was told."

"By whom?"

"A fearsome race of beings... the Builders."

"Were they human?"

"When I was a young boy, I thought them to be gods, but in the end, yes, they are only men and women."

On our first night it was Lothar who prepared a delicious supper of sage-roasted chicken and asparagus. Over dinner, Stanley recounted some of his previous adventures with Fynn, though I had heard the stories before: His journey along the Nile, and the incidents aboard the *Carpathia*... When he started reminiscing about his exploits with Brigadier Thomas during the Crimea War, it was time to excuse ourselves. I could see Geppetto growing restless and suggested we might take a walk. He was up from his seat like a shot and we meandered out onto the open field. The air seemed thick at first but thinned as we approached the top of the cliffs.

It was decidedly dangerous to get too close to the edge. In the darkness it was difficult to see where the three hundred foot drop began or the ledges ended. Nor could we see New York City from our vantage, but Geppetto was curious about a new bridge under construction to the north.

"But why build a new bridge— why not just repair the old one?"

"Well, I guess millions of people cross the river every day— maybe it was easier."

"Tell me about this number again, Patrick."

"Millions?"

"No, billions… I've been wrestling with the concept to no avail."

"Okay. Let's see… Say every person was a grain of sand. A pinch is a couple of hundred… It would take a few thousand to fill a spoon, millions would fill a bucket, and a billion would fill a bathtub…"

"So, a person for every star in the sky."

"Well, there are the stars we can see with the naked eye, and the ones we can see with a telescope— that's got to be trillions."

"How much sand is that?"

"A whole beach's worth."

Geppetto paused for a while, looking skyward. "Why can I not see the stars any longer?"

***

On our return, Madeline greeted us by the front door. She was outside having a cigarette. "Back already?" she asked with a smile. "Oh…" she replied to my long stare. "Yes, no smoking in the library anymore…" Madeline took us up to our rooms. I bunked in *Nietzsche's Nook* and Geppetto slept next door in the *Plato Academy* suite.

It was difficult to say exactly how much time passed in the library. It may have been days or even weeks. One morning, Brigadier Thomas had terrible news over breakfast. He had not mentioned anything previously, perhaps not to spoil the evening, maybe because he simply forgot, or, he had just received yesterday's paper from proper time.

"I suppose you've heard about Sand City by now, eh Patrick?"

"No— why?"

"It was in the newspaper, some sort of cataclysm has befallen your fair city."

"What?"

"It was splashed on the front page."

"Where's the paper?"

"Oh… sorry, in the kitchen. Lothar needed it to wrap some old fish heads."

"What did it say?"

"Hmm, what do I remember?" the Brigadier asked himself. "A terrorist attack— was it?"

I felt panic rise up. There was no wifi— no bars on my cellphone. I ran down the hill to my car, figuring the only source of news available was the radio. I also noticed the gate was wide open and neither Lothar nor Stanley were on duty this morning. I did get a signal. The news blared from the speakers. I sat with the doors to my car wide open and listened intently:

… the popular resort, summer home to 20,000 vacationers… Officials have not released casualty figures but they could number in the hundreds or thousands, one unnamed source has told us… An area as far south as Fairhaven has now been quarantined… While some still consider this a terrorist attack, no group has so far taken responsibility…

As far as I could tell, nothing was certain. Speculation ran rampant: Everything from an anthrax outbreak to a tactical nuclear bomb was mentioned. One odd thing: Aircraft were unable to fly over the scene due to plumes of electromagnetic interference.

Brigadier Thomas came down the hill a short time later, leading the ranks of Stanley, Lothar, and his new recruit, Geppetto.

"What news, Patrick?"

"None of it good." I turned to the brigadier. "What do they say happened?"

"Who?"

"All the geological experts here."

"Oh yes, an earthquake, I heard someone say. Or was it an anomalous seismic event? Perhaps an undersea volcano…"

chapter eighteen
cubed

It was late that afternoon when I decided to leave, having spent the day anxiously. I had walked far enough south to get a cell signal and tried calling everyone I knew in Sand City. No response— right to voicemail. There was nothing new on the radio about the disaster, just endless speculation.

I explained to Geppetto that he should stay. "You'll be safe here and these people are my friends. I trust them."

"I'd rather come with you."

"It could be dangerous. Besides, the library is a great place to catch up on modern history."

"When will you be back?"

"I don't know... a couple of days, maybe."

Geppetto pointed over my shoulder. "Who is that?" he asked and squinted for a better look. An expression of recognition crossed his face, and then fear. I turned to see a small figure trudging up the hill with fierce determination. They were heading straight for us and now I guessed it was a woman wearing a hooded sweatshirt. She was carrying something under her arm.

When the brigadier and Stanley came up behind me, Geppetto was already running towards the edge of the cliffs. The woman pulled away her hood and let it fall to her back. I saw Kali's smiling face. She looked at least ten years older than I remembered; her hair streaked with gray and dangling before her eyes.

"How did she get through the gate?" I asked.

"Despite appearances, security isn't that tight. Any hiker might hop the fence," Brigadier Thomas replied.

"I am here for Geppetto," Kali said as she brushed past us and brandished a shotgun.

"Why?" I called out.

"Now that he has learned to speak English, I will take him with me."

"Where to?"

"Somewhere you can't find him. He will translate the manuscripts."

"You have them?"

"I do, and there is much he can tell me, I'm sure of it." She faced us. "Do not interfere and I will leave the rest of you unmolested. I have only come for Geppetto."

"I have no wish to go with you," he cried out, taking several steps backwards.

Kali pressed on. Soon Geppetto was up against the edge of the cliffs. It was at least a three hundred foot drop. The bottom was already deep in shadow, only a waning sun skirted the top. He glanced over his own shoulder at the river below. A few more steps and he was a dead man; he would smash into the rocks, like all the Drummonds from the past.

"You have a choice, dear man, come with me now, or fall to your death."

"I choose to fall," Geppetto said. He seemed to leap off the edge and disappear from view.

Kali turned away in disgust and then stepped toward the brigadier and Stanley. She clicked back the shotgun. I had an idea though. Reaching into my pocket, I found Pavel's marble of time and turned it clockwise as far as it would go. With a single motion, I tapped it twice and flipped it underhand towards Kali's back. I was aiming for the deep crevice of her hood. I watched the marble slow along its way, like a stop action film, yet it was inexorably on course. Kali began to turn, but too late. The look of surprise on her face was precious.

She was trapped in slow-time and stood there as if a statue. While only a moment would pass before she found the device and destroyed it, hours would pass outside the bubble. My only thought was escape, but Brigadier Thomas had other ideas.

He leapt upon Kali, and to curious effect. It was as if he had hit an unmovable object and ricocheted to one side. He then plunged over the edge and disappeared from view. Kali stood motionless, though now she was hovering in mid-air. There was nothing between her and the bottom of the cliffs. For a brief moment, I thought I saw a smile cross her face. The bubble of time popped, and she fell like a stone to be dashed below at the river's edge.

Stanley and I rushed to the cliffs and peered down. There was a lifeless body sprawled at a horrible angle. I heard a low moaning though. Off to our left we spotted the brigadier face down on an outcropping of rock. He hadn't plummeted to his death after all. Stanley and I helped him up. He was injured, bruised and battered, and perhaps had a broken rib by the way he was clutching his side.

"You should be happier than you seem, Patrick," he managed to say.

"Why?"

"We've just eliminated Kali."

I gave him a look.

"Well, the loss of life is always regrettable, but think of her as an enemy combatant."

"Maybe..." I was hurrying in the other direction.

"Where will you go?" the brigadier asked over his shoulder.

"Home..." I replied and started back towards my car. "You should stay here and guard the library."

"Against whom?"

"Kali."

"Another Kali?" the brigadier asked.

I nodded and sprinted down the hill back to the entrance. To my surprise and great relief, I found Geppetto sitting in the passenger seat. He was grinning.

"How...?" I started to ask, "—never mind..." I dimly understood he had not fallen after all; he had just jumped and traveled half a *miglio* instead. I fired up the engine and tore through the open gates, northward.

***

It was a long drive to Sand City, even though we never made it that far, and it was pouring rain the whole ride. Geppetto marveled at the windshield wipers. I gently asked him about Kali. It was pretty clear that he had seen her before and recognized her, but refused to say more. When I glanced over I could see fear in his eyes. He did finally mention that Kali was fond of music, and I recalled something similar. We stopped only once on the way to grab a bite, and for gas. I was relieved that only unleaded was available.

Admittedly, I grew a little impatient with Geppetto. Everything was so new to him and he had so many questions. In the end, he decided that such a splendid civilization would doubtless last a thousand years. I didn't have the heart to tell him how unlikely that seemed, and was happy when he finally fell asleep. For me it was like a deja vu, only I was traveling north instead of south.

Early the next morning we were stopped at the border of Fairhaven. We could enter but go no further up the peninsula. Route 16 was completely closed. I also tried every back road I knew; they were all guarded as well, a barricade, a police presence, or maybe they were military. Scary in any case with black masks and helmets. I turned back and finally decided to find a room.

There was a vacancy at the Lucky Sevens Motel, under the shadow of the interstate. A familiar place to me, though the rate was double what I remembered. Geppetto was still marveling at the swimming pool in the courtyard— right where I left him. He hung on the chain link fence and looked in longingly.

"Sure, we can go for a swim later, if you want. Let's settle in first..."

Everything in the cramped room held new fascination for Geppetto. When I flipped on the TV and showed him how to use the remote, I lost him completely. He just stared at the screen fixated, and flipped through every channel available. I tried calling Detective Durbin on his cell and finally got through. He was also in Fairhaven. I'm not sure if he was trapped here like the rest of us, or ready to deploy into Sand City when the time was right.

"What happened exactly? Terrorists?" I asked.

"No one knows, or no one's saying..." he replied.

"You must have heard something."

"Military cordon... that's all I know."

"What about the other towns nearby?"

"I hear they're being evacuated one by one: Oldham and Garysville, all the way down the peninsula... They closed off Route Sixteen— northbound. You can only leave. Nobody goes in unless they're military."

"Wow."

"National Guard is all set up. More coming tomorrow."

"More?"

"Airlifted in, I heard— from different states." Durbin paused. "They won't even let me through, and I'm the goddamn Chief of Police."

I could hear his frustration. He was mostly worried about Ricky though.

"Yeah, Ricky's there and I haven't heard a thing in two days. All the cell phones are down."

"Maybe the tower's out again?" I suggested.

"It's worse than that, Patrick— and you know it."

"What about the rest of your family?"

"They're fine, luckily… here in town with me." Durbin paused again. "How about you, Patrick? You okay."

"I'm good."

"And Fynn?"

"He's in Sand City— haven't heard anything either."

"Okay…" Durbin paused to consider. "Remember the diner near the courthouse?" he asked. "Meet me there in an hour. I might have an idea."

"About what?"

"About getting inside."

***

Geppetto complained about being hungry and he had every right to. Neither of us had eaten anything since late last night.

"What kind of food do you like?"

"Anything other than what we ate before."

"Fair enough…" I laughed. "No preference though?"

"I especially enjoy food from the sea."

"Sure… What do you want to drink?"

"Wine."

"A little too early maybe… how about water?"

"Is it safe?"

"I'll get a couple of sodas…"

"What's that?"

"It's like fizzy nectar— very sweet… you'll probably like it."

On my phone, I found a local fish and chips place that was willing to deliver. I just had time for a quick shower. Geppetto followed me into the bathroom, but I asked for some privacy.

"Sorry…"

"If someone knocks on the door, that'll be our lunch. Just give them these…" I peeled off two twenties from a wad of bills and dropped the rest on the bed.

"What are they?" he asked, picking up the pile.

"It's money… umm, like ducats or florins…"

"Ah, not coins… but paper— that is very curious." He smiled. "What should I do with the rest? These bits of paper with hundreds on them?"

"Keep them safe, in your pocket."

"I've seen this man before."

"In person?"

"No… in a book, I think. He was flying a kite in a lightning storm."

"Sure, that's Ben Franklin."

"And why would such foolishness be celebrated by a portrait?"

***

Geppetto had spent a good deal of time marveling at the bathroom. I gave him detailed instructions on how the plumbing operated. He also decided to take a shower— something else he had never experienced. I could hear the water running. The TV was showing the same endless news about the disaster in Sand City. It wasn't news at all, just a replay of stock footage: ambulances and military cordons. The same rehashing of what they didn't know, and the same wild speculation presented by a parade of experts. I'd seen it all already. I pressed the mute button and lay back on the bed.

From my pocket I took out Pavel's dice and gave it a closer look. It seemed ordinary enough, black with white dots. On a whim I touched all eight corners. Nothing happened— it didn't start glowing or anything. Then I rolled it onto the bedside table. It clattered and a three appeared. I picked it up and held it in my palm. I could feel a slight tingle run up my arm. Then an odd sensation came over me, as if a thousand versions of myself all sat together at the same time.

But nothing else happened. I hadn't moved an inch. Well, almost nothing. The water stopped running in the bathroom. I guess

Geppetto was finally done. I waited a few minutes but heard nothing more. I grew a bit worried, then called out to no answer. Maybe he had slipped in the tub or something. I opened the door to find the lights off. No Geppetto, and the tub was dry. A few moments later there was a knock on the front door. I wasn't expecting anyone. When I swung it open, Ricky Durbin was there, standing and grinning.

"I thought you were in Sand City," I greeted him. "I was just on the phone to your dad. We're going to meet at the diner."

"What the hell are you talking about, Patrick? My dad is trapped in Sand City. I haven't heard from him in two days now."

I beckoned him inside. "Oh sorry. You're worried about him."

"Damn straight I am."

The dice... I thought, and almost said it aloud. Only now did I suspect that I had slipped into a parallel timeline. I also noticed my shirt was a slightly different shade of blue. "How did you know I was here?"

"I didn't, but I figured if you were anywhere nearby, this is where you'd show up." Ricky grinned again. "Besides, there's not a room in town that's not booked already."

"Do you know anything else, anything that's not on the news?"

"No... Just rumors."

"Could we sneak in? Take the back roads?"

"There's no way you're getting in unless you're military or a doctor... or maybe an EMT..." Ricky paused as an idea struck him. "We would need the proper vehicle..."

"Like?"

He laughed slightly. "Like not your Saab, or my Pontiac." He gave me a grin. "Come on, I have an idea..."

"Let me grab some stuff..."

The one thing I shouldn't have grabbed from the nightstand was the dice; it slipped to the carpet. A five. I picked it up. A tingling. It felt like a thousand shadows rushed by and merged into me. Geppetto came out of the bathroom dripping wet but fully clothed.

"Who's this?" Ricky asked.

"Oh, meet Geppetto, a friend of mine..."

***

I felt guilty about leaving Geppetto at the motel, promising to be back in a day or so. He took it well. In fact I'd never seen someone so enamored with a mini-bar before. I ripped out a page from the phone book— it had a list of local take-out places, and I taught him how to use the telephone.

"Do you understand?"

"Yes. Whenever I am hungry, I push any of these numbers into that machine and ask for food."

"Right, and just tell them what room you're in: eleven."

"And when they knock on the door I give them a special piece of paper." Geppetto smiled.

"That's right. Oh, and there's an ice box out around back."

"Ice?"

"Those little cubes of frozen water that you like so much."

"I shall explore my surroundings thoroughly."

"Well, don't go too far, and don't lose your key card."

"Good luck to you then, Patrick. No need to worry, I will spend my time in the glorious thing you call a swimming pool."

Before Ricky and I left, I paid for an extra week, just in case.

***

Ricky Durbin drove us up towards the ocean. I started to wonder if his idea had something to do with borrowing a boat. Instead he pulled into a small compound nestled in the woods. It was a cinder-block garage behind a chain link fence. No guards or anything, no one there at all.

"Wait here," he said and disappeared to the back of his car. I could here him rummaging around in the trunk; the sound of tools clinking against each other. A moment later he hopped the fence. I watched him pry open the garage door with a crow bar. It seemed empty, but he waved me over.

"Get that gate open, will ya?" he asked and pointed to the bolt cutters.

"What are you doing? Requisitioning a vehicle?" I asked.

Ricky laughed but was a little vague in his reply, "We're gonna need some extra gas."

By the time I got the gate open, Ricky came tearing out of the garage sitting aboard an ATV.

"What's this?"

"A rescue dune buggy, that the lifeguards use."

"What now?"

"We wait till it's dark."

"What, like use the flashing lights and sirens to fool people? Like we're on a mission?"

"I'm not sure that's going to work, Patrick."

"What's the plan then?"

"Stealth."

It was a harrowing ride, racing through the pine barrens along the back roads, though road was not the right word. We were lucky to have a full moon to guide us. The sandy trails were white compared to the underbrush and trees. Ricky used the lights sparingly to cross streams and bogs with caution. He had to shut everything down once when a helicopter flew overhead. We rolled to a stop under some gnarled branches to let it pass. After an hour or so we made it to the beach and the going got easier. We could see the shoreline clearly enough and the black Atlantic frothing in the moonlight. There were few other obstructions along the way.

By sunrise, we had made it as far as the Oldham breach. It now stretched far inland towards the bay and out of sight. Ricky turned off the engine and we looked across. The channel was far wider than either of us remembered, some few hundred yards, and it was filled with a treacherous swirling. In the middle it seemed as if the ocean was rushing inland, and with some force; while closer to either shore, the current was slower and looked to be a backwash that returned to the Atlantic.

"What now?" Ricky asked.

"Looks tough to cross."

"You mean swim?"

"You think the ATV could make it?"

"No, it's too deep. And I would not want to stall smack in the middle."

From where we stood there wasn't much to see of Sand City. That's to say, it looked completely normal; a few houses, sun, waves and a wide stretch of shoreline led to the misty north. If anything was wrong, it was that no one lounged on the beach on such a fine day. There were no umbrellas or blankets, no one frolicking in the surf.

I looked around our side of the breach. A quarter mile inland and still on the Oldham side there was a kind of boathouse. Not much more than some driftwood and a few panels of weathered gray ply board. There was a rack of boats though, I remembered. "Come on," I said and sprinted up the beach. Ricky followed. We hauled down a kayak and found a couple of good paddles. "What do you think?" I asked and added a hopeful smile.

"I'm all in, Patrick. Just row fast— okay? I don't want to get stuck in that current."

"Let's try over there. It looks narrow."

We slid into the slow water and paddled with as much strength as we had, cutting across the treacherous bit in the middle. It was easier than I thought, and we were on the other side after just a few minutes. Ricky and I dragged our kayak up onto the dunes, safe from the water's edge.

"Well?" he asked.

I pointed. "Let's go north and east. We should have a good view of the village over that hill."

He muttered okay and followed. I felt the wind kick up as we walked over the ridge, an ocean breeze. But I hadn't gone more than a few yards more when the air turned thick like jello. I could hardly breathe. I turned to ask Ricky if…

He was gone. Vanished. Not hiding. I couldn't even find his foot prints. "This is not good," I thought aloud, and began to retrace my steps. Maybe I had crossed some kind of invisible boundary. The kayak had also disappeared and the breach seemed somewhat less menacing.

I sat a long while puzzling over what just happen but failed to come up with a satisfactory answer. This was not some parallel present, that much I was sure of. I hadn't used the dice. Ricky was gone— but had he disappeared, or had I? It was either the past or the future— I was someplace else in time. For now there was little left to do but explore further.

Up and over the dunes I went, half climbing, half jogging, sprinting when possible. I came across nothing. No roads, no houses, no other structures. I should've been able to see the monstrous green water tower. Eventually, I made for Higgins Hill and looked down on the village. That too was gone.

I began to wonder: Had I just slipped into a distant past? And if I did, why didn't Ricky come with me? There was no good answer. This was a Sand City devoid of humans, and devoid of buildings, as if it had never existed. But I had just seen the news reports… It did exist, and everyone remembered… I had to admit the place was beautiful in its pristine state. An absolute paradise. I was wrong about the humans though.

Not more than a few minutes passed when I heard a noise, a kind of hammering. It came from a long way off and mostly to my north. I walked towards it, though cautiously, and it grew continually louder. By now I recognized the location; it was coming from Blackwater Quarry.

To remain unseen I edged along the high dunes, crawling on all fours among the stunted pine trees. I came around from the north and warily crept to the top of the cliffs. This was not the same quarry I remembered. It was deeper than I had seen, more like a giant hole. There was no water either. Below me were gangs of men digging with picks and shovels. They were barely dressed, and not in what I would call trousers.

As I watched for a time, something odd became apparent. The people along the edge of the quarry were moving at a normal pace, but those at the center seemed to have stopped completely, almost as if they were statues. I stared harder and longer, and after a while, I could see that they were indeed in motion, though digging at a snail's pace. I didn't know if they could see me, or at what speed I might be moving.

There was something very primitive about the whole scene. I could see coarse ropes tied to boulders, and a poorly constructed apparatus of rough hewn wood— maybe like a crane or a giant lever. At the center of the quarry was a black stone, a disk about twenty yards across— it was not primitive. This was a perfect circle and highly polished. Scores of workers were along its edge hammering away with absurdly small chisels, flaking off the tiniest bits of stone. It was difficult to be sure from my vantage, but the inner circle looked to be carved with some sort of writing or symbols, and perhaps a giant serpent encircled the entire perimeter.

At this point it wasn't too hard to guess I was in a very distant past. This was not some parallel present anymore. How I got here still wasn't clear. I scanned the area further. There was a small hut off to the side with a thatched roof. I saw the occasional worker go in and come out again. "The boss," I concluded, and from that moment my eyes didn't stray from the shadow in the wall that belied a door. Fifteen minutes later or so a slender figure emerged. Even from my vantage on the dunes I recognized her: Kali.

I crept back out of sight to consider my options. I did not want to be seen, nor caught and conscripted into hard labor. It seemed to me I had few choices available, though I toyed with the idea of using Pavel's dice again. It seemed like a bad move. What would that accomplish? It would only take me sideways, and a parallel timeline in a distant past was not something I relished. In the end my only recourse was to try to get back to the present, somehow. With that in mind I made my way back to the Oldham breach.

I walked for at least a mile to be sure I was far away from whatever swirling vortex must have sucked me in. If I did cross it again, I felt nothing unusual. Still no Ricky, no kayak, no dune buggy. There were buildings though. I could see the water tower again and the cell phone mast; there were familiar houses dotting the shore. I reckoned I was back in the present and yet there was not a single person to be seen.

It was my intent to roll the dice again, though a flat surface was hard to come by at the moment. I searched the beach and found a small piece of driftwood. I rolled a five, then picked up the dice. Nothing happened except for a slight tingling up my arm. Then the phantoms came, the rushing shadows. I felt as if I were one of them.

***

Next thing I knew I was coming out the door of Lema's Market on Commercial Street. I was carrying something heavy and looked down: a bag full of cat food, cans and kibble. My clothes were different as well, though familiar and clean. I had no other memories of this day. I could only recall how I had just arrived. The cube was still in my other hand, I clutched it hard. A parallel place. It all seemed pretty normal, and better than where I was before.

My mood was buoyant. Sand City was exactly as it should be, crammed with summer tourists of all shapes and sizes. I walked down Captain's Way back to my apartment. A car stopped by the curb; flashing lights came on and there was a friendly chirp from the siren. It was Durbin's Black Explorer. The window rolled down and Ricky peered out from the passenger seat. I was greatly relieved if not a bit confused.

"Hey Patrick— how's it going? Just got back, huh? How was New York?"

"New York?" I asked but didn't mean to.

"Late night road trip?"

"Oh, it was good… thanks."

"Hey, we're taking the boat out— Wanna come along?"

"Fishing?"

"There will be fishing, yes, and maybe a little drinking," Durbin the elder called out from the driver's seat. They gave me simultaneous, nearly identical grins.

"Sounds great— but I've got stuff to do. Maybe next time."

"Sure… Oh— Fynn's looking for you by the way."

I walked past the *Chronicle* office but was in no shape to stop and say hello this morning. I heard a small horn tooting and the buzz of an engine. I turned to see Anika glide to the curb on her Vespa. She looked as beautiful as I remembered, even in a helmet and sunglasses. She was also wearing a colorful Hawaiian shirt tied at the waist. It felt odd that I hadn't seen her in years— that's how it was for me at least, and I realized how much I missed her. To Anika, I might have been gone for only a few days.

"Patrick, hello…" she called out. "I haven't seen you much this summer. What have you been up to?"

"Oh… traveling a little."

"To where?"

"Here and there."

"With father?"

"Mostly…" I smiled. "Nice shirt…"

"Well?" she asked expectantly.

"What?" I replied and returned her smile.

"Hasn't father told you my news? I'm getting married next week… to Sven…"

"Sven the lifeguard?"

"Yes."

"Oh… congratulations." I gave Anika a hug but hit my head on her helmet.

"Seems a bit sudden, I suppose, but you know how these things are…" Anika laughed a bit.

"Not really… I do hope to meet him though."

"I'm sure you two will become fast friends."

"Where's your dad? I heard he's looking for me."

"Ha— who knows where he might be?" She laughed again. "Well, I've got to fly… I'm meeting Suzy for lunch."

"Suzy Chandler?"

"Of course, she's to be my bridesmaid." Anika gave me a friendly kiss. "See you at the house later?"

"Probably…"

I continued along to my apartment but felt like I was being followed. Fear and paranoia welled up. When I turned around, it was only a few school kids huddled together over their cell phones. They smiled at me, giggling, and snapped a photo.

***

Fynn was already waiting at my place, well, downstairs in the Depot Cafe having breakfast, devouring a plate of Tom's delicious home fries. I was also happy to see my Saab parked under the willow tree where it usually was. Inspector Fynn called out to me as I reached the back staircase.

"Ah, Patrick, there you are. I've been waiting. We have a flight to catch."

"To Japan?"

"No… to California… this afternoon."

"This afternoon?"

"Of course, Stanley is expecting us."
"Do you mean CalTech and Clair Patterson, the lead guy?"
"The very same."
"We already did that."
"What are you saying, Patrick?"
"Maybe a couple of weeks ago…"
"I see… well, we might do it again then. I'll ask you to indulge me."
"I'm not sure that's a good idea." I stopped to think for a moment. "The order of events is screwed up."
"Eh?"
"What do you remember about Hawaii?"
"I brought back some lovely shirts."
"What about our errand?"
"Successful by and large."
"What about Zvorkovo and Vasili Arkhipov?"
"Less successful, I would say."
"But we're still here."
"In this timeline, yes. Others were less than lucky."
"Do I have to learn Russian again?"
"Why would you? We're going to Pasadena." Fynn smiled. "Besides, you already speak Russian, don't you?"
"*Da, konechno…*" I paused. "*Gde moy kot?*"
"Your cat?" Fynn turned to me.
"I remember dropping him off at your house."
"Sorry, I don't share this recollection."
"I'm sure he's fine…" I said trying to convince myself, and then wondered if I had left enough food and water in his bowls. "When did you last see Lothar?" I asked.
"Eh?" Fynn turned to me. "I saw him at the amusement pier just yesterday."
"And Mortimer?"
"He is there as well and willing to help."
"That's not right. Didn't he jump through the revolving doors?"
"Not that I recall."
"Do you remember anything that happened at the *Hotel de Cirque?*"
"Yes, quite an adventure." Fynn seemed a bit confused by now. "But tell me, where is Geppetto? Is he safely secured at the library?"

"About that…" I hesitated, "…he's in a parallel timeline."

"Well, I think you have some explaining to do, Patrick."

I sat down at Fynn's table and ordered coffee. I took a long gulp then began to explain all that had happened. He was quiet for a time, then finally had a question:

"But are you sure it was the past that you saw at the quarry? It could just as easily been a distant future."

"Well, it was all very primitive— no technology."

"I see… still, it is not a certainty that progress and the future necessarily follow the same path."

"Why do you suppose Ricky disappeared? I mean he didn't travel with me…"

"But you said you saw him just an hour ago."

"Yes, but before that."

"It could be any number of reasons, I suppose." Fynn paused. "It might be simple causality."

"The past changing the present?"

"Yes… But I am recalling something the Arbiter said about the construction of these circles. Some components are built in the past and some in the future. Perhaps this is what you saw."

"But not in the present?"

"It doesn't seem so… and yet there is a rippling effect that you observed, parallel to here."

"Some sort of disruption?"

"It might be a lack of skill on Kali's part."

"What do you mean?"

"I don't suppose building a circle is an easy thing. There might be some room for error. It may also explain all the electrical outages as of late."

"Why would she want to build a circle of her own?"

"A question we must ask, I agree. It may be like the magnetic circle on the Mongolian steppes."

"Why would she want that?"

"What better way to lure unsuspecting travelers and then eliminate them?"

"A trap."

"It seems to fit with her intent." Fynn gave an anxious glance. "I do not wish to burden you further, but I also have some bad news."

"What's that?"

"Someone has broken into my house…"

"And?"

"And I can only guess they stole a large number of faxes."

"Faxes?"

"From Sebastian Clark."

"The manuscript translations?"

"It would seem so."

"That means Kali is here— she must've followed me."

"It's not at all your fault. She was bound to appear sooner or later." Fynn raised a grim smile.

"Is there anything going on at the quarry now?" I asked.

"Not that I know," Fynn replied. "Perhaps we might take a look tomorrow."

"Tomorrow?"

"You appear rather frayed around the edges, Patrick. You should rest. We'll speak in the morning, eh?"

"And what about California?"

"I'll call Stanley to reschedule our flight."

***

I was just happy to be home and found Zachary there waiting. He was as I remembered, all black and glossy with a tuft of white between his front legs. Wait, was that right? I also had a dim memory of him being completely white with a tip of brown at the end of his tail. Maybe it wasn't quite home, but it was close enough. A long nap was called for.

When I woke that evening there wasn't much to be found in the fridge. I grabbed a package of candy fish— fake crab, that is— and mixed it together with a plastic bag of creamed spinach. I poured the whole thing over a bed of egg noodles. It was nice to eat something familiar.

A bit later I was in the kitchen washing the few dishes left in the sink. My back was turned from the door. Behind me, as usual, my cat was sitting on the table. I heard something scrape against the wooden surface and I knew in an instant what it was: Pavel's dice. I turned to watch Zachary push it towards the edge with his front paw. He was just playing as any cat might. He swatted again and the dice fell to the tiles… I looked at him and he stared back defiantly. I glanced down at the dice. It was a six.

I picked it up and in that instant the scene changed. I had not moved an inch, but this was more than just a tingling in my arm. Searing pain came to me. Zachary was gone with not even a fading smile. The apartment was abandoned, as if I had never lived here, nor anyone else, at least not for a long time. The roof had all but collapsed. This was not a place I could stay. The air was acrid and stifling. I tried to wrest the sliding door open but it wouldn't budge. I finally broke through with a heavy iron frypan. Glass shattered everywhere. I made it to the deck and gasped for air.

chapter nineteen
carlos world

I sat huddled on my tiny deck catching my breath. There were no lights at all and I wondered if the power was out again. It seemed to be more than that. There were stars though, more than I could count. Geppetto would be happy. There was also a full moon just rising over the dunes. I could see the shadowy outline of Saint Albans in the distance, even though I didn't see the shoreline. I wondered what timeline this was, parallel yes, but obviously not a world with me in it.

I recognized most of the buildings around me, though something was off about them. They seemed too small. It was also freezing cold and it shouldn't be, not if this was still the present. An icy wind blew in from Serenity Bay. I heard no other sound, no one speaking, no music, no vehicles moving on the roads. Rolling the dice again in the dead of night was probably a stupid idea. I didn't feel as though I had much choice.

The dice fell from my palm... It was a four. I picked it up, then felt the searing pain again. I dropped to the ground in an instant and the reason was pretty clear. My spiral staircase no longer existed. Luckily the sand was soft and I landed well. I groped for the dice in the darkness.

There were some lights here, but they seemed to be open flames dotting the landscape, flickering in the distance. Things were definitely different. My eyes grew accustomed to the dimness and I could see shadows, shapes. Sand City was not at all what I expected. Next to me, was a line of carefully placed cylinders that rose to the sky. They reminded me of totem poles. Strange buildings also loomed above me and to either side. It was too dark to fully understand what I was seeing, but they were built in a style of architecture I had never seen. Towering conical structures, rounded and topped with steeply peaked roofs.

After a while, I heard people laughing, then I saw torches approaching. Within a few moments, several men were upon me, three burly Vikings, braided beards and helmets, each carrying a broadsword, a battle axe and round shields. From my vantage on the ground, I got a good look at their legs, clad in soft leather boots and grieves.

One of them spoke in a language I had never heard. I had no way to answer, and soon he began shouting at me. I stood up slowly and tried to smile. He had some sort of lantern with him and held it up to my face. He tried many languages, all of them unknown to me. I stopped him when he spoke something that sounded a bit like English, and managed to say, "Hello, and good evening."

"An Englander, eh? Had a bit too much mead tonight?" he replied with a laugh. They spoke among themselves; it was unintelligible to me, and then another man came forward. "An Anglo washed up on our shores, eh lads? You're very lucky we speak your language— otherwise you'd have been killed as a spy."

I took a wild guess as to where I had landed and said, "I have to speak to Carlos."

"Carlos?" the man was surprised by this. "Carlos, the First Prefect?"

"Carlos Santayana."

"And why would he want to speak to you?" The man laughed at the idea.

"He knows me well, and I know him."

"What's your name?"

"Patrick, Patrick Jardel."

"Are you an assassin?"

"Of course not."

"A trader then?"

"No."

"A traveler?"

"Yes, and a good friend to Carlos."

"Where are you staying?"

"Nowhere... I just arrived."

They conferred among themselves for a while and then split up. One of the men led me to a long flat structure. It looked a bit like a hotel. He ushered me into a sort of dark cabana with roughly paneled walls. There was a bed made of straw in the corner. Better than a prison cell, I thought.

"We've contacted the proper authorities, and I've been notified that the First Prefect himself is willing to meet with you."

"When?"

"Tomorrow. It seems you are something of a VIV after all."

"A what?"

"A very important Viking." He laughed and added, "Sleep well, Englander..."

***

All I had to wear were my wrinkled clothes, like they were slept-in, and they were, and I was also covered in bits of straw. The following morning I was awoken and escorted to a dining hall. It was a forbidding place, dark, with a huge table and old wooden benches on either side. A fire raged in the hearth. The room was otherwise empty except for a single man sitting by the blaze. I couldn't see who it was exactly until he rose and walked over to me.

"Welcome, Patrick. Welcome to the Town of Twin Towers."

"I hope you mean Sand City."

"In your parlance, yes."

It was Carlos, and as I remembered him, wearing a colorful poncho, and a sombrero that hung on his back. I was at a loss for words. He burst out laughing at my expression.

"How…?"

"You're lucky that I flew in two days ago."

"Flew in?"

"On what you call an airplane."

"I don't understand."

"I was told of your coming."

"By the Arbiter?"

"Yes. He said to trust only you."

"What about Chloe and Doctor Zed?"

"They could not be trusted. I had them executed."

"What?" My expression no doubt was one of shock and loathing.

Carlos laughed and slapped me on the back. "I'm sorry, Patrick, I could not resist such a joke."

"So they're okay?"

"Of course they are. They arrived centuries ago and we've built statues to them… Great heroes to our cause."

"You mean they're dead?"

"Let us use the word *departed*."

"But they came to get you. We need your help."

"And you shall have it." Carlos gave me a wide smile. "They told me all about Kali and her nefarious doings."

"Is this the present?"

"It's always the present, young Patrick, my amigo."

"That's not quite what I mean." I held out Pavel's cube in my palm.

"Ah, I understand perfectly now." Carlos gave a smile. "The present yes, but our calendar is not the same as yours."

"I'm guessing your history isn't either."

"Always with the joke, eh, compadre?" Carlos laughed again. "Things are indeed different from what you might expect. A long history… I have a book somewhere on my shelves. I will lend it to you."

"But last night… the Vikings with swords… and this place? It looks like Beowulf's Hall or something…"

"What you call Sand City is now a holiday park."

"A what?"

"A historical re-creation... Tourists come here to see how their ancestors lived a thousand years ago."

"Like a theme park?"

"Yes."

"So... not Vikings?"

"No, they are actors. Things elsewhere are quite modern. We have telephones, automobiles, planes and trains, and everything else you are familiar with."

"Still, it must be very different."

"Oh, it is, and I'm happy to show you around this great empire of ours." Carlos smiled. "Can you stay for a time?"

"I'm not sure."

"Why then are you here exactly?"

"Sort of by accident..." I paused to gauge his reaction. "We need your help..."

"Ah, sí, sí, the Señorita... If she were to appear anywhere, I would have her put to death."

"Kali, you mean?"

"Yes, the name she calls herself."

"She's hard to kill."

"I suppose you're right about that." Carlos grinned. "Well, we shall journey across space and time and hunt her down no matter where she hides. Think of the adventure, *mi amigo*..."

"Do you have any idea where she is?"

"None at all, that's the fun of it." Carlos gave me another wide grin.

"She might be closer than you think."

"What are you saying to me?"

"There's a quarry here in what I called Sand City... Do you have one too?"

"It hasn't been used in centuries."

"Something's happened though?" I guessed.

"Yes..."

"Is that why you're here, in Sand City?"

Carlos' expression changed, his smiled faded. "There's a good reason," he replied in a hushed tone. "Come along, I'll show you... *Andale, mi amigo*."

"Where are we going?"

"But of course… let's have breakfast, eh?" Carlos led me from the dark hall into the bright sun. From what I could see, Sand City was the historic town just as he had described to me at Fynn's party. There were long houses, forts with wooden pickets, ramparts, farms, and a boatyard replete with Viking ships.

"I would love to show you around my world. Travel, take in the marvelous sights, and meet its people. It is a wonderful place…" his words dropped away. "But I cannot leave at this time."

"When you say show me around, do you mean America?"

"It's not called that, but yes."

"What is it called?"

"*Verland*," Carlos answered. "The capital of our empire is what you would have named New Orleans."

"Why there?"

"It is the perfect location, central to both the Americas as you call them… Easy for ships to come and go… and the river is an excellent means of transport."

"What about hurricanes and flooding?"

"Always a problem, yes, but we've taken steps. We build above the flood waters, and we have an extensive network of canals and levees that drain into the natural wetlands."

"What else is different?"

"*Qué gran pregunta*," Carlos replied with a gleam in his eye. "Everything is different, all of history for a thousand years. But we have spoken about this before, eh?"

"Yes…" I muttered. It was a big question. I laughed slightly. It was good to see Carlos though, and I felt safe for the moment. "Do you have coffee in this world?"

We sat outside at a small restaurant and he ordered for me. Some sort of waffles with maple syrup, two eggs scrambled, and oddly seasoned bacon. I was ravenous and devoured everything on the plate. The coffee was exceptional.

"Imported," Carlos said, "the coffee…"

"From where?"

"Well, over the centuries we've opened trading routes with Europe, Africa and Asia… The English are good trading partners especially."

"What do you trade?"

"All and everything. They have tea and coffee. We have tomatoes and potatoes, and chocolate. They have rice and opium, we have cocaine and maize. They have rubber, we have lumber. We have tobacco, they have sugar… the list goes on and on, eh?"

I sat back with a second cup of coffee. "So… How did things unfold in the last thousand years?"

Carlos laughed. "A history lesson, eh? I can only give you the broad strokes, but feel free to ask any questions you might have."

"Let's start with the *Nina*, the *Pinta* and the *Santa Maria*."

"Yes… well, as I've told you, Mr Columbus appeared on schedule in *Guanahani*, but we were more than a match for him. He did not return to *Castile*."

"Where?"

"Spain… But he was well-treated."

"A guest or a prisoner?"

"In that time, the entire east coast was under a single hegemony, all the way to what you call the Mississippi. A kind of warlord had taken over… I've forgotten her name… Astrid the Beautiful, or was it Astrid the Cruel?" Carlos chuckled. "Daughter of an Iroquois Chieftain. She was not the most tolerant person."

"Was she part-Viking?"

"Yes. And she forbade all contact with the East."

"Europe, you mean?"

"It's quite an easy thing to sink a ship off the coast or simply wait for them to land. No one to my knowledge ever returned to the East with news of our existence."

"What about the Vikings still left in Europe? Or their ancestors?"

"There were rumors certainly, legends. But for those in the East, traveling to the West meant certain death. No one ever returned."

"What was done with them?"

"They were honored guests. Integrated into our society… We learned much from them."

"How?"

"Well, after Astrid was deposed, we instituted a very special policy," Carlos said with a smile and a gleam in his eye. "Whenever a visitor arrived from the East, we set up a school."

"A school?"

"A university, yes. A campus. Scholars would gather and study the new arrivals; learn about their culture, their religion, their languages and beliefs."

I thought about this for a second. "Kind of like an inoculation?"

"A good way to phrase it, yes." Carlos laughed. "We've tangled with them all, the Spanish, the Dutch, the English, and the Portuguese."

"Violently?"

"Not usually… I allowed many trading colonies in the sixteen hundreds to these Europeans. All were welcome— a vibrant interchange between cultures, but we dealt from a position of strength. We had them outgunned and outnumbered. It proved to be very profitable for everyone involved."

"How long did that last?"

"For centuries, and even to this day, we are happy to have immigrants from other lands, but on our own terms… From the West as well."

"Asia?"

"But of course…" Carlos leaned back in his chair. He went quiet for a time. "My single mission was to protect this land and the people who lived here."

"With Vikings?" I asked, not meaning to sound sarcastic.

"Yes… I could see no other way to do so." He leaned forward and stared at me. "But I had only the best intentions…"

"Like?"

"Well, the first change I made was to forbid slavery. Both the indigenous people and the Vikings were notorious…"

"Why did you do all this?"

Carlos leaned back. "Patrick, my amigo, I lived through what the Moors did to my land, my people… we were mercilessly subjugated."

"When was this?"

"The *Reconquista*… In your history it was from seven eleven to just before fifteen hundred. The last of the Moors were expelled on the very day Columbus sailed." Carlos paused. He had a hard look to his face. "My people, the Iberians, they took full advantage. I saw what we did to the inhabitants of the New World… We were just as savage as the Moors, even worse… unmatched brutality mixed with religious fervor and outright greed. I could not allow this to happen."

"That's when you decided to travel back? To change things?"

"Yes. My greater purpose was to save this land from the Europeans bent on plunder."

"And you succeeded?"

"Of course…" Carlos laughed. "I knew full well when I started that there would never be enough Vikings to conquer this vast expanse." He grinned. "They freely interbred with the indigenous peoples. Everyone here is a mongrel of one sort or another."

"Land of the free…" I muttered to myself.

"By the eighteen hundreds it was us who made the journey to the East. We appeared on their shores with a great armada."

"Ships?"

"No… Airships." Carlos smiled again. "Everything is splendidly modern. You should stay, this is a wonderful place… peaceful, harmonious, and a land of great abundance."

"It's disney-history," I muttered. "Like for the tourists."

"What do you mean to say, Patrick? I'm not understanding this."

"It's an artificial world, a world that you designed, not a world that evolved organically."

"You cut me to the quick, young Patrick. I should be insulted, but I am not."

"Sorry… but it's exactly what Kali is doing…"

"But why say something so cruel? There is a great difference between what I do and what the Señorita wants to accomplish."

"How so?"

"Think of it as a book. Yes, I've rewritten history, true enough, but it is your choice whether or not you wish to read the book, experience this version of events."

"And Kali?"

"She has burned every book, and then says, here, you must live inside the one I have written."

"I see your point."

"Well, we must not tarry." Carlos said abruptly and put a napkin to his mouth. "*Andale, mi amigo*, let's go for a walk."

We left the cafe and took a paved path that led to the north and slightly east. Sand City was unrecognizable, though tourists began to emerge from their hotel rooms, and soon enough the village was bustling, swarming with people walking along a network of sidewalks: indigenous people, Vikings, and tourists, the latter looking quite modern.

"Only a few days ago, there was a great cataclysm in this area," Carlos explained along the way. We followed a foot path towards the Atlantic side, then veered off to another that led north. "The electricity stopped flowing… a few seismic tremors, and a great wave hit the eastern shore," Carlos continued. "We were all but ready to evacuate when the next morning everything returned to normal…" he paused, "…More or less."

"It's Kali's doing," I said.

"What?"

"In a parallel timeline something similar happened… at the quarry. I was there and I saw her."

"What was she doing?"

"Building something. Probably a circle."

"To what end?"

"A kind of trap maybe?"

"What sort of trap, eh?"

"For travelers… that was Fynn's guess."

"I'm not so sure, it seems to be more than that," Carlos said. "But tell me, how is old Fynn?"

"He's good… we've been doing some errands for the Arbiter."

"He means well, I suppose…"

"Who?"

"That odd mechanical man."

"You know him then?"

"Yes, to a point. He has also asked for my help in this regard."

"What regard?"

"Ah, but I have been hunting for the Señorita, far and wide."

"And you trust him?"

"Ciertamente."

"Do you know Mr Temsik?" I asked

"Öde? But of course, he is a frequent guest of mine. Always visiting but never overstaying his welcome."

"Does he know about the quarry?"

"He does."

"Has he said anything to you?"

"No, but he did seem upset, and that's quite unusual in itself."

We approached the quarry from the high dunes. The area was roped off; obedient tourists wouldn't dare cross such a barrier. I could feel the air getting thicker, if that's the right word. Carlos felt it too; he acknowledged with a glance.

"We must not get too close," he warned. "I've tried to send people in, but no one has returned."

"You mean they disappeared?"

"Yes…" Carlos scrutinized my expression. "Something similar has happened to you, eh?"

"I lost a friend, sort of…"

"A swirl in time, I believe," he said. "Some may cross, others may not."

"Why?"

"Quite a mystery, eh, *compadre*? But you and I seem to be immune."

We crept closer along the edge of the cliffs and finally got a view of down below. Not really a good view; the bottom of the quarry was shrouded in heavy mist, a morning fog that refused to be burned off. We could see little to nothing.

"Do you hear that?" Carlos asked.

I listened and heard the soft tapping of a hundred hammers. It was a delicate, almost musical sound that echoed up towards us.

"Do you think it's the distant past?"

"I cannot say— it could just as easily be the future. I only know it is not exactly the present," Carlos replied in a whisper and led me back across the barrier. We returned to his world and headed down to the village.

"You are certain that Kali was there in the bottom of this hole?" he asked.

"I was certain… but not today, not here…"

"A risk I will not take. Besides, it would be foolish to attack her in such a stronghold."

"What's the plan?"

"Ah, the hunt must continue. Perhaps you might join me?"

"What hunt?"

"The hunt for Señorita Cero."

"Do you know where else she might be?"

"No, she is everywhere and she is nowhere." Carlos reached into his poncho and pulled out a tattered paper. "The Arbiter gave me a list. All pivotal points in history, so he claims…" He unfolded the page and handed it to me. "Where would you like to go first, eh amigo? Here, the Battle of Tours in seven hundred and thirty-two— that sounds interesting."

I looked over the list of improbable history. Things that seemed unlikely, things that were not necessarily inevitable. Some of them were more familiar than others:

Constantinople, 1453
"I remember this one… that's when it fell to the Turks."

"Oh yes, I was asked to lock a particular gate so that the city would not be conquered." Carlos smiled.

Next on the list was *Corsica, 1807*

"What's this?" I asked.

"Some jurisdictional problem, something to do with Napoleon's birthright."

"Why three dates for the Library of Alexandria?"

"It was burned many times, as you can plainly see." Carlos pointed: 48 BC by Julius Cesar, 273 by Emperor Aurelian, and 642, by an invading muslim army.

"And this? Jousting with Henry in fifteen thirty-six?"

"Oh, I was asked to go easy on him, and not knock him from his horse."

"Why would that matter?"

"Something to do with the Reformation, I think."

I went back to the list: *Washington DC, 1945, Truman or translator.*

"Regrettable, that one…"

"Why?"

"I am suppose to assassinate either of these people."

"What? Harry Truman?"

"To stop the atomic bomb from being dropped."

"Why is Gutenberg on this list?" I asked.

"He was brutally murdered in fourteen thirty-nine."

"By Kali?"

"It would seem so."

"Isn't that just delaying the inevitable?"

"What is inevitable?" Carlos turned to me.

"Books, printing presses…"

"Delaying perhaps, but also changing things, or even setting your history back a few hundred years."

"The Arbiter never asked us to do any of this."

"Us? Of whom do you speak?"

"Fynn, Mortimer, Mr Q… all the rest who've been helping."

"Nor would he."

"Why not?"

"These timelines are quite far from your own. Everyone you mention is comfortable with their history. Let's say they lack an adventurous spirit. They prefer to stay with what they know."

"And you?"

"Creating different histories is a specialty of mine. I'm quite good at it, and I'm happy to range far and wide. It matters little how things turn out."

"Well… I'd like to help, but I have to go back."

"I understand completely, Patrick." Carlos gave me an embrace. "Now that you know where I am, please return anytime as my guest."

"Thanks."

"And rest assured, we will stop the Señorita when the time comes. You have my solemn promise."

"When will that be?"

"Who can say, *mi amigo?*" Carlos laughed. "And how will you return?"

"I guess I'll just keep rolling the dice until things look familiar."

"Of course, if I were you, I'd stay a while."

"What do you mean?"

"The day is waning. It will soon be dark. Traveling at night— probably not a good idea. I'd wait till morning at least."

***

I had the notion that with one of these rolls I should end up back in Boulder Colorado. Pavel had said the *closest parallel timeline*, and that certainly seemed closer than others, closer than this. I could almost imagine Jamal Morris' friendly grin, one of Andy's stupid comments, or even a wink and a kiss from Cindy Ramirez. Any of these would be welcome. In the end I reckoned the *closest timeline* was a matter of geography.

Finding my clothes early the next morning cleaned and ironed, I decided to leave. I got a better look at the giant totem poles, all intricately carved, and most with frightening faces. Carlos was already gone by the time I woke up, called away on state business. I had breakfast in the same cafe, then found a quiet garden near to where I thought my apartment might be.

I rolled again. A five. I picked up the dice and hoped for a gentle tingling up my arm. It was not to be. A rush of pain came instead. Everything changed, though it seemed to change for the better.

It was a huge relief to return to a familiar Sand City. I didn't hope for perfect, just close enough to call home. It all seemed okay at first. The buildings were in the right place, it was a hot August morning, and the streets were filling with summer tourists. But I knew in my heart something was wrong. It was a hard jump here, I had felt the pain— it should have been a tingly replacement jump. And there were no phantoms to be seen in the corner of my eye. This was probably a parallel world where I didn't live.

Nonetheless I made a beeline to my apartment and bounded up the spiral stairs. The door was locked and I didn't have a key. I cupped my hands to peer in through the sliders, hoping my cat was there, or anything else familiar. Nothing was. The pictures on the walls were not mine, nor the furniture. If I had to guess, I'd say a woman lived here now. I could see girlie things, lingerie and knick-knacks that clearly weren't mine. I was somewhat thankful no one was home.

Nor did I see my Saab parked under the willow tree. A small feeling of panic set in. It seemed increasingly likely that I did not exist in this timeline. And if I had previously, it was probably better if no one saw me. I found an unattended bicycle— it was strikingly familiar— and I pedaled up Higgins Hill towards the dunes and the ocean.

Finding Fynn's house shuttered and abandoned only increased my anxiety. I rode back to the Oldham breach again. It was narrow enough to jump across, not that I did, and I could see the usual houses tucked away in the dunes. South Beach was dotted with umbrellas again. I could also see the green water tower to the west. This was better. I followed the bike path to the quarry. Everything there seemed completely normal. There were picnickers along the shore, and a few brave souls jumping into the black water from the edge of the cliffs.

Massive clouds rolled in from the east: a summer thunder storm, and I welcomed it. A respite from the heat, it felt wonderful to be spattered by rain as I biked over to the rotary in Oldham. It came to mind that only Mr Temsik could help me. I ran into the Cove Diner, now soaked in full blown despair.

"Is Öde here?"

"Who?"

"Omar."

"Hey, Omar, somebody here to see you."

"Can I help you, sir?"

I stared at him. It was Öde but it was not. He was not the Mr Temsik I knew. He seemed more like an empty vessel.

"Umm, what's the lunch special today?"

He gave an odd look and handed me the menu. I left hurriedly and full of embarrassment. There was little else I could do. As much as I wanted, I could not stay. I found a quiet spot and I rolled the dice again— a two— I picked it up and felt a tingling shoot up my arm. It was not at all an unpleasant sensation. A rush of phantoms swept by, funneling into me, almost like shadows converging. Better than searing pain, I guess.

***

In an instant it was easy to tell where I was: back in my apartment and laying on my own bed. All was not well though. I had no recollection of this life, not a single memory was accessible. I was still clutching the cube in my hand and looked around the room. A high peaked ceiling, the wood paneling, the skylight, all structurally the same. I could also hear the rain pounding against the roof. It was darker than it should be though, and a few things looked strange and unfamiliar. The furniture was definitely different. I saw a television but it seemed to be an antique, a small screen set in a wide wooden box.

I sat up and swung my legs to the floor to find I was wearing only loose pajama bottoms. Something was wrapped around my ankle as well: a metal cuff attached to a long bit of chain. A woman came from behind and slipped her arms around my waist. "Ah, you are awake again, eh Patrick?"

I turned in horror. It was Kali.

"What's the matter, darling?" she whispered in my ear.

I was repulsed and wrangled myself free.

"Don't you love me anymore?" she asked.

"No… This is all wrong."

"What's wrong?"

"Why am I chained to the bed?"

"Well, I don't want you jumping away again."

"I won't, I promise…"

"I'm sure we've had this conversation before."

"I don't remember."

"You've grown rambunctious as of late… Traveling back to the past and trying to change my world… Shame on you, Patrick."

"Won't happen again, promise."

She laughed, a horrible sound that I had heard before. "Of course it won't. I've sent for the doctor."

"What doctor?"

"I don't know his name… He's here to help though."

"Help with what?"

"Your achilles tendon. I can't have you leaping away anytime you want, eh?"

I got the general idea of what she meant and my slim hope that Doctor Zed would appear was immediately dashed.

"It's a great tragedy," Kali went on, "to lose a traveler like you… have you hobbled…" She sighed. "And after all the work I've put in, all those years of persuasion and guidance… Shame you aren't more obedient, Patrick. We could have done great things together."

"Why not just put me out of my misery?"

"I won't kill you, if that's what you're asking. I like having you around. You're one of the few people who can appreciate my efforts— with that memory of yours." She slid her face next to mine.

"What's for breakfast?" I asked and stared straight ahead, cringing inside. I felt frantic. I knew how I got here but I didn't know how to leave. A small comfort came; I could feel the dice in my clenched fist. Something she could never find.

Kali got out of bed and put on a robe. She came around to stare at me. "There's something a bit off about you this morning. You are not the same Patrick who fell asleep a few hours ago. What have you been up to, eh?"

"Nothing." I held up the chain in reply.

"What's the last thing you remember?"

"Going to work yesterday," I lied outright.

"What?" Kali tilted her head in disbelief.

"Maybe it was Thursday…"

"Seems your memory is beginning to fail after all," she said with disgust.

"You're probably right." I grinned. "Where's my cat?"

"What cat?"

"He used to live here with me."

"I don't like cats. I put him in a box outside on the curb."

"What kind of box?"

"The kind that Schrödinger uses." Kali laughed again. "You've arrived from somewhere, haven't you?" She held my face in her hand. "Where did you just come from?"

"The future."

"Which future?"

"A better one than this."

"And why have you come?"

"It was an accident. I was jumping to the past and just sort of landed here."

"I find that unlikely, Patrick, dear." Kali flitted through the room as if she felt imminent danger, but returned a moment later and stared at me with a hideous smile. "Tell me what is this future like, eh? I want to know all the details."

"Well, TV is different." I pointed to the large wooden box in the living room. "Not exactly a flat-screen."

"Now I know something is very wrong," Kali replied. "Such a thing is quite impossible. There are no transistors here, no chips, or worldwide networks… I've seen to it."

"What world do you mean?"

"Surely you recognize your own present?"

"It looks different."

"Different than what?"

"Yesterday."

"But you are here and I am here, it must be so—" Kali was interrupted by a deafening noise that arose from nearby. I knew it as the noon siren. Some things in this timeline had not changed. It persisted however.

"Don't pay much heed to that," Kali said. "Just another air raid drill." She laughed at my expression. "No, we haven't had an actual attack in decades."

I noticed a cane leaning in the corner by the kitchen. It had a brass elephant's head with its trunk curling along the shaft. I had seen it before. "Nice cane," I said.

"A gift from your friend Mr Mortimer."

"He's not my friend."

"No, I don't suppose he is." Kali eyed me briefly. "I didn't care for the design though."

"What do you mean?"

"The jackal's head…" She smiled. "I prefer it as an elephant."

"Have you seen him lately?"

"Mr Mortimer? No…"

"And where are we exactly?"

"I begin to understand," she said. "You've not come from the future at all… You've arrived from a tangent."

"A what?"

"A parallel place." She paused to consider. "You are a different Patrick entirely. Tell me though; how did you manage to find me—hmm? I would think this place is far from your usual haunts."

"The Arbiter sent me," I lied.

"What?" Her tone was shrill; she flitted across the room again, but soon calmed herself. "If you are indeed from a tangent, then this is even more interesting. There's much you can tell me."

"Like?"

"Where is Geppetto?"

"Who?"

"Don't be coy."

"He's not here… that much I can guess."

Kali slapped me hard across the face.

"You killed him two days ago in my tangent."

"Did I?"

"Dropped him off a cliff."

"What a shame…" Kali muttered and went silent.

"Why the circle here?" I asked.

"What?"

"At the quarry…" No sooner were the words from my mouth when I realized she had no idea what I was talking about.

"A circle, here…" she said softly and a terrible smile came to her face. "…Yes, why not? That's a wonderful idea, dear Patrick. Thank you."

"Uh-oh," I said, but I hoped not aloud. I clutched the cube in my hand all the much tighter.

"What's this you are holding so desperately, eh?"

"Oh, it's a good luck charm. My lucky dice."

"I never took you to be superstitious…"

The phone rang, a landline. Pretty sure it wasn't for me. Kali picked it up and just listened. A scowl came to her face. She hung up and turned to me. "I have an errand to run. I'll be back before you know it." She flitted through the room. I felt a kiss on the side of my cheek and she was gone.

I waited a long while; quiet came. All I could hear was the rain on the shingles. I tested the limits of my chain. I could make it to the bathroom, the shower, the sink and the toilet. In the other direction I was able to walk to the fridge and the stove, though not all the way to the washer-drier. It was possible to sit at the kitchen table, and I could make it a few steps out onto my deck. I could go no further though. It was the end of my tether. I clutched the dice hard in my hand. I had to leave, but I also had to stay and find out more.

Outside in the rain, Sand City looked different; the view had changed dramatically. I couldn't see the bay anymore. Many of the old buildings had been torn down, replaced by concrete boxes. Where

Baxter Estates used to be, I could see high-rises, horrible things, cookie-cutter architecture. It reminded me of the Moscow suburbs. Many thousands of people must live here, and the whole place was probably spoiled. I wondered if they all had jobs.

A moment later, I felt Kali wrap herself around me again from behind. I slithered away in disgust. She had returned without a sound.

"Tell me about this world," I said.

"You're curious, eh?" She looked into my eyes. "Well, it is utopia, a place where everything is perfect."

"Perfect for whom?"

"Everyone who obeys."

"Who lives in all those apartments?"

"Many thousands of workers. The military, your US Navy, for the most part. Sand City is a strategic location."

"How long have I been here?"

"All your life, I would imagine," Kali replied. "I found you years ago, writing propaganda for the *Center*."

"The what?"

"Your little newspaper..." Kali said, but then went silent for a while. She simply stared at me, almost as if she felt pity. "Have a seat, Patrick... I'll make us a cup of tea while you read."

"What?"

"Catch up on things."

I said nothing but sat at the kitchen table. It looked about the same as usual. Kali put a book down in front of me: *History of the Twentieth Century*. I leafed through the slim volume with both fear and curiosity.

"This should answer all your questions, darling boy," she said and turned to the stove. "Written by a friend of yours..."

I looked at the author: Gary Sevens.

"I wrote this?"

"I suppose you did in the past."

Kali came over and opened the book to page forty-three. "I thought you might like to read about Hawaii."

chapter twenty
no returns

War in the Pacific

After Pearl Harbor, America, for its part rested on her laurels. It was at least a victory for propaganda. Our forces were heroic beyond measure. A tactical victory, one might say, though in actuality the Pacific fleet suffered a strategic defeat that would take years to fully recover from. The destruction of oil fields and dry docks was the real disaster. None of this was brought to the attention of the public. The mitigated attack had left the fleet at Pearl more or less intact, but the loss of the *Enterprise* and the damage done to *Lexington* was a severe blow. War was declared on this date of infamy, December 7th 1941.

For their part, Japanese military leaders revised their strategies after the debacle. They chose a new target: Midway, and conquered it easily with a small invasion force. The Johnson Atoll fell a few months later. Gradually entrenching their positions with flak guns and a sizable force of dive bombers and zeros, the islands became like aircraft carriers that didn't sink. Nor could they sail.

One by one, every island that could be taken in the Pacific was; even a few of the Aleutians in the North. In less than a year Imperial Japan dictated America's strategic efforts, and those were now decidedly defensive. America's number one aim was to get the islands back, one by one. The greatest fear being the development of Japanese long range bombers stationed at Midway...

I was about to read further when Kali called out, "I forgot, there's no tea. I can make a hot coco though."

"No coffee?" I asked almost absentmindedly and read on with a kind of morbid fascination:

The Atlantic War

At the end of 1941, when the United States formally declared war on Germany, there was little they could do against Fortress Europe. Moreover, entry into the European theater had been delayed by nearly a year, and by then it was too late. There was no where to go. Britain had fallen and the repercussions were enormous. North Africa was locked up, Egypt occupied, and the Sudan. The Suez canal was in German hands. Oil flowed freely into the Nazi heartlands. Turkey, Baghdad and Tehran soon fell under Hitler's sway. A vast swath of territory from the northern Sahara to the Indian Ocean was given over to the Italians to administer.

Spain joined the axis in early 1942, under the leadership of El Caudillo, aka General Franco. He promptly marched into neutral Portugal and effectively closed off all access to the eastern Atlantic. With Lisbon gone, there was also no exit for the thousands of remaining refugees. It was however the perfect excuse to seize Portuguese territories: the Canary Islands and the Madeira archipelago—and the Americans did so readily.

The next viable strategic port was in the Azores. A port the Americans vowed to take. Operation Gray began in the summer of 1942. With a landing force of 30,000, the islands were quickly secured and the US gained a toehold in the strategic shipping lanes. There was little Spain could do to retaliate, and the Germans chose a policy of non-engagement for now.

I flipped through the pages and came across a chapter on Britain. I already knew that history. It only confirmed what Fynn and I had seen in the newsreel, though I learned it took a further two years to subjugate the British Isles amidst fierce resistance. And the Royal Navy had remained largely intact.

Despite this, at least on paper, everything that had been British was now German, the colonies, that is. Fully a quarter of the planet's population and about a third of its landmass were handed over to Nazi control. Hitler's gift to Tojo: Burma and everything east of India…

Kali sat down at the table and poured out two cups of hot chocolate. "Not what you expected, eh?"

I said nothing but sipped my coco and read further:

The Pacific Theater

All eyes turned to Australia, the last bastion of Britishness. The allies mutually decided it could not— and would not— fall; though in actuality, Japanese strategic intentions remained largely inscrutable. A three-pronged approach was quickly developed: defense, supply, and emigration. By and large they were successful and exceeded all expectations.

The first battles were fought for the Solomon Islands and Papua New Guinea in late 1942. Southern shipping lanes had to remain open at all costs. Gradually, the north Australian coast became the most heavily fortified place on the planet: the Malay Line, though the only major city under direct threat was Darwin. To the west and south, from Perth to Melbourne, and from Brisbane to New Zealand, the populace remained relatively safe from attack.

A mass emigration ensued from existing and former British colonies. Vast convoys sailed virtually unmolested, protected by a burgeoning American Navy. Bodies were needed for soldiers and industry, for defense and farming. *The Aussie deserts would be transformed*, said the propaganda. Most immigrants came via the western ports of Canada, Vancouver and Victoria. And later, from Cape Town in South Africa, and even the Indian subcontinent once the Germans had begun their southern advance.

During this time, the Japanese strategy of harassing the Panama Canal took its toll. The only lane between two vast oceans was choked off by the repeated sinking of numerous ships on their western approach. The damage was caused by an endless fleet of Japanese midget submarines, which more often than not, managed to avoid detection.

In response, the US signed treaties with Ecuador, Peru and Chile, gaining access to their ports. The canal might shut down but the Pan-American Highway never did. It was Eisenhower who oversaw the tripling of America's infrastructure: trains, roads, bridges and highways. War materials could reach either coast in a matter of days.

On the eastern seaboard, by early 1945, V-3's were hurled across the Atlantic to rain destruction on the East Coast of America, and there was little the US could do to counter the effects. And while the Atlantic Sea Lanes were still a dangerous place, interference from

German wolf packs had been dulled, thanks to airpower, and new sonar and radar technologies.

Across the world, India fell to the Germans in 1944. A line was drawn with Japan. Despite the historic handshake between German forces in India, and Imperial troops in Burma, this was to be a sticking point in years to come. The Nazis had easily taken the former British colony while Japan had solidified its gains throughout China. Later, by the 1970's, this enormous border became a flash point between opposing superpowers.

I flipped through the pages and found a chapter titled, *South America: Secrets, Spies, and the Second Pope*. I was about to read on when Kali snatched the book from my hands. "This is more interesting, darling Patrick," she told me, and presented a different chapter, *The Fall of Russia*:

Operation Barbarossa was more successful than could be imagined. Beginning in the Summer of 1941, with Britain all but secure, Hitler turned his armies east. Moscow was taken directly, no dilly-dallying. The oil in the Caucasus's was then secured. Leningrad was all but raised and Stalingrad fell a year later. The remnants of the Red Army fell back behind the Ural Mountains.

"Ah, the Germans, yes... Kali said while looking over my shoulder.

"It sounds like you admire them."

"I admire no one. I do recognize their brutal efficiency."

"You spent some time there?"

"I never met the führer personally, but I had his attention by whispering into the ear of another: Heinrich." Kali gave a small laugh. "For a time, I was the official astrologer to the Reich."

"Really?"

"Not being Aryan, my presence was merely tolerated, though I had an uncanny knack for being correct each and every single time."

"About the future, you mean?"

Kali smiled. "Yes, my advice was always correct and usually heeded."

I went back to reading:

There were continuing skirmishes in Siberia, a few lingering

Russians. A joint Nippon-German operation cleaned the area up by the early 1950s. The Russian nationality was all but extinct, and the idea of a Soviet or Bolshevik certainly was. Across the continent, Slavs became slaves; the Nazi's had unlimited free labor and resources for at least a generation to come.

I skipped ahead until I found: *The Armistice and War's End*

In April 1945, FDR's last words were, "The Center must hold." He was referring to the central continents, surrounded on one side by the West, Nazi fascism; and to the East, the Imperial Dynasty. His Vice President, Henry Wallace aka… the *Negotiator*, took office a few days later. The US remained a bastion for freedom, individuality, and tolerance— though some would complain, it was nearly overcome with immigrants.

Diversity was its strength, others would say. The ethnic and national remnants of displaced people from all across the world lived in enclaves throughout the Americas. It was a vast cultural mosaic and they held the memories of their origins alive in light of overwhelming force elsewhere.

At President Wallace's disposal were the new atomic weapons, available for use in the summer of that year. He chose two targets: the first was Corvo, an Atlantic island about one square mile in size, the northernmost of the Azores, and uninhabited. All the world was invited to watch, the Germans and Japanese especially. It was all but obliterated. A second demonstration, the following week, removed the Bikini Atoll from the map. Two months later, armistice talks began…

"Oh, I like this part," Kali said over my shoulder and thumbed a few pages. I read on in horror:

The Post War World

Hitler died in 1962, in his sleep, and at age seventy-three. With new leadership, there was a "softening" towards the conquered races. Ethnic groups and nationalities were no longer to be exterminated, but 'should be placed in service of the Reich.' And after a generation or so, some autonomy crept in. Administrators from other European nations stepped up to fill the sputtering bureaucracies. "Paris will always be Paris..." as it was famously said by General Rommel. London had not fared as well.

There were rumors of atrocities: death camps, slave labor, mass extermination, and sterilization on an industrial scale. Nothing was ever proven, and few believed the persistent stories. Such inhumanity was without parallel, most people would say. When it came to unmatched brutality, it was difficult to decide which was worse, the Nazis or the Japanese Empire. For at least a generation, the overlords were feared and loathed.

"Regimented societies, I would call them," Kali made a comment. This history had left me reticent; I went back to reading:

A terrible new truth did come to light as the years passed. Throughout the occupied lands, the first generation had been called *collaborators*; their descendants were labeled *opportunists*; and with the third generation coming of age, they were now considered the new *elites*, prosperous and wielding power, albeit under the oppressors' direction.

Such was not the case in the Center, as it came to be called. A diverse, vibrant culture remained— unruly and chaotic, but in the end still ruled by a semblance of democracy. The standard of living was certainly higher, though it was no less militaristic than the other two powers; and all seemed to be on a constant war footing.

"Blast these Americans and their high-minded ideals," Kali interrupted again.

"What do you mean?"

"They cling to their belief of exceptionalism. Freedom, liberty, equality... I never expected they would actually attempt to put them into practice. I thought these were only soothing words."

Both new empires suffered from the same basic problem. There were simply not enough Germans, nor enough Japanese to run things properly. The idea of racial purity had not worked out in practice.

Many Aryans took wives of other races in Europe, the Ukraine, and across Russia. And Japanese men did much the same in Asia. Three generations later, one's social status usually depended on how much of a mix you were...

***

"Finished the book, Patrick, darling?"

"I've read enough."

"Chock full of good ideas, don't you think?"

"I wouldn't say that."

"Ah, but it's not the version of history you were expecting."

"You're doing all this crazy control-the-world stuff from my crappy little apartment?"

"No. I don't live here. You do. I just stopped over to say hello..." She laughed.

"Why make a world like this?"

"The place where you normally abide is impossible to control."

"Why?"

"I had to do away with the corporations that run things in that timeline. They are bothersome, overly complicated... Hard to keep track of, hard to manage. One company always buying another, or merging into something else."

"What are you talking about?"

"Rampant capitalism, of course... I found it very difficult to stop its inception."

"When was this?"

"That's the problem. It began springing up in the sixteen hundreds. Damn the Dutch and all those English shopkeepers. There was very little I could do to prevent it." Kali moved closer and stroked the side of my face. "They have one overriding principal that I cannot get around. So infuriating, they are unbendable when it comes to that rule."

"Which is?"

"Turning a profit for their shareholders. They can be incredibly short-sighted, seeing ahead for only three months at a time."

"What?"

"Quarterly profit and loss statements."

"And in this world?"

"Industry is under the thumb of governments. The latter is much easier to control. They are prone to react to crisis, all in the name of duty, patriotism, security, or any other irrational notion you can conjure."

"What's it like now?"

"It's taken three generations but a new oligarchy has risen in that time. It's far easier to influence a few families than the masses…"

"Who are they?"

"Many grew wealthy during the war." She smiled. "And so much has already been forgotten…"

"How much has been forgiven?" I asked.

"It amounts to the same thing." Kali laughed and she may have been right. "A perpetual cold war…" she went on. "It's lasted some seventy years, but things are generally quite stable."

"What do you get out of all this?"

"Well, dividing the world into three parts makes it easier to manipulate. Easy to pit one side against another. In any group of three, it's usually two against one," she considered. "Soon enough there will be only two distinct players." Kali smiled. "We shall see who falls first."

"Who are you rooting for?"

She ignored my question but said, "I have but one regret regarding this timeline."

"What's that?" I asked, able to think of hundreds of others.

"Humans have not gone into space, only a few rockets with bombs attached to them."

"Why would that matter to you?"

"It concerns us all, Patrick. Here, there is no awareness of the planet as a whole. In your more familiar timeline, there was one picture that changed it all."

"What picture is that?"

"A photograph of the earth from space rising above a lifeless moon. Do not underestimate its impact."

"You're saying it was a good thing?"

"For the planet to survive, yes… and such is in my best interest. Where else would I have to live?"

***

The following morning, Kali was away, or so I hoped. I had already tested the chain. There was no chance of breaking free, though I knew where my tether ended. It was just long enough to let me out onto the deck. I made a run for it. The chain snapped to the end halting my progress. I tumbled through the sliding doors, most of me at least. The dice fell from my hand. I stretched out my arm. It was just beyond reach, the metal band around my ankle cut through towards the bone. Then I heard Kali running across the floor. With a final effort, the cube was in my palm. The tingle arose, and more pain, but at least I was elsewhere, free from Kali.

An odd thought crossed my mind. For the first time I wondered what happened to my parallel self when I slipped away… Did that other me vanish? Or did he just revert to who he was before.

***

I was still on my deck, what was left of it. The Depot building had all but collapsed in on itself and was half buried in sand. Only the iron stairs seemed intact, the spiral nautilus, now a stairway to nowhere.

High clouds covered the sky. There was no sun, just a meager patch of brightness where it should be. It was bitterly cold as well, dead of winter cold— but this was August, or should be. This was my present, I reminded myself…

I was still in my pajamas, freezing, hardly dressed for the weather. Nothing was growing except for a few lingering tufts of dune grass and some spindly pines hanging on for dear life. Clearly, there was no one here alive.

I scanned the horizon. Serenity Bay had been swallowed up. Everything was covered in sand including the streets. I could hardly see the village, just a few structural items poking up from the dunes, a caved-in roof, or a broken steeple. Not exactly the Sand City I remembered from my present. There was no sign of the water tower or Baxter Estates. Saint Albans was an empty husk, and now far from any shoreline.

Back on the ground, something caught my eye. A brown shape scuttled nearby, then another. Bugs… Too many, and much larger than I thought possible.

There was no reason to stay. Luckily the sand I was standing on was frozen. I cleared off a flat spot and hoped for the best. Just as I was about to roll the dice again, something else caught my eye. A man was walking towards me, and from quite a long ways off. Even from this distance I could see he was wearing a red fez. It was Öde Temsik.

"Ah, there you are, Patrick. I thought you'd be joining me sooner or later."

"What is this place?"

"It's best I don't tell you… though ironically enough it's one of Kali's timelines."

"How did you find me?"

"You found me, I'd say."

"That's not a good answer."

"Alright, well, I knew exactly where you were in the present, only not which present. So I searched them all."

"All?"

"Enough of them to find you. I thought you'd be happy to see me."

"I am."

"Good. Now we must go."

"Where to?"

"Away from here." Öde paused to smile. "If I could take you anywhere, where would it be?"

"Home… back to my original timeline."

Mr Temsik hesitated. "What would be your second choice?"

"Someplace warmer… where there's people."

"Ah then, utopia here we come."

"Utopia?" I asked.

"I will remind you that by definition, utopia is an imaginary place."

"I'd rather go somewhere real…"

"Whatever you decide, you must do so quickly. This is no place to linger, not without a geiger counter."

"How do we leave?"

"Do you have your dice?" he asked and brushed a smooth spot in the hard sand. "I've learned a few tricks over the years…" Öde looked up at me and I handed him my black cube. "Even Pavel couldn't have guessed… It's so simple really. If you roll the dice with one hand and pick it up with another, nothing happens. Use the same hand and you slip away to somewhere new."

"There are two of us," I reminded.

Öde laughed and held up his own white dice. "I have a plan for that as well. Trust me. One person rolls them both, but the other person picks them up… this prevents either of us from blinking into a parallel present."

"Then what?"

"We wait until doubles are rolled, then we will be traveling to the same place, so we both pick up a dice."

"Simple as that?"

"Yes."

"What happens if we don't roll doubles?"

"We try again until we do."

Mr Temsik rolled first: a six and a one. I picked up the dice, and like he said, nothing happened.

"I ran into you in another timeline," I said and rolled: a five and a two.

"I can't say that surprises me… There are many versions of myself, some in the past, but mostly in the present. My receptacles, you might call them."

"Receptacles?" I asked. "Well, he wasn't quite himself…"

"No, I don't suppose he was."

"How much does he remember?"

"I'm not sure we ever had that conversation."

"Is it like a soft jump?" I asked and picked up the dice again.

"A soft jump?" he asked. "What's that?"

"Like reincarnation."

"No. They have no memory of my visits. I like to call them placeholders." Mr Temsik rolled a four and a three.

"Placeholders?"

"It's comforting to know I can always go back and take refuge. They hold my place in the present, so to speak. There's hardly a timeline where I don't exist."

"So, no hard jumps for you?"

"Not that I can remember."

"Tell me about where we're going." I rolled a five and a four.

"A better world, a place where the best of human nature outshines the worst."

"Paradise?"

"Well, there are no gas powered leaf blowers."

"What?"

"They've all been banned. And no beverages in cans."

"Not even beer?"

"Especially not."

"What about plastic bottles?"

"They're made of something else… something that dissolves into nothing after a time."

"Biodegradable?"

"Oh yes, we're all aboard with Rachel Carson, Jacques Cousteau, and the Attenborough brothers."

"Who?"

"Well, perhaps they are from before your time. Let's just say we've recognized that our earth is a singular place, and as such, needs to be cherished." Mr Temsik rolled double sixes. "Ah," he exclaimed. "Well, off we go then…" He smiled. "We must pick up our own dice simultaneously… Ready?"

I felt a tingling up my arm. No pain this time. In the next moment nothing changed but our surroundings. Sand City was back to normal, more or less, and Mr Temsik was still there, now sitting opposite at a picnic table. I was wearing completely different clothes. My pajamas were gone, replaced by a simple shirt and jeans.

"It looks pretty much the same," I said, looking around, "except for that giant sea wall."

"It is the same… except for the rising sea levels," he replied.

"What happened?"

"Unintended consequences. A kind of hyper-industrialization occurred after the war. An attempt to raise living standards."

"Which war?"

"World War Two."

"Who won?"

"The allies as you call them, though the rest of this world is quite different."

"How so?"

"Well, haven't you ever dreamed of wondrous undersea cities?"

"I have, but I didn't think they be built because of rising sea levels."

"Ah, the ingenuity of humankind, eh? Never fails to amaze me."

"I thought we were in the present."

"Indeed we are... but the polar ice cap is a shadow of its former self."

"Meaning."

"It's melted away for the most part."

"What about all the polar bears?"

"Bipolar bears, do you mean? Well, the penguins aren't very happy about that... having new neighbors and all."

"What are you trying to say?"

"Many bears were relocated to Antarctica."

'Okay, things *do* seem different." I paused for a moment. "There was no searing pain— I live here in this parallel place?"

"You *did*. We were great friends."

"What do you mean did?"

"You've just replaced that version of yourself."

I had to think about that. "What happens when I leave?"

"Do you mean *if* you leave?" Öde asked and smiled. "Well, who can say?"

"What else is different about this version of the world?"

"Many things of course... but the major difference goes back to one day in history."

"When's that?"

"Not so long ago... The twenty-first of July, nineteen forty-four by your calendar, there was a simple change."

"What happened on that day?"

"Henry A. Wallace was nominated for Vice President."

"As opposed to?"

"Harry Truman."

"And that changed things?"

"Indeed it did..."

"How?"

"It resulted in an entirely different geopolitical evolution."

"How so?"

"There was no Cold War to speak of. Instead, there was a generally benign competition with communism, a space race especially—and eventually, cooperation…There are people living on the moon nowadays, and on their way to Mars."

"Americans?"

"All nationalities."

"What about the Iron Curtain?"

"Made of paper in the end, especially after Stalin was assassinated."

"What else?"

"Well, it's quite a list… No atom bombs were dropped— not on people anyway. Hmm, what else? After the war, former colonies were afforded sovereignty and autonomy. Many lines on the map were changed."

"Meaning?"

"Artificially drawn countries were modified to better reflect ethnic boundaries."

"Such as?"

"Oh, geography is not my strong suit, I'm afraid. A few new countries in Africa emerged… the Kurds got their own nation, the Armenians, bits of Europe were redrawn, and there is no south or north this or that."

"What do you mean?"

"Oh, like North Korea as a separate place."

"What about China?"

"Hmm, Chairman Mao did not come to power."

"And economically?"

"Well, I would describe it as scrupulously regulated capitalism… free trade, fair labor practices, eco-friendly products and processes, and all adhering to global standards…" Mr Temsik paused to consider. "I would also say fewer things have been privatized."

"Such as?"

"Prisons for one, healthcare for another."

"Governments?"

"Yes, of course, and in a variety of flavors."

"Terrorism?"

"Not to speak of. Very few religious zealots out and about."

"Sounds great and all, but it's not really utopia," I complained half-heartedly.

"Perhaps not, but it is quite pleasant, wouldn't you say?"

"I guess…"

"If you prefer, I can take you to a different utopia, though it is quite far from here."

"Where is it?"

"In the distant past… It's a version of history wholly unrecognizable to you. No Roman Empire, no burning of the library in Alexandria. No America, no English, no slaves, no colonization."

"Why is it in the past?"

"Doesn't exist any longer. It's been snuffed out."

"By Kali?"

"What can I say, except probably. Though, it is so far from your normal history, I think only Carlos has spent time there."

"What about his world, his Viking Empire?"

"Oh yes, that's also quite a pleasant place, certainly a utopia for those living in what you call North America."

"Not for others?"

"Who am I to say?"

"So there's no utopia in my present?"

"I'm afraid not, this is as close as it gets." Mr Temsik hesitated for a moment. "There is one other place… It's not so far in terms of years, but very far in terms of culture."

"Where is it?"

"In the future, a few decades from here."

"My future?"

"I've not seen you there."

"What's it like now?"

"In transition, I would say. First, a great cataclysm must be overcome."

"Like what?"

"Would you like to visit?"

"I'd like a cup of coffee first."

Öde laughed. "That is something we do have. The diner is still nearby, though I do not work there anymore."

***

The Cove Diner was no different than what I was used to. Mr Temsik was a regular, I guessed, since the waitress led us to a booth and brought two cups of coffee over without a word. I half expected Durbin to come through the front doors, or anyone else I knew.

"Yes, Sheriff Durbin is indeed here in this present. I know him, but not that well."

"Sheriff Durbin?"

"He has the same fondness for pancakes."

"Okay, so tell me about this utopian future," I said and slurped down my coffee.

"You wish to travel there?" Mr Temsik asked and sat back in his seat. "I for one am looking forward to it."

"You've been there?"

"Oh yes, I spend much of my time there. It's quite peaceful."

"And the cataclysm you mentioned?"

"I would call it a worldwide revolution. Utter chaos for a time… the complete overthrow of capitalism."

"Wow."

"Indeed. Let's say it is a new world that has been patched together from a variety of ideas. A mishmash of things, from the past, from the present, and from the future."

"Like what Carlos does?"

"Yes… But what history is not like this? We always take ideas from the past and try to make them work in the present day."

"Carlos helped with this?"

"Indeed he did."

"What kind of ideas do you mean?"

"Justice, equality, fairness, liberty… things like that."

"Socialism?"

"No."

"Communism?"

"No again. There is globalism, though it's not at all what you might imagine. We are all simply cognizant that we share the same world and have laws that forbid people from damaging the earth."

"What constitutes damage?"

"It's all written down in a big book." Mr Temsik smiled and handed me a menu. "Ah, but let us have something to eat, eh? I'm hungry." He motioned for the waitress. "The spinach pie is rather good. Not too much dill. I recommend it."

"Sounds delicious."

"It is a world based on language," Öde began after he placed our order.

"What, so everyone speaks the same language?"

"Not at all. There are some six or seven thousand languages across the globe. It is the cultural boundary which is always respected."

"The Tower of Babel," I remarked and started in on my second cup of coffee.

Öde chuckled. "The various peoples of the world have organized themselves into small groups, mostly along ethnic and linguistic lines."

"What about government? A central government."

"We have democratized power."

"What does that mean?"

"It is shared equally. No one person has power over another."

"What if two or more people gang up on someone?" I asked.

"Oh yes, that best describes how government used to operate, but everyone's vote does not have equal weight." Mr Temsik leaned forward. "While most matters are voted upon, there are three tiers of engagement: things that have local impact, regional, or global impact."

"So, a kind of democracy?"

"You might think of it as a card game."

"What, like poker?"

"Local matters trump regional matters, but global matters trump all."

"I'm not sure I get that."

"Well, if you are living here in Sand City, you wouldn't get a vote on whether or not to build a well in some remote Mongolian village."

"Unless it had a global impact…"

"You're catching on." Mr Temsik smiled. "If our imaginary well was to go so far as the molten core of the earth, you might get some say on the matter…"

"A vote?"

"Yes. Proposals are weighed against their impact. Most things never reach such a threshold."

"Who decides?"

"As I mentioned, one of the three councils, local, regional, and global."

"Who gets to vote?"

"Nearly everyone, but abstaining votes matter as well— inasmuch as they are tallied."

"Why?"

"If there are more abstaining votes than yeas or nays, the matter is shelved. Back to the drawing board, one might say."

"What about apathy? People who don't vote."

"It's their choice entirely." Mr Temsik smiled. "But voting is easy. It's something we do every day... like social media in your world." Öde took a sip of coffee. "It's been decentralized, across the whole planet."

"How?"

"Simple technology, already available even in your usual present."

"Cell phones..." I muttered to myself.

Our spinach pie arrived and a side of fries. "Hunger is something we should all feel— it's in our nature," Öde said with a grin. "Though the future has done away with famine, disease, and warfare."

"How?"

"Easy. With food, medicine and sport..."

"Sport?"

"In place of warfare."

"Like violent gladiators?"

"No, it's been sublimated over the years."

"So, like golf?"

"Golf is not a sport. It is a game." Mr Temsik laughed. "Human nature cannot be quelled by imposing laws. There are some things that cannot be done away with... instincts that we are hard wired for..."

"Like?"

"Greed, laziness, curiosity, fear, even aggression and violence."

"Is there violence?"

"There is. It is part of our nature, a hallmark of our species." Mr

Temsik paused and took a few fries. "I will only say the young are generally more violent than the old."

"The young?"

"Specifically, males of a certain age, from adolescence to their mid-twenties. This is clearly recognized and even indulged to some extent."

"What about hard core criminals, murderers, psychopaths— how do you deal with them?"

"With some difficulty. They are not sterilized, if that's what you're asking. They are merely sequestered."

"Not eliminated?"

"By no means... I suppose whatever makes them that way is important to our genetic makeup— though I am not one to say why. Their lack of empathy, the abandonment of morals and ethics, the violence... it must have some evolutionary benefit, or such characteristics would not have survived for so long in the gene pool."

"So how do you deal with them?"

"Their access to technology is limited."

"That's it?"

"They are provided with food, water, shelter..."

"Like a prison?"

"There are no bars on the windows, no guards or wardens."

"What about fences?"

"Only the vastness of the ocean. They live on an island."

"Which island?"

"Greenland has been set aside for them."

"Sounds cold."

"These people have lost their rights as citizens."

"No such thing as rehabilitation?"

"Of course there is, but it is a choice, not a demand placed upon them." Öde paused. "I never said it is a perfect world."

"I guess not."

"We offer education instead of indoctrination."

"Meaning?"

"It's better to learn how to think than what to think."

"What about nonviolent offenders?"

"Economic crimes?" Öde asked.

"Sure, like burglary or embezzlement."
"There is no money."
"What?"
"Time is the new currency."
"How does that work?"
"It's a bit complicated."
"Is everyone's time worth the same?"
"Of course not… a skilled surgeon's time is worth more than a shopkeeper's."
"A shopkeeper?"
"Many people enjoy this as an occupation."
"But you said there was no money."
"Goods and services are purchased by giving up a bit of time."
"What if I wanted to live in a nicer house?"
"Nicer than what?"
"Nicer than my neighbor's."
"That is your prerogative. You could earn it by working hard and sacrificing many hours, if that's a priority for you."
"Giving up more time?"
"Yes, and making your time more valuable by gaining skill and experience throughout your life."
"What about all the dirty jobs no one else wants to do?"
"Such as?"
"I don't know… Not everyone can be a surgeon or… a poet. Somebody has to drive the buses, take out the trash, or, run the bureaucracy."
"We have uncomplaining robots for such tasks."
"Not sentient robots?"
"No, they are more like a toaster. It was decided that giving robots any sort of intelligence, or indeed sentience, was a bad idea."
"So, it's a highly stratified society?"
"I would say the opposite. People follow their inclinations, their innate talents. The world can't have too many poets." Mr Temsik smiled.
"What about religion?"
"There are many religious people. Again, it seems to be an innate human need to believe in the divine. Yet, it is not comparable to

religion in your present, nor your past."

"Why not?"

"It has no power other than its spiritual insight. No economic power, and they do not dictate policy. There are no sprawling institutions, no hierarchy to speak of. Generally, it is a quest for spiritual freedom, a search for the mystic, the transcendent. You are free to follow whatever doctrines you choose. Adherents may influence others but only with their ideas and their passion. They cannot compel others to their beliefs by means of force."

I sat back, trying to take in everything Mr Temsik had described. It did sound idyllic, utopian even. I still had a lot of questions, a lot more to think about. "So what's next for this new civilization?"

"Terraforming keeps people very busy and probably will for years to come."

"Terraforming?"

"Making the earth more like a garden, less like a desert… From there… well, if we have a destiny at all, then perhaps it is to bring life to dead worlds, to other planets…"

"Sounds like we're spreading a disease."

Mr Temsik let go a long laugh. "Perhaps you're right, Patrick."

***

The waitress came by with more coffee and I asked for a slice of cherry pie. Öde ordered an ice cream sundae. I looked around the diner to see if anyone was listening to our conversation. No one seemed especially interested. "This utopia of yours… or even this present… it's not someplace you'd invite Kali to, right?"

"Absolutely not… I would say she is an unwanted guest no matter what."

"Have you seen her here, maybe at the quarry?"

"Yes. Our paradise will soon be disturbed, it seems to me."

"Can she be stopped?"

"That is the question, dear Patrick." Öde sat back in his seat. "Tell me, have you spoken with Mr Sato?"

"Not yet."

"Ah, but this is imperative."

"Where is he?"

"Japan of course."

"A lot of people live there. How would we find him?"

"We?"

"Fynn and I."

"I can help with that…" Mr Temsik replied but said nothing further for the moment.

"I'm still not sure what Kali is after," I said.

"But you have met her?"

"Yes…"

"I would say she desires control. She wants a world where everything is stable and predictable."

"That doesn't sound so bad."

"Ah, but life itself is change, without it there is only entropy. Stagnation and death will eventually follow."

"Doesn't she realize that?"

"Kali sees only the present."

"I'm not convinced."

"Why not?" Öde asked.

"She seems like an opportunist."

"Ah… and a clever one at that. I regard her as extremely adaptable."

"What do you mean?"

"Whatever timeline she finds herself in, she's able to craft it to her own needs."

"For example?"

"Well, she might not like the idea of your worldwide spider web— the open exchange of ideas and information… But she's able to put it to good use. Kali will make it serve her own aims, spreading lies and mistrust if she wants."

"Is that what she's doing in my usual timeline?"

"She's no fool, and has a keen eye as to what's inevitable and what's not."

"So she's all about control?"

"Yes, and she is constrained only by the mechanisms that can control the world…"

"Like?"

"Politics, economics, religion, the military…"

The waitress sauntered by with our check. Mr Temsik paid with a currency that looked a bit different than I was used to.

"Well, enough of Kali," Öde said abruptly and looked at his watch. "We'll have to get you back home. Do you remember what you rolled when you first used Pavel's dice?"

"A three."

"I've learned over the years that if I can roll the same number twice in a row, I'm right back to where I started."

"Pavel never mention that."

"I doubt he even knows... It's just one of those quirky things..." Öde smiled and rolled both dice: double threes. He picked them up with his other hand and rolled again: double threes. We both picked up a single dice and I felt the pleasant tingle run up my arm.

A moment later I was sitting in exactly the same spot, the same diner, but Durbin and Fynn were also there. The dice rattled against the table. It was a three. They looked up at Omar.

"Oh sorry, gentlemen, I didn't mean to drop that... More coffee?" he asked.

I heard Fynn telling Durbin that we were off to Tokyo tomorrow, some sort of police conference... I clutched the dice still in my hand. I found something else, a scrap of paper Öde had slipped into my pocket. It read: *Shinjuku Gyoen Gardens, 11:15 AM.*

PART VI

chapter twenty-one
umami

It was an uneventful flight if not long, about fourteen hours. No stops and little turbulence. Fynn stayed buckled in his seat for most of the journey and slept through half of it, though he seemed to enjoy his meals. First-class made it all the more bearable.

"I do hope my language skills are up for the task," he confided over sushi.

I had decided not to eat mine. "What do you mean?"

"I'm the first to admit my Japanese is a bit rusty."

"I thought you've been to Japan before."

"Not since the Edo period, I'm afraid to say."

"I'm guessing it's changed a little since then."

Fynn laughed. "Indeed, I was a *Nanban*."

"A what?"

"A southern barbarian." He raised a smile. "Later, I was promoted to *Kōmō*… the word for Dutch, though meaning *red-haired*."

"When was this?"

"At the turn of the seventeenth century. But I stayed for many years in a trading colony called Hirado, and later, an odd place named Dejima."

"Why was it odd?"

"It was an artificial island built especially for trading with foreigners in Nagasaki."

"What did you do there?"

"I learned about the Japanese, their language, their culture and traditions."

"Did you run across Mr Sato back then?"

Fynn chuckled. "No, our paths did not cross. You must understand, Patrick, even back then Japan was densely populated. Millions of people, I would have to guess."

"Tell me about your previous visit."

"I was aboard a Dutch vessel— when was it? Just before sixteen hundred. While bound for the west coast of South America we got terribly lost… Our navigator, an Englishman named Adams— or was it Williams— well, no matter, eventually he guided us through the Straights of Magellan, and through some treacherous storms, I might add… After many travails we eventually washed ashore in Japan."

"And?"

"We were immediately taken prisoner."

"But you survived."

"Of course, in fact we flourished." Fynn sat back in his seat and closed his eyes. "It's a long and boring story, Patrick…"

"I'd love to hear it. Not like we're going anywhere right now."

"I certainly hope we are," he replied. "Speeding through the atmosphere at some many hundreds of miles an hour— yes?"

"Yes."

"Well then, please wake me again after we land…"

***

At security all I had in my pockets was a cell phone, a set of keys, and a single dice. I forgot to bring Edmund's pocket compass, nor did I think I'd need it. The only baggage we had to wait for was the bear claw cane. Luckily it came around the carousel before anything else and we were able to make a speedy exit from Narita Airport.

It was another hour's drive into central Tokyo, and part of the route took us alongside a large bay, following a complicated system of tunnels and elevated two-lane highways. I found it disconcerting to see our driver in the passenger seat. As we got closer, the city was a study in neon. Scrolling lights flashing odd symbols— odd to me at least— only a few English words and logos were recognizable.

Our car took us to Hotel Century Southern Tower in downtown

Tokyo. We had separate rooms on the twenty-eighth floor. It smelled of cigarettes, and Fynn didn't like being up so high, despite the panoramic views of the city. My room overlooked a skyline and a park below; next to me was a large building with a clock tower. The hotel seemed exceedingly modern.

Next morning I was knocking on Fynn's door. I had felt the hotel shaking during the night, and asked him about it.

"Nothing to worry about… such minor earthquakes are common."

Fynn's room had a view of Mount Fuji, at least its snowy cap. It seemed quite far from here.

"Last erupted, the sixteenth of December, seventeen- oh-seven," Fynn replied to my unasked question.

"Are you ready to go?"

"Where are you taking us, Patrick?"

"The park."

"Now? It hardly seems a good use of our time."

"It will be, I promise."

Fynn thought for a moment. "Who told you Mr Sato would be there?"

"Öde mentioned it."

"What did he say?"

"It is the only place where Mr Sato can still find peace."

"What do you suppose he meant by that?"

"Not sure… and I'm not sure how to get there either… Subway or taxi, you think?"

"I'd prefer a taxi rather than cramming into a subway car."

We started down the long corridor to the elevators, but I had to make a sudden u-turn.

"Where are you going, Patrick?"

"Sorry, I forgot my shoes…" I looked down at my own feet covered in complimentary slippers.

***

It turned out the Shinjuku Gyoen National Garden was in walking distance. Fynn and I wandered a few city streets along the way, hoping for a late breakfast. My initial impressions were that of a friendly, polite people who kept to themselves, and they were well regulated pedestrians. We passed a mall full of vending machines though I couldn't quite make out what they were dispensing, and it seemed to me as if all the prices were listed in pennies. Fynn, in his infinite wisdom, had already converted dollars to yen. There was a small admission fee to the gardens.

After half an hour of strolling through a typical if not beautiful urban park, we spotted Mr Sato on a bench by a giant tree. He was very old, onwards of eighty years. He had lost most of his hair, and that which remained had turned white. Only his rimless glasses were unchanged. Last time I recall seeing him, he was wearing a tall top hat and an old fashioned formal collar. Today he was dressed in a simple white shirt under a vest.

"Mr Hideki Sato?"

"Yes. Who are you?"

"I am Fynn and this is Patrick-san."

He stared at us for a time, then rose with some difficulty, to bow graciously. "Welcome to Japan."

"What?"

"Are you not tourists?"

"Of a sort," Fynn replied. "And thank you."

"As such I am duty bound to be hospitable." Mr Sato nodded and gave us a knowing smile.

"Feeding the pigeons?" I asked.

"No, I don't particularly like pigeons. Peck, peck, leave not a crumb on the ground..." He glanced over. "If it were up to me, I'd let feral cats roam through the park." He gave me a grin. "But I'm here for the flora."

"The what?"

"Notice that tree?"

I looked over at a thick trunk and a gnarled set of roots. The branches were covered with curious fan-shaped leaves, green, but tinged with yellow tips. It loomed over us by some fifty or sixty feet.

"Well, I've known this particular ginkgo since I was a young boy. We were saplings together."

"How long ago was that?"

Mr Sato sighed. "Going on six hundred years now... It is the only tree in the park that survived the war, the bombings, the fires, and the destruction."

"Miraculous," Fynn commented.

"Indeed… And if you don't mind, I will sit again, eh?" Mr Sato lowered himself back onto the bench. "Some of the oldest living things on the planet are trees. Many have lived for thousands of years."

I noticed that Mr Sato held onto a cane. It had the brass head of an elephant on top; its trunk curled down along the wooden shaft.

"You keep staring at my cane, young man."

"Oh, sorry… It's—"

"A gift from my wife… She picked it up in Rangoon some years ago— when Rangoon was still called that."

"Does it—?"

"It does nothing but support my weight. These old legs are not what they used to be." He smiled again. "Tell me, young man, which is more complicated, a person or a tree?"

"I would guess a person."

"Everyone always says that, but they are wrong. I've spent a good portion of my life talking to plants."

"What do they say?"

Mr Sato laughed. "Very little. They don't use words like you and I… But, by listening, I've learned much about what we call intelligence, and especially sentience." He turned to us. "All my life I have been searching for *Yūgen*."

"What's that?"

"It's difficult to define exactly… Let us say it's the feeling that *all is right with the world*."

"And how's that going for you?"

Mr Sato laughed again. "I have come to believe it can only be a temporary experience. It is our nature as sentient beings not to remain in the present for too long." He bade us to share the bench, and we sat next to him at a respectful distance.

"You're equating sentience with the passing of time?" Fynn asked.

"I am indeed. Our extraordinary ability to project ourselves into the past or into the future is the only thing that makes us aware of our present."

"Would you grant sentience only to humans then?"

"Not at all, all living things are sentient… but with this argument comes the nature of intelligence and consciousness." Mr Sato bowed his head. "Which creature is the first to have even a modicum of self-awareness? Is it a bird? A fish? An insect? Where do we draw the line?"

"And flora?" Fynn asked.

"Plants do not have the kind of intelligence we wish to see, the kind we might understand… yet they are most certainly sentient. And what is this thing we call intelligence, eh? Does anyone know? We always assume it comes from the top down, but what if intelligence emerges from the bottom up?"

"Meaning?"

"Many complex systems operating independently, but adding up with a kind of synergy."

"The whole greater than its parts?"

"Yes. Flora or fauna, we are all a collection of separate cells, each performing its own function, largely unaware of what the other cells are doing, and yet, from this multitude emerges a single being— what we call a consciousness."

"I'm not sure what you mean," I admitted.

"You are little aware of what your blood stream is doing at the moment, eh?"

"Well…"

"That's the odd thing about self-awareness… all the billions of cells working separately, unaware of each other for the most part, and yet it adds up to consciousness… An illusion to be sure, but a glorious one, don't you think? It is nature's ultimate feedback mechanism."

"What does that have to do with plants?" I asked.

"I have come to wonder if plants live only in the present and nowhere else." Mr Sato turned to me. "Plants have no words to use, so they are believed to be non-sentient. But this is our bias more than anything. How do they experience the world, or time, for that matter? Does the winter go by quickly for the tree, dormant as if asleep?"

"I never really thought about it before."

"It would not be correct to say they have a conception of time, certainly not as we perceive it. And yet they are surely rooted in the *perfect present*. They can feel it passing… the swaying of branches in the gentle breeze, or a fierce wind… the sunlight that falls upon them each day, the nourishing rain… Their experience is entirely different from our own."

"It doesn't sound that different."

"Time only moves forward for those people who live in the western cultures. For most living things time doesn't flow at all."

"What does it do?"

"It is cyclical… Life has adapted to reflect time in its seasons… it marks the transit around our star in an endless repetitive pattern, or a spiral perhaps…"

"A spiral down?"

"Eh? No, things spiral sideways more than anything." Mr Sato sat silently for a time. "Well, gentlemen, if you wish to continue this conversation, we must move to there," he said and pointed across the path to a different bench.

"Why?" I asked.

"Why?" he repeated and stared at me. "Must there be a reason, young man?"

"It's just that you sound so definite."

Mr Sato softened his expression with a smile. "Perhaps I am tired of squinting into the sun. That bench offers more shade." He slowly got to his feet and Fynn and I helped him over the curb. No sooner had we sat again when there was a terrible noise: a sharp, long cracking sound. A large branch split off from the ginkgo tree and fell on the very bench we were just sitting at. It would have certainly caused injury if not instant death.

I turned to Mr Sato in disbelief. "You knew that was going to happen?"

"I had an inkling it would, yes." He gave a throaty chuckle. "Well kind sirs, it's been a pleasure to converse with the both of you, but I must be on my way," Mr Sato said. "I do hope you enjoy your visit to my country." He shifted his weight and seemed ready to stand up again.

"Wait. Don't you remember us?" I asked.

"No… All you foreigners look alike to me. Let me have a good look at you."

"We are friends of Mr Temsik."

"Who?"

"Öde."

"Oh yes… the man who rescued me." He gave us a glance. "Not tourists, but travelers, eh? I only ask to be left alone, unless you are here to kill me again."

"What?"

"Aboard that dreadful steamship. "You set the bear against me."

"We did not," Fynn replied.

"No? I was sure it was you."

"We mean no harm," Fynn assured. "It was Kali Shunya who wished you dead— perhaps you know her now by the name Reimu."

"Reimu? My granddaughter?" Mr Sato seemed surprised and a bit confused. "But why do you mention her?"

"Kali Shunya goes by many names."

"Reimu tells everyone she is my granddaughter— I thought it must be true by now." A befuddled look crossed his face. "I will say she is the spitting image of my wife from long ago."

"How long ago?"

"We were married during the occupation, just after the war."

"Did you have children?"

"Children?" Mr Sato peered up at us through his glasses. "Not that I remember."

I turned to Fynn and spoke in Russian: *"How can Kali be his granddaughter?"*

"She cannot be." Mr Sato turned to me with a tight smile. "It's perplexing, I'll admit."

"But you were married to Kali?"

"No, I was married to Reimu."

"This is the name Kali goes by."

"How could it be her? She was so young, as young as my granddaughter."

"Where is she now?"

"Who can say? She's like a ghost, that woman… always flitting from here to there."

"What do you mean exactly?"

"Reimu is very busy running her business these days. She has no time for me any longer."

"What business is that?"

"So many things, I can hardly remember... lately it's something to do with mining operations."

"What sort of mines?" I asked.

"Kiku-ishi, xenotime, pure yttrium— a rare earth element."

"What does she hope to do with it?"

"But how can I know her intent?" he replied to Fynn and seemed almost angry. "I can only tell you what she's done. It is up to you to discern her motives." Mr Sato fell silent for a long while. "She has made so many promises to me, but has delivered nothing."

"Who has? Kali?"

"No, Reimu, my departed wife. She is the *mononoke* who follows me everywhere."

I turned to Fynn for a translation. "A kind of troublesome ghost," he explained.

Mr Sato nodded.

"What things has she promised?" Fynn asked.

"The sword, for one..."

"Which sword do you mean?"

"She promised to find and return the fabled *Honjo Masamune* to its rightful owner."

I gave Fynn a puzzled glance.

"He means the samurai sword of power. You might think of it as the crown jewels for Japan."

"One cannot put a price on that..." Mr Sato said and gave off a sigh. "She has sworn to retrieve it."

"Did she?"

"Not as of yet."

"Where is it?"

"Lost."

"When was it lost?"

"Most people say during the occupation. The Americans probably have it."

"Are you certain?"

"No." Mr Sato gave a sigh.

"What other promises has this *mononoke* made?"

"The restoration of our history."

"Did she change things for you?"

"I don't think so… I can still recall being a slave."

"A slave?" I asked.

"Yes, a Portuguese slave… centuries ago."

"Can you explain?"

"Someone meddled in our past… at the end of the so-called Edo period. Two hundred and fifty years of progress was thwarted."

"Do you mean a Japan that never went into isolation?"

"Exactly that." Mr Sato glared at Fynn. "To stop building ships, to forbid the reading of foreign books, cultural contacts, new technologies… Ah, stability perhaps, but I call it stagnation. Things should be very different for us." There was a harsh quality to Mr Sato's tone. "It was all Tokugawa Ieyasu's doing. The Shogun who wanted to cut us off from the rest of the world…"

"There is a place where that never happened," I said.

"What?" Mr Sato turned to face me again.

"It's an excursion from the *Hotel de Cirque*."

"An excursion?"

"Like a vacation…"

"You've been there?"

"No… but you could."

"How?"

"Come back to the hotel with us. Clark will fix you up."

"Where is this hotel?" he asked.

"Quite far from here," Fynn answered.

"I don't feel like traveling, honestly; but thank you for the kind offer."

"Can you tell us what Reimu has in store for the future?" Fynn asked, trying to steer the conversation.

"I know nothing of the future, sorry to say."

"What about the present?"

"I know even less about that." Mr Sato gave a throaty laugh. "I have little to do with the company anymore, and now they leave me be, that's all." He paused uncomfortably. "Except for the bodyguards."

"What do you mean?"

"This is the only place I can find peace nowadays."

"Peace from what?"

"The bodyguards— it usually takes them hours to find me... I expect they will soon enough, and our conversation will end."

"Do you have any idea how your inventions are put to use?"

"What inventions?"

"Your plants, the hybrids."

"I did all that work such a long time ago, I can hardly remember."

"They are from the manuscript though?"

"Yes... the book that Reimu gave me... drawings of curious plants I had never before seen, but I could not make any sense of the words..."

"Can you tell us about these plants?"

"Over the years she gathered many specimens for me. Plants with unusual properties."

"Where is this book now?" Fynn asked.

"Gone... disappeared entirely."

"When?"

"Around the time when my wife was murdered."

"She was murdered?" Fynn asked. "When?"

"A long time ago now..."

"How does all this relate to the present?" I asked.

"Of course it has to do with the plants," Mr Sato replied and glared at me.

"Can you explain this to us?"

"No, not really, unless you're well-versed in genetics. I only know she's devised a way to alter them, splicing genes, making two plants into one."

"What does it do?"

"It grows like any other plant."

"What effect does it have on metabolism?"

"Ha—" Mr Sato gave a guttural laugh. "This I cannot say with precision."

"How about in a general sense?"

"It alters one's perception of time."

"In what way?"

"Such a large question, Patrick-san," he replied. "I have dedicated my life to understanding how time operates."

"Have you reached any conclusions?"

Mr Sato laughed again. "No, I have a good deal of humility left in me. What I have studied concerns the perception of time, not time itself."

"And how do we perceive it nowadays?"

"Ah! A life that rushes by so quickly that it seems no more than a dream… Clearly the pace of life has quickened."

"Did you hope to find a way to slow things down?"

"No, we must find a new way to keep up with it."

"What, like fast-time, slow-time?" I asked.

"It's not as simple as that, Patrick-san. It is more nuanced."

"What then?"

"Hmm, I would use the example of a dream to illustrate."

"Like a dream when you sleep?"

"Yes… You might have a dream that goes on for hours, many things might occur, much time seems to pass. But when you awake, hardly a minute has gone by."

"To an observer, you mean?"

"I do. Only a few seconds of REM sleep has passed. Would you call this fast-time or slow-time?"

"Neither, I guess."

"It cannot be neither," Mr Sato said solemnly. "It must be one or the other…" He added a smile. "Or at least both."

"Both?"

"If you lived through the dream, you have slowed time down immeasurably. You've stretched a few seconds into hours. But if you are the observer, time has sped up. A lifetime might pass in just a few moments."

"You're saying it's a matter of perspective."

"Yes, very nuanced indeed. The whole matter is quite paradoxical."

"Dreams aside," Fynn said, "often, I've fallen asleep for what seems like only a moment to wake and find the sun rising."

"A perfect example of fast-time," Mr Sato said and smiled. "You compressed many hours into the blink of an eye…" He turned to me. "What do you think of that, Patrick-san?"

"Me?"

"If you were to fall asleep with your eyes open, it would be a strange sensation indeed. You might glance over at the clock and see its hands moving at some speed."

"Fast-time, yeah, that makes sense."

"Or does it? Perhaps Mr Fynn has slowed time by taking his blink of an eye and stretching it into many hours of restful sleep?"

Fynn started laughing.

"This is more than just nuanced," I complained.

"As I have already said, it is not about time itself, it is about our perception. But Policeman Fynn has struck at the heart of the matter."

"What's that?"

"It's all about one's mind, our ability to concentrate, focus, and place attention. This is what affects the perception of time. While asleep, there is little sensory input, nothing to focus upon, and time seems to pass very quickly indeed."

"So fast-time is fairly common?"

"Yes. If you limit your attention, the hours may go along quickly."

"How?"

"Any number of ways… a few cups of saké will do the trick." Mr Sato smiled. "Or, if you are single-minded and concentrate on one task alone, time will seem to rush by."

"For instance?"

"It could be anything: reading a book, watching a television program, or being deep in thought."

"And the opposite?"

"Yes… slow-time, a rare thing to be sure."

"Why is that?"

"To slow time down is a difficult task. And it is fraught with so many terrible connotations, depending on your personality. An example might be pain."

"Pain?"

"Yes, emotional pain or physical pain can make the minutes seem like hours… Or, one might be filled with doubt and remorse, and time slows to an excruciating pace. An eternity has passed and yet you look at the clock and only a few minutes have gone by."

"Such has a ring of truth to it," Fynn remarked.

"I'm not so sure…"

"Do you not think impatience makes time travel more slowly?" Mr Sato asked. "The feeling of anticipation or worry can stretch time out to an almost infinite measure." He smiled again.

"I guess…"

"Imagine a schoolboy watching the second hand tick in his classroom. Or a salaryman, waiting for the clock to strike six." Mr Sato turned to me. "Anxiety and fear have much the same effect… though, each person is different, true to his or her own nature. Anguish, guilt… boredom, monotony, depression— they all exist in slow-time."

"It sounds like a very negative place."

"A rare occurrence when it's not." He gave me a sad smile. "I was in a car wreck once, and it unfolded in what you would call slow-motion. I was acutely aware of what was happening, and powerless to stop it, I will add. And yet, the scene unfolded with such delightful slowness. I could see every detail, every event, every cause and effect…"

"Slow-time."

"By any measure, yes, though it is not sustainable."

"Why not?"

"Something to do with human metabolism. In such a state, a person's brain is working far faster than usual, processing every aspect… You have a thousand thoughts in a moment rather than a few dozen."

"It's paradoxical," Fynn commented, "that in slow-time, one's mind is moving so much faster."

"Indeed." Mr Sato gave a big smile and bowed his head. "There is a third way to perceive time," he continued. "And that is to remain mindful of the present only."

"How does that work?"

"Well, meditation is the ancient practice. One's focus is everywhere at once: on your breathing, the cool air that glances across your skin, the song of birds and insects, the swaying of leaves… The *blissful-now*, one might call it."

"Only meditation does this?"

"Not necessarily; playing a sport is like this, or taking an arduous hike, perhaps even, a long hot bath."

"But not a sustainable state of mind?" Fynn ventured.

"I agree… the merest distraction is enough to thrust you back to the normal flow of things."

"What distraction?" I asked.

"Glancing up at a clock, I might say... Ah, but to remain in the blissful present— this is something Reimu was interested in," Mr Sato said. "Hence the concoctions."

"What concoctions?"

"From the plants... one to experience fast-time, and one for slow-time."

"So really, you're just altering people's minds."

"You might put it that way, but it is one's mind that measures how time flows."

"And why is any of this different from alcohol?" Fynn asked. "A glass of beer or rice wine. It seems to have the same effect on people."

"It is not much different... nor is it different than drinking a cup of tea or coffee, or a sugary tonic laden with caffeine."

"What does this new Sweet Water do?"

"You've heard of it already, eh?"

"We have..."

"This is a bit different. It keeps one in the everlasting moment where you can experience *Yūgen*."

"What, like meditation in a bottle?"

"Only a westerner would say such a thing." Mr Sato looked at me and chuckled. "To find the perfect balance was a difficult task."

"You mean dosage?"

"You might put it that way."

"And you did all this for Kali?" Fynn asked.

"Who?"

"Reimu, your granddaughter..."

"My reasons were noble, I assure you, but I will admit I've made a terrible mistake." Mr Sato paused for a long while.

"What were your reasons?" Fynn persisted.

"It seems silly when I say it, but I only wanted to converse with the flowers."

"How?"

"By synchronizing my perception with the flora all around us."

"The blissful-now?"

Mr Sato nodded but said nothing further.

"It's all gone awry," Fynn said softly.

"Yes… and I fear the company has some dreadful intent nowadays."

"Which is?"

"What no one has noticed is the genetically altered spearmint that's used in its manufacture."

"Spearmint?"

"Yes, tiny leaves that grow in the wild."

"And to what end?"

"Certain compounds have been added to react with plastic."

"What plastic?"

"From the bottles… Such chemical combinations will cause untold havoc."

"What sort of havoc?"

"Well, the effects are cumulative, I will say. They are injurious to a person's immune system, among other things."

"Does this new drink cause sterility?" Fynn asked.

"Yes. Within a few generations, the world's population will be cut in half."

"Why would she want that?"

"Reimu aims to save the world. Sustainability… she has called it." Mr Sato let off a loud sigh. He seemed suddenly anxious and glanced around the park. "Even here, she will find me eventually."

"Who?"

"The spirit who haunts me daily… the voices in my head…"

"Kali?"

"No, the ghost who makes promises."

"Who exactly is making all these promises?" I asked.

"The *Hannya*, perhaps she is the spirit of my dead wife."

"Can anyone else see this spirit?" Fynn asked in a quiet voice.

Mr Sato turned to him. "No… She is indistinct, her form shimmers, I cannot see her properly most times."

"Tell me, Mr Sato, do you have a photograph of your wife?"

"I have no such thing. Nor do I need it. She haunts me every day."

"How did she die?"

"She was murdered, as I've said."

"When exactly?"

"So many years ago, I've forgotten…"

"Can you tell us what happened?"

"She was in the shop... alone... someone came in and killed her. It was all thoroughly investigated at the time."

"Why was she killed, do you know?"

"By the yakuza, I was told... thugs."

"Was it a robbery?"

"No. Who would want to steal what we sold? Little trinkets, flowers, and a few bonsai trees..."

"And when did you first meet your wife?"

"During the occupation... It was love at first sight and we married after only a month. She was not from a good family though... Indeed, many called her a foreigner— no offense, of course..." Mr Sato hurried a smile. "But... I broke with tradition, because I was in love."

"It may be possible to prevent her murder," Fynn said. "When did you see her last?"

"Hmm...The last time I traveled? I can hardly remember. I cannot jump anymore, not with these legs... Ah, when I was a younger man..."

"You might come with us."

"Eh? Oh, a *Umarekawaru* jump... "No, that's not for me."

"What's a *Umarekawaru*?" I asked.

"A re-live, a soft jump," Fynn answered, then turned back to Mr Sato. "Your knowledge of that present may be invaluable to us."

"How so?"

"In preventing the crime."

"You mean go back to before she's dead?"

"This would be our plan."

"As much as you tempt me, I cannot. My time is at an end. I am tired. This is something you must do on your own."

"Very well," Fynn replied. "But you may give us some details, if you please."

"I can hardly remember anymore."

"Surely, you would want to end her suffering? Her restless spirit?"

"Yes..."

"Tell me then, please, Mr Hideki Sato, when did your wife die?"

"The first day of spring in nineteen sixty-three."

"And how might we find you back then?"

"I'd probably be at the shop."

"What shop?"

"The shop that Reimu and I had together. Here, I will write down the address." He motioned for a pen and paper. "There is an alley off Kira Street and there you will find some shops... I used to have a stall there..."

Two men appeared on the path, both with sunglasses and identical suits. They walked towards us at a brisk pace. Mr Sato had noticed them first. "As much as I have enjoyed our conversations, gentlemen, I must be going now." He rose from the bench and gave us a long graceful bow, then shuffled off towards the waiting men.

Fynn and I remained on the bench for a while longer. He was deep in thought, then finally turned to me. "Mr Sato thinks the spirit that haunts him is a kind of *shiryō*, the souls of the dead."

"You don't believe him?"

"No. It is more likely to be an *ikiryō*, the soul of the living."

"You mean Kali."

"Exactly right, Patrick... whispering in his ear all these many decades."

"Ghost or not, we're being followed," I said quietly.

"What do you mean?"

"Every time I look behind us, I'm seeing someone lurking in the shadows..."

"Can you be more specific?"

"A man, a tall man. I haven't seen his face though."

"Are you sure?"

"Yes."

"Another of Mr Sato's bodyguards perhaps?"

"I don't think so... I first saw him in the lobby."

"Here at our hotel?"

I nodded.

"Well, we'll lose him soon enough."

"Why is that?"

"We're off to twenty twenty-one."

"Now?"

"Yes, we must travel to the future and see about these plans of Kali."

"Sweet Water?

"We will attend this unveiling to understand her larger aims, eh?

There is still much we can learn, no doubt."

* * *

It was a simple matter to find a quiet place to jump. Fynn set the cane and we leapt on the count of three while both holding the bear claw. We arrived in Tokyo again, this time in 2021; things had changed very little. I wondered if progress was slowing down.

"It's only been a few years, Patrick. I don't know what you expected."

"Well, I can't get a wifi signal anymore…"

"Your phone may be incompatible or even obsolete."

"What's next?"

"The event is not until tomorrow evening."

"The grand unveiling?" I asked.

"Yes, we should go back to the hotel, and hope my credit card has not expired."

"You're joking, right?"

Fynn smiled. "We must find the location that Mr Q provided me. I'll ask the concierge. They can be most helpful in this regard."

* * *

The following evening, Fynn and I set off to the grand unveiling of *Umami-Water*. A driverless auto-taxi got us close, but we had to walk part of the way as the roads had been closed off. Outside corporate headquarters, we came upon a perfectly staged media event. A full blown gala with music and lights, lots of neon, smoke and lasers. Giant TV screens dominated the sky from their scaffolds.

Under them, a large crowd had gathered on the plaza, many thousands if I had to guess. They spilled out onto the nearby streets. Above it all was a giant logo: *H-2-OO*. I have to admit it was cleverly designed, with a large capital H, the number two, and a small letter "t" followed by two O's.

"It's remarkable that so many people can get so worked up over a bottle of water," Fynn commented as we approached the scene. "I've never seen such a fanfare."

"And no one notices that this new soft drink has been created by a giant pharmaceutical company?" I asked with some sarcasm.

"No one seems overly concerned," he replied.

"A place where the truth no longer matters…"

"What's that, Patrick?"

"Oh, just something Öde said."

"I recall in great detail what Mr Quandary told me," Fynn continued. "With this new drink, Kali will take over the Asian market in less than a year. India is after that, then Europe, Africa and the United States. By this point, she already has governmental approval. The ingredients are completely innocuous… or so it would appear."

"But they're not… according to Mr Sato."

"And I believe him."

"How did she get away with it?"

"This new beverage is priced at half the going rate. I suppose it's irresistible in that regard. And like all nefarious plans kept from the public eye, it's been carefully masked by shell companies."

It was incredibly loud when we got close. Loudspeakers blared with pop music. A lot of people were dancing by now, and most everyone was holding a bottle. To my ear, some of the singers seemed to be emulating Mickey Mouse. The lyrics were generally unintelligible and even Fynn chose not to attempt a translation.

Laser lights shot overhead, odd figures sifted through the crowds passing out free samples. They all had giant heads, not real heads. Some I supposed were anime characters, most of whom I did not recognize. Human water bottles also milled about, most of them had feet. An icy cold bottle was thrust into my hand, and into Fynn's as well.

All the while, loudspeakers would randomly blare out words in English, like, "Relax…" It would cut through the music. I had to guess English was a second language for the announcer. "…Sweet Water…" the voice cried out slowly and musically. "H-Too-Ohhh…." came next, the *oh* was carried till his breath ran out.

Fireworks went off from the top of the building and the crowed oohed in awe. The music subsided and someone took the stage. I listened to the curious mix of announcements. Admittedly, I didn't understand a word: High squeaky voices brimmed with enthusiasm, and low gravelly voices imparted utmost seriousness. The crowd hung on every syllable and cheered at the end of every pause.

We never even got close to the stage, but on the giant TV monitors, Mr Sato was visible, perhaps as the elder figurehead. He was bound to a wheelchair. Kali was by his side, though she looked quite different than usual, now dressed in a yellow latex outfit with bright green trim. Her hair was blonde and other colors, spiked high over her forehead. Oddly, she also wore yellow earmuffs, and looked more like a cartoon character than a person.

"Well?" I asked and held up my free sample. "Mr Sato said the effects are cumulative. I'm sure one sip won't do much harm."

Fynn gave me a look, one eyebrow raised.

I unscrewed the cap and took a mouthful. It was absolutely delicious: just like fresh water with a hint of sweetness, honey maybe, and a tinge of mint. The combination of flavors was so subtle as to be exquisite. I took another sip, I couldn't seem to help myself... Not at all like a flavored seltzer, more like spring water with an extra something. I could see how it might become addictive— a staple like ordinary water, but with a slight punch to it.

Fynn was still staring at me. I had finished the bottle and already wanted more.

"Well?" he asked.

"It's wonderful..."

"And how do you feel?"

"Wonderful..."

Fynn took me by the arm and led me away from the crowds and the fanfare, probably for my own good. "That seemed like a worthless undertaking," he said as we left the scene.

"Why?"

"We've learned little, eh?"

"Well, I'm guessing it will be a very popular drink."

"Hmm... And to put a stop to any of this, we need to go back again."

"Back where?"

"To the nineteen sixties, to find Mr Sato's wife or Kali as the case may be."

"Why there?"

"We must retrieve the manuscripts if possible."

chapter twenty-two
ballpark figures

Fynn and I returned to the Shinjuku Gyoen National Garden. It was dark and closed. We scaled a tall iron fence and dropped to the other side. I struggled with it, Fynn made it over easily.

"Hurry along, Patrick. We'll be spotted by the authorities within moments." He led me to a rustic bridge that crossed a manmade pond. "Here, a good place to jump," he said but seemed hesitant.

"What?" I asked.

"I have a terrible admission to make."

"Which is?"

"In the end, I thought it a better idea not to have the cane fixed."

"Why?"

"With all these errands as of late… and my considerable concurrency in any given era…"

"I understand completely." I smiled. "Are we going to make doubles again?"

"I certainly hope to."

"I'm guessing you have a concurrency back in nineteen sixty-three."

"Indeed I do… and yourself?"

"Not that I remember."

"I was far from here, let us say," Fynn replied with a tight grimace. "Another word of caution— Pavel has explained to me that the cane is designed for one person to use, not two. With both of us jumping, it does not always function as anticipated."

"Well, let's hope for the best."

***

I can't speak for Fynn, but for me it was a hard jump. We arrived only a few yards from where we left, though deftly missed the pond and came to land on the shore. It was a bright sunny day, probably around noon. The park was now ablaze with cherry blossoms, and Tokyo changed the instant we settled. Not really, it was us who had changed. We were now some sixty years in the past.

Everyone was dressed pretty much the same, but not the same as when we left; all the men at least, in black or gray suits with skinny ties. There was an astonishing conformity among them. I saw fewer women on the streets as well; those I did see, were dressed in modernish skirts and blazers.

"What day is it?" I asked as we brushed ourselves off.

"Thursday, the twenty-first of March, nineteen sixty-three, as said by Mr Sato."

"How is that possible?"

"Eh?" Fynn turned to me with a questioning glance. "Oh yes, we must presume it is a timeline that Kali has not yet obliterated."

"Maybe we should have arrived a day earlier? Before Mrs Sato was murdered?"

"I thought about that," Fynn replied. "But I did not want to interfere with events. They should unfold the way they were meant to, eh?"

The park looked more or less the same, though Mr Sato's tree was a bit younger and the leaves were but small green buds. I noticed fences along the walkway, low iron hoops half embedded in the ground and interlaced with each other. Fynn pulled out the scrap of paper Mr Sato had given him; the address of his shop.

On the nearby roads, there were fewer cars, many more motorbikes and three-wheelers. The streets were awash with the whine of two-stroke engines. "Kei cars," Fynn called them; "rice burners," others might say.

It was hard not to notice massive construction going on throughout the city. Everywhere I looked, I could see giant dangling cranes. Every other rooftop had one it seemed, and they looked precarious to say the least, wobbly and ready to fall at a moment's notice. I also guessed that Japan had recently discovered poured concrete and cinderblocks. A sad thought crossed my mind: the remaking of Japan in our own image…

Fynn and I found the address with some difficulty. We wandered for nearly an hour and he asked for directions several times. We finally turned off a broad avenue to find the alley full of ramshackle shops. One side was bound by a massive curving wall and above it, I could see windows a few stories high. They were all painted over, broken or boarded up; and I thought it might be a warehouse or a factory. Lower down, temporary stands were set along its walls; sellers of trinkets and all manner of things. And food vendors... It smelled delicious if not unfamiliar. I was eyeing various selections and asked Fynn if he had any local currency. He had come prepared and handed me several heavy coins.

"They're silver dollars, American," I said, a bit confused.

"Yes, legal tender and readily accepted here in Tokyo, I will guess."

The vendor examined the coin closely then smiled and bowed. It was acceptable to him and I even got change back. I had decided against fish on a stick, a whole fish that was, head to tail; and instead tried what Fynn called, "yakitori" — skewered meat, or shish kabob by any other name. I can't say for certain what kind of meat it was. I also tried the rice dumplings with a sweet soy sauce, and *Takoyaki*, fried batter, filled with— I wasn't sure— but they were delicious.

The other side of the street had simple two story structures all attached in a row. They lay in the shadow of the massive warehouse. They were shops mostly, and seemed more established, having signs on them— not in neon though. I couldn't read a single one and pestered Fynn as to their meaning, until his patience ran thin.

"Did you see the man with the tattoos when we first entered the alley?" he asked.

"No."

"Likely, the local yakuza enforcer."

I had seen someone else loitering. A man with a hat pulled down over his face. He posed a familiar figure, but I said nothing for now.

The alley wasn't exactly a straight road, but made a wide arc. The place was crowded with shoppers milling about and lingering beside the storefronts. Though I could not understand a word of what was said, it seemed to me a lot of haggling was taking place. We passed many shops along the way, none of them seemed out of the ordinary. There was a tea room, a couple of ramen stands, a vegetable market, an open-air butcher and a fish place. One stall was covered in newspapers and magazines, and another displayed a table crammed full of transistor radios. We passed a furniture maker and I took some interest in a beautifully crafted step tansu, elmwood, a cabinet in the shape of a miniature set of stairs.

The crowds grew thin as we walked on and soon enough we seemed to be the only pedestrians. No one else had ventured this far, to the last few shops in the alley. Beyond, the rest of the buildings looked derelict, abandoned perhaps, but the narrow alley curved back around to the main boulevard. It seemed impossibly dark, yet I could see some cars in the distance driving along Kira Street. I could also hear hammering. Metal against metal, a hard rhythmic pounding.

"A blacksmith," Fynn commented.

Not much later we saw a man leaning against the doorway, hardly dressed with just a pair of baggy pants, and a cloth wrapped around his forehead. He was sweating profusely, a cigarette dangled from his lips. He eyed us with some suspicion. Fynn tried the door to an adjacent shop but it was locked. The man called out to us. I had no idea what was said. Fynn walked over to him and bowed in greeting.

Surprisingly, he spoke perfect English: "If you have arrived for the Olympics, you are a year too soon."

"We are here to buy a bonsai tree."

"Hideki Sato is not in the shop today, nor it would seem, is his lovely wife... It's odd that it should be closed today of all days."

"Why of all days?"

"It is *Shunbun no Hi*." The man gave us a huge smile.

I turned to Fynn for a translation. "The celebration of Spring."

"The equinox?" I asked.

"Indeed... though Tsaku is also absent."

"Who?"

"Mr Sato's cat. He's usually wandering among us, especially on such a lovely day."

Fynn faced the man again. "And you, kind sir?"

"Me? Well, I am a blacksmith. I have the stall next door." He nodded over his shoulder. "I make swords for tourists and ceremonies. I am Kenshi, Sakurai, at your service." He smiled and bowed graciously. "But please, most people just call me Mr Kenshi."

"I see a great many shops here," Fynn said, "but not many people."

"They don't come down to this part of the alley— too far from the main road," Mr Kenshi explained. "Though, the lovely Miss Hana is doing well today... Next door..." he pointed to a dress shop. "Sold many a paper umbrella, I've heard."

"And Mr Sato's shop?"

"Reimu Sato sells flowers, *kiku* and alike, and they do a brisk business this time of year."

"Kiku-ishi?" I asked.

"If you prefer rocks to flowers, that would be Miss Suki's place, the House of Mirrors." He pointed a few doors down. "She sells gems and minerals of all shapes and sizes."

"And that one?" Fynn asked pointing to the adjacent door.

"Oh, the Catalog Shop. They'll sell you anything you need for the right price."

"Such as?"

"Everything in the catalog of course... or you can place a special order if it is necessary to you."

"What sort of things?"

"Memorabilia, nostalgia, historical items... mostly." Mr Kenshi gave a small bow. "It's run by Mrs Ambrose."

"Mrs Ambrose?" Fynn asked.

"Yes, a foreigner in our midsts. A very nice lady though. Would you like to meet her?"

"Perhaps later, thank you," Fynn replied. "And your shop, Mr Kenshi? May we come inside and browse?"

"Sure... why not, come have a look if you're interested..." He led us inside with several bows.

It was a tiny place, but behind the shop I could see an open courtyard with a small furnace at its center, bellows and all. I also noticed an anvil and hammers of different sizes. To either side was a low iron fence. It separated one courtyard from the other. At the back of the shared space, all the shops were bound by a common wall about three feet high. It was covered by some sort of vine with green leaves and seemed to run the entire length of the alley. Behind that was a virtual forest of bamboo, though only as a thin strip a few yards deep— beyond it, the ordinary buildings of Tokyo rose up.

Inside Mr Kenshi's shop was an impressive array of swords and daggers, many katanas hung on the wall. Fynn took some interest in one in particular.

"This one strikes me as extraordinary."

"You have a good eye, sir. That sword is a work of art— not from my labors— I was only asked to restore it."

"A thing of beauty," Fynn replied. "And all these others?"

"Dull-bladed replicas, I would call them, for the tourists to buy."

"Tell me, please, will Mr Sato be back to his shop this afternoon?"

"Oh no, of course not, Hideki-san is at the game."

"What game is that?"

"The baseball game."

"How would we get there?" Fynn asked.

"Ah... take the streetcar on Kira Street, number eighty-seven, southbound, two or three stops only. You can't miss it, there's a large playing field visible from the road."

As Fynn and I made our way back to the main boulevard we were stopped by a man loitering in the alley. He was no stranger. It was Mortimer. He wore a charcoal suit and a matching trilby.

"Well, well, if it isn't Fynn and Patrick... Welcome," he said, stepping out of the shadows. "I'm surprised to find you here."

"Where else might we be?" Fynn asked.

"Scotland."

"Doing what?"

"Admiring its rugged beauty, I would guess."

"What makes you say such a thing?"

"Not what but who. Mr Temsik said you'd be there."

"But we are not."

"As I can plainly see... An odd little man, that Mr Temsik, though he implied you would need my assistance."

"I'm sure we will not," Fynn said harshly.

Mortimer held up his index finger. It had a black mark and a small cut that had not healed well.

"Ah, perhaps I'm being hasty," Fynn amended his tone. "Last we saw, you were exiting through the revolving doors at the hotel."

"A dreadful battle to be sure... an endless ordeal to thwart this doppelgänger of mine. Enough to say, I prevailed and my lesser self was disposed of."

"Disposed?" I asked.

"Thrown into the abyss of time…"

"And how did you escape from Russia?"

"The end of the world, do you mean?"

I nodded.

"Traveled back a few years to search for my cane, and unsuccessfully, I will add… Eventually, I ran into my double and he got the better of me. Stole my eyepatch and the room key. It took me years to make my way to the *Hotel de Cirque*."

"And why are you here exactly?" Fynn persisted.

"I am only here to retrieve my cane."

"Somehow I doubt that."

"Have you found it yet?" Mortimer asked. "I've heard that one of the shopkeepers has it in their possession." He nodded up the alley.

"Who told you this?"

"I've befriended a few locals." Mortimer gave us a smile, not a friendly one. "I was also told to find Mr Sato… And if I'm able, I'll happily put a stop to Kali as well."

"Mr Temsik asked you to do this?"

"Not in so many words, but his intent was clear enough."

"You already know how difficult killing Kali has proven."

"It's enough to kill Mr Sato. All Kali's plans will come to naught if I do."

"What if he is innocent?"

"None of us are innocent." Mortimer gave his thin smile. "And Kali? Is she here?"

"Not that we've seen," Fynn replied.

"I was hoping I might borrow your cane then."

"I'd prefer not to lend it to you."

"No matter, I'm not going anywhere for the moment."

"How long have you been here?" I asked.

"Me? I've only just arrived. Not an easy destination, as you have no doubt discovered." Mortimer smiled at Fynn and I. "Tell me, have you located Hideki?"

"Yes."

"Mind if I tag along?"

"It's best if you don't."

"I might make the promise to refrain from injuring him— though that may prove difficult if I learn that he has my cane."

"He does not, of that I can assure you. He has no interest in such devices."

"No? I've heard otherwise."

"From whom?"

"As I've mentioned, some of the locals."

"Well, rest assured, Mr Sato's interests lay elsewhere," Fynn said.

"And where exactly?"

"At a baseball game it seems. Patrick and I are going there now to meet with him."

Mortimer seemed hesitant, glancing at us both as if to determine our actual intent. "Alright then… Be seeing you," he said and walked back into the alley to disappear among the shoppers.

* * *

The one thing that had not changed about Mr Sato was his rimless glasses. We spotted him in the bleachers behind home plate. I also saw he was clutching the jackal cane. In this era he was in his late thirties, a good ten years younger than I'd seen him on the *Carpathia*, and a good deal thinner. Fynn and I climbed the stands and sat down on either side of him. He was startled at first but a smile came to his face.

"Oh yes, I do recognize the both of you quite well. You are the detective, Fynn, and you are the wireless operator, Mr Jardel— Patrick-san, if memory serves. It's been sixty years at least." Mr Sato paused to bow his head. "And by the look of you, I can guess you're travelers."

"Yes— the three of us— eh?" Fynn replied.

"And why, I might ask, did you set that ferocious bear upon me?"

"It wasn't us. It was Kali."

"Who?"

"Kali Shunya… though she may go by another name."

"What name?"

"Reimu."

"Ha. Why would my wife wish to kill me, eh?" He chuckled. "Of course, she's angry at me from time to time… I am not the perfect husband, I suppose."

"Your wife is a traveler as well?" Fynn asked.

"She is… or she was…" his voice trailed off. "Ah, but this is the only place I can find peace nowadays."

"Peace from what? Not a ghost?" I asked.

"No, of course not. I mean my wife… she is not at all fond of baseball."

"And the cane— is it yours?" I glanced over.

"Oh, it's Reimu's. I twisted my ankle this morning and borrowed it for the day."

I stared off into the field. It was kind of weird to watch a baseball game in the middle of Tokyo. The players had numbers I could recognize, but the names on the back of their jerseys were unintelligible.

"We've been playing baseball for nearly a hundred years now…" Mr Sato said, noticing my attention. "There, you see number nine in right field, he is Japan's Roger Maris. And there on first base, number six, is our version of Mickey Mantle, a wonderful switch-hitter."

"Is this like a major league team?" I asked.

"No, not at all. It's an industrial team. I am part owner and as such, I'm obligated to watch." He chuckled. "It's not important though, it is a— how do you say it? A practice game."

"A preseason game?"

"Yes, that's it exactly. I am here to evaluate the new players."

I heard the crack of a bat. A man ran to first. "Safe-ah," cried the umpire. I definitely heard an extra syllable.

Mr Sato turned to me. "I have been watching players for years and years, and I've come to the conclusion that some seem to sense time differently than others. They are better hitters and fielders, pitchers too…"

"Locked in the zone," I said.

"What?"

"It's an expression that Americans sometimes use."

"Ah yes, seeing the ball," Mr Sato agreed. "So you understand how one's perception of time can be altered."

"A little… fast-time, slow-time, and the perfect-present," I said.

"Eh?" Mr Sato stared at me for quite a while. "And where have you two just traveled from?"

"Here and there…"

He laughed, though a bit nervously. "Fast-time is easy enough. A bottle of saké will do nicely," Mr Sato said. "Drink yourself into a stupor and wake up the next morning— that's fast-time for you."

"And slow-time?"

"Good for the hitter," he replied and nodded towards the field. "He can see the ball coming to the plate and he knows where it will be. This is where he swings… and why we concentrate on batting practice so much." Mr Sato laughed.

"So it becomes second nature," Fynn commented.

"Exactly. The difficulty lies in consciously slowing down time in one's mind. It seems to be an impossible task— especially when you are waiting at the plate for the next pitch."

"Anticipation," I said. "The hitter isn't really slowing time down. He's just guessing where the ball will go."

"Do you think so, Patrick-san?"

"Sure, nobody bats a thousand."

"There may be something in what you say, and yet we've had winning seasons for the last two years. And we will again." Mr Sato smiled. "We've also beaten most every major league team we've come up against."

"What's your secret?"

"I require that all the players drink a special tea before the game."

"A special tea?"

"It's not unlike regular tea, but it slows things down for the players."

"Time?"

"Only the perception of time. Things seem to move slower, especially baseballs."

"Does Kali know about this?" Fynn asked.

"Who?"

"Your wife."

"No, like I said, she is uninterested in the game."

"Where did you come across this special blend of tea?" Fynn asked.

"I brewed it from one of the plants in the book." He turned to face Fynn. "That's why you're here, isn't it? You've come about the manuscripts."

"They hold some interest to us, yes. What can you say about them?"

"Much and little," Mr Sato replied. "I had an impossible time translating these books, I will admit as much. The language is very foreign to me... it's not Portuguese... or Latin..."

"Where are they now?"

"Gone, disappeared about two weeks ago."

"From where?"

"The shop."

"Stolen?"

"I can't think by whom.... besides, I've made copies of all the drawings— the plants, I mean to say."

"And what do you make of them?"

"Species I've never come across before."

"What do they do?" I asked.

"Do?" He turned to face me. "They grow... like plants. I have some back at the shop."

"Where did you get them?"

"Reimu found them for me— but that was years ago, before her accident."

"What accident?"

"Fell down the stairs and broke her leg. Walks with a limp now, the poor woman..." Mr Sato gave off a sigh. "She used to travel often, scouring the world to bring me specimens..."

"The specimens from the manuscript?"

"Yes, though I am beginning to suspect some of them are hybrids."

"Where did she go exactly?"

"I can only say we were separated for a long time... years, it seems to me."

"And where did you go?"

"Me? Nowhere. It was her that disappeared... To the south, I think..." He smiled. "I'm quite content where I am."

As Mr Sato was speaking, I could feel a slight vibration. It seemed to be coming from under my seat and it was getting stronger. The benches were shaking. I looked around to see some of the players lose their balance, stumbling; the short stop fell to the infield.

"What was that?" I asked, alarmed.

"Just an earthquake, a small one," Mr Sato explained and then reached for a tattered notepad. He made a few marks.

"Recording the tremors?"

"No, the short stop... he lost his footing."

"We went by the shop earlier," Fynn said, "but it was closed. Where is your wife, Mr Sato?"

"Not there, you say? That's surprising to me. She's no slacker, my wife."

"Where do you suppose she's gone?" Fynn persisted. "I fear she might be in danger."

"Danger, you say? No, I'm sure she can look after herself." A worried look crossed Mr Sato's face.

"Nonetheless, we should check to see she is safe."

"Safe from what?"

"I would say from whom."

"Ah... yes, a different traveler, a malicious one. Tell me then, Policeman Fynn, what do you know that I don't?"

"I fear the worst."

Hideki Sato said nothing more but rose from his seat. We headed back to the alley on foot and at quite a pace despite Mr Sato's reliance on the cane. We reached his shop in just a few minutes. He went to the door and started banging, calling out Reimu's name but there was no answer.

"Do you not have a key to your own shop?" Fynn asked.

"No, Reimu has the only copy. We'll go around to the back. This way..." Mr Sato took us through to the adjacent shop, the sword smith's. Mr Kenshi looked up at us as we passed but said nothing. Hideki Sato gave him more of a nod than a bow and hurried by. Fynn and I followed a few steps behind. Sakurai caught up with us in the courtyard and we all vaulted over the low fence.

The backdoor to the shop was firmly locked as well, though it was rather flimsy, built from a wood frame and glass panels. Mr Sato jabbed his elbow through the glass and reached in to unlatch the door. He called out, "Reimu... Reimu..." in a loud, frantic voice, and looked about in a panic.

We followed him in more cautiously. The place seemed undisturbed. It was filled with exotic plants that were probably unknown to most botanists. I saw flowers and tiny trees displayed under tasteful lights. There were also several paper paneled doors elegantly partitioning different sections of the shop; it seemed a bit like a maze.

Mr Sato had already bounded up a set of stairs that led to an apartment, still calling out for his wife. We heard muffled shouts and creaking floorboards from below. He returned a few minutes later, alone, and in complete despair.

In the meantime, Fynn had found something, or someone. One of the paper-paneled doors lay off its hinges. Under it was a body. I helped him move the panel and we found a woman lying face down on the floor. She was wearing a red and gold embroidered kimono, and I could see a small bit of blood dripping from her ear.

Sakurai Kenshi and Mr Sato rushed over. Fynn felt for a pulse and shook his head. With great care, the inspector turned her over. It was Reimu. It was Kali Shunya. She was dead, very dead. Mr Sato let out a great sob of grief and turned to Sakurai for some small comfort. Fynn and I conferred in low tones:

"It's Kali. It's Reimu," I stated the obvious.

"And a Kali who is vulnerable."

"What do you mean?"

"Her prescience has not saved her in this case."

"A double, you're saying?"

"Perhaps a version that lacks Kali's formidable skills. She has been stabbed in the ear, as you can plainly observe."

"We've seen this before," I said quietly.

"Yes, with Vadim Arkhipov," Fynn replied and checked the body. He felt her wrist and then put the back of his hand to her face. "She is still warm to the touch. I will guess she has died within the last hour."

"Why would Kali murder her own double?"

"Indeed. It seems Reimu is the victim and Kali is the perpetrator." He turned to me with a look. "I don't see her motive, I'll admit that."

"But she was killed the same way as Vadim."

"It would appear so... A shame Doctor Zed is not here to confirm this."

"They're leave-behinds," I said.

"What?" Fynn turned to me.

"What Madame Madeline has been saying for all these years. Kali jumps to the past, makes a double and then moves on— that makes her a leave-behind."

"She is using Mortimer's cane, you are meaning?"

"Yes."

"What you say makes a bit of sense. She would have trouble traveling to Japan; her weakness is geography. But she only has to arrive once and then go back and forth between different presents."

"It means she cannot re-enter one of her doubles… she can't soft jump back into them."

"You may be correct, Patrick, and this might be to our advantage."

"Still… why kill her own double?"

"She is unpredictable, eh?" Fynn said. "Though, we cannot assume Kali is the murderer even though it seems likely. We must rely on the evidence." He started to examine the area. Nothing else seemed amiss. Near to where Kali had fallen he found a mat on the floor where tea had been laid out. It was set for two, and cold to the touch. One cup was empty, the other almost full. I saw lipstick on the edge of both of them.

Hideki Sato sat on the futon, inconsolable for the moment. Luckily, Sakurai Kenshi knew where the saké was stowed and poured out several cups, enough to take the edge off Mr Sato's grief. He left him there and walked over to us.

"I saw her not an hour ago…" Mr Kenshi said.

"Does she always dress like this?" Fynn asked.

"Only for a special occasion or a holiday."

"We must call the police."

"The police? No, I will call Mr Wada, the yakuza representative," Sakurai Kenshi said.

"The time for protection has passed."

"You may be right…" He went for the phone on a nearby desk.

We were not completely alone in the shop. I heard a small meow from under one of the display tables. A ginger cat with stripes, looking a bit like a miniature tiger, sauntered out and wound between my legs.

"It's Tsaku," Mr Kenshi called over. "And he seems to like you, my friend."

Inspector Fynn continued his examination of the shop. He first went to the backdoor, the one Mr Sato had smashed to gain entry. "This door can only be secured from the inside," he observed, then strode over to the main entrance. It was also firmly locked. He bent down and picked something up.

"What's that?" I asked.

"The key," Fynn replied, "to the front door, and a rather old fashioned one."

"A locked door mystery?" I asked. "Or some kind of ritual suicide?"

"We shall see…"

"Pretty sure we know who else could've done this," I said in a quiet voice.

"Who?"

"The locked door— who else could it be?"

"Kali, you are meaning?"

"No… Mortimer. He jumps in from the future, kills Kali, and jumps away to the past… He was just hanging around in the alley…"

"Mortimer doesn't have his cane," Fynn reminded. "And he seems happy enough to remain in this present for now." The inspector walked over to Hideki still sitting on the futon. "Tell me, Mr Sato, how does this lock operate?"

"Which do you mean?"

"To the front door… you mentioned only your wife had the key."

"Yes… it can be locked from either side— it's the same key."

"So it's quite possible that someone could have locked it from the outside?" Fynn asked.

"I would say yes. But where is the key?"

"I found it just by the door, as if it fell from its place."

"What are you leading to?"

"This may not be a locked door mystery after all."

"But that is the only key, and if it was there on the floor… then the entrance was locked from the inside."

"And the backdoor?"

"It's not usually locked at all."

"What about the basement?" Fynn glanced over to a door by the stairs.

"It's bolted from the inside as you can see. No one has been down there in years."

"Is there another key to the upstairs rooms?"

"No— there is no lock on that door. No customer would ever be so rude as to enter our domicile."

"This is where you live?"

"Yes. Most everyone lives right above their own shop."

Fynn and I went up a rickety staircase to the second floor. The upstairs apartment was tiny and cramped. A corridor led to a galley kitchen, and a bathroom with only a shower. Off to one side was a small dining area and an even smaller room for sleeping. Two large windows overlooked the alley.

"No one has gained entrance from here," Fynn observed. "The shutters are all secured from the inside, and I see no signs of tampering."

Outside each window was a balcony, if it could be called that. It was hardly deep enough for a person to stand and lean against the railing. There was a third room, a kind of an attic used for storage; I saw a few steamer trunks at the end of the hallway. Fynn tried to open them but they were locked up tight.

***

The police arrived in due course, only two officers at first. They flanked either side of the door and said nothing to us, staring straight across the room stone-faced. A few minutes later a man strode in with a loping gait. He bowed to the officers and then looked around the shop, moving his head rather than his eyes.

"I am Detective Watanabe, Daisuke, of the Tokyo Prefecture," he announced in a gruff, gravelly tone. "I ask that none of you will leave until we have spoken first."

Despite the sound of his voice, he was a young guy, barely thirty, if that. Probably grew up in the middle of the war. He was wearing a plain suit, somewhat shiny it seemed, but it fit perfectly, and he had a skinny black tie. The detective sized us up with an expressionless gaze. There was a trilby in is hand, but I doubt he ever wore it. I watched him move around the room, examining the scene of the crime, lifting a few items here and there with a pen he had taken from his pocket.

He also spent some time hunched over the body. When he rose to his full height again, I realized he was taller than most Japanese men I'd seen, gangly, that's to say. He had spiky hair on the top of his head;

his sideburns seemed a bit too long, and his shoes a bit too pointy.

Detective Watanabe conferred with the two uniformed policeman, quietly barking orders it seemed. They bowed and headed upstairs to conduct a thorough search. We could hear them from below, stomping about, opening cabinets and alike. The detective loped over and turned his chin up, giving us all a good long look.

Fynn presented an identification badge.

"Well, a chief inspector for the Hong Kong Police," Detective Watanabe said in perfect English.

"Retired…" Fynn replied with a gracious bow.

"I am honored, good sir." He returned the gesture, then took a notepad from his pocket and scribbled something. "What can you tell me about this unfortunate occurrence?"

"It is as you see… The four of us broke into the shop to find Mr Sato's wife lying dead."

"The door was locked?"

"Both the back and the front."

"And the key?"

"I found it on the floor, there…" Fynn pointed.

"How do you suppose she was killed?"

"There is a small trace of blood coming from her ear. I believe she was stabbed by something very long and very sharp. Perhaps, a hypodermic needle."

"Hmm…" He looked at Fynn. "…and you have seen something like this before?"

"I have. Just last year outside of Moscow."

"Well then, a locked room, a murder, and no witnesses…"

"There is one witness," Fynn replied and nodded over to the cat who was now curled up on the futon.

The detective raised an eyebrow and went over for a closer look. "I wonder what you might tell us if you could speak," he muttered, then turned back to Fynn: "Well, we have no suspects… This could prove to be a troublesome case."

"Surely, there are suspects, Detective Watanabe," Fynn replied with a grin.

"Yes, I suppose there are always suspects." The detective returned the smile though it didn't seem that friendly. "And how are you acquainted with Mr Sato?"

"We have some business together, import, export," Fynn lied.

"And you are?" He turned to me.

"Patrick, Inspector Fynn's colleague."

"Ah, an American, eh? Maybe gangsters have committed this crime." He laughed and gave me a wink.

"Tell me, please, Detective Watanabe, is this the first murder in the area?"

"Yes, as far as I know... But what do you mean, sir?"

"Here in this alley. Have there been other incidents?"

"A few burglaries here and there. This has to do with the crime, you think?"

Fynn smiled. "Probably not— it is more my own curiosity."

"I would have to check the records at the station," the detective replied and then noticed the jackal cane leaning against a desk. "This looks quite valuable," he commented and called out to Mr Sato. "We should first determine if robbery is the motive. Was anything taken?"

"Not at first glance... though there is little of value here, eh? Who would want to steal a miniature tree?" Mr Sato replied from his place on the futon.

"You should look more closely... and upstairs in your apartment. It is important to know if anything is missing— even if it only had sentimental value to you or your wife."

"I'm not sure I am up for the task of inventory."

"Of course. Take as much time as you need."

"With your permission, Detective Watanabe, I would like to speak to the other shop owners nearby." Fynn bowed. "And in your presence, if you would."

"Are they our suspects?"

"Everyone is suspect when a murder has taken place, but I am supposing they may have heard something, or saw something untoward."

"Which shops do you mean?"

"On either side of this one," Fynn explained.

The detective turned back to Mr Sato.

"Yes, I am the middle shop," he confirmed. "To my left is Mr Kenshi and Miss Hana's place. To my right is the Catalog Shop and Miss

Suki's House of Mirrors..."

To the surprise of everyone, and especially Mr Sato, the telephone rang. It was a jarring, old fashioned sound. He rushed over to the desk to answer, and as he listened, a terrible expression crossed his face. "It is Miss Hana Kei," he called to the rest of us. "Someone is accosting her at this very moment."

"What?" the detective cried out.

"She is alone in her shop and terrified. Someone is trying to break in her door. We must hurry..."

Detective Watanabe snapped his fingers and the two policemen sprang for the door. The rest of us followed. As we left, I noticed Mr Kenshi took something small from a nearby table. I caught a glimpse, it looked to be a woman's lipstick.

Two shops over we could see a man, and he was indeed banging on the door with some ferocity. One of the policeman blew his whistle. The man spotted us and quickly sprinted up the alley. He jostled through the crowd of shoppers to disappear from view. With a nod, Detective Watanabe sent his men after him.

Mr Sato and Sakurai Kenshi ran to Hana Kei's shop. The latter tried the door with no success and called out her name repeatedly. There was no response for quite a while. Mr Kenshi turned to us with a look of frustration. "We should break it down," he said. "She might be injured."

"Wait a moment, if you please," the detective said. "I hear something from within." We all stopped to listen. There were soft footsteps, and the latch on the door began to rattle.

"Who is there?" a tiny voice called from inside.

"It is only me, Sakurai, and I have the police here... You are safe now."

The door opened a crack and Miss Kei peered out. She glanced at us all in turn. It was difficult to read her expression though; her face was painted a pure white. I couldn't even see her eyebrows. In contrast, her small lips were a bright red, and some sort of elaborate mascara lay above her eyes. Hanna Kei was stunning if not beautiful.

She shuffled back into the shop, her steps hampered by a lavish but constraining silk kimono. It had a high waist band with some kind of weird square bow at the back. We followed her in slowly. Miss Kei was slender and barely five feet tall. She had the most lustrous black hair I'd ever seen; it was almost indigo, as if it glowed with a dark blue aura. It was probably very long as well, now piled up at the back of her head with an elaborate cloth held together by a set of hairpins.

I didn't understand a word of what followed. She sat quietly on a mat with her hands folded. Mr Kenshi on one side and Mr Sato on the other, both on their knees, consoling her. Miss Kei spoke with a tiny voice, and although she spoke not a word in English, I felt compelled to listen attentively to every syllable. It was child-like, singsongy, and hypnotic. She almost sounded like a small girl of five or six. Fynn was also listening closely, and Detective Watanabe paced about, asking the occasional gentle question.

I looked around the shop to see various kimonos for sale, and accessories: swathes of silk, hats, headdresses, makeup, and paper umbrellas— all things associated with traditional garb. They held little interest and my attention returned to the sound of Miss Kei's musical utterances.

* * *

"Accosted by a ruffian," he summarized as we left the dress shop. "She managed to push him out the door and then called Mr Sato for help." Fynn seemed less than satisfied by the encounter. I could tell he didn't quite trust her.

"Ah, did you not notice her slippers?" he asked.

"No."

"The silk was scuffed and splattered with mud."

"What does that say to you?"

"It says she was not in her shop all day as she told Detective Watanabe." Fynn took me along the alley to Mr Sato's shop, two doors down. "Let's have another look around, eh?"

I followed him upstairs to the apartment again. It seemed the same, though every door in the place was wide open, including the shutters and the closets. The trunks were still closed, but Fynn raised an eyebrow.

"What?"

He walked over to the largest of them and opened the lid. "Wasn't this locked last time we checked?"

"Pretty sure it was."

We went back downstairs and out into the courtyard. Fynn took some time to examine the ground. I hadn't noticed before but each yard reflected the owner's personality. Mr Sato's was a garden. Mr Kenshi had a forge with an anvil. Next to his was Miss Kei's; devoid of anything it seemed. On the other side, I looked over the low fence to see a patio with a few metal chairs and a table. Furthest from us was a zen garden with white pebbles punctuated by larger rocks of a different color.

In Mr Sato's garden, Fynn observed a few muddy footprints.

"They're probably from when we all ran here from Kenshi's shop," I said.

"No, look, they are quite small, and they are going in the opposite direction." He followed them to the iron fence and then peered across into Mr Kenshi's place. "There…" he said and pointed, then a moment later he vaulted over. "A woman's scarf," Fynn said and held it out. "I do not remember seeing this before."

"Who does that belong to?"

"We must find out, but quietly."

"Ah, there you are," Mr Kenshi called out from his backdoor. "Detective Watanabe is looking for you. He requests your presence at the district station."

"And where is that?" Fynn asked.

"Up the alley to Kira Street, make a left, it's only a few doors down."

The inspector turned to me. "Something else I noticed, or failed to notice," Fynn said in a quiet voice.

"What's that?"

"Mr Sato's cane… it is no longer in the shop."

I smiled. "Tsaku the cat is also gone."

chapter twenty-three
dreadful device

Detective Daisuke Watanabe was waiting in his cramped office. As a policeman led us to the back room I could hear typewriters incessantly clattering. They were manned by many white-shirted bureaucrats, diligently filing reports.

"I hope you don't mind, but I telephoned Hong Kong to check your credentials," the detective announced as we entered and sat across from his desk. "Impressive to say the least, Chief Inspector Tractus Fynn, and I am honored by your presence. My department and its resources are at your disposal, good sir."

"That's very kind, thank you."

"So… have you made any breakthroughs in the case?" Watanabe asked but with a sense of humor.

"I have," Fynn replied. "It's most likely that Mrs Sato was murdered by one of the nearby shopkeepers."

"And not by Mr Sato himself?"

"It would be helpful to check his alibi."

Detective Watanabe read out a written statement: *Every Saturday, I leave the shop in the afternoon. I walk up to the corner and catch the one-oh-five to the playing fields.* He leaned back in his chair and put his hands behind his head. "Well, I have checked… My men tell me Mr Sato was indeed at the baseball game exactly as he says."

"This is where Patrick and I first met with him."

"Alright, he's in the clear then," the detective said. "We've also apprehended Mr Wada— the man seen banging on Miss Kei's door."

"The fellow with the tattoos loitering in the alley all day?" Fynn asked.

"Eh? Yes, that's the man. Mr Wada, Gesuidō— a neighborhood thug." The detective clicked his intercom and spoke in Japanese. He turned to us again. "I'll have him brought up. You'd like to speak with him, I am sure."

Watanabe led us to a small interrogation room. A table, a few chairs, and a ceiling fan that was slowly turning. He stopped outside for a moment. "It is generally known that the *Ryū ga Gotoku* control this alley of shops. What you call the yakuza. A certain Mr Akaname is in charge."

"And there's nothing you can do against this man?"

"My hands are tied by local politics." Watanabe held his chin up.

"A protection racket?" I asked.

"I believe they call it insurance nowadays." The detective gave a hapless grin. "This one, Mr Wada, is just local muscle. All the shops pay him protection. It's like a tax."

There was already someone seated at the table. He had oily slicked-down hair with a lick that fell across his forehead. Gesuidō Wada was not a handsome man by any measure. He wore a high-collar shirt and long sleeves. When he first spoke, his voice was an octave higher than I expected. I also noticed he was missing two of his fingers.

"What does that mean?" I asked Fynn.

"Disloyalty, usually."

Watanabe bade the man to roll up his sleeves. His arms were covered in bizarre tattoos. The detective said something in his rumbly voice… Fynn translated as the interrogation proceeded:

"You wear this shirt, but even on such a hot day?"

"Why not? I hear it's supposed to rain later."

"Alright then, tell me, Mr Wada— Why did we find you at Miss Hana's door earlier?"

"I thought she was in trouble."

"Trouble?"

"That's my job. I protect people."

"You haven't answered my question."

"Well— she called me on the phone. Said she had some difficulty…"

"What kind?"

"She didn't say."

"And you came running? A man like you doesn't stand a chance with a beauty like her."

"Did you go inside Miss Kei's shop?" Fynn asked.

"No, the door was locked, like I told you."

"And Mr Sato's shop?"

"What of it?"

"Did you go inside?"

"Sure, lots of times." He added a slimy grin.

"Today?"

"Maybe... He is late paying his dues."

"But what sort of man would take retribution by murdering someone's wife. Have you no honor?" the detective erupted in anger and paced the room.

"What are you talking about?" Gesuidō Wada looked over at him.

"Reimu Sato has been killed today."

"What? It's the first I've heard of it."

"What time did you visit Mr Sato?" Fynn asked calmly.

"Early this morning. He owes a fair amount in gambling debts. Hideki Sato likes to bet on these baseball games of his."

"And later that afternoon?"

"Well, I tried, but the shop was closed and the door was locked."

"What time was this?"

"Two o'clock, I'd say."

Fynn seemed satisfied and nodded to the detective. Gesuidō Wada was escorted elsewhere.

"Well, what do you think?" Watanabe asked as he led us back to his office.

"He is not our killer," Fynn replied.

"Why not?"

"He's more likely to resort to brute force, not an elaborate plan with locked doors."

"I agree, though I'll keep him here for the time being." The detective sat behind his desk again and leaned back in the chair with his arms up behind his head. "What is your next step, Inspector?"

"I'd like to interview the adjacent shopkeepers," Fynn replied. "I'd be pleased if you could join us."

"You have my blessing of course, and I'd like to, but I have my hands full already. As we speak, I've got my men checking into the backgrounds of these very people." He leaned forward again. "They may have criminal records."

"Is there anything you can tell us about them?"

"They are known to me, somewhat... A few weeks ago we had to see about a fracas between Mrs Reimu Sato and Miss Suki, the owner of the Shop of Mirrors.

"What was it about?"

"A real cat fight. It took several officers to break things up… Some sort of tryst, if I recall."

"Between whom?"

"I can't say exactly, though many names were bandied about. Jealous lovers, I suppose." The detective paused to smile. "It seems to me Reimu and Miss Tanaka were also rivals for someone's attention."

"Who is Miss Tanaka?"

"Sadako, Mrs Ambrose's assistant, a woman far too ambitious to my liking."

"And what can you tell us about Mrs Ambrose?"

"Oh yes, the foreigner in our midsts, to be sure, but we like her nonetheless. She's proven herself to be a good person."

"Who else holds your interest?"

"I am immediately suspicious of Mr Kenshi."

"Why is this?"

"Perhaps it is my own prejudice, but he is a southerner. You may not notice that he speaks in the Kansai dialect. I will only say they are not the most trustworthy of people."

"Let's see where the evidence takes us," Fynn cautioned.

"Such men… they worry me," the detective continued. "He might be a go-getter, or a con-artist… They can be cavalier at times, too informal, lacking respect, and perhaps a bit sloppy…"

"Surely his work does not suffer from such an attitude," Fynn observed.

"No, he is a master tradesman, I am forced to agree."

"We will keep your warnings in mind," Fynn said, and with a glance to me, started for the door.

"Chief Inspector Fynn, there is one other matter," Watanabe called out. "I went through the records as you asked. I will say it is generally a quiet area. Very few incidents to report." He swiveled in his seat and rolled over to a file cabinet. "Ah, here we are… well, this is quite interesting… It seems there were multiple deaths some years ago—before my time."

"And?"

"The Tokyo utility company was attempting to install an electrical transformer on the corner of Kira Street. Eleven men died in the process."

"Died of what?"

"Electrocution, it says in the report. In the end it was decided that the transformer would be located elsewhere. Even in modern Japan, there are some who remain superstitious."

"Meaning?"

"It was generally concluded that a *Kami* thwarted the installation of the electrical transformer."

"A *Kami*?" I asked.

"A Shinto spirit."

"A ghost?"

"An unintended short circuit, says the official report."

"How was the matter resolved?"

"The equipment was installed three blocks north on Yamato Street instead."

***

Fynn and I returned to the alley. Our first stop was the House of Mirrors, two doors before Mr Sato's place. A woman named Sasayaki Suki greeted us as curious customers when we entered. She spoke to Fynn at length in Japanese and there was a fair amount of bowing back and forth.

Her voice was quite extraordinary, though I couldn't understand a word. She spoke like an old woman, yet there was nothing old about her. She was probably in her late twenties and very pretty. Miss Suki had dark hair, long to the shoulders, and oddly, a thin streak of white started at her forehead and went all the way to the back. She wore a dark blue blouse with tiny yellow dots spread across it, and a tan skirt.

Like her voice, Miss Suki was thin and wispy. She barely spoke above a whisper, and I strained to hear her words. It was a monotonous tone devoid of hope, as if it held a terrible resignation about the world. Every syllable was relentlessly tragic.

The shop also seemed strange to me. There were gems and minerals of all shapes, polished slices of rock, each displayed on a reflecting tabletop. On the walls hung mirrors of all sizes and it made the store look much larger than it was. In the far corner I found a single bonsai tree illuminated from below. It was centered between two perfectly aligned mirrors that stretched out to infinity. Miss Suki walked over to me.

"We are here on behalf of Detective Watanabe," Fynn said from across the room.

"Ah, the man is a paragon of virtue, and a selfless public servant…" She said in a sorrowful voice but gave us an incongruous smile. "He telephoned to mention you would be stopping by." Miss Suki turned to me. "And you must be the American he spoke of."

"Your English is excellent."

"Thank you, it was compulsory at the school I attended." She bowed in my direction. "The tree is a gift from Hideki Sato," Miss Suki said to my unasked curiosity.

"You know him?"

"Of course, Hideki Sato is one of my best customers. He has an insatiable appetite for xenotime. He's bought dozens of crystals over the years," she explained in a tone that mixed both woe and apathy.

"Detective Watanabe has asked us to look into the murder of his wife, Reimu Sato."

Miss Suki said nothing to this, nor did her expression change. "Murdered, eh? I won't say I'm surprised by this turn of events, nor especially sadden by it."

"No?"

"I detested the woman, as did everyone in the alley. I suppose there will be many suspects for such a crime," she remarked in an unwavering monotone.

"Who then would she invite to tea?" Fynn asked.

"You might ask who would accept such an invitation. Not I, certainly."

"Mrs Ambrose?"

"Hmm… if it suited her purposes, I would say yes… And I did see her by the front door," she added in a whisper.

"What time was that?"

"I would guess about two o'clock or so." Miss Suki paused and walked nearer to Fynn. "And not much later than that, I saw her assistant Miss Tanaka jumping the fence in the courtyard."

"Where was she going?"

"To Mr Sato's shop, I would imagine."

"Detective Watanabe mentioned something about a tryst. How did you come to be involved?"

"That's rather a personal question."

"Indeed, yet we are investigating a murder, eh?"

"Well, if you must know the truth, Sakurai Kenshi and I were engaged to be married some months ago, but I broke it off when I caught him cheating on me."

"With Reimu Sato?"

"She's nothing better than a whore," Miss Suki whispered with hardly any inflection.

"And did her husband know?"

"Probably not, nor would he care. Hideki is always sniffing around Hana Kei." She closed her eyes for a moment, then continued, "After our break up, Kenshi started spending his time at the Catalog Shop, flirting with Mrs Ambrose and her assistant, Miss Tanaka."

"It all sounds quite complicated."

"Not to us," she replied in a bland voice.

"And who is Mr Kenshi seeing at present?"

"Now he's sleeping with Miss Kei, the jealous little tart."

"Jealous of whom?"

"Everyone… Don't be fooled by her sweetness," Miss Suki cautioned in a relentless monotone. "I've heard she is a fallen woman. Killed her own father, it's said…"

"That sounds quite dreadful," Fynn commented.

"There are rumors up and down the alley that Miss Kei is with child."

"Whose child?"

"Anyone might be the father, even Mr Wada."

"And when did this tangle of lives begin?"

"Hmm… Not long after Reimu's accident. She was laid up for months, and it seemed to me that her personality changed."

"How so?"

"She became a wanton woman."

"What was she like before her accident?"

"Certainly more aloof."

"Is this when you first saw her with a cane?"

"Yes."

"The head of a jackal?"

"Is that what it is?" she asked. "Well, Mrs Ambrose certainly had a keen eye for it. Hideki Sato wanted to sell it, but Reimu would have no part of that."

"Tell me, Miss Suki, was anything stolen from your shop?"

"Today, do you mean?"

"No, in the last year or so."

"Now that you say it, yes. A large kiku-ishi."

"How large?"

"It was one of our centerpieces, as big as my hand, I'd say, twenty centimeters."

"When was this?"

"A few weeks ago."

"What can you tell us about it?"

"A rare piece, quarried north of Mount Funabuse in the Gifu Prefecture, at a hill called Maru-Yama. A crystal of xenotime and zircon arranged in a radiating, flower-like pattern."

"What used to be here?" I asked, pointing to an obvious blank spot on the wall.

"Hmm?" She turned to look. "Yes, my *Ungaikyo*."

"What's that?

"It's difficult to translate to English. Perhaps you might call it a possessed mirror, or a mirror ghost."

"Sounds scary. What does it do?"

"Ah… it reflects things as they are, rather than how you'd like to see them."

"And where is it now?" Fynn asked.

"Oh yes, another thing that went missing from my shop recently."

***

"Well?" I asked as we made our way out into the alley again.

"I suppose we are lucky that she is a busybody…"

"Why?"

"We've learned much just by listening, eh?" Fynn smiled. "Though,

Miss Suki doesn't strike me as entirely stable. It's quite possible that she murdered Reimu in a fit of passion."

"Do you really think so?"

"No… She doesn't wear lipstick," Fynn replied.

"On the teacups, you mean?"

He turned with a smile. "You noticed?"

"I noticed something else."

"Yes?"

"I'm pretty sure I saw Mr Kenshi take something from the crime scene."

"A lipstick holder," Fynn said. "I observed this as well."

Next door was the Catalog Shop. We had been informed that Mrs Ambrose was half a foreigner, her mother was Japanese, her father an Austrian. She was also a widow, her husband long since dead. "A woman of obvious intelligence, shrewd perhaps," Detective Watanabe had said.

On entering, it was easy to tell this shop was different from the others. The door opened onto a kind of foyer with a centrally placed desk. The rest of the area was screened off, and little else could be seen.

A woman sat before us with her hands folded. It was Sadako Tanaka, the shop assistant. She seemed mildly surprised by our appearance and spoke to Fynn in Japanese. She was young, in her mid-twenties, athletic, and dressed in a simple white shirt with a pleated skirt to the knees. Short, bobbed hair framed her face with two long spikes on either side. She was wearing heavy make-up and bright red lipstick.

Miss Tanaka's voice was immediately grating. It had a shrill, eager quality. She hadn't said much, but already her replies were too loud, obnoxious almost. Of course, I didn't understand a word. She disappeared with a bow and then returned to say Mrs Ambrose was not receiving customers unless they had an appointment. This time she spoke in halting English.

"We are not customers, young lady. We are from the police and we are investigating a murder."

Miss Tanaka disappeared again. We could hear her speaking with Mrs Ambrose nearby. The other woman, though unseen, had a beautiful voice, perhaps the very opposite of her assistant's. It was mature but musical, intoning up and down. She was saying something of grave significance. Whether it was important or not, I couldn't know, though every word seemed steeped with meaning.

"This way, please." Miss Tanaka reappeared and led us through the rooms which mainly consisted of cabinets filled with tiny drawers, as might be found in a library. There were a few glass cases as well, though they seemed empty.

We met with Mrs Ambrose in her lavish office. She was peering into a small mirror as we entered, reapplying her lipstick. Her face held an exquisite symmetry and her smile, though cunning, was alluring. It seemed as if she had somewhere else to be and barely gave us a glance.

I noticed henna-red streaks in otherwise dark hair which had a bit of curl. She also had a good figure and was taller than most. Mrs Ambrose wore a shimmering blouse and matching skirt with a slit up the side.

"How may I help you today, gentlemen? I do hope you will be brief, I have an important appointment to keep."

"We are here on behalf of Detective Watanabe," Fynn explained.

"Oh, he is the very picture of laziness and corruption," Mrs Ambrose said in a tone that was almost convincing.

"And who is it that says such things?" Fynn asked.

"It's a well known fact up and down the alley," she replied in perfect English, and her voice was quite wonderful to hear.

"We are interviewing all the nearby shopkeepers this evening."

"As suspects or witnesses?" she asked and added a husky laugh.

"That depends upon your reply." Fynn smiled. "Miss Sasayaki Suki claims she saw you entering Mrs Sato's shop earlier this afternoon."

"Utter nonsense. Why would I visit Reimu? We didn't get along at all."

"Nonetheless…"

"What time did you say?" Mrs Ambrose asked, not expecting a reply. She had a condescending way about her, as if she knew far more about any situation than you could ever hope to. "Hmm, I may have knocked on her door around two o'clock, but there was no reply."

"What was the nature of your visit?"

"Unfinished business, I might say."

"And your shop is adjacent."

"Separated by a brick wall, yes." She laughed again in her husky manner, though it felt as if she might be laughing at us.

"Did you hear anything untoward?"

"I will tell you one thing I didn't hear after one o'clock: Sakurai's incessant hammering."

"Sakurai?"

"If I knew Mr Kenshi was to make such a racket every day, I'd have asked for a shop further away from his."

"Nothing else?"

"The wall is quite thick. I heard nothing else," Mrs Ambrose said. "You might tap that walking stick of yours against every brick, but you will find no opening, if that's what you hope." She eyed Fynn's bear claw cane. "I will say also, that's an interesting piece." Mrs Ambrose forced a smile to her face. "Perhaps you might sell it to me, hmm? I'd like to feature such a thing in my catalog."

"It is not for sale," Fynn replied politely.

"Anything can be acquired for the correct price," Mrs Ambrose said.

"Such as Reimu's cane?"

"I remember it, I won't say I don't… an exquisite piece, the head of a jackal in brass."

"Was it for sale in your catalog?"

"Who told you this?"

"Mr Sato."

"Hideki-san is mistaken."

"When did you first see this cane?"

"Reimu had it after her accident, it was some years ago."

"How did she hurt herself?"

"Coming down the stairs from her apartment. They are quite steep. I haven't seen it since though."

"Did she mention how she acquired it?"

"Not to me. Shouldn't you pose that question to her husband?"

"Perhaps if we might browse through this catalog of yours?" Fynn inquired.

"Quite impossible, I'm afraid."

"Why is that?"

"The new version is due from the printers any day now."

"And last year's edition?"

"Obsolete… things have been sold, new items have been acquired. It no longer reflects what we have in stock." Mrs Ambrose reached behind to some shelves and drew out a thick book. She slammed it down on her desk. "Feel free to glance through it…"

"Where is your inventory stored?" Fynn asked instead.

"The basement."

"Might we have a look?"

"Of course not."

"Ah, but we are investigating a murder. It's possible the killer may have gained access to Mr Sato's shop through the basement."

"I doubt that completely. It is locked at all times."

"I see… well, I'd hate to trouble Detective Watanabe with such a trivial errand. He tends to be overly scrupulous." Fynn gave his best smile. "All we're asking for is a quick look."

Mrs Ambrose sat stone-faced for a time but considered Fynn's request. She finally called out to her assistant. "Sadako, please show these gentlemen to the basement, if you would."

There were several locks on the door. Miss Tanaka undid them one by one and then led us down a narrow flight of stairs. She went first and flipped on the lights, what there were of them. Most of the huge room remained in shadow, but it seemed larger than I could have imagined. The nearest wall was nearly a hundred yards away. This was an underground warehouse. It was filled with innumerable boxes and crates, shelves upon shelves of dusty, unidentifiable items.

By the stairs, I noticed a few things showcased in glass display boxes… a sword, an umbrella, and a faded mirror with a gilded frame. In the far corner were racks of clothing and it smelled of mothballs. I could see clothes and military uniforms from every era in history.

"Surely, this basement extends far beyond the confines of the shop," Fynn said to Miss Tanaka.

"Yes, yes, it does. Mrs Ambrose leases the space from all the stores above us."

"Is there any access to them?"

"The stairs are in place, but all the doors have been nailed shut—years ago."

Fynn nodded to me. I knew what he wanted and checked each staircase leading up. Miss Tanaka's description was accurate. I did find something though; it was Tsaku the cat. He sauntered over to Miss Tanaka and jumped into her waiting arms.

"How did you get here, little tiger?" Fynn asked. "Is there some crawlspace we don't know about, an air duct of some kind?"

The shop assistant giggled slightly. "Oh, I invited Mr Tsaku… it gets quite lonely in the cellar and we've become good friends."

"Where did you find him?"

"Wandering around in the courtyards, not an hour ago." Miss Tanaka blushed. "Is there something in particular you need to see?" she asked.

"No, not really…" Fynn replied and strolled through the room, examining anything of interest that caught his eye. "Have you ever seen a brass cane for sale in the catalog?"

"I remember seeing something— was it an elephant perhaps?"

"Was it sold?"

"Yes, yes, a number of years ago, though I couldn't say who bought it."

"I am also wondering about Mrs Ambrose's whereabouts between one and two o'clock this afternoon."

"I don't intend to say anything to you, Mr Policeman, sir. Nothing that would undermine my employer."

"What would you say to Detective Watanabe?"

"Even less. I value my position, and even more so, I value my life."

"You are afraid of the detective?"

"Not in the least."

"Has Mrs Ambrose threatened you in any way?"

"She doesn't need to. A simple glance is enough."

"And I don't suppose you'd like to see Mr Akaname involved, eh? Or even Gesuidō Wada."

"Why would they be?"

"Discord at one of the shops…" Fynn suggested.

"It would be nothing new to them."

"I see… Well then, a vacant store would need to be rented. Or perhaps it would be in need of a new proprietress?"

Miss Tanaka paused for a moment. "Mrs Ambrose had me make

her a key."

"What kind?"

"To a front door, I would guess. It's old fashioned, and all the shops have one that's similar."

***

We returned to Mr Sato's shop as evening waned. Fynn double-checked the door to the basement and it was indeed bolted. "Surely no one passed through this door," he reaffirmed.

"Two things are now missing," Hideki announced as he appeared from the courtyard, "the cane and my wife's favorite scarf."

"Are you certain?"

"Of course, I've searched the place thoroughly."

"And nothing else?"

"No."

"What about the steamer trunk upstairs?"

"It's for traveling. It is empty inside."

"Why would it be locked?"

"I could not say."

"Tell me, please, Mr Sato, about this telephone on your desk?"

"What of it?"

"I noticed a similar telephone upstairs. Is it on the same line?"

"No, it's our private number."

"Another question: was Tsaku inside or outside when you left for the baseball game this afternoon?"

"My cat? Well, he was out and about, on the prowl as usual."

"And would Reimu let him back inside?"

"No. Regrettably, she did not like cats at all."

***

That night Mr Sato gave me the downstairs futon, but he had a question: "Tell me something, my friend Patrick-san, where is your head when you sleep?"

"Pardon?"

"I am lending you my bed, but which direction will you face? East, west, south or north?"

I had to think about that for a second. "South, I guess."

"Oh, that explains a lot."

"Why?"

"People who sleep facing south usually suffer from memory loss."

"Really?"

"Those who face north fare little better, unless of course you are living in a different hemisphere."

"What about east or west?"

"It's best to face the setting sun, you'll always remember your dreams in the morning."

"What about east?"

"Such leads to incurable despair."

"How do you know all this?"

"Careful observation, and I ask people the very same question I just asked you."

I slept well enough despite Mr Sato's dire warnings and had the downstairs shop to myself. There was little chance of coffee the next morning and settled for tea. Hideki had laid out breakfast, such as it was: miso soup and some kind of rice porridge, or maybe it was fermented soybeans. He then busied himself watering his garden in the courtyard and tending to the various plants that filled the shop. Detective Watanabe arrived bright and early, and with news:

"We checked the tea for poison. Nothing there but a strong sedative."

"A sedative?" Fynn asked.

"Indeed, some kind of horse tranquilizer."

"And the lipstick?"

"Yes... though it's sold up and down the alley. Anyone might wear such a color... even a man."

"A man?" I asked.

"Such would be a very clever ruse, eh? Something we would not suspect."

Fynn chuckled. "It would be clever indeed, but I am gaining a clearer picture of what may have happened... My prime suspect is now Miss Hana Kei."

Detective Watanabe seemed surprised by this. "How is such a thing possible? My money is on Mr Kenshi or even Miss Suki— she has a nasty streak…"

"They may be involved around the edges but they are not murderers."

"Of course, I'd prefer to arrest Gesuidō, though if you say he's innocent, I'll set him free."

"He is at worst an unwitting accomplice in this affair."

"How so?"

"Hana Kei used him as a diversion. She called him on the telephone and asked him to visit her directly."

"And I would guess he complied with such a request."

"Yes," Fynn agreed. "At that point she called Mr Sato and begged to be rescued."

Detective Watanabe thought for a moment. "Ah, but she called him from the private line. I am beginning to understand. She was here the whole time, hiding. When we were distracted, she left Mr Sato's shop and returned to her own, then opened the door when we knocked."

"But where was she hiding?" I asked.

"Upstairs, in one of the trunks."

"Miss Kei is rather petite," the detective considered.

"She also stole the cane," Fynn said.

"Where's it gone?"

"This, I don't know yet."

"Well then, let's pay her another visit and see what she has to say."

***

After breakfast, Fynn, Watanabe and I strolled over to Miss Kei's shop. He posted two patrolmen outside the front entrance. It was already open and we found her inside with Sakurai Kenshi. She seemed to be dressed exactly the same as yesterday. I guessed we had just interrupted an argument, as I heard harsh words when we entered, and they were both red-faced. The two detectives began questioning her, gently, it seemed to me, though I understood little. Fynn later explained the conversation in detail:

"And why do you suppose Mrs Sato's scarf was found in the courtyard?"

"I have no idea at all," Miss Kei replied in her tiny voice. "Perhaps the wind blew it there. Besides, are you sure it's hers? I have a dozen like it in my shop. They're quite popular."

Fynn meandered around the room and found something under a pile of fabric. He gave it a close scrutiny. "And this?" he asked, holding up the jackal cane. "How did it come to be here?"

"Reimu lent it to me some days ago."

"I know that to be a blatant lie," Fynn said. "Mr Sato had it with him for most of yesterday."

"Did you murder Reimu?" Detective Watanabe asked directly.

"No. Why would I? She was a friend," Miss Kei replied but shot an angry glance at Kenshi, who was seated beside her on a cushion.

"And was Reimu a friend to Sakurai Kenshi, as well?" the Tokyo detective barked and glared at the two of them.

Fynn intervened with a calmer tone, "But you were there that afternoon, eh?"

"Yes, I did have tea with Reimu-san, I will admit this now," Miss Kei began in her childlike voice. "I called a little after one o'clock. She invited me in and we sat for a while. But after only one or two sips of tea, I felt myself becoming drowsy. I saw it in Reimu as well. Her head was lolling back and forth and her eyes lost their focus."

"And then?"

"And then... yes, well, the next thing I heard was someone banging on the door, calling out Reimu's name. But she did not hear. She was laying next to me asleep or dead."

"What did you do?"

"I ran upstairs to hide, and successfully I might add."

"Where?"

"In one of the trunks. I was able to latch it from the inside."

"I will admit the ruse with the telephone call was rather clever."

"Thank you, Detective Watanabe," she said and bowed with humility.

"And the cat, Tsaku?"

"I saw no cat."

"Why steal the cane?" Fynn asked.

"I knew that I could curry favor with Mrs Ambrose. She has asked about it many times and I could tell how she coveted it greatly."

"Were you hoping for something in exchange?"

"Yes… the umbrella she stole from me."

"She took something from your shop?"

"Yes," she repeated in her tiny voice.

"Was there something special about the umbrella?"

"It has a spirit attached to it, a *Kasa-obake*."

"A *Yōkai*? What does this spirit do?"

"When properly unfurled, it will protect one from the ravages of time."

"I see… and how is such a thing known to you?"

"From my ancestors. The umbrella has been passed down for generations."

"Why would Mrs Ambrose want such a thing?"

"She is compulsive in that regard. Her taste for acquiring objects knows no bounds."

"And why would you take Reimu's scarf?"

"She was clutching it in her dead fingers. I thought it might be important."

"Was it?"

"Not that I could see…" She shot another glance at Mr Kenshi, another angry one it seemed.

Detective Watanabe walked behind Mis Kei as she sat on the floor. I watched him bend over to stare into the back of her head. It seemed like odd behavior at first, then he reached into her headdress with two delicate fingers and pulled out one of the hairpins. I'd seen something like that before, almost like a hypodermic needle. He held it up for all to see.

"This would be the murder weapon," he ventured. "There is still dried blood on the tip of it as well."

Miss Kei seemed unaware that such a thing was in her hair. To our surprise though, she leapt from her cushion and lunged at Sakurai Kenshi. She had another weapon in her sleeve, a small curved dagger which she jammed into his shoulder. We rushed over and pulled her off. She was sobbing now. The wound was severe but probably not life threatening.

The mounting evidence was now impossible to ignore. When arrested, Hana Kei called out in her singsongy voice: "I'm innocent, innocent, the culprit roams freely. After I'm gone, I shall haunt you all for the rest of your lives."

***

Fynn and I sat in the courtyard of Mr Sato's shop drinking tea. Hideki himself had disappeared, on an errand, he told us.

"That about wraps it up," I said to Fynn.

"I suppose..." he replied, though noncommittally. "I cannot say I'm entirely satisfied with the outcome."

"No?"

"I believe Miss Kei's account of events. Her story is in line with the evidence. If you remember, one tea cup was empty and the other was not."

"But she stabbed Mr Kenshi," I pointed out.

Fynn was about to reply when the backdoor opened. I turned to see Mortimer standing there. He walked over and snatched the jackal cane from the table. "Well, thank you for this, Tractus," he said, and then clambered to the top of the courtyard wall.

He gave his thin smile and leapt off. Mortimer didn't disappear though; instead, he landed roughly on the pavement. He could hardly mask his displeasure, and took a closer look at the cane. "The inside mechanism has been removed."

"The functioning cane is no longer in this era as far as I can tell," Fynn explained.

"You're saying it was though?"

"Yes. It seems Kali was here with it and then left behind a double... a shell of her former self."

"That's who was murdered?"

"It would appear so."

"And my functioning cane?"

"It likely has the head of an elephant now."

"What are you saying?"

"Perhaps Kali did not care for the jackal."

"So where is it?"

"If I were to guess, I'd say in the early days of the occupation."

"Why then?"

"Mr Sato mentioned it... Kali's previous visit, perhaps her very first appearance in Japan."

Mortimer considered for a moment. "Still, I'm intent on traveling back a few years to the time of Mrs Sato's accident… I will find my cane there."

"And a formidable version of Kali, no doubt. Besides, it may be an impossible task. I cannot say exactly when your cane was replaced."

"I've heard Mrs Ambrose from the Catalog Shop has it in her possession."

"Who told you this?"

"Her assistant, Miss Tanaka."

"And you've met Mrs Ambrose?"

"I have, under the guise of a curious customer."

"What did you discover?"

"Mark my words, Tractus, there is something unsavory about that woman."

"I will not disagree," Fynn replied.

Mortimer slumped into one of the nearby chairs. "And you and Patrick… where are you off to now?"

"Mr Sato has a cottage in the south island of Kyushu… our next destination."

"I will meet you there."

"I would welcome that," Fynn said. "Here, let me jot down the particulars…" He reached for a pen and paper.

"Well, gentlemen, I have a few other avenues to explore," Mortimer announced and stood again. "With a bit of luck, I'll see you soon." He gave a quick bow and disappeared over the courtyard fence.

"Where did you say we're going?" I asked Fynn.

"We must travel back further."

"Why?"

"Of course, to retrieve the missing manuscript. And I would like to meet this Kali of the past."

"What?"

"Mr Sato said they first met during the occupation. We shall go and investigate."

"What occupation?"

"The occupation of Japan."

"Will I have to learn Japanese?"

Fynn smiled. "Such won't be necessary. We can reprise our roles as American servicemen."

"I'll need a uniform."

"We both will," Fynn replied. "Perhaps you'd like to outrank me this time, eh? Now we must find a place that will sell us such things."

"The Catalog Shop," I said.

"Of course, you're right, Patrick."

***

We returned to the Catalog Shop the following evening. "I didn't expect to see you again," Mrs Ambrose said in her lavish voice. Her assistant was absent. "I was told the investigation had concluded."

"It has. Miss Kei has all but confessed to the murder of Reimu Sato."

"Confessed, you say... well, that's welcome news."

"I'm sure it is to you."

"What are you implying?"

"You murdered Reimu Sato."

Mrs Ambrose gave Fynn a look but said nothing for a time. Finally, she smiled and asked, "Why would you think such a thing?"

"I believe you meant to acquire the cane, though it slipped from your grasp. You had set Miss Kei to this very task."

"That's absurd... And you can prove nothing of course."

"No," Fynn admitted and cast his eyes down.

Mrs Ambrose gave a husky laugh. "Miss Kei is more clever than I gave her credit for... I was sure she would be found inside and presumed guilty of Reimu's murder."

"How did you kill Mrs Sato?" Fynn asked.

"I am not saying I did, but it would be a simple matter, hypothetically speaking. I would have a key to the front door. They would be unconscious. I would prick her ear with a deadly syringe."

"Where would you acquire this device?"

"Such things are in the catalog. They are in great demand and sell for a good price."

"And the jackal cane?"

"An object of extreme value, I was told."

"By whom?"

"A customer from a few days ago, a foreigner with an eyepatch…"

"The cane wasn't there though."

"No."

"And then?"

"I would lock the door and return to my shop."

"What about the cat?"

"The loathsome creature slipped between my legs and followed me in through the back door."

"And the book that's gone missing?"

"Oh, I acquired it some weeks ago. It will also fetch a good price. It looks to be quite rare." She laughed. "So, what do you intend to do, Mr Policeman?"

"There is little I can do," Fynn replied. "Nothing I could say to Detective Watanabe would lead you to the gallows…" He paused and then quite unexpectedly raised a smile. "Besides, we are here on a different matter. My friend and I need to purchase some clothing, uniforms from another era."

"We sell clothes from all periods," Mrs Ambrose confirmed. "What may I interest you in this evening?"

Inspector Fynn explained our needs rather vaguely, but enough to entice Mrs Ambrose to take us down to the enormous basement. He also asked about getting identification papers from that time period. Mrs Ambrose arched an eyebrow and seemed a bit suspicious at first, but then bowed and smiled. "Such can be obtained for the right price."

"Navy uniforms would suit our purposes."

"The American Navy? That poses additional difficulties."

"How so?"

"Every officer is assigned to a particular ship. I would have to obtain paperwork for such."

"Army then… Air Corps would be fine. The rank of colonel and a captain. And we would need blank papers: transport orders, requisitions and alike… from the highest levels."

"They will be signed by the supreme commander himself," Mrs Ambrose promised.

We found appropriate uniforms that fit pretty well, though they did reek of mothballs. In the end Fynn was a lieutenant and I was a captain. "Officers are asked fewer questions," Fynn told me. We also found period duffle bags.

"This will take some time, you understand…" Mrs Ambrose said. "Check back tomorrow, please." She smiled. "And I'm afraid to say, gentlemen, your requests will not come cheaply. What do you propose in payment?"

"What would you accept?" Fynn asked.

She glanced at the bear claw cane. "That would be adequate payment for my services."

"What?"

"I would like to add it to my collection."

"Collection?"

"In the catalog…"

"Such is too high a price to pay for some old uniforms, documents, and a duffle bag," Fynn replied. "Though, I might offer this instead…" He took off a gold ring from his pinky. I had never seen it before. There was a large red stone at its center and five smaller stones surrounding it. Mrs Ambrose raised an eyebrow. She was clearly interested and gave it a thorough inspection.

"For this, I can give you a few period overcoats. It doesn't appear to be worth much… I'll throw in the duffle bags for nothing."

Fynn seemed to reluctantly agree.

***

"What just happened in there?" I asked once we left the shop. "And what's with that ring?"

"I've made a terrible mistake, Patrick. "Hana Kei is simply a thief, not a killer."

"You believe Mrs Ambrose murdered Kali."

"She has said as much… and she's correct that it would be impossible to prove to the satisfaction of Detective Watanabe."

"What are you going to do?"

"I seldom resort to this. And it is not something I do lightly. But when justice cannot be served, something else must be done…"

"The ring?"

"It is a form of judgement."

"What's that supposed to mean?"

"It's too terrible to speak about, Patrick."

"What does it do?"

"It's a way of imprisoning the guilty for their crimes."

"How does it work?"

"It traps you in a loop. The same year passes endlessly, over and over again."

"What? Kind of sounds like the Flatlands Prison."

"It's not dissimilar. The days go by as usual, but the year remains constant. Eventually the wearer of the ring grows old and dies."

"Nothing changes?"

"Very little. Perhaps only what others do in that year."

"What do you mean?"

"The device has no effect on them of course, so they might say or do anything."

"What happens if you take the ring off?"

"Things go back to the way they were, only whatever time has passed cannot be reclaimed."

"And no one notices that the same year is passing over and over again?"

"Most do not."

chapter twenty-four
occupational hazard

It was an easy jump back from Mr Sato's little shop. We went to the courtyard and used the wall that was just at the correct height. Fynn set the date on his cane to 1946 and we leapt together. Our landing proved more difficult. He found himself atop a pile of wreckage some distance from me. I fared little better, landing in the alley, an alley now filled with debris that had spilled from the destroyed buildings.

I climbed up to help Fynn dislodge himself. He was trapped under a broken door. I lifted it and he scrambled out while carrying something in his hand. It wasn't the cane, but a sword.

"How did you know that was there?" I asked.

"I didn't… just a hunch, let's call it." Fynn smiled. There was more to this then he was telling.

"A gift for Mr Sato?"

"Indeed, if we can find him."

"What about the cane?"

"We must find that as well. It should be nearby." Fynn sifted through the rubble and soon spotted the brass bear claw poking out from behind a bookshelf. We climbed back down to the alley and found what was left of the main boulevard. He pointed south and we started to walk.

By the look of things it seemed to be early winter. Fynn guessed we were roughly in the same place where the park had been. There was no sign of it any longer. It had been obliterated by American bombers. There was little else for miles. What had once been a city was now low-lying ruins. To the horizon, everything was pretty much leveled. I could only see twisted metal, slabs of crumbled masonry and dead trees. Some brick foundations rose above it all, punctuated by iron staircases that led to nowhere. Oddly, a few smokestacks remained intact or at least partially.

"So… this is what the apocalypse looks like."

"Yes," Fynn replied with a grim sigh. He pointed again. "We need to continue south."

Amidst the devastation and along the roads we came across miserable lines of people on foot. They were as silent as the landscape and heading to some unknowable destination. A lucky few rode past on bicycles, some sat in wooden carts and wagons; they rattled by endlessly. I saw no animals though, it seemed that the carts were designed for people to pull. Far off, I spotted an old train going by. It was overflowing with passengers, many hanging onto the sides of the cars or perched on the roof.

We came across the hulk of a destroyed building. It must have been large, with its guts spilling out onto the street as a giant pile of debris. Mostly though, it was charred wood and splinters. There were droves of people milling about, some of them sweeping with brooms; others carrying things, or methodically digging through the giant pile. Everyone was dusty and covered in grime. Not a single person spoke, nor wore a smile.

I also noticed quite a few telephone poles remained; I could see them in the distance, but not enough it seemed. Nearby, we passed a gang of men, six of them in a familiar position, valiantly trying to resurrect one as if it were a flagpole. Re-attaching the wires would be someone else's task.

We traveled away from Tokyo into the countryside, though it hardly mattered. It was bleak and depressing everywhere. Fynn and I walked for hours and barely a word passed between us. The roads were not completely devoid of motorized vehicles. Once and a while a jeep would rumble by or a big American car. "US military," I said. "But they don't seem to care about anyone."

"I for one am glad they are not stopping."

"Maybe we could flag one down?"

"I'd think better of it, Patrick. We have no identity papers that would make sense to them."

"Well, what now?"

"We continue south to the Kyushu Province. And it's quite far."

"We're walking there?"

"For now… until we can think of something better."

"A vehicle maybe?"

"Such would seem necessary."

"How? Do we steal a car? Buy one?"

"Even if we did, petrol seems to be in short supply," Fynn said. "We may have to resort to bribing someone, I will guess."

"Do you have funds?"

"Of course," he replied. "But getting to the southern island is problematic to say the least." Fynn trudged along. "It's some three or four hundred miles to the south and east. There will be little chance of avoiding Hiroshima or Nagasaki."

"Why not call Stanley?"

"What?" Fynn was astonished by my question but chuckled. "Fetch him from across time and space? And to what end?"

"He could have a plane ready and waiting. You know, US Army Air Corps or something."

"I suppose it could be done, but it would be an awful lot of effort," he protested.

Coming towards us, north along the road, a noisy car passed by—if car is the right word. It rattled and sputtered, then stopped a few yards behind us. "Occidentals!" the driver called out. "What are you two doing on the road? It's not very safe for westerners."

We jogged over. The driver was not Japanese, not by the look of his flaming red hair and freckled skin.

"Who are you? Not the military as I can see by your clothes."

"We're journalists," I lied. "We got separated from the press pool."

"What's that?"

"The international press pool."

"Oh, I'm not a member, sorry. I'm an independent, a freelancer."

"What brings you here?"

"Photography," he said and nodded to a backseat piled with equipment: tripods, metal boxes, and an old fashioned movie camera.

"Nice car," I commented.

He laughed. "Yes, a *Yonki*, a woodpecker, it's called. Formally, a Kurogane, Type Ninety-Five— I was lucky to acquire it."

"I'm Patrick and this is Fynn."

"A pleasure to meet you. I am Hollis Indigo." He paused to look us up and down again. "Might I give you a lift somewhere?"

"Where are you going?"

"Hiroshima."

"But it is to the south," Fynn explained. "You're traveling in the wrong direction."

"Am I? Well, I do feel a bit turned around," Hollis admitted. "The map says I should go north and west, but it seems like I've just come from there."

"If I may," Fynn said and turned his map clockwise. "You have it upside down. Hiroshima is south and east of us. Not a place you should go."

"I have to. It's my profession."

"What profession compels you to go to such a place?"

"Newsreels… I've seen bombed cities all through Europe, filmed them all, London, Berlin, Warsaw…" His voice trailed off. "I've never seen devastation like this, except maybe Dresden."

"I hear things are much worse in Hiroshima and Nagasaki, where the atom bombs exploded," Fynn said.

"Yes. I've also been told that. They've been cordoned off... I doubt I'll be able to get close enough for a good photo, let alone moving pictures."

"What of the *Hibakusha*?" Fynn asked.

"The who?"

"The survivors."

"I've heard reports... victims with terrible burns..."

"I wouldn't go there," I cautioned.

"Why not."

"Radiation. Umm, X-rays..."

"What's that?"

"Like Madame Curie... they can be harmful to you... and your equipment."

"How do you know so much about it?"

"I have an uncle... he's a scientist."

"Alright then, thanks for the warning," Hollis said, though I doubted he would take my advice. He did beckon us aboard his odd vehicle, and cleared some room in the backseat for Fynn to sit. It was by far the worst journey I'd ever taken. This was no natural disaster, it was the wrath of the Americans, as it had rained down from the skies. And yet, somehow the people persisted, they survived, shell-shocked and stumbling about in broad daylight.

"I've seen terrible things back in Tokyo," Hollis told us along the way. I strained to hear his voice over the sound of the engine. "Many people starving right on the streets, pan-pan girls on every corner, and a thriving black market... Ha, a renaissance for the yakuza, you might say." He turned to give me a grim smile. "In the end though, the Japanese are not a broken people, though a people resigned to their fate nonetheless."

Hollis Indigo took us as far as Kobe. He dropped us at a fishing village before the road turned eastward. From there Fynn was able to hire a boat to take us further south. We traveled at night and usually without engines, the local fishermen deftly avoiding any entanglements with US Navy patrols. We hopscotched along the east coast and finally crossed over to the southernmost island of Kyushu. We managed to stay well clear of the atomic cities.

Once Fynn was satisfied that we had traveled far enough south, our journey turned inland and west again. He was able to procure some rudimentary camping equipment: a backpack, bed rolls and cooking gear. Military surplus, if I had to guess. Provisions were courtesy of the US Army, repackaged K-rations found on the black market, and I never knew spam could taste so delicious. I saved the biscuits and a chocolate bar for later.

It was several days more of hard hiking through the mountains. Usually we'd avoid the roads entirely; though we did hop a lift on a truck full of laborers heading south. I began to see the occasional smile now and then; our journey was becoming bearable, almost pleasant. The weather grew milder and I was very much surprised to find how rural and beautiful this part of Japan was. We passed many terraced farms sculpted into the mountainside, and quaint villages undamaged by the war.

The people we met along the way seemed more curious than alarmed by our presence since we were not military. Most of the time, Fynn pretended not to speak Japanese at all. We were *Nanban*, southern barbarians.

***

"You've come to the crux of things, Patrick."

"The manuscript?"

"Yes, but which version? The one that Mr Temsik took from the back of your car? Or a different copy obtained by Kali?"

"Or the fax from Clark."

"What fax are you talking about?" Fynn asked.

"Oh, that happened in a parallel present; you might not recall."

"I don't, though I suppose it's possible since I did eventually receive a fax from Clark."

"When was that?"

"Shortly before we left."

"Well… Why not just ask Mr Sato outright?"

"On every occasion when the subject has arisen, his replies have been vague and unhelpful. He might easily lie, or mislead us. I'd like to see the thing with my own eyes."

"You don't trust him completely."

"As we have traveled further back, I've noticed his love for Kali has increased. It seems wise to exercise caution."

"I agree… and it still leaves the question about the other two volumes. The one about architecture, and astronomy, I think."

"If copies have been made, they must be retrieved, hence our next destination."

For days we hiked across the mountains, through dense forests and groves of towering bamboo. We crossed many a gorge, and sometimes just stopped to watch the roiling mist along the peaks. Eventually we reached a tiny hamlet called Soyō, somewhere just south of Mount Aso.

"How do you know exactly where Mr Sato lives?"

"Ah, from aboard the *Carpathia* of course. While you were manning the wireless station, Mr Sato and I had many a long conversation in the forward lounge."

***

It was early afternoon when we found Hideki Sato. Some miles from the tiny village we came across a clearing, a meadow almost, and just beyond on a low terrace, a cottage could be seen tucked away into the mountainside. It was rustic, but elegant in its simplicity, a tiny house with a high-peaked roof. To get there we had to cross a deep ravine, a scar in the mountains. And we had to cross on a rickety bridge made of nothing more than bamboo and reeds. I peered down through the gorge and could see a stream far below. I felt a touch of vertigo.

Hideki Sato greeted us on the porch to his cottage. He was wearing a drab kimono and a wide-brimmed straw hat. "If you will kindly remove your shoes, it would be greatly appreciated." He bowed. "All hail the conquerers…"

"We are not conquerers," Fynn replied.

"All hail our benevolent occupiers." Mr Sato bowed again but refused to make eye contact. He was younger than I had seen him previously, and quite a bit thinner, though his rimless glasses were the same. I believed him when he told me he was six hundred years old or so— no doubt like most travelers, he had a younger placeholder from somewhere.

"Don't you know us?" I asked.

"All you Americans look the same to me, I'm sorry to say."

"Well, you cannot be blamed for that. Besides, we are Canadians," Fynn said and turned a smile in my direction. "And… we come bearing a gift," he added as he took the bundle from my hands and gave it to Mr Sato.

Still kneeling, Hideki carefully undid the chords that held together the bit of frayed cloth. He picked up the sword in its sheath and carefully examined it, taking a few minutes to fully scrutinize the carvings and workmanship. He looked at Fynn, astonished. "It cannot be. It's impossible…"

"I don't know that it's genuine, but it is an exquisite piece of work—yes?"

Mr Sato slowly, reverently, drew the katana from its sheath. He held it up to the sun. It reflected and gleamed, like out of a story book. He seemed unable to find words for a time. Finally he spoke: "And what must I do in return to deserve such a gift?"

"A few hours of your time, some conversation, and perhaps something to eat and drink."

"Of course, of course, I am being a terrible host, please come through…" Mr Sato slid open the paper door and ushered us inside with a generous bow. He seemed quite elated, almost giddy, and broke into a cheerful laugh.

The inside of the cottage was sparse but beautiful. I had an odd observation: the plastic of the future had been replaced by lacquered wood and ceramics: vases, bowls, cabinets, and bookshelves mostly. There were no windows, no glass at least, only a few large openings in the wall that could be shuttered. It was basically one large room divided by paneled screens. The floor was made of planks perfectly fitted together, and was scrupulously clean.

At the back was a wonderful garden, walled on two sides and hewn from the very heart of the mountain. It seemed both ornamental and practical, as I could see flowers and vegetables, herbs and hedges. I was also surprised things were so green for the middle of winter. Nearby lay a small natural pool. I watched wisps of steam coming off the water.

In the center of the courtyard was a cast iron fire pit. The ashes were still smoldering. I could see shimmers of heat rising and a few embers. I felt it's lovely warmth and cupped my hands.

"It's a terrible shame, but for now, such a treasure must be hidden from view," Mr Sato declared and walked over to a cabinet.

"Why is that?"

"Your General McArthur, the Supreme Commander, has issued a decree: All katanas must be turned in and melted down for scrap."

"No exceptions?" Fynn asked.

"One exception at least, your gift to me." He put the sword away and latched the doors.

"It doesn't seem like you get many visitors here," I commented.

"You'd be surprised, Patrick-san."

"You remember me…"

"Indeed I do. I know you both now. It was not so long ago we were aboard the *RMS Carpathia* together."

"An eventful voyage, wouldn't you say, Mr Sato?"

"Not that I recall, Mr Fynn… But please, make yourself comfortable. I will first brew us some tea, eh? We have much to talk about…"

"What about Ursula?" I asked.

"Who?"

"The dancing bear."

"Oh yes, performing her tricks on the foredeck. Quite amusing… and that Russian fellow— what was his name?"

"Öde Temsik," Fynn answered.

"No… something else…Viktor, maybe…" Mr Sato's voice trailed off as he busied himself with a kettle. "Well, on a bright note, after that voyage I decided to leave government service— and I'll add, before things got out of hand."

"Meaning?"

"My nation's endless hostility, its imperial ambitions… Meaning, the war tribunals will soon begin in Tokyo, and the criminals will be brought to justice."

"How did you survive the war?"

"I was wounded in Manchuria, nineteen thirty-three, and sent home." Mr Sato invited us to sit on a few cushions as he brought over a teapot and cups. "It's true I am isolated nowadays… But, from time to time the villagers come and ask to be healed. I help if I can…

there are many herbs and cures from my garden… for a variety of ailments."

"How is it so green in the middle of winter?"

"Nearby are underground hot springs… the water keeps things warm in just this particular area."

"This is all that sustains you?"

Mr Sato laughed. "I have a large sack of rice, so I am fine for the next year or so."

"Where is your wife, Reimu?" Fynn continued his questions.

"Eh?" Mr Sato turned to him. "Well, she's out hunting bears."

"What?" I wasn't sure I heard him right.

Mr Sato gave me a wide grin. "I'm joking of course, though not about the bears, such creatures do roam the forests." He poured out three cups of tea. "Reimu won't be back for days, weeks even…"

"Where has she gone?" Fynn asked.

"Traveling to the north."

"That is clearly a lie…" Fynn countered. "We've just come from there. It's a wasteland."

"Perhaps north is not the right word. She's on the other side of the mountain, gathering firewood." Mr Sato smiled. "She should be back anytime now."

Leaning up against the wall in the corner of the room I spotted a cane. I had seen it before: the brass elephant's head with a curling trunk.

"We are here about the books," Fynn said flatly.

"Of course you are and I'm delighted. I am very glad to have visitors, and the two of you, no less. A most fortuitous arrival indeed." Mr Sato gave us a wide smile. "Since you both speak English so well, you might help me with my translations."

"Translations?" I asked.

"Into Japanese."

"What language is it in now?"

"A kind of English, I would say."

"Where are the manuscripts?" Fynn asked.

"The manuscripts? Like a book, do you mean? Oh yes, those are largely indecipherable. I am talking about the new collection of loose pages."

Fynn shot me a glance. "How did you come across these pages?"

"From my wife, Reimu... she gave them to me, not a week ago it seems."

"May we see them?"

"Yes, yes... of course," Mr Sato replied and sipped his tea. "Most interesting they are, especially the pages on botany. It's been a great boon to my work."

"And what work is that?" Fynn asked.

"Studying the plants from a different earth."

"A different earth?" I was surprised.

"That's how it seems to me. I've never encountered anything like these... The leaves of one plant, the roots of another and the flowers from yet a third... Someday I'll graft them together to find the end result."

"I thought they were hybrids."

"Hybrids, eh?" Mr Sato paused for a time. "Well, now that you say that, I must revise my thinking." He smiled. "I have held the idea that the plants in the book have the ability to alter one's perception of time."

"How would that work?" I questioned and started to wonder if Mr Sato was stalling.

"Ah, well you might ask. I have embarked on an exciting field of study."

"What would that be?"

Mr Sato's eyes lit up; they were gleaming. "I have devised a method of detecting the cosmic pace of time. We might call them gravity waves. We all know how gravity can affect time, eh? Einstein has told us this... Slowing us all down in its thickness."

"And?"

"Oh, every so often an enormous ocean of gravity rolls across our solar system and brings things to a standstill."

"It's sort of a moot point, isn't it?" I countered.

"Why is that?"

"If things have slowed down, they've slowed down for everyone in a relative sense. No one would notice."

"You're correct, though it might explain why history travels at a different speed than time itself." Mr Sato flashed a smile. "The distance between the past and the future can only be called the present."

I laughed, then thought a bit harder. "So, you're saying the present might persist for a very long time."

"Between related events, certainly— centuries even."

"Like in terms of cause and effect?"

"Exactly. Daily events add up to history but not when one is immersed in it."

"In the present, you mean?'"

"Yes. And yet there are moments that most people regard as historic— history seems to speed up."

"That's mostly done in hindsight," I said.

"You sir, wield logic like a samurai wields his noble sword. You have cut my argument to shreds." Mr Sato gave a long laugh. "Of course, there are other occasions when time is very much less dense and things proceed along at a breakneck pace."

"No one notices that either, I guess."

"Not usually, and exactly why I wish to concoct the potion on page forty-three."

"What?"

"From the manuscript."

"We would very much like to see these translations," Fynn persisted.

Mr Sato rose and walked over to the far wall of the cottage. I could see a low-to-the-ground writing desk surrounded by towering stacks of papers and books. A lantern burned nearby. He returned and handed Fynn a stack of pages. A quick glance made it clear that they were modern faxes, the translations sent by Clark and the Arbiter, probably stolen by Kali.

"Ah, but first we shall eat something, eh? We have so much to discuss… I will prepare a great feast in your honor," Mr Sato announced and moved towards the edge of the courtyard, to what might have passed for a kitchen.

Fynn took the time to look through the fax pages and handed them off to me one by one. I couldn't make much sense of them, English or not.

"Well, this bit seems to be a construction manual," Fynn said quietly.

"For what?"

"On how to build a circle."

"What kind of circle?"

"I'm not sure I understand it at all…"

***

"Wild rice, and legumes from my garden… and a special sauce of my own recipe," Mr Sato said rather proudly as he set three bowls down on the floor. I was starving by now and looked around for a fork. There was none. I wrestled with the chopsticks. "This is delicious…" I said after a few mouthfuls. "What kind of meat is it?"

"Best you don't ask. Many different creatures roam the forest around here and some get caught in my snares."

His comment did little to quell my appetite and I kept on eating.

"Tell me, my gentlemen, have you just arrived from the future or the past?"

"The future," Fynn replied. "Have you traveled there yourself?"

"No… But everyone has knowledge of the future… or at least what it might bring. It is often incomplete and sometimes completely wrong, but it is readily available."

"How so?"

"One only needs to look at other people's lives, to understand how they lived them. We can see them begin and end, and we can make inferences about our own future."

"Other people?" I asked.

"Other people who have lived and died throughout the ages. Surely we compare ourselves to them and take lessons from their lives? I believe it something most people do, and nearly every day… if not famous people in history, then family members, ancestors and alike."

"That's not quite the same thing as traveling to the future."

"I hardly see the difference." Mr Sato smiled. "Of course, I am most eager to travel to the past. Perhaps I can entice you to join me."

"Where is it you'd like to go?" Fynn asked between mouthfuls; his appetite seemed no less abated either.

"To just before the so-called Edo Period. If Shogun Tokugawa Ieyasu had not come to power, I might guess that Japan would be an utterly different place. And there are several opportunities to thwart his rise…"

"Is that something you wish to do?"

"Yes, I've spent months planning such an expedition. I could certainly use your help."

"For what reason?"

"I'd wish to see a Japan that never went into isolation," Mr Sato explained. "Ah, how the world would be if our progress did not end so abruptly."

"A way forward to conquer all of east Asia?" Fynn asked.

"I'm not saying that at all. I am saying Japan's presence would be known across the world. We would have embassies in all the major capitals. Our own modernity would keep pace with the west."

"For good or ill."

"As you wisely say, Mr Fynn." He gave a polite bow. "Of course, I would have changed things the first time around, but I was otherwise indisposed."

"How so?"

"I was captured by the Portuguese and sold into slavery. Jesuits, I think they were."

"When was this?"

"The late fifteen hundreds by the west's calendar. It was a terrible voyage. Most of my comrades died along the way… down in the holds… the women were separated from the men. They were never seen again. Forced to be concubines, I was told."

"Sounds awful," I commented.

"I didn't see the sun for a month… but eventually they brought us up onto the deck. They wanted us alive, at least some of us… We were a novelty to them, I suppose."

"What happened then?"

"We arrived in Lisbon some weeks later, a wondrous place, I will admit." Mr Sato paused with a sigh. "I was sold to a nobleman by the name of Fillippo Sassetti. He took kindly to me, and I seized the opportunity to learn the western languages."

"You became a translator?"

"I did." Mr Sato chuckled. "I twisted my tongue into positions it had never known before— very difficult at first— but once I learned Portuguese, the other languages were easy to master."

"How long were you there?"

"Twenty years at least, and it took nearly as many to voyage home. I made a harrowing escape and stowed away on an English merchant ship. It took me as far as Calcutta, and the rest of the journey was overland. I will say I learned much along the way…"

"Such as?"

Mr Sato sat back and laughed. "It set me on my life long quest."

"The study of time…" I said.

"Well, yes. But how could you know such a thing?" Mr Sato turned to face me.

"We talked about it before even though you don't remember." I smiled and bowed.

"Well, I began to realize that time is only how we perceive it… and that all life sees it in a completely different manner. From there I sought to communicate with all creatures, and even plants."

"What did they tell you?"

"Creatures communicate according to their nature and their needs."

"Like?"

"Hmm… If I were to listen to a cat, he would likely say, *Hello, how are you today? Do you have any meat for me?*"

"What about a dog?"

"He may say the same thing, though over the course of many years, I have learned that cats are quite different."

"Different from what?"

"Let us say dogs." Mr Sato gave me a smile.

"Why?"

"Dogs live in the present with great precision. They rarely consider past events, except as habitual routines, recurring patterns. Nor do they think much about what's to come."

"What if they're waiting for their owner to return?"

"Ah yes… they are anxious, then ecstatic when their master returns— but both actions are very much in the present."

"And cats?"

"From my experience, they abide slightly in the future."

"How is that possible?"

"Well, they seem to have a sort of precognition. They are quite adept at anticipating events."

"Psychic?"

"I'm not sure about the word you're using…" Mr Sato turned to me. "Though I will say, it's quite easy to put a picture in a cat's mind. Probably because they don't respond to words very well."

***

After supper, Mr Sato cleared the room and went back to his cabinet. He removed the sword again, reverently, and gave it more scrutiny. "Even this noble katana, it's blade is destined to rust."

"Destined?" I asked.

"Basic chemistry tells us this. It is iron's imperative. It does not choose to interact with oxygen, it's simply the way the world is."

"But it has no knowledge of its own destiny," I protested. "It's an inanimate object."

"Do you have knowledge of your destiny?" Mr Sato asked with a chuckle. "But along comes another bundle of molecules in the form of a sword smith or a samurai. He makes a pact with the iron. He says, 'I will rail against your destiny. You shall not rust. You shall remain pure, sharp, shiny, and deadly.'"

"It's only temporary though…"

"And what is permanent, Patrick-san?"

***

"Now what?" I asked once Mr Sato had disappeared back to his garden.

"Yes, the vexing question, Patrick. How do we return to the present? And do we bring these with us?"

"Where do you mean in terms of geography?"

Fynn laughed. "As you hope, a return to Sand City."

"I'm happy to hear it, but why exactly?"

"We still have to locate Geppetto. And I grow concerned that Kali has decided to play things out on your home turf."

"What makes you think that?"

"The odd goings-on at the quarry for one, her appearance at the library; and Geppetto, as I've mentioned. Somehow he is the key to all this."

"So… a jump to the present and a tedious flight back?"

"Perhaps… Or a boat to North America, then a jump." Fynn raised a smile. "Any return will be problematic. Even the cane is little help since we must also travel to the other side of the earth."

"What about Kali? She's going to show up sooner or later."

"I have no wish to encounter her," Fynn replied. "We have the faxes and the manuscripts. That should suffice in thwarting her plans."

"What are you going to do with them?"

"I'm not sure… I'm loath to destroy them entirely, though putting them in safe keeping is a great risk."

"The Amsterdam bank?"

"It may well come to that." Fynn paused.

"I say burn them… At best they're only copies, at worst they're forgeries."

"Yes…" he replied softly, and after some long hesitation Fynn threw the first manuscript onto the fire pit. It flared up suddenly, leaving a peculiar odor. Mr Sato noticed what we were doing and was appalled to say the least. He came running over, shouting in Japanese.

"I am sorry, Hideki Sato," Fynn said to him and tossed the other two books onto the flames. "We must save the future from a great calamity."

Mr Sato was speechless and gave Fynn a searching look; then just watched as the faxes were fed to the fire, page by page, ensuring they were fully burned. We heard another hue and cry. It came from behind us. When we turned, Kali was at the front door. She was dressed in khaki jodhpurs and a matching shirt. She did not take off her shoes, but blinked from sight. In an instant Kali was by the fire pit, staring down at the ashes. "You feeble-minded fools," she shouted.

Before I could even think what was happening, Kali already stood next to Fynn and thrust a triangular knife into his ribs. She stepped back. There was blood everywhere, dripping from the short blade and spreading across Fynn's shirt. He crumpled to his knees and fell to the pavement.

I immediately thought to rush over with assistance, but the same happened to me. Before I knew it, Kali was at my side. I was nothing more than a piece of meat. I felt the blade cut through me, a sharp pain coursed through my gut. Oddly, I felt surprised more than anything as I hit the ground.

Kali stood over us and looked down. "I've missed your vital organs, in case you're wondering," she explained. "You will both bleed out slowly... I only let you live so that I might ask some questions."

Mr Sato stood by horrified, and helpless it seemed, but he was looking at something else across the room. A shadow passed through the door. Kali, not sensing any more danger, stayed in the present instead of flitting into the future as usual. So focused on revenge, she did not notice that Mortimer loomed in the doorway. He was still in his gray suit and trilby. I guessed he did not hike here as we had. Oddly, he started whistling a tune, an unfamiliar melody. That caught Kali's attention, and for a moment she seemed distracted, almost flustered.

I pulled out my cell phone and turned it on. There was of course no service but it glowed and displayed its cryptic icons. It dropped to the ground with a clatter. Kali came rushing over to investigate this miraculous device and snatched it from the bricks. "What is this thing you have?"

In that moment, Fynn tossed the bear claw cane to Mortimer who now skulked by the cabinets. He caught it deftly. "Double yourself," Fynn called out, breathless.

"I thought it was fixed," he responded.

"I lied."

"Eh?" Mortimer asked and stared at Fynn. In another instant he was gone. Kali blinked over but she was too late.

"I'm not sure that was such a good idea," I said mostly to myself, but I was wrong. A silence came across the cottage. It seemed like several minutes went by. All I could hear was the rain starting outside, pounding against the roof. I looked over at Fynn who was now sitting against the wall. He had dragged himself into the living room. All the while Kali flitted here and there, into the past and the future, and back to the present, seeking potential dangers everywhere. She paid little attention to us though.

A moment later, Mortimer reappeared in the doorway. He gave his thin smile, and then another Mortimer materialized, and another. Only one held the cane. The others were charging at Kali and she was forced to defend herself. One of them kicked over the fire pit. Embers went sliding across the floor and into the cottage. It would soon be ablaze. The paper screens started to burn furiously.

Kali fled to the grassy meadow with several Mortimers in pursuit. I lifted Fynn into my arms and we struggled to a standing position, both of us leaning on each other, both of us bleeding badly. We staggered to the door and away from the fire which had begun to creep up the walls of the cottage.

In the corner of my eye, I saw Mr Sato retrieve his precious katana, but he also took something else: the elephant cane. He rushed over to help Fynn and I. The three of us climbed off the porch and into the clearing. It was soggy and slippery, soaked with rain. We fell more than once.

"See how dark the forest has become. Get yourself across the bridge and to the woods beyond. Hide, hide, my friends. She can't kill you if she can't find you," Mr Sato whispered and then set off wildly across the clearing with the elephant cane held high. This got Kali's attention.

Distracted by the Mortimers, she had no chance of intercepting Mr Sato. He flung the cane as far as he could and it landed unseen into the chasm. We could all hear it clattering against the rocks.

"You foolish little man," Kali screamed. "You shall die with the rest of them." An instant later, she blinked up next to him and Mr Sato had a mortal wound. His left side opened up like lamb chops, flesh and muscle were exposed to the open air. Blood began to pour from the gaping slash. The fabled katana fell to the wet grass.

There was one means of escape. I still had Pavel's dice in my pocket. I could roll to a parallel place and hopefully a better one. Of course, I thought better of the idea; I couldn't just leave Fynn behind. We hobbled closer to the bridge. Mortimer ran interference in his own way. I could see at least half a dozen doppelgängers now. They descended on Kali from all sides and she was compelled to retreat for the moment.

"I wish I knew which way to jump," Fynn whispered as we reached the bridge.

"What?"

"A safe way to escape. I have not seen the stars for several nights and I've even lost track of the days. I know not which direction we should go."

I looked over to the clearing. I could see Mortimer's doubles falling now, cut down and slumped in the wet grass. "Let's just get across and figure it out later."

"As you say," Fynn turned and tried to raise a smile. "Away from here is all that's important."

We started across the flimsy bridge. "This is no place to jump from," I said, peering down into the gorge. A stream was rushing by but it didn't seem very deep and was crowded with boulders.

"We may have little choice," Fynn replied and pointed to the meadow. Kali saw us and began to march in our direction.

"But…" I was about to protest when I felt the bridge sway and pitch. I looked over. One of the Mortimers was hacking away at the vines with Mr Sato's katana. He held the bear claw cane in his other hand. The last thing I saw was his thin smile as we began to fall. "Bon voyage," he called out, and it echoed along with us as we tumbled through the void.

PART VII

chapter twenty-five
stone soup

I can't speak for Fynn, but I was expecting a moment of searing pain. It never materialized, just a pleasant drifty feeling came over me. I was back to somewhere and to someone familiar, though neither is the right word. I found Fynn on the ground next to me. He looked different and it wasn't just the beard. His hair was black, not a trace of gray or white.

"Well?" he asked while brushing himself off. "What do you think?"

"You're twenty years younger than usual."

"What?" he asked and felt his own face. "Well, there's no mirror available, but I will say that you look just as I remember." Fynn glanced down at his clothes and I did the same. We were both wearing kilts and I'd guess of the same tartan.

"We're alive at least," I pointed out.

"And in the past," he added.

"I think we're lost."

"Nonsense. I know exactly where we are, more or less." Fynn raised a smile.

"We've been here before… and together… a soft jump for both of us."

"So it would seem." He turned to me. "What do you remember about this place?"

"Nada," I replied.

"Perhaps all our memories will come rushing back to us after a while."

"I'm not sure I want them to."

"Nonetheless, it would be useful to remember."

"Did Mortimer send us here?"

"I would not say that exactly."

"Was he trying to kill us when he cut down the bridge?"

"No… I believe he tried to save us. He seemed to know we'd be traveling somewhere."

"Somewhere far away," I muttered.

"A simple axiom, Patrick: the further we fall, the further we travel."

"Do you think he's dead?"

"Mortimer is clever at the very least. He may have found a way to defeat even Kali."

"What about Mr Sato?"

"I fear the worst…"

We surveyed our new location. Fynn and I stood in some tall reeds, baked brown by the summer. The ground beneath our feet was like a wet sponge, squishy at every step. What was land and what was water wasn't exactly clear, and my boots were leaking. We were in some sort of bog. Fynn pointed to higher ground where a few gray rocks poked up from a hill. We started off in that direction.

"*Blàr Chùil Lodair*," I said after a few cautious steps.

Fynn stopped in his tracks. "You just spoke in Gaelic."

"Did I?"

"Yes. You said, 'the Battle of Culloden…' and I understood you."

"Not a language you normally speak?"

"Not for centuries."

"Maybe I was here once… with Chloe or her sister Lilly… I think it was around the time of Culloden."

"I can say the same, though I don't recall seeing any of you at the time." Fynn resumed his pace. "And the season is wrong."

"What?"

"It looks to be late summer. The infamous battle took place in April."

"So— are we before or after that?"

"This is the important question, Patrick."

"It has to be before…"

"Why do you say that?"

"I remember leaving right after the battle… I was wounded and

Chloe took care of me, Lilly too."

"They were both present?"

"Cohabiting, you might say."

"What do you mean?"

"They shared the same body." I paused. "But from here, I jumped back to Modena— to get you out of the dungeon."

"That, I do recall…" We walked on for a few yards and Fynn asked, "What else do you remember about this place, Patrick?"

"I escaped to here from the Flatlands…" I paused again. "…And maybe a few things Mr Temsik mentioned."

"Such as?"

"He seemed to think this was the first time we ever met."

"Well, that's quite unexpected. Did he say anything else?"

"Not really." I hesitated for a moment. "I am a little worried that we night be changing history; well, the past I mean."

"It's likely, but in the larger sense, I doubt it will matter much."

"I wonder if it changes *your* history."

"I see… and you're afraid that a new sequence of events will not lead you back to the Italian Renaissance."

"Well… yes."

"But I am here and you are here, so things worked out for us both— already, in the past; it's a matter of record."

"Or a matter of memory."

"I have a vague recollection of being lured here," Fynn said.

"Lured by whom?"

"By what… the Scottish Enlightenment, it was called, though I may have arrived a few years too early."

We scrambled up the hill for a better view of our surroundings and rested a while against the gray rocks. "Check your pockets," Fynn suggested.

"I'm not sure I have any."

"Well, I found this…" He held out a purse with a few odd coins. "This is a *Louis d'or*, French currency, I believe," he said and held one up.

I searched myself to find a plastic lighter and the pocket knife that Fynn had given me so long ago.

"Anything else?" he asked.

"No."

"Luckily, I also have half a loaf of stale bread and some kind of dried fish in my pouch."

"What now?"

"We must figure out exactly where we are and when, in order to return home."

"Home?"

"Sand City and your favorite timeline."

"How?"

"I will need a compass and something like an astrolabe."

"Something?"

"Well, a maritime sextant will do the trick, or perhaps a land surveyor's equipment. And, I'll need to watch the stars tonight." Fynn pointed to the horizon. "A distant shoreline, I would say. Let's head in that direction."

***

We trudged along the coast for days, following the cliffs that rose and fell, and sometimes found ourselves right along the beach. We never saw a soul except for an occasional ship out at sea, sails fully unfurled. I was happy enough that we did pass a few streams along the way; the water was cold and sweet. And most nights, I was glad to be wearing a woolen blanket. Fynn grew concerned that our direction was west and not north like he supposed. He was beginning to wonder which ocean lay to our right.

The next afternoon we came upon a rural town, a village just at the edge of the water. It was a bright sunny day and fairly warm. There were fishing boats and even ships with their sails stowed. Up on the hill loomed a ruined castle, though quite a few substantial houses could be seen along a broad street. They were all hewn from the same gray stone, and judging by the amount of chimneys, they all had massive fireplaces. Each had small, sparse windows.

"Yes, now I recall this place," Fynn announced. "It is Nairn, or *Inbhir Narann*. Founded by the Norseman, many hundreds of years ago."

We made for the town and I hoped for something to eat. I was ravenous by now. Not only was our food supply gone, but, except for our dinner with Mr Sato, I hadn't eaten properly for weeks.

"Some of my memories are returning," Fynn told me. "We must find High Street. On one end people speak Gaelic, and on the other, Scots."

"Which end is which?"

"The highlanders speak Gaelic and the rest speak Scots."

"Scots?"

"A nearly unintelligible dialect of English."

"We haven't eaten in days," I reminded him.

"Yes, our most pressing concern, I agree," Fynn replied and led me into a blacksmith's shop.

"I was hoping for a pub or a tavern," I said as he opened the door. A large man with a beard took notice:

"Well, well, Clan MacPherson, eh? I can't say any of you fellows have ever graced my establishment before— though I'm honored... And what brings you gentlemen so far afield?"

"We are wayfarers heading south. We've stopped in your fair town for a day of rest."

"There's not much more south you can go... Edinburgh, you must mean. Well, I'd take the high road... the low road is crawling with the king's men and his sympathizers." He spat to the ground.

"We shall heed your advice; we are cautious travelers if nothing else."

"And from a long way off, I'd say." He looked us over again. "Why are you dressed as such?"

"We've only just returned from Darien," Fynn explained.

"From where? Darien, you say?"

"The colony of Caledonia."

"Well, well, the other side of the world," the shopkeeper gave Fynn a long look. "A great misadventure, my father spoke of it often. I thought there were no survivors."

"Only a few..."

"And is that how they dress there?" The man asked and let go a laugh.

"It's been a long journey."

"You might say that. Going on thirty years, it'd be..."

"I was but a small lad when my family first departed," Fynn

explained. "Trying to escape the seven-ill-years... I've spent a long time in the colonies."

"And him?"

"He's part savage."

"An Indian, eh? I've heard tell of such people."

"Why is he with you?"

"He's been indentured to me."

"Why doesn't he speak?"

"He's mute... nor does he understand half of what I say."

"So long as he's not English." The man spat to the ground again.

"We've been at sea many long months and it's embarrassing to say, but I've lost track of the date," Fynn said. "Can you tell me what the year is?"

The ironsmith laughed a bit. "Year of our lord, seventeen thirty-two."

"And it is July?"

"No, it'd be the twentieth of August."

Iron implements of all kinds hung from the rafters and I could hear someone hammering in a nearby courtyard. We looked around the shop and the blacksmith seemed a bit nervous. "I should be making broadswords and flintlocks, not pots and pans," he called out.

Fynn had but a few coins, enough to buy a large iron cauldron and a tripod to hang it over a fire. He also insisted on a good number of spoons, a few small bowls, and a huge ladle as part of the deal.

"Gold, aye, it surely is, but I've not seen this denomination before. It's not coin of the realm."

"As I've said, we've traveled far and wide."

"Be you a Jacobite or something else?"

"Something else," Fynn replied. "But I'm no lover of the English, nor what they've done to this land."

"Can you fire a musket or swing a sword?"

"If it comes to that, yes." Fynn gave the man a smile. "Can you tell us, kind sir, are there any stone circles nearby?"

"You mean to say standing stones?" He seemed perplexed by the question, as was I. "There'd be the old Clava Cairn by the river— tis not a place you should go."

"Why not?"

"Well, you might go, but you wouldn't want to tarry... tis the abode of witches."

"We will be watchful."

"Aye…" the blacksmith seemed skeptical. "Follow the Nairn up for eight miles. It'll take you near enough."

***

Fynn and I lugged the cauldron and tripod along the cobbles of High Street towards the center of town. We were on our way towards a communal fountain. Not really a fountain, just a pipe with a continuous trickle of water that emptied into a ditch. The street widened into a sort of central square. My questions began to mount.

"I can't explain it exactly, but I seem to understand this language."

"How is such a thing possible?" Fynn turned to me.

"I must've lived here longer than I thought."

"What do you suppose jogged your memory?"

"Necessity?"

"Most curious."

"Okay, maybe understand is an exaggeration… but some of the words are familiar, even whole sentences."

By now, we had attracted some attention from the townsfolk. A few called out and even started to follow us. I was still wondering what Fynn had in mind.

"No, I have not taken leave of my senses," he said. "We are both here and yet neither of us can recall anything of importance…"

"So?"

"So… I'm supposing there is someone else here who knows us, knows our story, and I mean to draw them out."

"Someone? Like Chloe or Lilly?"

"If they are here…"

"Who then? Mr Temsik?"

"This is what we hope to learn, eh?"

"Or Kali?"

"No. I can't imagine why she would be in such a location." Fynn paused. "It seems to be an insignificant time and place to alter history."

"We're closest to Culloden."

"Yes, but now we know it's still a decade away from the battle."

Fynn paused. "And even if the outcome is different it would have little impact on history."

"No?"

"As you can already see, Patrick, Scotland is a depleted place. Bonnie Prince Charles has no chance of taking over the entire island."

"And why ask about the standing stones?"

"Something that sticks in my memory."

"Well… there are a lot of stone circles in the not so United Kingdom."

"This I will not disagree with… and they were all built around the same time— let us say late neolithic, some five thousand years ago."

"Maybe that's why Kali is here."

"To change prehistory?" Fynn was astonished at the idea. "Such seems reckless and unpredictable even for her."

"I don't know. I'm just trying to think out loud."

Fynn gave me a weary nod. "Yes… well, let's put our minds to it, but first things first… Give me a hand, please." We dragged the heavy cauldron over to the fountain and filled it up about halfway. "I've paid too much for this, I suppose, but it will serve us well," he said and added a smile.

It was easy enough to set up the apparatus and start a fire with scraps of wood gathered from the road. I set it aflame with my lighter. Fynn found three large stones and washed them carefully in the fountain.

By now, a few people had noticed our activity and wandered over for a closer look. With some flair for the new audience, Fynn dropped the stones into the pot as it began to boil, one by one and with a dramatic flourish. A man came over to ask what we were doing. He may have spoke in English, but it was barely intelligible to me. Fynn seemed to understand his questions.

"I'm making soup of course, and there'll be plenty to go around."

"With stones?" the man questioned.

"Think of them as potatoes," Fynn replied with a grin. He reached into his pouch and drew out a handful of wild scallions that he had gathered along the way. "A bit of garnish will make it all the more delicious." He sprinkled them in from a great height and began to stir again.

The man laughed at this notion, but considered the idea. "A wee bit of salt would flavor the soup, but I'd not want to waste it on stones alone."

"Save your salt, good sir," Fynn answered in a loud voice. "We're not boiling brine from the sea. We'd be making something sweet and savory."

"Looks a bit thin," a woman called out from the gathering crowd. She added a cackle.

"Aye," said another. "If only you could put in half a cabbage…"

"Indeed. And perhaps someone has an old bone we could simmer?"

"I may have an old mutton shank— hardly fit for a dog," a young woman from the square called out.

"If you might part with it, we would all benefit from its delicious marrow." Fynn tasted the soup and made a funny face. "We need some garnish, to be sure," he announced. "Turnip greens, wild onions, or cabbage would do nicely."

"Aye, and a measure of oatmeal to sprinkle in," someone said and handed Fynn a small burlap sack.

"Thank you, Madame, it will thicken the soup nicely."

"Or a potato or two?" someone offered. Fynn took them graciously and sliced them into the pot.

"Even an old fish head might add a wee bit of flavor," another man shouted, laughing.

"I'd prefer not to make fish soup… What do you all say?" Fynn called out to the crowd.

"Aye, we'd like something meaty," a man yelled and a chorus of townsfolk agreed with a cheer.

"I might have a small sack of offal in the larder… I was going to make haggis but it's starting to rot in this warm weather."

"It would be a welcome addition," Fynn replied with a smile.

Soon enough the soup was thickening and simmering with such a delightful aroma, others in the town came out to see what was going on. More ingredients were added: turnips, more potatoes and carrots. I could smell freshly baked bread from somewhere. A young boy came over with an armload of loaves. He presented them shyly. "Compliments of the baker," he said.

Fynn took them graciously and gave the boy his last few coins. "We have a feast before us, good ladies and gentlemen," he announced to the crowd. "Who will partake?" A small cheer rose and people started lining up. Fynn happily doled out the flavorsome supper to all comers, myself included. It ended up less like a soup and more like a hearty stew.

As the eastern sky grew dark, a stranger wandered up High Street with a fiddle under his chin. He gave us a smile and a nod, then began to play a sprightly tune. I could hear a few drums joining in from somewhere. A few minutes after that, a young lad and a lass came careening out of the crowd onto the open square. They were dancing and people started clapping in time. Others soon joined in. A flask was passed around and I took a sip of strong whiskey. People were singing now as the sun began to fade. A few torches were lit and a large bonfire.

I heard a soft rumbling along the cobblestones and turned to see some men rolling a barrel of ale toward the festivities. High Street became a celebration and I guessed half the town had turned out, as there were at least a hundred people milling around the central square.

There was a figure lingering in the shadows though. I almost recognized her, or thought she was familiar at least. I saw a tumble of black hair. She was dressed in a white frilly blouse and long skirt. When she stepped into the firelight I was convinced it was Chloe… She was here to rescue us. The Arbiter had sent her, I was sure. I was wrong though. I also noticed some of the townsfolk seemed wary of her. They stayed well clear, indeed, even shunned her. Only a very few would tip their hats.

***

It was quite late when the evening's frolic came to an end. Many people had fallen asleep right there on the cobbles. Others were helping their mates stagger home. The woman I thought to be Chloe approached us. "Well, gentlemen, 'twas a fine soup and a glorious evening— for that, I thank you." She added a small curtsey. "And I'll say you're a sight for sore eyes."

"You know us then?"

"Aye, you'd be Mr Fynn and Patrick. What say we have a conversation about such things?"

"And are you Lilly or Chloe? Or a bit of both?" I asked.

She raised an eyebrow and came closer. "I've not seen Chloe in an age," she replied, "though I do expect a visit shortly." The woman sidled up to me and draped her arms around my shoulder. "We should find a less public place though. Follow me to my cottage, if you will."

She wasn't quite the Lilly I remembered. First of all, she wore no glasses, and her hair was loose around her neck. It seemed to me, she had gone native, speaking in a thick brogue. I wondered what else was different about her.

Lilly had a lantern and set it aflame with a tinder from the dying fire. She led us out of town and we walked in silence for nearly an hour until she stopped and pointed to the south. "If you look closely enough, gentlemen, you'd be seeing Lady MacBeth peering from the ramparts." She laughed a little. "There'd be Cawdor Castle, but we should steer clear. Mustn't trespass."

"How far is your cottage?"

"Another hour's walk from here, or so."

We followed the river Nairn for a time until it began to narrow into not much more than a stream. There was a heavy mist along the banks. The lantern reflected as a dome of light. If anyone was nearby, they'd be certain to see us coming. Lilly knew the path by heart. We left the river to cut across farmlands, and hopped over several rock walls. She led us over a few gentle hills to a spot that was familiar to me, the Clava Cairns, and her cottage.

The glen was not quite like I remembered. The woods seemed the same, the stream, and the cottage with a thatched roof. But down the path, the standing stones were different. I counted nine of various heights, but now toppled as if some giant had thrown them here and there. At the center was a pile of fist-sized rocks embedded in the ground, more an oval than a circle. Something was wrong though, most had been dug up and scattered about.

"Welcome to the *Na bi a-nis*, gentleman," Lilly announced as we entered the clearing.

"The what?"

"The ne'er-now," she replied in English.

"Why is it called the never-now?"

"Hmm, I suppose it's a place where the days will never come to pass."

"Where are these days?" Fynn asked.

"Far to the future, if I had to guess."

"How does that work?"

"It doesn't anymore, Patrick," she answered. "I can only tell you what did happen anytime you might enter the ring of stones."

"What?"

"Time seems to stop."

"Inside the circle? Or outside?" Fynn asked.

"Both, I reckon... Outside, it all goes by in a blur, as if it be water rushing past."

"And this is a place for traveling?"

"Aye, it was. Takes you anywhere you'd want to be— curious thing though— it only takes you to the future."

"Are you sure?"

"Took me years to figure out how it all worked," Lilly replied. "And that said, anybody's future is this thing's past."

"Meaning?"

"You'll travel, verily, but you'll never feel a prick of pain. It's always a soft jump to somewhere you've been before."

"Such seems an impossibility," Fynn said.

"Aye... I can't say why it works, only how." Lilly climbed up to one of the fallen stones and sat cross-legged.

"The place is a ruin," I said.

"'Tis at that, and I won't say I'm not glad to see you both." Lilly smiled. "There's been strange goings-on as of late."

"Such as?"

"That woman, firstly."

"And who would that be?"

"I was hoping you could tell me. A slippery one, she is... Took me under her wing— or wanted to. I'd have no part of her."

"Why not?"

"I didn't care for her much, that's all... Of course, that's not what she thought." Lilly gave us an ominous smile.

"When was this?"

"Near on twenty years ago. She showed up with an army of diggers."

"Diggers?"

"Lowlanders to be sure…. they desecrated the place."

"What are you saying?"

"It's an ancient cairn, maybe three, four thousand years old. Someone important was buried here."

"That's a long time ago," I commented.

"Aye… still, it's a desecration."

"What exactly did she do?"

"She dug something up, didn't she?"

"What? Old bones?"

"'Twas more than that… a kind of talisman, I'd say."

"A talisman?" Fynn asked.

"Aye, a sort of a disk as big as your hand outstretched… and made of some metal I'd ne'er seen before."

"Metal?"

"Not brass nor silver, copper or gold."

"Where has it gone?"

"Now there's a story for you," Lilly replied. "I pried it from her cold dead hands."

"What?"

"Aye. I couldn't touch her at first, all that flitting about…"

"It's Kali," I said.

"I think she called herself Katy…" Lilly commented. "It all changed right after she found the talisman though. She settled down and became rather ordinary."

"You killed her?"

"Aye. I didn't like her at all, though I gained her trust first…" Lilly's mouth moved into an unpleasant smile. "Then I stabbed her in her sleep. 'Twas an easy thing to do."

"How long was she here?"

"Seemed like twenty years… Endless ranting, prattling on about British shopkeepers taking over the world. Nipping capitalism in the bud, or some such nonsense…" Lilly gave a laugh.

"She might have as easily blamed the Dutch for that," Fynn said under his breath.

"Also declared she was here to ferment an uprising... Aye, and there'll be another none too soon."

"Jacobites?"

Lilly nodded. "I found this on her person." She unfurled an old piece of parchment and handed it to Fynn.

"What is it?" I asked.

"A registry of names, many of them crossed off— not that I recognize them all— but most of the families are known to me," Lilly explained.

Fynn struggled to read in the dim light. "All of these names are familiar to history," he said and started down the list: "Hume, Watt, Maxwell, Dewar, Carnegie, Ross, Macleod..."

"A hit list," I said.

"Pardon?" Fynn asked.

"A list of people to assassinate."

"What makes you say that?"

"Patrick be right. She even tried to recruit me for the task, but I'm not in the habit of killing random folk."

"Look at this name: Adam Smith..."

"Aye, but he'd be just a young lad, not even laid eyes on a gold sovereign yet."

"Tell me, my dear, did Kali have a cane with her?"

"Do you mean with the brass head of a jackal on top? A wee bit like Mr Mortimer's?"

"He was here as well?"

"No. Haven't seen the likes of him in an age and a day." Lilly smiled. "But there was nothing special about her walking stick. She was ancient, could barely take more than a few steps without it."

"How old was she?"

"She wasn't an old woman when she first appeared, I'll say that much. Spent too much time in the never-now, I'd guess."

"Not a place to linger in, eh?" Fynn asked.

"No. But she was an old hag when I did her in. I don't think she would have lived many more years."

"And how long have you been here?"

"Me? Tis hard to say, I might jump from here to there, but I always return."

"And this talisman… where is it now?"

"Gone it is." Lilly gave us a pained expression and hopped down into the clearing. She paced back and forth. "Not a week ago, it was… there'd be a strange figure gliding through the woods. Taller than a man, robed in a dark cloak and wearing a pale mask… an eerie sight if ever there was one."

"The Arbiter," I said.

"A friend of yours, Patrick?"

"I wouldn't say that."

"What did he want?" Fynn asked.

"Said nothing the first few nights, just here to spook the natives, I was starting to think. But then he demanded the talisman in that mechanical voice of his… I laughed to his face. What's in it for me? I asked."

"What did he say?"

"Not a thing, but the next second I know, my sister Chloe pops in for a visit. Snap, she's in my head and I'm her puppet. She hands over the disk to this specter and a moment later they've both disappeared again."

"Where is Chloe now?" I asked.

Lilly laughed at the question, but bitterly it seemed. "Long gone, she is, aye… But you've hit the nail on the head, Patrick."

"Why is that?"

"I travelled all this way and back just to find her. I ne'er did though… till that night."

"And you got stuck here?"

"You might put it that way. I cannot travel the way things be now— look at the place…" She gestured with outstretched arms. "Aye, since that foul woman dug up the talisman. Nary but a ruin now. It'll take me years to set the stones standing again."

"What can we do to help?" Fynn asked.

"To go anywhere, gentlemen, we've got to travel back to a time before the talisman was stolen. I'm not a good enough jumper for the task, and was hoping one of you were."

"How far back would we have to go?" Fynn asked.

"Some years only," Lilly replied. "And I have this, which I'm sure would be a help." She unwrapped something and handed it to Fynn.

"My old astrolabe," he observed with a smile.

"Aye, you left it here on your last visit."

Fynn looked up at the black sky. "A clear night to see the stars... It should be a simple matter for us all to travel back."

***

It was a hard jump for Fynn and I, though I can't speak for Lilly. Nor did we all land together. I was some miles from where we started but found the river Nairn and followed it back to the glen. Fynn was already waiting.

The circle looked very different now. Not a ruin, but fully restored. The nine standing stones were perfectly aligned around the center cairn. Each was a different height and arranged in ascending order from lowest to highest, like a spiral staircase made for giants. The tallest stones had steps cut into their sides, and all of them were flattened on top with just enough room for a person to stand. I also noticed a stone block near the cairn, oblong and studded with several regular depressions. It looked to be some kind of sacrificial alter.

I was about to enter the circle, but Fynn held me back.

"Not a good idea, Patrick," he said. "We should wait for Lilly to return."

"How do we get back?"

"To our familiar present?"

I nodded. "Is it possible to jump across the Atlantic?"

"I would not want to risk such a journey. We may have to book passage... Besides, I'm not entirely sure when we are." He gave me a frustrated smile.

"So it's going to be complicated..."

"No doubt."

"You're both being silly lads," Lilly scoffed. She had overheard us and stepped into the glen. "Inside the circle is the never-now. There is no future, nor a past."

"What are you trying to say?" Fynn turned to her.

She laughed. "The ever-now, the never-now, call it what you want. It amounts to the same thing. Time doesn't pass inside there."

"How do we travel then?"

"You'll see soon enough, but first we've got to check the calendar." She gave us a smile and beckoned with a finger. We followed her back to the cottage. Outside, Lilly stopped near a large flat rock. She pointed to a line of scratches. "I keep a tally of the days here… Give me a moment… Ah, today is the eleventh of August, seventeen-oh-one."

"Are you certain?"

"I am. There's the last mark I made."

"It was a soft jump for you?"

"Aye, Patrick."

"Where did you disappear to?"

"Went to Nairn for provisions. Come along inside and I'll cook us all some breakfast."

***

Lilly was not forthcoming about how the circle operated, despite Fynn's constant questions. I was happy enough to eat the oatmeal and sausages she had prepared.

"It's best if I show you, that's all," Lilly said. "Besides, I'm not planning on traveling anywhere for the time being."

"What did you tell Kali about this circle?"

"Not a word, 'twas none of her business. Nor did she seem to care—fixated on the talisman, she was."

We returned to the circle and stepped inside together. I had felt something like this before. It was like walking into an atmosphere made of jello. Looking back outside, I could see a world rushing by at such a pace, it was no more than a smear of color and light.

"Don't be distracted by what's going on out there, Patrick. We'd be needing your help here inside." She turned away and called out, "Alright then, Mr Fynn, just count the years."

"The years?"

"From seventeen-oh-one to where you'd rather be." She laughed.

"To the future, you mean to say?"

"From here, it matters not where you're going."

Fynn did a quick calculation. "Three hundred and seventeen."

"You'll be jumping from there." She pointed to the third standing stone. "Each pillar takes you a century through time," Lilly explained and then turned to the cairn and started removing a few fist-sized rocks. "We'll be needing eight stones... a white one there in that trough, and seven more, there." Lilly piled some rocks on what I thought was the alter. "Just the black ones," she cautioned.

A wide smile cross Fynn's face as he began to understand the process. He walked over to help. I also came to a dim understanding and figured this to be some sort of prehistoric abacus.

Lilly stood back satisfied for the moment and pointed to the stones stacked on the alter. "White rocks for decades, and black rocks for years..." She patted the unused depressions in the alter. "Pebbles go here...these be for months and days, but I'll warn you, getting yourself to the exact day never seems to work very well."

"And what will you do?"

"Me?" Lilly laughed. "I'll just wait here for that Kali woman to show... for the first time." An unpleasant smile crossed her face. "Well, gentlemen, mustn't tarry inside the circle. I'll only wish you *tilleadh thu gu math*." She blew a kiss as Fynn and I climbed the third pillar, and then leapt off into oblivion.

chapter twenty-six
back again

I was waiting on a long line at the post office when Fynn burst through the door. "Did you hear the ruckus outside?"

"No, what ruckus?"

"All those little birds chattering away."

"Where?"

"In the hedge by the sidewalk."

"I didn't see them."

"Nor did I, but I heard them well enough."

"What were they trying to say?"

"I only wish I knew." Fynn smiled. "And what brings you here this morning, Patrick?"

"I'm mailing a letter to Mr Quandary."

"It has little chance of arriving."

"You're probably right, but it's worth the price of a stamp at least."

"I see… And you are hoping for his assistance?"

"Maybe that's too strong a word. His advice, or a different perspective on things."

"And what is the topic of your dilemma?"

"The quantum of events."

"Have we not discussed this at some length?"

"Yes…"

"Did you check your box?" Fynn asked.

"Not yet."

"This might make it easier for you."

"What?"

"Your key… you forgot it at the house."

I checked the number: 1933. "Thanks."

"It's more than likely that you've already received a reply from Mr Q."

"I haven't mailed the letter yet."

"Nonetheless…" Fynn smiled.

There was something in his expression I couldn't quite understand. Then it swept over me like a flood, a rush of memories and experiences. Like being whacked over the head with a deja vu stick. We had just returned from the standing stones— at least that's the last thing I could recall.

"Well?" Fynn asked in a whisper.

"I may need to sit for a second or two."

He pulled me from the line and took me back outside. "Hurry along, Patrick, we have much to do."

"Like?"

"We must check the quarry, find Geppetto, and see about Lothar's welfare."

"Lothar?"

"Mortimer may still be among the missing, eh?"

"So?"

"I have some concern for our giant friend. I would hate to think he's living on his own."

"Fair enough…" I agreed, and followed Fynn to the parking lot. "I wonder what day it is?"

"It's Thursday. I noticed the calendar in the post office."

"You mean only three days have gone by since we left for New York."

"Yes. Welcome to my world, Patrick."

"Have we gone to Japan yet?"

"More importantly, we should ask if the faxes have been stolen from my house?"

"You remember that?"

"I do… Kali must not get her hands on the translations."

"Did we just soft jump into the future?"

"No. I've said time and again, it's impossible."

"I've seen a lot of impossible things lately. How was this not a soft jump to the future?" I persisted.

"I am equally baffled. I do not understand the concept of Lilly's never-now." Fynn walked on a bit. "I can only say we are back to where we belong, and everything appears as it should be."

"Maybe not everything…" I said and pulled a copy of the *Chronicle* from it's metal newspaper box. The headline read: *Quarry Condos Ready to Rise*

"What's the matter, Patrick?"

"The headline… construction at the quarry. That can only mean one thing."

"Kali is already here," Fynn replied in a solemn tone and quickened his pace along the path towards the parking lot. We didn't get very far since we were now followed by a small crowd of admirers. Someone came over and asked for Fynn's autograph.

"Why would you want such a thing?" he asked.

"You're famous— well, internet famous. We all know that you're a time traveler."

"This is preposterous," Fynn replied with a smile. "You're mistaken, kind sir. I am nothing more than a retired policeman."

"But we all saw the pictures, the photographs…"

"Photoshop," I said to the man.

"What? Oh…" he muttered. "Well, could I have your autograph

instead?"

"Mine?"

"Sure, the sidekick… better than nothing."

I scribbled something in his notepad, just hoping that would make him go away.

"This is an untenable situation," Fynn said quietly as we walked towards my car. "We have things to do, tasks to complete— we can not be followed by a gaggle of interlopers."

I nodded in agreement but said nothing more. We finally made it over to the amusement park and out onto the pier. Mortimer's stall was open but unattended; there were ping pong balls scattered everywhere. The clown faces with their mouth's agape stared back lifelessly. Up along the boardwalk was a ruckus of another kind. I could see Lothar at the concession stand and he seemed to be arguing with the corn dog vendor.

"Uh-oh," I said as Fynn took me by the arm. We rushed over to intervene though it was too late. A crowd had gathered to watch the show and the police were already on the scene. Three officers were putting handcuffs on the giant's wrists.

"Now what?" I asked.

Fynn held me back. "Luckily, Chief Durbin owes us a favor, eh?" He smiled. "Let's see what we can do…"

***

In a moment of searing pain later, Fynn and I were standing in the lobby of the *Hotel de Cirque*. A smiling Clark was waiting and greeted us brightly, "Welcome back, gentlemen, welcome to the future."

"At least there is one," I grumbled to myself. "When are we?"

"Far from where you were, I would imagine," Clark replied and walked over to us.

I glanced down at his new prosthetic feet. "That's not a very good answer," I complained.

"Oh, well, I'd say you're about two hundred years from your usual present."

"Not very crowded today." I looked around the empty lobby. It seemed newly renovated and shockingly modern.

"Closed for a whole week," Clark said. "It's a bit like a holiday for me."

The Arbiter himself glided towards us. "Policeman Fynn, and Mr Jardel. Are you ready?"

"Ready for what?"

"To eliminate Kali once and for all."

"How?"

"The Circles of Null have been restored. We will return to a far distant past and stop her there."

"We?"

"Yes… anyone who wishes may join me. Come, the others are waiting," he said and swept across the marble floor. The others included Pavel Mekanos and Edmund Fickster, Doctor Zed, Chloe, Mr Q and Lothar. There was no sign of Mortimer. For a moment I puzzled over which Lothar— not the one we had just left on the boardwalk— and I wondered how that was possible.

Fynn and I sat at the table with the others and I could smell fresh coffee. I helped myself to a cup, but it seemed a bit off. I also ate some of the odd crackers Clark had laid out. They tasted bad, artificial and unidentifiable. So much for the cuisine of the future.

The Arbiter began to drone in his mechanical voice: "Welcome all… We can now embark on the journey to erase Kali from the past, present and future."

"Which Kali?" I asked.

The Arbiter glided over to me. "What do you mean, Mr Jardel?"

"There seems to be more than one."

Fynn chuckled. "What Patrick might mean is that we've encountered several duplicates in our recent travels."

"Have you?" the Arbiter asked.

"Probably created by using Mortimer's cane, though they seem less formidable than the original."

"These duplicates will also be eliminated in one fell swoop," the Arbiter responded.

"That's not really what I meant."

"What then?"

"I remember what you said about the first Kali…" I turned to look up at his porcelain face. "You banished her before the pharaohs… but you also sent one to the distant future— remember?"

"Today that will be rectified."

"So there are at least two, if I remember right."

"Yes, you are correct, Mr Jardel."

"So which one are we hunting for? The original, or her leave-behind?"

"They pose the same threat."

"Okay, still… we should be clear about this."

"It is impossible to stop Kali in the future, as you hope."

"Why not?"

"The future has not arrived. She is not there. She may never be. It is only possible to stop her in the past."

"That's the plan?"

"Yes."

"How do we know she didn't make it back to the present?"

"Who?"

"The Kali of the distant past."

"That's impossible."

"Why?"

"She has long since turned to dust."

"Are you sure?"

"It seems unlikely she could return."

"However improbable, Patrick is correct. It must be considered at least," Mr Quandary spoke up.

"We know she can only jump a hundred years at a time, right?" I said.

"That seems to be a certainty," Fynn agreed.

"So how far back was she sent exactly?"

"Thirteen thousand years…" the Arbiter replied with some hesitation. "Though she was banished in the summer of three thousand, one hundred and two."

"BC?"

"Yes, BCE by your calendar."

"And what were you doing back then, all those millennia ago?" Doctor Zed asked. "This is not very clear to me."

"Ah yes… our expedition," the Arbiter replied. "We traveled there to ignite the Bronze Age."

"Seriously?" I was stunned.

"It was necessary… It all happened in the blink of an eye, historically speaking; though that blink took several hundred years."

"And Kali was with you?"

"Regrettably, yes."

"Say, how big was this expedition of yours?" the doctor inquired further.

"A very small entourage, I assure you…" The Arbiter fell silent for a time to hover back and forth across the lobby floor.

"Okay, so…" I broke the awkward pause. "How's my math, Lothar—it would take Kali about a hundred and eighty jumps to get back to this particular present."

"One hundred and eighty-three," Lothar corrected me.

"It's certainly doable, no?" I looked around at the other travelers. "Fynn and I jumped back from the fifteenth century. It only took us a week or so…"

"That was a mere five hundred years," the Arbiter declared. "Eighteen millennia is a different thing entirely. And for most of that time there was not even a hint of civilization," he explained. "Much could go wrong."

"And to jump so linearly, with such focus and determination. It would take years if not more," Doctor Zed observed.

"She is nothing if she's not determined," Lothar said quietly.

"Who among us at this table has not made so many journeys?" Fynn pointed out. "Patrick is correct, it is more than a possibility."

"Are you saying we have two Kalis to contend with?" Chloe asked.

"I'm not saying that at all… we just can't be sure which is which, or where they might be."

"It might explain certain things," Lothar said.

"Such as?"

"Her inscrutable agenda."

"Well, it seems to me that with whatever technology she possesses, she can jump at will and with great precision," Edmund spoke up for the first time and glanced around at the others. "What can you tell us about her origins? And perhaps the nature of this device she employs?"

"Does it even help to stop this Kali from the past?" Mr Quandary asked. "It's the one from the future that followed Patrick and I who seems to be the real threat."

"From Siren City..." I agreed.

"Exactly. I will travel back and ensure she is not sent to the future," the Arbiter repeated.

"Won't that change everything?" I asked.

"Can you be more specific?"

"Give me a second..." I paused to collect my thoughts. "I jumped there to save Mr Quandary, to the future, Siren City. Kali followed us back... that's when the trouble started. So, if I don't do these things, everything changes."

"You are worried that Policeman Fynn will be dead?"

"Yes."

"It's a risk I'm willing to take," Fynn called out.

"Well, I'm not." I turned to him. "Where is she from originally? We should stop her there."

"No one knows her exact origin. She just appeared one day... and from there everything began to stagnate," the Arbiter responded.

"When was this?"

"After the Dark Time, it was said."

"Ah, the place from which no traveler has ever returned," Fynn commented. "A few hundred years from our usual present."

"It is well beyond that time," the Arbiter said.

"Was it like a renaissance?"

"No. More like a phoenix rising from the ashes..." The Arbiter glided across the floor. "I lived through her reign," he intoned mechanically. "For a thousand years nothing changed. Every day was more or less the same, yesterday or tomorrow. It was impossible to tell one from another."

"Are you sure that was in the future?"

"But why ask this question, Mr Jardel?"

"Seems to me, that's what the distant past was probably like."

The Arbiter paused for a while as if to process my idea. "You are meaning before recorded history, your fore-bearers, your ancestors?"

"Sure... Before progress started to kick in. Things probably didn't change much for thousands of years at a time."

"Your point?"

"The distant future sounds a lot like the distant past."

"Ha!" Mr Quandary blurted out a laugh. "Patrick might be onto something. You may have thought you were in the future, but in reality, you were in the past. It's happened to me on more than one occasion."

"We need to know more about these circles, and these Builders…" Pavel Mekanos spoke up in protest. Edmund started nodding and all eyes turned to the robed figure.

"Are you a Builder?" Fynn had a question.

"I am the Arbiter, the last of my kind."

"Is Kali a Builder?"

"Some have speculated this to be true."

"What can you tell us about them?"

"It is said they exist outside of time."

"Then they must exist outside of motion as well," Pavel remarked caustically.

"Perhaps they exist beyond time," Lothar suggested.

"Beyond?" Chloe asked. "If that were so, they should be able to intervene at any point in history, past, present, or otherwise."

"If they still exist." Lothar turned to her with a smile.

"How is that possible— to exist outside of time?" I asked.

"Hmm, you've got me there," Pavel said and gave a double laugh. "I don't suppose it's likely at all— not the way we understand physics."

"Perhaps physics is wrong," Mr Q said.

"You might think of it this way," Edmund began and raised his hand a bit. "Take a lonely photon, speeding through the universe for a billion years. It reaches a telescope and is detected, reflected— seen, as it were… But, from the time when it left— all those years and miles ago, to the time it arrived, not a wink of time has passed."

"What?"

"For the photon…. traveling at the speed of light, no time passes at all. Einstein talked about it at great length."

"Photons have no sentience," Pavel said.

"True enough, and they are neither particles or waves, they are both. They have no mass and yet, they have varying frequencies… and as such they are capable of carrying information to any present."

"I'm more interested in how the circles were built… and why," I tried to change the subject.

"It was their intent to ensure humankind's survival by creating many separate timelines." The Arbiter glided nearer.

"What?" I turned to him.

"The Builders…" he said but then fell silent.

"For me, the important question is: when were these circles built?"

"I agree with Chloe," Fynn said and glanced over with a nod. "From my experience they all seem to be quite old. *Ancient* is the word I would use."

"Exactly when they were built is a matter of conjecture," the Arbiter admitted. "The historical records have been lost. It can only be said they first appeared within one precessional period."

"Twenty-six thousand years?"

"Yes, that is a good approximation."

"And they just appeared out of nowhere?"

"Such is their nature, once constructed and completed, the circles span all timelines."

"The centerpiece," I muttered. "But they were built in the distant past, right?"

"Yes, at least partially."

"How could that be?"

"Perhaps an ancient civilization rose and fell long before we can imagine," Doctor Zed suggested.

"Like an Atlantis thing?" I asked. "But there's absolutely no trace of them, no evidence."

"The circles. Are they not evidence enough?"

"Aside from that, you're saying an entire civilization rose and fell, and then was obliterated from the archeological record?"

"It's a possibility."

"But they've left no trace of themselves, not a single artifact."

"What would you hope to find?"

"Broken bits of pottery, some ruins."

"You are presupposing much, Mr Jardel. What would be left of your civilization in twenty-five thousand years or so?" the Arbiter asked.

"Plastic."

"At best that lasts a few thousand years. There would be little trace of it."

"How about all the buildings?"

"Concrete is not as permanent as you might hope. And the iron and steel? Well, it may leave a faint imprint buried deep in the sediments." The Arbiter hovered over me. "All that will be left of your civilization are deadly atomic isotopes, a plethora of glass bottles, and a few bits of metal."

"That's it?"

"Some things made of rocks or porcelain may also survive…" He looked down at me through his mask. "If you leave a legacy, it will be all the space probes drifting among the stars or abandoned on the moon."

"How far in the future are we talking about?"

"One precessional period," he replied. "Exactly as in the past."

"The Stone Age?"

"Yes, and aside from a few cave paintings, all that remains of the upper paleolithic is clay, stone, ivory and bone," he went on. "I mean of course the indigenous peoples."

"Indigenous peoples?"

"I will suggest an advanced civilization was transplanted from the future. They traveled back to construct the circles."

"The Builders, you mean."

"Yes."

"That's the only possibility?"

"It's the most likely one."

"So… somehow humans persisted… they survived long enough to stay alive into the far, far future," Lothar said.

"If the Builders are human," Mr Q commented.

"Why would they put these circles in such weird places?"

"How do you mean, Mr Jardel?"

"Well, most of them are at sea level in our present."

"Your point?"

"Sea levels vary over the years, especially many years."

"There's something in what he's saying," Edmund came to my defense. "Take the circle at Sonny Ming's as an example… if it was built so long ago, well, that part of Long Island was underwater or covered by a giant glacier."

"I can only suppose the Builders had this in mind from the start.

Likely, they wanted the circles found and used in a particular era, when, as you say, sea levels provided access."

"Okay, that does sort of make sense."

"Over geological time sea levels have fluctuated by hundreds of meters. Twenty-six thousand years ago, sea levels were much lower, perhaps by a hundred meters," the Arbiter explained further.

"So how is this not Atlantis?" I asked.

"This myth has nothing to do with our previous expedition, nor the Builders," the Arbiter responded and glided towards the elevator doors. "I must prepare for a few minutes. We will meet outside on the path in half an hour."

***

A few others disappeared too, Clark, Chloe, Mr Q and Lothar went off in search of their own preparations. Doctor Zed remained in the cafe, Pavel, Edmund, Fynn and myself.

"You might be right about Atlantis, Patrick." Doctor Zed came over and sat next to me. "I'm quite an aficionado on the subject. Though, I'd place it firmly before the Bronze Age."

"The Arbiter's first expedition?"

"Yes. It all comes down to what Plato said in the *Timaeus* dialogue."

"Doesn't he say Atlantis existed some nine thousand years before his own time?" Edmund asked.

"He's prone to exaggeration. Nor do I believe it was the size of Libya and the Anatolia combined," the doctor replied. "Besides, there is a large difference between what Plato said and what others have added to it."

"Like who?"

"Well, Ignatius L. Donnelly, for one."

"Who's that?"

"A pseudo-scientist and a congressman of your nation." Doctor Zed gave me a wide smile.

"Many of the stories claim Atlantis was the mother of all civilizations," Pavel cut in.

"I doubt Plato ever said that." The doctor turned to him. "It's a terrible mishmash of ideas. It could be anywhere…"

"Doesn't it have to lay beyond the Pillars of Hercules?" Fynn asked.

"Yes, and I do wish the pillars of Hercules would stop moving about."

"What?"

"Well, for some they are at Gibraltar, to mark the beginning of the Atlantic Ocean. For others, it is the passage between Sicily and the Italian mainland. For Odysseus, it's in the Peloponnesos. For Jason and the Argonauts, it's the Bosporus Straights…"

"I'd say the legend is based on the ancient Greek city of Helike, near Corinth," Fynn observed. "It's been around since the early bronze age and suffered a catastrophic tsunami in three seventy-three BC— an event Plato would have heard about."

"It could simply be Marseilles, a Greek colony," Edmund proposed. "Or, some would say, Atlantis is a historical reflection of Tartessos."

"Or its biblical equivalent, Tarshish," Doctor Zed agreed. "I might guess it to be a vestige memory of the Minoans after Santorini erupted."

"Some say Sardinia," Edmund countered.

"Or north of Cadiz where the Phoenicians mined for Orichalcum," Mr Mekanos added.

"What's that?" I asked.

"The metal of Atlantis," Pavel explained. "No one can say for certain what it was. It may have been a simple alloy of bronze, or some sort of rare earth mineral."

***

With some ceremony, we set off to the Circles of Null. It was about two miles from the hotel according to Clark. A bleak afternoon greeted our entourage, low clouds hung above us and implied rain— all color had been washed from the landscape. We were a procession more than anything, following the Arbiter who led the way along a narrow path that cut through the dunes.

"Fixing the circles seems like a dangerous thing to do, reckless even," Fynn confided to me as we walked.

"Why?"

"Anyone might now gain access, Kali included."

When we arrived I noticed the entire area had been fully restored, not just the circle to the past, and not just dug out by Lothar and myself. It was impressive: a triangular causeway intersected all three circles, and I could see two columns about three feet high. I could also make out a sculpture on the ground, the whole place was ringed by a huge snake eating its own tail.

"The ouroboros," Mr Q said as he came up from behind.

The Arbiter in the meantime had glided to the middle of the first circle, presumably the one that led to the past. With his arm-like appendage, he placed a silver disk at its center, then hovered back to us. "The exact date of Kali's banishment is lost to history and the vagaries of the calendar," he announced. "I will travel back some six thousand years to just before this event. Lothar has helped me calculate the correct timeframe."

"I'll volunteer to travel with you," Doctor Zed spoke up. "Any other intrepid adventurers?" He glanced around at the group but none of us seemed willing to take the risk.

"Your service is appreciated, Doctor, but I will ask you to remain."

"Why?"

"I have no need of a physician. And if someone in the present, or someone in the future suffers injury, your expertise will be needed." The Arbiter hovered towards the first column. "Since the journey takes one so far, it is difficult to arrive on an exact day."

"Does the same go for your return?" I asked.

The Arbiter swiveled to face me. "No. The return circle has been well-calibrated. I won't be gone for more than a few moments."

"But how will you return?"

"I cannot be sure I will."

"Why not make a leave-behind of yourself?"

"Meaning?"

"Jump to the future first, just in case..."

"I'm not convinced this is a good idea."

"Why not?"

"I doubt there is a future in which to live." He raised his appendage-like arm. "If Lothar will do the honors..."

The giant easily pushed the stone column into position. I noticed the other pillar in the nearby circle kept pace. They were perfectly synchronized. The Arbiter raised himself to the top, like some mechanical specter, his black robes flowing. "If all goes well, you will be standing here, wondering why…"

It seemed a cryptic thing to say, but I took his meaning nonetheless. If he was successful, he would simply disappear into the past and stop Kali. And there would be no reason for us to be gathered. Still, I hoped we'd remember, at least some of us.

"I shall return momentarily," the Arbiter said.

"How momentarily?" I asked.

"Eleven seconds by your time." He pointed with his mechanical arm. "There, at the center of the return circle."

By some means, the Arbiter propelled himself from the top of the column and went into free fall. I expected him to vanish into thin air, and he did. Lothar began to count aloud in the eerie calm, "One, two, three…" His voice broke the silence along with a soft wind. "…ten, eleven—"

We all heard the crash and saw a cloud of sandy dust. There in the return circle, in a heap, was the Arbiter. What was left of him at least, a torn black robe, his porcelain mask shattered yet revealing no face. We rushed over for a closer look, but Fynn took Lothar and I aside. "Gentlemen, quickly," he cried out. "You must move the marker to its furthest increment…" We obeyed and pushed the stone column to the end of the precessional period. The other pillar followed suit. Fynn then rushed to the center and removed the silver disk, with the hope of rendering the Circles of Null useless.

There was no Arbiter any longer. Instead we found some kind of mechanical harness that a man might stand in, though its occupant was now absent. He was dead or had been dismantled. I for one was disappointed to find ordinary wheels on the bottom. After the initial shock of what happened, we couldn't help but speculate on events:

"If he were killed in the distant past, there would be no robe, no mask— perhaps only a few rusty metal fragments," Pavel observed.

"So what did happen?"

"Or when?" Edmund asked and glanced over.

"Seems to me he was killed the moment he arrived and thrown back to our present," Mr Q offered an opinion.

"Maybe he traveled but the apparatus did not," Doctor Zed

proposed.

"Well, my question is: who was he? Who was inside?" Fynn asked.

"What do you mean?"

"Surely, it was someone sitting or standing inside what must now be called an apparatus."

"The mask, the voice… clearly it is someone we know who wishes not to be recognized," Mr Q proposed.

"He once told me there were three Arbiters," I said.

"Are you saying this might not be him?" Chloe looked at me.

"I'm just remembering something he mentioned."

"I'd guess it's Carlos Santayana," Edmund declared.

"Why him?"

"It seems like he might fit inside."

"My bet's on Mr Temsik," I said.

"Why say that?"

"I don't know… just a guess."

"You're meaning a doppelgänger?" Fynn asked.

"I say it's Kali herself," Mr Q ventured.

'That's preposterous," Lothar disagreed.

"Is it? She's been leading us on a while goose chase all this time."

"It may be someone we simply do not know," Fynn concluded.

***

We carried what remained of the Arbiter back to the hotel. Lothar did most of the heavy lifting. As soon as it came into sight, we could tell something was terribly amiss. Clark let off a gasp of alarm and leapt across the sand on his new and improved feet, all the while crying out in despair.

The hotel lay before us as a ruin. Sand had piled into the lobby through the broken glass entrance. Even the revolving doors were askew and off their hinges. The great center dome had cracked and mostly caved in on itself. Only one of the corner turrets remained standing. It seemed to me the damage had occurred centuries ago.

Clark was especially despondent; it showed on his face. He wandered around the derelict hotel in a kind of daze, checking on the damage and muttering to himself. The elevator was inoperable, nor could he be sure if the upper floors existed. He did however drag up some stores from the basement: tins of assorted food, though probably long past their expiration.

"It's late. I say we all get some sleep and see what tomorrow brings," Fynn tried to encourage the group and most everyone agreed.

We had no choice but to spend the night in the ruins. The ground floor was more or less intact. Clark and Fynn found rooms behind the kitchen. Lothar and Mr Q staked out what was left of the Conservatory, though there was broken glass everywhere, and not a single rhododendron had survived. Doctor Zed curled up by the backgammon tables, though Pavel and Edmund disappeared entirely.

In Chloe's room, I checked the closet. There was still a swirling void beyond the door, but this time I heard a kind of wobbling whistle that was not present before. Later that night I wandered out to the lobby with half the hope that Mr Temsik would appear to explain everything. I waited for about an hour to no avail, and eventually went back to bed.

***

"Good morning to you all," Pavel Mekanos greeted us in what was left of the lobby. Clark was already awake and sweeping the sand away from the entrance.

"I have good news," Pavel continued, and seemed especially cheerful. "Edmund and I were up all night tinkering with the apparatus."

"Which apparatus?"

"The Arbiter's."

"And?"

"Well, yes, I think we can get it to work. I can at least send Patrick and Fynn back to Sand City."

"To what end?"

"Well, from what you've told me, surely that's where Kali is to strike next."

"Mr Q and I will return with you," Lothar said, smiling, excited at the prospect.

"That might not be a good idea," I cautioned.

"Why not?"

"There's already a version of you in our present… and, well… he's not quite the same."

"The other version of Lothar, you must mean," Mr Q interrupted our conversation.

"What?"

"The lobotomized version… after the surgery of nineteen twenty-seven." He turned to his companion. "Patrick is right, Lothar; you shouldn't risk such a jump."

"What about the rest of us?" Doctor Zed asked. "If Kali is on the attack, you'll need all hands, eh?"

"I cannot ask any of you to risk such danger," Fynn said.

"But we must. We must help. We must put an end to her," Pavel declared stridently.

"How would the rest of you all get there?"

"By other means, I suppose… we'll figure something out," Edmund said. "If we could make it to your birthday party, I'm sure we can make it now…"

"What about poor Clark?" Chloe asked in a whisper. She turned to him. "Won't you come with us?"

"No, I shall remain here," he replied in a despondent tone. "I might be of help in another way."

"What way?" I asked.

"Someone must stay behind and keep and eye on the Arbiter's apparatus, hmm? And…" Clark held up a handful of room keys… "You might slip one of these into Kali's pocket," he suggested.

"To what end?"

Clark tilted his head and stared at us all. "Given the state of the hotel, it should send her flying into a wall, splattered if you will." He paused to grin. "Another reason why I should stay. I'd very much like to see that."

chapter twenty-seven
suspect traveler

Pavel and Edmund were true to their word. The Arbiter's apparatus returned us to the past, exactly eleven seconds before we were plucked. I was staring at the clown heads when all the memories of this present came rushing back. Fynn took my arm to lead me down the boardwalk, but in the opposite direction than I expected.

"What about Lothar?" I pointed.

"We cannot prevent what's about to happen, but we can pay Detective Durbin a visit."

A short time later we were standing in the Sand City Police department. The desk sergeant ushered us into Durbin's corner office.

"I thought you two were on your way to Japan," the chief greeted.

"Sadly, the conference was cancelled at the last minute," Fynn replied.

"Really? What happened?"

"A minor earthquake… but we are here to ask a favor," he continued.

"Sure. Just name it." Durbin sat back with a grin.

"It's in regard to Lothar."

"Who?"

"The sad-faced giant with a penchant for corn dogs."

Durbin thought for a moment. "Oh him… Lothar's his name, huh? He hasn't said much. Well, I got him in lockup until the county decides whether or not to bring charges." He leaned forward and scrutinized Fynn. "What can you tell me about this fella?"

"He is under our care, let us say…"

"You know this guy?"

"We know his brother," I said.

"His brother?"

"Sweetest guy you ever met."

Durbin shuffled through a few papers and picked one up. "According to witnesses, the altercation started over condiments."

"Weird that he likes mayonnaise so much, but he's pretty much harmless, so long as he's well-fed," I replied.

"We were hoping you could release him into our custody," Fynn added. "I will post bail if necessary."

"You guys are kidding, right?" Durbin looked us up and down. We stared back without a word. "Okay, I owe you a favor, I guess. You're just damn lucky the vendor is not pressing charges."

We found Lothar in a cell and there was no mistaking the crescent scars on is forehead. The door rattled as it unlocked and he stepped out to give us both a bone-crushing hug. "How are you feeling?" I asked.

"Lothar happy," he responded and gave me a wink. "Lothar hungry as well…"

I wasn't a hundred percent sure he was back to normal, if that's the right word.

"All things considered, I'm feeling fine despite a nagging headache." He smiled down at me.

"Do you remember everything?"

"I remember Pavel sending me back…"

***

The next day I had an errand of my own to run. Stanley Livingston kindly flew me down to New York in his single engine Cessna. It was noisier than I expected. A cab took me from LaGuardia to Brooklyn and it cost an arm and a leg. I found the address Mr Ming had provided, a huge block of apartments off Shell Avenue and not so far from Coney Island. I will admit the neighborhood filled me with disconcerting feelings, almost like memories, though nothing I could put into words.

I let myself into the old building, there was no security at all. The elevator was broken so I climbed the stairs and then knocked on the door to apartment 987. There was no one home apparently, at least no one answered. It came as a relief. I didn't really know how this meeting was going to unfold anyhow. I turned to head back downstairs, but as I started down the hall, the adjacent apartment door opened a crack. A woman called out: "Who are you looking for, sonny?" The language was Russian.

"An old friend…"

"A friend of yours, or a friend of your mother's?" the voice continued.

"What?" I asked, not sure I had heard right. "I'm looking for Valentina Bulgakov. Do you know her?"

"Are you the cops?"

"No."

"Who are you then?"

"Like I said, a friend."

"She's not here anymore." The door open a little wider and I could see an old woman in a house robe peering from within.

"Where is she?"

"You speak pretty good Russian."

"Thanks, so do you."

She laughed at that. "Valentina's gone. Moved away almost ten years ago."

"Did you know her?"

"Sure… I was her next door neighbor since the nineteen-eighties."

"Where did she move to?"

"Florida. A trailer park, maybe. She closed up shop."

"What shop?"

"She owned the florist's on Neptune Avenue."

"When was this?"

"After her kids disappeared."

"Disappeared?"

"You know, moved out on their own…" she laughed a bit nervously. "Oh, a long time ago, the twins…"

"The twins?" I asked.

"Sure, probably about your age by now."

"Identical twins?"

"No… I don't think so," she laughed a little. "Couldn't be more different those two…"

***

Fynn texted. He needed me back in Sand City. I'm not sure why. I flew back with Stanley from LaGuardia to Fairhaven. Conversation was difficult and neither of us felt very talkative. As we traveled above the Long Island Sound, I recalled a conversation from the *Hotel de Cirque*. Stanley would meet his doom in the waters below, or did in 1999. I tried not to think about it, nor did I mention a word to him. When we landed, Fynn called on the phone:

"Where did you go, Patrick?"

"Oh, to visit an old friend."

"Who is that, if I may ask?"

"Do you remember Valentina?"

"Of course, Grigori Bulgakov's lovely daughter."

"Well, she was…"

***

A few days later, I was surprised to get a call from Chief Durbin. I thought it might be about Lothar who was resting comfortably at Fynn's house. The chief wanted me in his office as soon as possible, though he refused to say exactly what it was about. Not another crime spree as far as I knew… A police matter, I concluded, but admit to being baffled and curious. I biked over the next afternoon.

"Thanks for coming in, Patrick," he greeted me with a large coffee and led me into his office. "I'm pretty sure you know why I called you in here today."

"Umm… not really."

"No?" Durbin sat back in his chair, arms folded behind his head. He gave me a big squinty grin. "I know about you and Fynn."

"Know what?"

He leaned forward and opened the side drawer to his desk. Durbin pulled out a large folder, and on top of that was a tattered book. I had seen it before: his grandfather's diary. "I was cleaning out the attic the other day… Found a journal written by Sheriff Durbin, my grandfather."

"What does it say?"

"More than I want to believe… and I was mighty surprised to find your name in it."

"My name?"

"Yeah, and some other guy… Gary Patrick Stevens— or was it

Sevens? Hmm, I've heard that name before..." Durbin gave me a look. "He has a byline in the *Chronicle*."

"Once and a while..."

"You know him pretty well, don't you?"

"We've met."

"Well my grandpa's journal describes his first encounter with some guy named Patrick in nineteen thirty-three... Let's see... Finding an indigent at the quarry, later identified as a fugitive, and... a Canadian Mountie." He looked up at me. "Then he found him washed up on the beach a couple of weeks later, and there's this odd incident at the Saint Albans pool. Somebody jumping into thin air."

"Sounds interesting."

"I have to admit, when I first read this, it gave me a weird feeling."

"What kind of feeling?"

"Deja vu... like I read it before."

"That *is* weird."

"That's all you're going to say?"

"Well, I get that feeling a lot."

"I bet you do." Durbin grinned. "Care to explain any of this?"

"Not really."

Durbin started putting pictures down on the desk and sliding them towards me, one by one. The first I recognized: outside the rooming house on Fourth Street. "This is also from nineteen thirty-three. That's my grandma Daisy, her sister Elsie... and that's you, Patrick..." he said while pointing.

I was about to reply but he held up his finger.

"This is from Saint Albans," he went on, and slid another picture towards me. "That's Elsie again. She was a nurse. And that's you with your arm around her. That's Fynn... and, oh yeah, there's your buddy Lothar."

I said nothing.

Durbin held up another photo of Elsie and I standing in front of the Rio de Janeiro School of Music. "How is that not a picture of you?" he asked.

"What would I be doing in Rio?"

"What would you be doing in nineteen thirty-five is a better question." Durbin went quiet for a while. "All this has to do with Fynn somehow, doesn't it?" he asked.

"What makes you say that?"

"Nothing strange happened till he first showed up."

"What about the stuff in your grandfather's diary?"

"Okay, besides that." Durbin handed over a faded document.

"What's this?"

"A record from the War Department... Gary Patrick Stevens, Killed in Action: North Africa, nineteen forty-two."

"Actually, I wasn't killed, just missing." I paused to smile. Durbin just stared at me. "Okay, wow, got to say, you've been pretty thorough."

"You know me, Patrick. I won't rest till I get to the bottom of something— that's why I became a cop."

"Still doesn't really prove anything."

"No?"

"Did you show this to anyone else?"

"Not yet."

"But Ricky did."

"He may have... posted some stuff on social media. No one pays attention to that crap."

"What does Ricky have to do with this?" I asked.

"Nothing."

"Something..." I countered. "How did you find all this?"

"Okay, you're right. Ricky knows a guy who knows a guy... and well, eventually we got the facial recognition software to scan old pictures."

"Old pictures?" I asked.

"Historical archives— a pretty big database..." Durbin reached into his drawer and pulled out another stack of photos. He read each caption as he handed them across the desk:

1965: Pasadena, the CalTech shooting. "That's you, that's Fynn. You took a bullet, huh?"

1941: Los Angeles, movie premiere. "That's Bogart and Bacall... And that's you and Fynn in the background."

1941: Hawaii, three days after Pearl Harbor. "Made the paper that time: *Colonel Fynn Routs Enemy Spy, Honolulu Advertiser.*"

1903: The *RMS Carpathia*, maiden voyage. "A wireless operator— are you kidding?"

1946: Japan. A famous photo by Hollis Indigo. "Nice hat, by the way."

"It's all photoshop," I said.

"Okay… how about this?" Durbin slid his tablet over to me. "Look at the video. One second you're standing there with Fynn and the next second you're both gone. Care to explain that?"

He had set it to loop. All I could see was Fynn and I at the pier blinking in and out of existence.

"Looks like you're gone for about ten seconds until you walk out of the frame."

"It's just a glitch."

"Nobody else disappeared in your glitch. Look at those kids there eating ice-cream, or that guy sitting on the bench…"

"We just went around the corner for a slice of pizza."

"I'm not buying it, Patrick."

"Okay, you're right."

"What?" Durbin seemed surprised. "You're not going to deny any of this?"

"No."

"Hmm— I didn't expect you to say that…" Durbin paused for a long while. He leaned back in his chair again and started to swivel. "So, does this mean I have to believe it's all true?"

"Yes."

"Wow."

"Maybe we should talk to Fynn."

***

After a quick call, we drove directly to the house on the dunes, my bike in the back. Fynn was waiting for us on the deck. I noticed a hot tub had been installed, but didn't remember it being there before.

"Yes, it was Lorraine's idea. A wonderful place to relax on a cool evening under the stars." Fynn smiled. "It's a great shame that the sun does not set in the east."

"What?"

"This would be a magnificent spot to watch the setting sun, eh?"

"Where's your friend, the giant?" Durbin asked, seeming impatient.

"Lothar, do you mean? Oh, he's taking a stroll along the beach with Asta and Lorraine." Fynn motioned for us to sit. "I suppose you have many questions now, Chief Durbin. But let me offer you something to drink before we get started. A scotch maybe?"

"Sounds perfect." Durbin gave his usual grin.

"Well then," Fynn began the inevitable conversation, "I must first say, your diligence, your investigative skills and dogged pursuit of the truth are unparalleled."

"Meaning?"

"In all my long years, no one else has discovered my secret."

"That you can time travel."

Fynn raised a smile. "Yes."

"And Patrick?" Durbin shot a glance.

I sat back grinning. "Fynn's taught me a thing or two."

"He's being modest…"

"Okay then, how does all this work?" Durbin persisted.

"You'll understand if I say it's complicated, eh?" Fynn chuckled. "I'd rather not go into a lengthy explanation of quantum entanglement."

"Neither would I." Durbin sat back and took a gulp from his glass.

"We might consume this entire bottle of scotch and still fall short of a satisfactory explanation." Fynn lured Durbin with another glass. "Perhaps you have some questions?"

"You knew my grandfather?"

"Yes, a fine man, the Sheriff was. He helped Patrick and I out of a jam."

"In nineteen thirty-three?"

"Yes, our first visit to Sand City."

"Did you change the past?"

"We did indeed, and for the better one can only hope."

"Is that what you do? Go back in time and fix things?"

"For the most part, yes."

"What about the future?"

"Who can say what it might bring, eh?"

"And now, the present?"

"I can only say how pleasant my life is at the moment. My wife and daughter, my good friends, a fine evening— why would I want to go anywhere else?"

Durbin thought for a moment. "That's not what I meant, really. I'm getting the feeling that the present is messed up somehow. There's something else going on, something bad."

"I will not say you're wrong," Fynn replied and drained his glass. "All travel is a matter of memory, Detective Durbin. Memories often persist into the present."

"Is that what I'm sensing?" Durbin took another sip.

"If it can be remembered, it's very likely that it has happened."

"Well, I do have some weird memories."

"Such as?"

"It's more like a dream than anything... Some kind of trial at Blackwater Quarry... Mel's husband was there, I think... Some bodies on the beach... the Pontiac T-thirty-seven..."

"What else comes to mind?"

"It's funny, I sort of remember us sitting at a diner in Fairhaven. You got up on the table and jumped— then just disappeared. I turned around and everything was back to normal." Durbin looked over at me. "You were just sitting there eating your sandwich like nothing happened."

"You remember that?"

"Like I said, I sort of remember... That was just a dream, right?"

"Probably."

"Do you recall having me arrested for murder?" Fynn asked.

"Yeah, I do... sorry about that."

Fynn laughed. Durbin turned to me again. "I also remember going out on my boat and sinking... Did that happen?"

"Sort of."

"What about Mrs Domino?" Fynn asked.

"You know, it's strange, I never liked that woman..."

"This is why it's important to trust one's intuition, eh?" Fynn said.

"Ricky, my son, also has some weird memories. Remembers two Patricks." He glanced over. "A dead one and another one he gave a ride to..."

"That was complicated," I replied. "But, it's all okay now, right?"

"I guess..."

"Ricky, though not intending to, has made things difficult for us,"

Fynn said. "We've always tried to remain in the background."

"*We?*"

"Travelers..."

"Yeah, sorry about that... Still, nobody believes what's on the internet. It's like—" he interrupted himself and looked down at his phone. "Well, talk about coincidences... It's Detective Mitch." He put his phone on the table. "Hey Mitch, how are you? Let me put you on speaker... I'm sitting right next to Patrick and Fynn."

We could barely hear her voice:

"Hey guys... Glad you're safe and sound and back at home. Just gotta say thanks for all your help."

"Our pleasure," Fynn called out.

"Well, case closed is all I can say from here..." There was a pause. "Pretty much..."

"What news can you give us?"

"Found the perp. Well, her apartment in West Babylon. Found the car, a two thousand fifteen Kia Optima, leaking radiator fluid like a sieve. Also found a whole box full of automotive emblems... A couple of shotguns too, and a mess of explosives."

"Explosives?" I asked.

"Sure... she's the one who blew up Sonny Ming's place."

"Are you certain?" Fynn asked.

"Very. Got her on video. A regular terrorist. Goes by the name of Rien Ekkert..." There was another pause. "Haven't found her yet."

"Mad Maxine, you mean," I said.

"You know something, Patrick?"

"Umm, I might..." I hesitated. "Thing is, I think she followed me to the Palisades."

"Really now? You mean by the Hudson River."

"She had an accident... fell to the bottom of the cliffs."

"Well, well," Mitch said, and added a small laugh. "That's worth checking."

"You got anything else for us, Mitch?" Durbin cut in.

"Not much. This lady worked as a driver... for Otas Construction. They got a satellite office in Garden City..."

"And?" Fynn asked.

"I swung by to see what's up. It looks like they're in the business of contracting foreign guest workers for specialized projects."

"That is very helpful. Thank you, Detective Mitch," Fynn said to the phone.

"I'll call you later, hon," Durbin signed off. He took another sip of scotch and gave a wide grin. His expression changed however and he rubbed his brow. "Mitch told me about this road rage killer, so, well, thanks for helping her out." He glanced at us both. "Her other case though... the Gilgo Beach murders... It nearly destroyed her career and definitely affected her personally..."

"Yes?" Fynn asked.

"Couldn't you do the whole travel back in time thing and find out who the perp is? Fix things for her, maybe?"

"I suppose I could find one of the victims, and follow them for a week or so..."

"Before they were killed, you mean?"

"Yes."

"You can do that?" Durbin asked.

"It would be no simple matter."

"You should go back to the first victim then."

"We do not know who the first victim is. There may have been many others, but their remains have not been discovered."

"Well? Will you do it? It would mean a lot to Mitch."

"I'm open to ideas," Fynn replied. "And it will take some careful planning... But can we discuss this at a later date?"

"Sure, but why?" Durbin glanced at us both, assessing our expressions. He sat back. "Something's up, I can tell," he answered his own question.

***

Once Detective Durbin had left, the deck was ours again. Evening was approaching and I heard a noise. Someone was laughing. It was Anika. She appeared from the dunes into the light.

"I suppose you heard every word, eh, my darling daughter?"

"I did... the poor man. I'll guess he's feeling overwhelmed right about now." Anika walked over and gave us both a kiss.

"He's been very thorough, I'll give him that," Fynn said. "But it is an impossible situation. Something must be done," he added with impatience.

"You should be happy, father; you're a celebrity."

"I prefer my anonymity, my darling."

"I'm tending to agree with your dad. It kind of sucks. I can't even go into the grocery store without being followed and shot."

"Shot?"

"Cell phone cameras, selfies... Not to mention autographs."

"Maybe it's time that all the people in the world come to accept there are travelers among them," Anika replied but masked a giggle.

Fynn looked at me, and I at him. "No," we said in tandem.

"Alright. What would you have me do then?"

"It's a simple matter, my dear. This all centers around Durbin's diary," Fynn explained. "We need you to go back and find it before he does."

"Thievery?" Anika asked.

"Patrick can take you back."

"What if something goes wrong and I alter the present?"

"That's exactly what we want." Fynn smiled. "We're quite sure the diary is in his attic."

"Hmm..." Anika considered. "Have you ever been to this house?"

"Once or twice."

"What is it like?"

"Just a normal house."

"How would I gain access to the attic?"

"Oh... There's a set of hideaway stairs."

"What's that?"

"Umm, you pull a cord in the hallway and the stairs drop down and unfold."

"Sounds noisy," Anika commented. "When do you want me to do this— now?"

"The sooner the better," Fynn said.

"We should wait..." I blurted. "I know it sounds crazy but we might need Durbin's help. Nobody knows this town better than him."

"There is something to what you say, Patrick." Fynn poured another scotch and sat in contemplation. "Things as they are, we might retrieve Durbin's journal at a later time, after he's lent us some assistance." He turned to his daughter. "Tell me, my dear, any strange goings-on since Patrick and I have been traveling."

"Nothing too unusual… I read something about the dragonflies, or was it the *vuurvliegjes*?"

"Fireflies?" I asked.

"In any case, they've all disappeared. Don't you read your own newspaper, Patrick?" she scolded.

"I thought there were too many…"

"Too many what?"

"Fireflies."

"Perhaps they've eaten all the dragonflies then?" Anika suggested.

"That doesn't seem possible."

"Where is this?" Fynn asked.

"At the quarry. They're building something, apartments, I think. The whole town is in an uproar."

"We should go see," I said.

"No, we should wait," Fynn replied in a quiet tone, "till the others arrive." He turned to Anika again. "Anything else?"

"Not that I can think of."

"Did I mention we'll be having guests?"

"Guests?" Anika echoed.

"Just for a few days…" Fynn smiled. "Friends of Lothar— you know most of them. They were at my party."

"Sounds like fun." Anika gave us a bright smile.

"How's Sven, by the way?" I shot her a glance.

"The lifeguard?" She examined my expression. "Are you jealous, Patrick?"

"Maybe a little."

"Don't be. He's moving to Florida in September, once the season is over."

"I thought you were getting married."

"Don't be silly."

***

The next morning I biked down to the Sand City *Chronicle* office on Captain's Way. I'm pretty sure it was Hector Diaz's bicycle— not that he would mind. It was Friday, and for the staff of the newspaper, it was a day of rest. The weekly edition was out on the streets, the cycle would begin again, though not till tomorrow. I remembered the rhythm of that life all too well. The door jingled when I entered.

"Hey, Patrick, long time no see."

"How are things, Miriam?"

"Good... now that all those faxes have stopped coming in."

"Oh, sorry about that. Won't happen again."

"Better not."

"Where's Melissa?"

Miriam smiled, something she rarely did. "In her office talking to Eleanor."

"Eleanor— really?"

"That's right, the gang's all here... Amy, Jason, Frank, Pagor, Joey. They're probably waiting for you."

"I didn't know I was expected."

It was a pleasant reunion, not that I was a complete stranger. I stopped in most every week to drop off my editorials, and sometimes, just to say hi. Though, it was a rare treat to see Eleanor again, my former boss. She looked well. Donald Pagor slapped me hard on the back. "Patrick," he boomed. "How are you these days?" He started in with loud conversation. Others joined in. Melissa came around with a tray of lemonade. We all toasted. As far as I could tell, this timeline seemed correct and normal.

After a time, I took Joey Jegal aside and asked about the Blackwater Quarry.

"Haven't you been reading my stories?" he asked.

"Mostly... What, they've opened the quarry again?"

"No... they're draining it. Gonna build condos."

"Really?"

"Yeah. Planning Commission meeting a couple of weeks ago. I saw the architect's drawing. Have to admit it looks like a cool project. All these little attached units nestled along the wall, built right up against the cliffs."

"How did they ever get that past the zoning board?"

"Chamblis and his lawyers, I guess."

"But it's a county park, state land..."

Joey just shrugged.

"You're in favor of this?"

"I don't know... progress, right?" He looked up from his desk with a weak smile.

"So, they started construction already?"

"Absolutely, clearing the whole place out. You do not want to get stuck behind a gravel truck going down Route Sixteen— they're leaking rocks, chipping windshields— upwards of fifty a day, I heard."

"Where are all the trucks going?"

"Fairhaven, building a seawall on the east side of town, I heard."

"And where did they get all the construction workers?"

"You mean where do they live?" Joey asked and smiled. "Doing a story on that for next week's edition."

"Well?"

"Some weird immigration thing going on. Guest workers. Seems they couldn't find enough local help."

"What are you talking about, Joey?"

"Tent City."

***

Fynn and I had a final errand. We had to find Geppetto.

"Maybe he's better off where he is," I said.

"Lost in a parallel timeline, you mean to say?"

"He's not lost exactly. He's at the Lucky Sevens Motel."

"We can only hope this is so."

"Well, it's someplace Kali won't look."

"But we need to speak with him again."

"About what?"

"He must know something about this circle that Kali is building— how it operates... or even, how to stop it." Fynn paused for a moment. "We will use your so called *dice of destiny* to find him."

"No, that's not a good idea."

"Why not?"

"Trust me on this..."

"Do you still have it?"

"Yes, but I don't know how, or why." I reached into my pocket and held up the black cube with white dots.

"Alright then. How do you suggest we find him?"

"Maybe a quick jump back to Babylon?"

"Inadvisable. We must find him in the present. Where did you see him last?"

"Room eleven."

"What was he doing?"

"Taking a shower."

It was easier than either of us could imagine. Fynn and I drove to Fairhaven that afternoon and found Geppetto under the shadow of the interstate. He was floating in the pool on a colorful raft surrounded by an entourage of crackheads and prostitutes.

"I'm glad you've arrived. Come meet my new friends…" He greeted us poolside.

"Are you okay?"

"Okay?" he asked.

"Alright?"

"Yes, of course, but I'm down to my last scraps of paper."

"What?"

"The paper with a picture of Mr Franklin on it. Only a few portraits of Washington remain."

***

Fynn and I returned to his house on Dune Road. Geppetto had slept the entire drive from Fairhaven, curled up in the back seat. He seemed pleased with his new surroundings, the sprawling beaches, the endless waves, and the familiar faces.

Lounging out on the deck we found Pavel Mekanos and Edmund Fickster, eating from a plate of nachos. Mr Quandary had also arrived, now laying on the hammock with a book in hand. I hurried over. "How's Lothar doing?"

"Ah, Patrick, good to see you once again. Lothar is as well as to be expected."

"Meaning?"

"Given that part of his brain has been removed, he's coping admirably."

"Where is he?"

"Inside, resting," Mr Q replied, but something crossed his face. "Frankly, Patrick, I'm a bit concerned for him…"

"He's not okay?"

"He should not linger here; let's leave it at that."

"Where should he go?"

"To a time before nineteen twenty-seven."

"Before his… surgery?"

"Indeed."

"Has anyone seen Mortimer?" Fynn asked at large. No one had.

"I doubt he'll show up."

"Why is that, Patrick?"

"He's probably dead."

"I've often thought such only to be surprised."

"Well, if he did survive Kali, he has a functioning cane, the bear claw. There's no reason for him to come back."

"You may be right."

I heard a thud on the sand and looked to see Doctor Zed landing in the dunes. He brushed himself off and strolled over. "I'm not too late to the party, I hope?"

"Not at all," Fynn replied in greeting.

"I feel just like Mr Columbus, arriving on your shores for the first time." He gave us a huge smile.

"Where's Chloe?" I asked.

"She should be right behind me," the doctor replied and looked over his shoulder.

She was not. I ran across the dunes to the beach and found her in the water.

"I'm drenched," Chloe called out from the surf, and then let go a laugh. "The water is lovely though. Why don't you join me for a swim?"

***

Fynn's wife, Lorraine, and his daughter Anika were away for the weekend and well out of harm's way. That evening, the travelers gathered in his living room. We had no definite plan. We weren't even sure Kali was in our exact present, though it seemed more than likely. That she was constructing some new circle at the Blackwater Quarry was a good guess. What that circle might do, how it might function, was a matter of fierce debate:

"…We cannot say, as the translations have been lost again," Pavel explained.

"Again?" I asked.

"In the ruins of the hotel."

"We'll have to rely on what you can recall about them," Fynn said. "You and Edmund have studied the manuscripts at some length, eh?"

"Yes…" Edmund replied but seemed hesitant. "It could be any number of designs… We'd have to get a closer look to say anything for certain."

"Do you think it's some sort of trap?" Fynn asked. "A way to lure travelers to their demise…"

"It seems she's already accomplished that," Doctor Zed commented in a dry tone.

"How do you mean?"

"Well, all of us here, together again, and locked in your living room," he replied with a nervous laugh.

"Ah, but we face the same peril no matter where or when we are…"

"What of Öde Temsik? Surely, he would want to be a part of this?" Pavel said more than asked.

"We cannot be sure of his intentions. Nor have I seen him as of—"

"Step one is reconnaissance," Edmund cut in. "Brigadier Thomas would say as much."

"He's right," Pavel agreed.

"Where is the brigadier?" Mr Q asked.

"Nursing his wounds and keeping an eye on the library. Madeline is with him."

"And Sonny Ming?"

"There as well."

Mr Q had another question: "What of Carlos Santayana? Were we not assured of his assistance?"

"I'm sure he'll be along. He's a man of his word," Fynn said. "But I agree with Pavel and Edmund. We need to get a closer look at this circle."

"Tonight? Under the cover of darkness?"

"No. There would be little to see. I suggest we go tomorrow at dawn. Who's with me?"

General agreement echoed through the room, but Geppetto stood at that moment. "I will not go," he declared. "I have no wish to encounter this woman you call Kali. She is a Builder, she is fearsome, and she will kill us all."

"A Builder? Are you certain?" I asked.

"Yes. I've met her before in another world, another time… She cannot be stopped…"

All eyes turned to Geppetto. He was clearly distraught. Chloe sidled up beside him to give comfort.

"It's perfectly understandable," Fynn said softly. "None of us here will ask you to put your life in jeopardy. Though…" he added a smile, "you might tell us what you know about the circles, hmm?"

"Yes… What more can you say? How they're constructed, and most importantly, how they're activated," Pavel chimed in. "There were many words lost in translation."

"I don't remember everything," Geppetto replied as a caution. "One needs *quillerixt*. It must be present to set the circle in motion."

"What's that?"

"A difficult thing to translate. Not even your alchemists had a word for this… a 'dull-silver' metal is the best I could say in English."

"Might he mean yttrium?" Edmund asked.

"Absolutely. That makes perfect sense," Pavel concurred. "Though, he might mean germanium."

"Or tellurium…"

"How do you stop a circle?" I asked, hoping to avoid the entire periodic table.

Geppetto turned to me. "What do you mean?"

"The off switch."

He thought for a moment. "Oh, I can remember writing a footnote about it… the thing that prevents a circle from turning," he said hesitantly.

"What thing?"

"Not a thing maybe, I only recall the exact proportions of salt to water."

"What are they?"

"Let me think for a moment… yes, it was two scoops of salt to one *greshlik* of water."

"What's a *greshlik*?"

Geppetto shrugged helplessly.

"Sounds rather vague to me," Pavel complained.

"I remember the taste well enough," Geppetto added. "With a bit of work we might get the correct proportions."

"I don't think it will come to that," I said.

"Why not?"

"Seawater. That's what stops a circle."

"How do you know, Patrick?"

"I don't for sure, but it's a pretty good guess."

"Why?"

"They were all built near a shoreline— there must be a reason for that."

"I think it's a good supposition. Certainly worth considering," Fynn said. "And we've also observed how Kali seems keen to avoid saltwater."

"Have we?"

"Yes, at the Cocos Islands."

"It's all well and good, but how do we confront Kali to begin with?" Mr Q interrupted. "Stopping the circle seems secondary, eh?"

"You raise a good point," Fynn replied. "And why Edmund and Pavel have come from the hotel heavily armed."

"What?"

Fynn gave an expansive gesture towards the two. "Gentlemen…"

"Yes, well, some of you may recall these…" Pavel held up a stack of poker chips, "when used properly, they will take you out of harm's way. Flip it and catch it and you'll find yourself a quarter of a mile from where you were."

"Meaning?"

"You can move out of her way in a jiffy…"

"For use in the outdoors only," Edmund added with a smile. "And be sure your path is free from obstacles."

"Can you demonstrate?" the doctor asked.

"Not in the living room," he replied.

"Thanks to Mr Geppetto for the idea..." Pavel bowed in his direction. He passed out poker chips to everyone. I took a few, as did most everyone else.

"Also note the side effect: holding the chip prevents one from traveling in time," he cautioned.

"I don't believe Kali has the power to send someone through time," Mr Q said.

"Right..." Pavel replied, "though, I thought they might prevent *her* from traveling."

"Any marbles?" I asked. "Bubbles of slow-time?"

"No, we've run out... not that they've proven all that reliable."

"It did work once or twice."

"And these?" Doctor Zed asked, picking up a bell from a pile on the table. He began to ring it, but Pavel rushed over to muffle the sound.

"Sonny Ming gave us the bells. Ring it for ten seconds or so and you'll find yourself at the bottom of his school."

"What good would that do?"

"You'll be trapped under several tons of debris."

"So, you mean ring it and hang it around Kali's neck?"

"That might work."

"And, courtesy of Sebastian Clark," Edmund said and held out a handful of room keys from the *Hotel de Cirque*. "Also rather dangerous at present."

"What would we use these for?"

"Against Kali. Clark promises instant death if used... she'd be smeared up against the wall."

"If one could get her to jump, that is."

"Well, if not her, then her minions."

"What minions?"

"I don't suppose you could build a circle all by yourself. She must have help of some kind."

"I've also made these..." Pavel had a bag full of plastic pens."

"It's a pen."

"A ball point, yes. But click it twice at the top and you'll find yourself back at the hotel— such as it is... It ties into the Arbiter's apparatus. Quite safe."

"Think of it as an escape hatch, if you will. When you feel threatened, press the button twice," Edmund explained.

"What if you click it once?"

"That's for writing."

"Impotent weapons, all, it seems to me," Mr Q complained.

"Did you also bring the centerpiece?" Fynn asked.

"Yes... though I'm not sure what use you'll put it to."

"Nor do I at the moment... but thank you, Edmund and Pavel..." Fynn paced the living room. "We are up against the unknown and cannot guess what may or may not help us in the hours to come."

"Have you a definite plan in mind?" Mr Q asked.

"We must employ the same strategy as in Zvorkovo: Make a future that is impossible for Kali to predict, and impossible for her to escape."

"You mean more than one future," I said. "A diversion."

"Yes... but stay well clear of her. If she gets too close feel free to jump away... Our strength is in numbers, our ability to distract her—that is your only task. Do not put yourselves in danger."

I was startled when the doors to the living room burst open, as were we all. A looming figure appeared, backlit by the hall light, his face in shadow. He lumbered forth and a few of us gasped. It was only Lothar though.

"Sorry I'm late, I fell asleep again. What have I missed?" he asked with a smile. Relief flowed through the room and Lothar made his way to the table for a snack. "Lothar hungry," he said, though not meaning to. A look of frustration crossed his face.

"How are you doing there, Lothar?" I asked once he had finished his sandwich.

"It's like cohabiting with a simpleton and it's getting worse. Sometimes I cannot restrain my urges."

"What urges?"

"Dark, violent ones..."

chapter twenty-eight
kali's quarry

Fynn promised to wake us all before dawn. I had trouble sleeping the whole night, even though I did like being in the hammock under the stars and wrapped in a blanket. I heard voices. They came from out on the dunes, a heated exchange, and I recognized the language as Spanish. I could only make out a word or two and sat up for a better look.

There were two men conversing, but they were indistinct. The taller of them wore a long flowing robe; the shorter man had a sort of halo around his head. At a certain angle it glinted in the dim light. One man handed the other something, then they parted. The taller of the two started in my direction.

"What was that all about?" I asked when Fynn stepped back onto the deck.

"Eh?" He turned, a bit surprised. "Oh, you're awake, Patrick..."

"Who was that?"

"Carlos. He's come to help."

"How?"

"Such remains to be seen."

"What did you give him?"

"The centerpiece to the circle."

"You trust him."

"I do."

"What's going to happen?"

"Neither of us is sure… but we have agreed on when."

"When?"

"He has returned to his parallel present, but he will act when we do, at exactly sunset."

"That's the plan?"

"For now." Fynn smiled. He pulled his robe closer though I could see he was still in his pajamas. "Give me a hand in the kitchen, if you would."

"What?"
"We must prepare breakfast for ten."
"Ten?"
"Detective Durbin is joining us in the morning."
"Make that eleven... Lothar eats for two."

* * *

The entire gang walked up to Blackwater Quarry, though we took a circuitous route along the high dunes. Edmund went on ahead to check for temporal anomalies. He rushed back to report everything he had seen so far was firmly in our present. We broke into groups of three to allay suspicion, and I had urged Mr Q to leave his top hat at the house. It was our intent to remain unseen. We circled round to the east, so that anyone looking up at the rim would also have to contend with a bright rising sun in their eyes.

The nine of us gathered slowly. Fynn, Chloe and I arrived first and found a secluded niche atop the cliffs. Pavel, Edmund and Doctor Zed came up behind us, and a few minutes later, Richard Durbin, Lothar and Mr Q crouched among the rocks.

The scene below gave me a start. This was not the quarry I remembered. It was all but dry. A few workers seemed to be pushing shallow puddles towards a sewer grate with broad brooms. I could make out a perfect circle nearly twenty yards across. Pretty sure I could see a faint ouroboros carved around the whole thing. The circle was inscribed as well, though it was difficult to be sure from this distance.

The derelict steam shovel remained, but as a rusted hulk, having spent decades underwater. It had been moved off to one side where the picnic grounds used to be. I had seen it in action once, and I also recalled when Mortimer clambered on top to escape justice.

"To power a circle of this size, I would guess an enormous amount of yttrium would be required," Pavel observed from his vantage.

"How much?" I asked.

"Depending on its purity, well, several hundred kilograms."

"And it's highly toxic," Edmund added.

"Logistics might be our savior then."

"What do you mean, Patrick?"

"A truck, a van, a boat— some kind of vehicle would have to transport it here."

"Ah, I see what you're saying… there maybe a way to prevent its arrival."

"Exactly," I said with a grin.

"Hate to say it, Patrick, but its already in place. Look there along the ring in the middle… the gray, silvery edges."

"We're too late?"

"I would say so."

"Can you see a centerpiece?" Fynn asked.

No one could, we were too far away. Nor had the early light reached into the depths of the quarry. Surrounding the entire construction site was a tent city. Small, red, two-man tents were haphazardly pitched; some bright, others faded in color. There were too many to count.

"How'd she ever get that past the zoning board?" Durbin asked, not expecting a reply. I nodded over with a smile. Workers began to emerge from the tents, stretching and yawning. They were all dressed in gray jumpsuits, many of them held yellow hardhats. From this distance, they all look the same, as if part of an extended family: broad, flat faces, and dark straight hair cut in a bowl shape. They seemed driven by habit, lining up at a communal washroom and meandering over to what looked like an open-air commissary.

I wondered aloud if this was just Kali's workforce or something more like an army. None of them appeared to be carrying weapons.

"Where are they all from?" Chloe asked.

"And how loyal might they be?" Fynn remarked.

"What do you suppose she's meaning to do?" Doctor Zed seemed too excited. "Will that whole legion down there jump to some future time and wreak havoc?"

"Or the past…" Mr Q suggested.

"Well, the odd thing is, I don't see anywhere to jump from," Edmund said.

"Meaning?"

"No raised platform or anything." He adjusted his goggles. "I don't believe it's a circle for traveling."

"What then?"

"We would need to get closer to know for certain," he replied.

Fynn shook my arm and pointed. Down below, Kali emerged on the scene and walked to the center of her circle. She was dressed in a jumpsuit of her own, though it was immaculately white and tight fitting. We watched as she placed a silvery disk in the middle, then took a few measured steps to the outer ring. Oddly, she began to walk, though she was not actually moving. It was more like a circular treadmill. I noticed the ring she traversed began to spin, to turn in place. She built up some speed then lightly stepped off. I could see the ring still turning though.

It was several minutes before it lost momentum and began to slow. When it finally stopped we all heard a sharp click, as if some mechanism had snapped into place. Kali returned to the center of the circle, and it now seemed slightly raised, almost like a platform. She repeated her ritual at least three times, then took the disk and disappeared into the maze of tents.

"Well?" I turned to Edmund and Pavel. "What kind of circle is it?"

They both shrugged, but Edmund said, 'She may be trying to calibrate it…"

As we sat from our vantage, something curious occurred. Out of nowhere, a deer popped into view along the edge of the circle. It sniffed the air and trotted off on its merry way.

"Did you see that?" Durbin whispered.

"I did."

"A trick of the light," Mr Q said. He was wrong though. As we continued to watch, it happened again and again, at least a half a dozen times.

"Does this kind of stuff happen to you every day, Patrick?"

"No…"

"Can you explain this?" Durbin asked.

"We need to get closer."

No one had thought to bring binoculars. Edmund took the goggles from around his neck and handed them to me. "Next best thing," he said and smiled. I tried them on and the scene came into perfect view. I saw Kali, and beside her, a tall man.

"Trouble," I said, and handed the goggles to Fynn. "Look who's down there: Mortimer…"

"Not trouble, Patrick. Betrayal, it would seem."

"Wait, I know that guy," Durbin said when it was his turn with the goggles. "He runs a concession on the pier…" He turned to me, confused.

I shrugged.

Pavel had been peering through the goggles for some time and finally had a question: "See that, over by the hill, just beyond the tents? It looks to be a pumping station attached to a large hose."

"And?"

"Well, it seems as if they need to keep the place dry."

"Could we sabotage it?"

"We could, though it might take several days to fill back up."

"Is there a way to pump seawater into the quarry? Test Patrick's theory?" Mr Q asked.

"There might be…" Durbin said.

"What?"

"There's a fireboat… an old tug at the marina. It's designed to pump water from the ocean and spray it on fires and stuff."

"It could never reach the quarry."

"No… but the pump works. If we could attach it to a hose, bingo…"

"Where are we going to get a hose that long?"

Durbin smiled. "It's already there, as your friend just pointed out—we only need to pump the water in the other way."

Pavel handed the goggles to me and pointed. "The pumping station, there. Disconnect the largest outgoing hose…"

"Where does it lead?"

"Up to the beach is my best guess," Durbin said. "We find the end, hook up the fireboat and start pumping in the opposite direction. Should flood the whole place in a couple of hours."

"I think we have a plan," Fynn said and raised a smile. "How long would it take to make all this happen?"

"At least four hours… Maybe more, to sail around the north point and all…"

"Better get started."

"We need manpower."

"For what?"

"The boat, the pump, the hoses…"

"Can you make some calls?"

"I can..." Durbin gave his grin. "And I'll take Lothar with me. He can do the heavy lifting."

The giant smiled broadly; he had taken a shine to Durbin. "Lothar carry things..."

"I will also come with you," Pavel announced. "Pumps and plumbing are among my specialities."

Down below, the army of workers spread out to their stations around the construction site, all in yellow hardhats and white dust masks. Soon the air filled with the din of machinery: bulldozers, dump trucks and diggers, the incessant alarms of vehicles backing up, and jack hammers. It was time to leave.

∗∗∗

Our strategy was set, somewhat. One team was already aboard the tugboat, and presumably sailing into position. The second team, comprised of Edmund, Fynn, Mr Q and I, would sneak in under the cover of darkness. We would have to slip past the army of guest workers to disconnect the pumps and the hose. I still wasn't exactly sure what Fynn had in mind though.

"Sunset, eight-oh-one by the clock," he told me.

"Why then?"

"This is the time Carlos and I have agreed upon." Fynn stared at me for a long while. "Our entire plan relies on an old axiom."

"What's that?"

"Quite simply, two objects cannot occupy the same space and time."

"What does that mean?"

"It means we must cross our fingers and hope for the best."

"You're talking about the centerpiece..."

Fynn said nothing in reply but gave me a dark smile.

∗∗∗

Edmund had spent his time well, much of it in Fynn's garage scrounging for tools. He was pleased to find everything he might need, including a heavy pipe wrench. Geppetto was by his side all the while. I could hear them chattering the whole afternoon. He emerged

from the garage holding an old portable stereo.
"What's this device, Patrick?"
"It's for playing music."
"Such a marvel... can you show me?"
It took some time to find enough D batteries but I finally got it working. Geppetto was delighted.
"I now recall that music is a weakness," he said.
"Whose weakness?"
"Kali, of course. It is very distracting to her."

***

Over a quick lunch on the deck, Edmund was able to draw some conclusions about the circle we had seen, though he cautioned that nothing was a certainty: "I'm starting to see this as a *difference engine*."
"A what?"
"It's a difficult concept to explain..."
"But not impossible," Fynn urged him on.
"No..." He smiled. "It takes what is different between two timelines and combines them... or, said in another way, it *equalizes* them."
"How?"
"Hmm... Think of Shrödinger's cat: it must be either alive or dead, it cannot be both. If it's alive in one timeline, then it's dead in another."
"And the circle?"
"Well, the outer ring that we saw spinning calls up a parallel timeline, a parallel present."
"What, like the Wheel of Fortune?" I asked.
"I suppose... though when it comes to a stop the two timelines are combined in an additive sense."
"The cat you mean?"
"Yes, in either case it would be alive."
"Why not dead?" Fynn asked.
"Ah, well if the outer ring were to spin in the opposite direction— clockwise— then the differences between the two timelines would be subtractive... hence a dead cat."
"Do you think Kali understands this?"
"Quite impossible to know that..." Edmund paused. "Ultimately

though, if you spin the circle enough times, all parallel presents would merge into one."

"How many times?"

"Hard to say..." Edmund gave me a helpless expression. "Many thousands though... Maybe Lothar could do the calculations."

"This is Kali's dream come true..."

"And why we must stop her," Fynn concluded.

Our third team ended up being Chloe, Dr Zed, and Geppetto, who had now found his courage. Their job was to act as a diversion at the appointed time, or should things go awry beforehand. They would station themselves along the rim of the quarry and were armed with several powerful flashlights, and a very large stereo.

***

The sun had not quite slipped into the bay when we returned to the quarry, but it was already a dark place steeped in shadow. A few lanterns flickered on, and things seemed quiet. We made our way down the cliff face in silence. On the ground the construction site was harder to negotiate than any of us expected. It was a maze of tents. We knew the general direction of the pumping station and began to creep south.

A tall figure appeared directly in front of us. Even in the shadows, he was easy to recognize: Mortimer. He was holding a gun, the largest revolver I had ever seen, like something out of the old west. He walked towards us and tucked it back into his belt.

"There you are... I was beginning to worry."

"About what?"

"That you'd show up at all."

"Why are you here?"

"To help, of course." He thrust out his index finger. It was black and scarred.

"How did you escape from Japan?"

"I doubt we have time for a long story, Patrick," he replied. "Simply, once Mr Sato was dead, and you two had fled, there was little reason to remain. I jumped away."

"With the cane?"

"Yes, thanks for that." He held up the bear claw for a moment. "Funny thing, this Kali doesn't seem to remember a bit about our little fracas."

"But what brought you here?" Fynn asked.

"Well someone had to get close to Kali and figure out what she's up to."

"And?"

"I'll admit, she has not been forthcoming."

"I doubt you've earned her trust again," Fynn commented.

"What does this circle do?" I asked.

"Nothing as far as I can tell, aside from causing a few deer to pop in and out of existence… oh, and various insects." He paused and looked us over. "Well, if you have something in mind, it's best we hurry."

"Can you take us to the pumping station?"

"I can, follow me…" Mortimer beckoned us with a wave. "Darkness is our ally," he said.

"What do you mean?"

"Kali may be able to see the future, but she cannot— as far as I know— see in the dark."

"It should be a cinch," Edmund whispered along the way. "We need only to disconnect the hose and open those four valves so that the water might travel in either direction."

"Which ones?"

"The backwash valves." He pointed.

It was as easy as Edmund said. We each manned a valve and turned it counterclockwise, then uncoupled the main hose. With the task complete, we decided on our next move: escaping. Only Fynn didn't want to leave. He had something else in mind. "The rest of you can go," he said. "You've done what's needed…"

Somehow that wasn't acceptable, though at that moment Edmund dropped his heavy wrench. It clattered against a piece of sheet metal and made a terrible din. Not long after, workers appeared, one by one, and from every direction. They encircled us. Their ranks grew deeper by the minute. All I saw were their numerous grins reflecting in the dim light. We were soon surrounded by a thousand smiling workers. Kali stepped out in front of them.

"Well, well…" she called over and put her hands on her hips. An instant later, she was by our side, then started flitting here and there, almost like a ghost. She stopped again right in front of us. "Gentlemen, welcome to the end of history."

"What?"

"Well, the end of your history."

Fynn goaded her: "Yes, we see the elaborate circle, but it does nothing, it has no function at all."

"No?" Kali asked in a shrill tone then laughed.

I knew he was stalling for time. Rather, manipulating events so that they would coincide with the moment he had determined: 8:01, sunset.

"Bring them," she ordered. "They shall witness this for themselves."

A group of workers led us to the edge of the circle. Kali placed the centerpiece and began her ritual. The outer ring was set in motion, then she stepped off. It made a clicking noise, a kind of ratcheting. Once it started to wind down, three things happened simultaneously. Luckily, they all served to distract Kali.

First was the sound of a tugboat and it was unmistakable, though it came from a long way off. I heard two toots, a deep throaty sound. Fynn heard it as well. He turned to me with a hopeful smile. A few moments later we could hear water rushing in from somewhere, the hose near the dunes filled and started its wild dance of pressure. A small pool of water appeared at the edge of the quarry and it was seeping towards us.

Also at that moment, up along the rim, lights shone, some of them danced along the cliffs. It was only Chloe, the doctor and Geppetto, but in the darkness it seemed like many more. Then the music began. Geppetto had chosen Holst, *The Planets* and it began with *Mars*… I had heard this before. I saw Kali stop in her tracks and tilt her head. She was listening intently and it seemed she couldn't help herself.

Nearer to us, something was wrong with the circle. At the center, the disk began to glow. It went from orange to red to white hot in a matter of seconds, and then seemed to melt and drip from place like liquid mercury. I could only guess that Carlos had kept his promise. Another centerpiece was in the same location in his parallel present.

The air got thick, and certainly warmer. It was obvious that something was building, some sort of pressure. On instinct we all stepped back from the circle, Kali and her army of workers included.

She had not seen any of this coming despite her prescience. Kali looked elsewhere though, intent to avoid a puddle of water that was creeping towards us all. I saw Mortimer's thin smile. He sought to take advantage and pulled out his pistol. He took aim and let off several shots. None of them hit the mark. Kali was too quick for him. In another moment, she kicked his legs away. He fell to the ground. She snatched his cane and tossed it some distance. An instant later, Kali was holding the gun and emptied it into him. Mortimer was dead.

Impossibly, the quarry began to fill at an alarming rate. A wild torrent rushed in. The rest of the water had come from somewhere else, apparently from a parallel timeline. And amidst the roiling waters, a shape emerged— it was a ship... rising up with the spray, a Viking long boat. It rocked and swayed, then settled to the shore at an odd angle.

I knew it to be a re-creation, and the warriors aboard, though steeped in lore, were decidedly modern-looking with helmets and heavy armor. On the bow, I could see a familiar figure wearing a sombrero and poncho. It was Carlos Santayana.

An assault team waded ashore. "We will fill the air with lead," Carlos called out to Kali. "There is no where to hide."

"But you will not, you will not injure your good friends," she called back and slipped in behind us for protection. We immediately had the good sense to lay flat on the ground. The Viking army let loose a barrage of gunfire, but she easily avoided harm. Her army of workers however knew enough to flee and did so in every direction. When the shooting stopped I glanced over to see where Kali was. She wasn't, she was gone entirely.

Durbin and the rest, namely Pavel and Lothar, returned a few minutes later, bedecked in heavy wading gear. They scrambled down the cliffs from the high dunes. I could see Lothar was holding a small axe; Durbin held a rifle. Behind them I saw Chloe, the doctor, and Geppetto all make their way down, though more cautiously.

"Wow," was all Detective Durbin could say and repeated it several times as he looked around at the chaos.

"How did you get here so fast?"

"We came ashore to hook up the hoses," he replied with a grin.

"Wow… This is going to be tough to explain tomorrow."

"If there is one," I muttered.

An eerie calm had come, but all was not right, nor had all of this finished, I knew it in my core. I noticed first that the Vikings began to disappear; they simply blinked from existence. Pop, pop, pop, like popcorn in reverse. I expected to hear a noise but there was none. By the time we realized what was happening they were all gone. Carlos Santayana was the last man standing.

Kali reappeared without warning and was by his side an instant later. She was holding a curved sword and it seemed familiar to me. She hacked away at Carlos mercilessly. Blood flew everywhere; her face and jumpsuit were covered in red splatter. Mr Santayana dropped to the ground, dead.

Foolishly or not, Durbin fired a warning shot. He was about to shout something but Kali turned with her hideous grin. She raised her arm and snapped a finger. A moment later he disappeared.

"Where's he gone?"

"Erased from history." Kali laughed. "You've forgotten who you are dealing with. I am unstoppable…" she whispered in my ear and I felt her hand slide across my face. In the next moment she was standing a few yards away. Geppetto had also disappeared, though I suspected he had wisely gone into hiding.

Kali was now alone, her army dissipated, her circle rendered useless, and her plans thwarted. But she was not defeated. Carlos and Mortimer were both dead, and likely we were next. For the moment she remained out of reach, dancing in and out of the present, and around the rusted hulk of the steam shovel, as if it were her own private stage.

"Well… all the travelers I know in one place. This should be a memorable evening," she called out, dangling her legs from the steam shovel. "And I see you've brought Patrick, my one true ally."

"What?"

"Darling Patrick, with me every step of the way. Have I said thank you?" she asked.

"What are you talking about?"

She laughed and flitted in my direction. "Hmm…Present in Hawaii, eh? At Zvorkovo, in nineteen sixty-two… In Pasadena when Professor Patterson was shot. On the Cocos Islands when the tower was destroyed…"

"It's just a coincidence," I protested.

She smiled and continued, "In the library at the time of the fire. At the bank prior to the explosion, and at Sonny Ming's school. And now, here in Sand City…. Need I go on?"

"But, but…" I was at a loss for words, my mind was racing.

"I have manipulated him every step of the way." Kali laughed. "He had no awareness at all, no idea he was doing my bidding each and every time."

It almost seem plausible but I knew in my heart it was not true. I turned to Fynn and he raised an eyebrow.

"The culprit, right under my nose the whole time," Fynn shot back in a seething tone. "I have been betrayed." He also gave me a wink, unseen by Kali. Next, Fynn did something odd; he gave me a shove that nearly knocked me to the ground, and then backed away as if I were a pariah. He started throwing curses at me from another language.

This seemed to amuse Kali at the very least. She flittered nearer with a smile on her face. When she did, Fynn lunged and grabbed her by the arms, then dragged her kicking and screaming towards the water's edge. He never made it that far. Kali wriggled herself free. He was suddenly holding onto nothing, and in the next instant, she had plunged a sword deep into his ribs. She stepped back from the water's edge as I rushed over. The sword had pinned Fynn to the ground and there was red everywhere.

He grabbed me a round the neck and held his face to mine. "You are my friend, Patrick. It has been a great privilege…" he sputtered up a mouthful of blood. "Keep Anika and Lorraine safe, if you can…"

"I'll try, but I don't know how."

"Get her to the water," Fynn said. He raised a smile for a final time and closed his eyes. He was gone.

"Who's next, hmm?" Kali asked but obviously knew the answer. She looked at Chloe. "Her, I think," she said and pointed. By the time I turned my head, Chloe was no longer there. She had disappeared.

"What did you just do?"

Kali laughed. "I've erased her as well."

"But—"

"Your memories of her might linger but I assure you she is gone from this present. Will anyone remain?" she asked and raised her hand again. She snapped her fingers twice and gave me a hideous smile.

I turned to see Pavel, then Edmund, just vanish. "What are you doing?" I screamed.

"I am traveling to the past and finding your friends. I am eliminating them and returning here in the blink of an eye. It's a simple thing for me." She seemed to flicker in and out of existence. "Who's next?"

Doctor Zed was. He raised a bushy eyebrow— it was the last thing he did before disappearing.

"Stop, please."

"Sorry, Patrick. It's too late for that. Mercy is not something I believe in."

Mr Q disappeared next. I expected his top hat to fall to the ground but it was gone as well. This was the time to panic, but I didn't. Instead, I leaned up and whispered into Lothar's ear. He listened carefully. "You understand?"

The giant nodded and gave me a smile, then started to trudge towards the western face of the quarry.

Kali laughed. "I have no fear of this lumbering goliath…" she said and blinked away from his path. He paid her no attention at all and continued slowly on his way. "Where is he off to though, I wonder?" She raised her arm again as if to make him disappear, but I had the notion that he'd be more difficult to locate in the past than the others.

"Lothar is hungry," I called out. "He's going to find dinner," I added in a bland tone.

She turned to me, trying to assess my expression.

"Why am I still alive?"

"I enjoy your suffering; you do it so well. And it gives me pleasure."

"Now what?"

"We will wait for Öde Temsik."

"Are you sure he'll show up?"

"Of course."

"Why?"

"He must also be eliminated."

"Okay..." I said and stared hard at her. "Except, you forgot one thing..."

"What?" Kali shouted, and seemed confused for an instant. I had already flipped Pavel's poker chip into the air and in her direction. She had no time to think and caught it reflexively. A moment later she traveled a *miglio* to the west. She was hurled against the nearby cliff and ended up at the water's edge, knee deep. Kali pulled herself ashore, but it was not over. Lothar was there waiting. He raised his axe and cut off her arm with one well-placed blow.

I was already rushing to the scene. The severed limb fell to the ground, but oddly there was very little blood. In fact, there was none. I looked at Kali crumpled on the ground. She was alive, clutching her own forearm. Next to her was a severed limb, not exactly a human one, but a device of some sort, the source of her prowess.

I felt the giant's hand on the top of my shoulder. "Kali gone," he said.

I looked up at him with a smile. "Yes... gone... and all our friends too."

"Patrick is Lothar's friend."

"Yup, just the two of us now."

"Lothar hungry..."

"We're not all gone," a voice said. It was Geppetto, and he peeked out from behind a large boulder on the cliffs. He climbed down to us. "Someone else is coming— look..." He pointed and I saw a pudgy figure walking towards us from the bike path. He was wearing a red fez and a blue pinstripe suit. It was Omar the waiter, Öde Temsik.

Geppetto was alarmed at the sight of him. Terrified, I would say. He looked over at me. "I have no distinct memory of ever seeing him before and yet in my heart, I fear him greatly."

"Why is that?"

"He is a Builder."

"Shouldn't leave this just laying about," Öde said and held up the bear claw cane as he sauntered over. He gave us all a nod and then looked down at Kali. "You're the last one," he said.

Kali turned to him with a sneer. "What?"

"Only one Kali remains: you. I've seen to it. All your duplicates have been eliminated."

"That's impossible."

"Every tangent, every present has been scoured. It was a grim task, but they are all gone."

"They proved useless to me anyway, stuck in their present, unable to travel." She laughed at Öde. "You've done me a great service in the end."

"Wait, you killed them all?" I asked.

"Yes. I traipsed through all the other timelines, past, present, and future. Even if I missed one or two, they seem to be powerless versions."

"How did you do it?"

"Ha," Öde chuckled. "Lured by the promise of the manuscripts… quite a simple matter." Mr Temsik took a bell from his pocket and rang it for several long seconds. He placed it around Kali's neck and blew her a kiss goodbye. A moment later she disappeared.

"Won't she just re-do all this?"

"No. If she were able to, we'd be living in her world right now." Mr Temsik smiled.

"I have some questions."

"I'm sure you do, Patrick."

"Who was the Arbiter?"

"No one knows…"

"Was it Kali all along?"

"Doubtful…"

"You?"

Mr Temsik laughed. "No."

I thought for a moment. "What about my car?"

"Oh yes, the flat tires. You and Fynn were leaving a day too early. I was forced to delay your departure."

"Why?"

"Sunday was my day off at the diner."

**

The world had been saved, I suppose, but it felt less than satisfying.

My world had been destroyed, shattered. Nearly everyone I knew and cared for was dead or erased from history. I sat alone on the edge of the quarry, on a low ledge just where the cliffs began. My mind began to race. There was no good world going forward.

Mr Temsik appeared below me. Beside him was Lothar and Geppetto. They were all holding one of Pavel's pens. "We've come to bid adieu, Patrick," Öde called out.

I jumped down to the sand. "Where to?"

"Back to the hotel for now, such as it is…"

"And you promise to take care of my friends?"

"I do. You have my solemn vow."

I embraced Lothar and Geppetto, and said sad goodbyes. They clicked their pens twice and blinked away.

"And you, Patrick? What's next? You could come with us…" Mr Temsik offered.

"No… thanks…" I hardly had any words left to speak.

"You're not thinking very clearly, Patrick. You've worked yourself into a panic when the solution is obvious."

"What, what can I do?"

"Simply jump to the recent past, a soft jump will do nicely. Everything will be reset."

"That's it?"

"You will need to jump to a time before you met Fynn."

"What?"

"Sorry to say, it's true."

"Will I remember any of this?"

"Who can say?"

"But what about all those strange parallel lives? What if I jump back and end up in one of those?"

"Do you recall living through any of them?"

"Not exactly."

"There you have it. Jump back to a familiar time and you'll be back to a life that has familiar memories."

"Easy as that?"

"Yes."

I don't know how long I sat at the quarry after Öde left. I felt myself descending into a fugue state. I was disassociating from reality…

Hours passed certainly, though it seemed like days. I had never felt so utterly alone.

***

I was in the middle of a dream when the persistent telephone pulled me out of my slumber, and it seemed too early, way too early. It was the land line; that hadn't rung for weeks. Probably the cable company, always trying to upgrade my service. Damn those people. How many times do I have to remind them I don't even have a TV— just signed on for the internet.

"Hello?" I answered, picking up on the fourth ring. "Oh, hey El, good morning. Why are you calling on this line?"

"All the cell phones are down... the tower collapsed, remember?"

"Oh right. What's up?" I asked and started the heater. It clicked three times and I heard the burner gently swoosh to life. The smell of kerosene... nothing like it. My loft-like apartment was freezing as usual. A mid-March day and way colder than it should be. On the phone was Eleanor Woods, my boss, the editor-and-chief of the Sand City *Chronicle*.

"Umm... Why are you calling me, Eleanor? It's like seven, barely."

"Were you asleep?"

"Of course I was." I looked up at my ceiling. The skylights were frosted over with rain, though it did seem like dawn might be breaking.

"It's Detective Durbin. He wants you down at Boxtop Beach as soon as you can."

"What for?"

"Pictures."

"Pictures of what?"

"A crime scene."

"Holy crap."

"That's right, another murder... Some big shot inspector was called in from Amsterdam, Interpol, or some such nonsense."

"What's his name?"

"Fynn, or something."

"Okay, I'm on my way..." I lied and started thinking about a cup of coffee. I moved to the kitchen. My strange dream lingered though, a vast dream. There was no way to recollect all the tiny details, and yet it refused to fade. I put water on to boil and looked over at the table. My cat was staring up at me. There was something else too…

"That wasn't there before," I said aloud and saw a single dice with white dots on it. It all came rushing back. There was also a note underneath which simply read: *Happy Travels.*

———

AUTHOR'S NOTE:
I sincerely hope you have enjoyed reading this story. And now, I implore you to take a moment to click the "like" button, add a few stars, or, if you have the mind to: write a brief review. In the modern world of ebooks, these simple actions mean the difference between life and death. My other books and more information can be found at this link:
http://kmackdesign.com/books/allbooks.html

You may also follow Tractus Fynn and his exploits on twitter:
@TractusFynn

Thank you.
—MK Alexander

About the author:
MK Alexander has been writing fiction for more than 20 years. He is a long-time reporter and editor for various newspapers, and worked for The *New York Times* for over ten years. Winner of the BBC Short Story Award. Recent published titles include seven novels, three novellas, a biography, and a short story compilation.

Other Titles by MK Alexander

Tractus Fynn Mysteries:

Sand City: Murders Book 1
A failing newspaper, a resort town, a time traveling detective... and murder of course.

Jump City: Apprentice Book 2
How does a Mongol horde help solve a baffling crime in Colorado and save FDR from assassination? Inspector Fynn and Patrick charge through history, past and present to save America from itself.

Low City: Missing Persons Book 3
Intrepid reporter Patrick Jardel returns to the present to find his best friend Tractus Fynn has gone missing. Also missing is the beverage known as coffee. In this alternate timeline, Patrick travels across the globe and through history to save his partner and restore the present.

Cold City: Cold Case Book 4
Tractus Fynn has been murdered and it's up to Patrick Jardel to solve the mystery and somehow bring his best friend back to life. To do so, he must travel to the past, present, and future, and far afield, from the shores of the Aral Sea to the *RMS Carpathia*.

—

The Farsi Trilogy
When the CIA has a clever cyber-war program to shut down Iran. But things never go according to plan. Meet Aydin Llewelyn, computer genius, deadbeat and accidental spy. Can he and his ex-girlfriend make it to Tehran and save the day? Find out in this fast-paced, amusing, twisty tale of travel and intrigue.

Jekyll's Daughter
A faithful sequel to the famous horror classic: *The Strange Case of Dr. Jekyll and Mr. Hyde,* by Robert Louis Stevenson. The story picks up some 25 years later as Henrietta Jekyll comes upon her father's old journals and takes it upon herself to recreate his notorious formula with unexpected results.

Genre Jam, Volume One: Death & Injury
A compilation of five short stories resulting in death or grievous harm. A mix of genres, from science fiction to urban fairy tales.

Random Sacrifice
A highly original espionage thriller about Libya, its infamous dictator, and strange events that take place on a summer day in 1981.

My New World A Teenager's WWII Odyssey
A biography of Mary Cotsis, centered around her World War Two experiences as she escapes from the Nazi Occupation of Greece and travels to America to begin a new life.

Proof

Made in the USA
Columbia, SC
05 June 2018